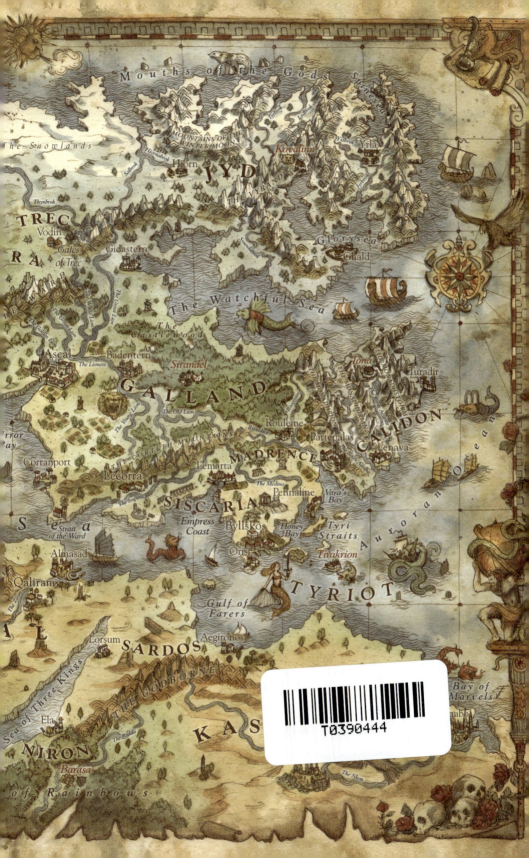

REALM BREAKER

ALSO BY VICTORIA AVEYARD

Red Queen

Glass Sword

King's Cage

War Storm

Broken Throne: A Red Queen Collection

Red Queen: The Official Coloring Book

Digital Novellas

Queen Song

Steel Scars

Novella Collection

Cruel Crown

REALM BREAKER

VICTORIA AVEYARD

An Imprint of HarperCollins*Publishers*

HarperTeen is an imprint of HarperCollins Publishers.

Realm Breaker
Copyright © 2021 by Victoria Aveyard
Map art by Francesca Baraldi
Map © & ™ 2021 Victoria Aveyard. All rights reserved.
All rights reserved. Printed in the United States of America. No part of this
book may be used or reproduced in any manner whatsoever without written
permission except in the case of brief quotations embodied in critical articles
and reviews. For information address HarperCollins Children's Books, a
division of HarperCollins Publishers, 195 Broadway, New York, NY 10007.
www.epicreads.com

Library of Congress Control Number: 2020950478
ISBN 978-0-06-287262-3 — ISBN 978-0-06-309285-3 (special ed)

Typography by Jenna Stempel-Lobell
22 23 24 25 26 LBC 16 15 14 13 12
❖
First Edition

To those who seek and never find

REALM BREAKER

PROLOGUE
The Song Unsung

No mortal alive had ever seen a Spindle.

Echoes of them lingered, in places remembered or forgotten, in people touched by magic, in creatures descendant of other realms. But no Spindle had burned in an age. The last of them was a thousand years gone. The passages closed, the gates locked. The age of crossing ended.

Allward was a realm alone.

And it must stay that way, Andry Trelland thought. *For the good of us all.*

The squire attended to his lord's armor, ignoring the first drop of rainfall as he tightened the belts and buckles over Sir Grandel Tyr's broad frame. Andry's honey-brown fingers worked quickly over familiar leather and golden steel. The knight's armor gleamed, freshly polished, the pauldrons and breastplate worked into the likeness of the Kingdom of Galland's roaring lion.

Dawn broke weakly, fighting through the spring rain clouds bunched up against the foothills and looming mountains. It felt like standing in a room with a low ceiling. Andry inhaled, tasting the damp air. The world pressed down around him.

Their horses whickered nearby, thirteen tied in a line, huddling together for warmth. Andry wished he could join them.

The Companions of the Realm waited in the clearing below the hill. Some guarded the pilgrim road leading into the trees, waiting for their enemy. Some patrolled the temple overgrown with ivy, its white columns like the bones of a long-abandoned skeleton. The carvings on it were familiar, Elder-written—the same letters Andry had seen in mythic Iona. The structure was ancient, older than the old Cor Empire, built for a Spindle long dead. Its bell tower stood silent. Where the Spindle inside once led, Andry did not know. No one had ever said, and he'd never worked up the courage to ask. Still, he could feel it like a scent near to fading, a ripple of power lost.

Sir Grandel curled his lip. The pale-skinned knight scowled at the sky, the temple, and the warriors below.

"Can't believe I'm awake at this Spindlerotten hour," he spat, his voice unchecked.

Andry ignored his mentor's complaint.

"All finished, my lord," he said, stepping back. He looked over the knight, checking Sir Grandel for flaw or imperfection, anything that might hinder him in the battle to come.

The knight puffed out his chest. Three years Andry squired for Sir Grandel. He was an arrogant man, but Andry knew no swordsmen of his skill who did not also err to pride. It was to be expected. And all was in order, from the toes of Sir Grandel's steel boots to the knuckles of his gauntlets. The veteran knight was a picture of strength and bravery, the pinnacle of the Queen's Lionguard. A fearsome and stirring sight to behold.

As always, Andry imagined himself in that same armor, the lion across his chest, the green cloak over his shoulders, his father's shield on his arm instead of fixed to the wall in his mother's parlor. *Unused for years, covered in dust, nearly broken in two.*

The squire ducked his head, chasing away the thought. "You're ready."

"Certainly feel ready," the knight replied, resting gloved fingers on the hilt of his sword. "After too many days dragging my aging bones across the Ward. How long has it been since we left home, Trelland?"

Andry answered without thought. "Two months, sir. Near two months to the day."

He knew the count like he knew his fingers. Every day on the road was an adventure, through valleys and mountains and wilderness, to kingdoms he'd never dreamed to see. Alongside warriors of great renown and impossible skill, heroes all. Their quest was near to ending, the battle looming close. Andry did not fear a fight, but what came after.

The easy, quick road home. The training yard, the palace, my mother sick and my father dead. With nothing to look forward to but four more years of following Sir Grandel from throne room to wine cellar.

Sir Grandel took no notice of his squire's discomfort, prattling on. "Spindles torn open and lost realms returned. Hogwash, all of it. Chasing a children's story," the knight grumbled, testing his gloves. "Chasing ghosts for ghosts."

He shook his head at his battle-ready Companions, their garb and coloring as varied as jewels in a crown. His watery blue eyes lingered on a few.

Andry followed Sir Grandel's gaze. He landed on the figures with tight, rigid posture, their armor strange, their ways even stranger. Though they were many days on the road with the Companions of the Realm, some felt anything but familiar. Inscrutable as a wizard's riddle, distant and unbelievable as a myth. *And standing right in front of me.*

"They aren't ghosts," Andry murmured, watching as one stalked the temple's perimeter. His hair was blond and braided, his form broad and monstrously tall. The greatsword at his hip would take two men to wield. *Dom*, Andry thought, though his true name was far longer and more difficult to pronounce. *A prince of Iona.* "The Elders are flesh and blood as much as we are."

They were easy to distinguish from the other warriors. The Elders were beings apart, six of them in all, each one like a beautiful statue, differing in appearance but somehow all alike. As distant from mortal kind as birds from fish. Children of different stars, the legends said. Beings of another realm, the few histories told.

Immortals, Andry knew.

Ageless, beautiful, undying, distant—and lost. Even now, he could not help but stare.

They called themselves the Vedera, but to the rest of the Ward, to the mortals who only knew them from ancient history and fading stories, they were the Elders. Their kind were few, but to Andry Trelland's eye, they were still mighty.

The Elder prince looked up as he rounded the temple, meeting the squire's gaze with fierce emerald eyes. Andry dropped his face quickly, knowing the immortal could hear their conversation. His cheeks flushed.

Sir Grandel did not flinch, flint-eyed beneath his helmet. "Do immortals bleed, Squire?"

"I don't know, my lord," Andry replied.

The knight's gaze shifted through the rest. The Elders came from every corner of the Ward, emerging from half-forgotten enclaves. Andry had memorized them like he did courtiers, both so Sir Grandel would not embarrass himself in company and for his own curiosity.

The two Elder women were a sight unto themselves, warriors as much as the rest of them. Their presence had been a shock to the mortal men, the knights of Galland most of all. Andry still found them intriguing, if not awe-inspiring. Rowanna and Marigon were of Sirandel, deep in the Castlewood, as was Arberin. Andry guessed them to be close kin, with their red hair, pale foxlike faces, and purple chain mail, iridescent as snakeskin. They looked like a forest in autumn, shifting between sun and shadow. Nour came from Hizir, the desert enclave in the Great Sands of Ibal. They seemed to be both man and woman to Andry's eye. They wore no armor at all, but tightly wrapped yards of duskrose silk banded with a ransom of precious stones. Their skin was golden, their eyes bronze, rimmed in black kohl and lightning purple, while their black hair had been worked into intricate braids.

Then there was Surim, who had traveled the farthest of any, mortal or immortal. Bronze-skinned with deep-set eyes, he still wore the journey from Tarima on him like a heavy coat, his stout pony having carried him across the vast Temurijon steppe.

Dom was more oak tree and antler than anything else. He wore leather beneath a gray-green cloak, embossed with the great stag of his enclave and his monarch. His hands were bare of gloves or gauntlets. A hammered silver ring gleamed on his finger. His home was Iona, hidden in the glens of mountain-clawed Calidon, where the Companions had first assembled. Andry remembered it sharply: an immortal city of mist and stone, ruled by an immortal lady in a gray gown.

Sir Grandel's voice cut through the memory.

"And what of Corblood princes, descendants of the old empire?" he hissed, his words taking on a razor edge. "Spindlerotten, maybe, but mortal as the rest of us."

Andry Trelland was raised in a palace. He knew well the tone of jealousy.

Cortael of Old Cor stood alone, his boots braced on the broken stone of the pilgrim road. He stared, unyielding, into the shadows of the wood, lying in wait like a wolf in its den. He wore a cloak of Iona too, and antlers were molded across his steel breastplate. Dark red hair fell about his shoulders, like blood at dusk. He served no mortal kingdom, but there were slight lines of age on his face, on his stern brow and at the corners of thin lips. Andry guessed him to be near thirty-five. Like the Elders, he was of Spindleblood, a son of crossing, his mortal ancestors born beneath the stars of another realm.

So was his sword. *A Spindleblade.* The naked weapon reflected the sky above, filled with gray light, etched in markings no one alive could read. Its presence was a thrum of lightning.

The knight narrowed his eyes. "Do they bleed too?"

"I don't know either," Andry muttered, wrenching his eyes from the blade.

Sir Grandel clapped the squire on the shoulder. "Perhaps we'll find out," he said, stomping down the hill, his heavy armor clanging with each step.

I certainly hope not, Andry thought as his lord joined the other mortal Companions. Sir Grandel fell in among the North cousins: two other knights of Galland. Edgar and Raymon North were just as sick of the errant quest as Sir Grandel, their tired faces mirroring his own.

Bress the Bull Rider pressed in, his smile overwide beneath his horned helm. The mercenary needled the knights whenever he could, to their chagrin and Andry's delight.

"Though you will not take up the sword, you should pray to the gods before battle nonetheless," said a deep voice, smooth as thunder.

Andry turned to see another knight step from the trees. Okran of Kasa, the brilliant kingdom of the south, bowed his head as he approached, his helmet under one arm, his spear beneath the other. The Kasan eagle screamed across his pearl-white armor, wings and talons outstretched for a kill. Okran's smile was a shooting star, a flash against his jet-black skin.

"My lord," Andry replied, bowing. "I doubt the gods will listen to the words of a squire."

Okran angled an eyebrow. "Is that what Sir Grandel Tyr tells you?"

"I must apologize for him. He is tired after so long a journey, crossing half the realm in blistering weeks." It was a squire's duty to pick up after his lord, in object and in word. "He does not mean to insult you, or any other."

"Don't fret, Squire Trelland. I am not the kind to let buzzing flies bother me," the southern knight replied, waving a nimble-fingered hand. "Not today, at least."

Andry fought the impolite urge to grin. "Are you calling Sir Grandel a fly?"

"Would you tell him if I did?"

The squire did not answer, and that was answer enough.

"Good lad," the Kasan chuckled, drawing his helmet over his head, fixing the amethyst nose guard into place. A Knight of the Eagle took shape, like a hero stepping out of a dream.

"Are you afraid?" The words bubbled up before Andry could stop them. Okran's expression softened, bolstering his resolve. "Do you fear the thief and his wizard?"

The Kasan fell quiet for a long moment, his manner slow and thoughtful. He looked at the temple, the clearing, and Cortael at its edge, a sentinel upon the road. The forest prickled with rain-drops, the shadows turning from black to gray. All seemed quiet, unassuming.

"The Spindle is the danger, not the men seeking it," he said, his voice gentle.

Try as he might, Andry found he could not picture them. *The sword stealer, the rogue wizard.* Two men against the Companions: a dozen warriors, half of them Elders. *It will be a slaughter, an easy victory*, he told himself, forcing a nod.

The Kasan raised his chin.

"The Elders called to the mortal crowns and I was sent to answer, same as your knights. I know little of Corblood or Spindle magic, and believe even less. A stolen sword, a torn passage? All this seems a conflict between two brothers, not something to concern the great kingdoms of the Ward." He scoffed, shaking his head. "But it is not for me to believe what the Elder monarch said or what Cortael warned, only to stand against what could be. The risk of turning away is too great. At worst, nothing happens. No one comes." His warm, dark eyes wavered. "At best, we save the realm before she even knew she was in danger."

"Kore-garay-sida."

The language of his mother's people was easy to reach for, well taught in Andry's childhood. The words were honey on his lips.

The gods will it so.

Okran blinked, caught off guard. Then he broke into a smile, the full weight of it overpowering.

"Ambara-garay," he answered, finishing the prayer with a dip of his helm. *Have faith in the gods.* "You did not tell me you speak Kasan, Squire."

"My mother taught me, my lord," Andry replied, drawing himself straight. He was nearing six feet tall, but still felt small in Okran's lean shadow. Growing up in Ascal, Andry was used to being noticed for his darker skin, and he was proud of the heritage it showed. "She was born in Nkonabo, a daughter of Kin Kiane." His mother's family, a kin, was known even in the north.

"A noble lineage," Okran said, still grinning. "You should visit me in Benai, when all this is done and our lives returned."

Benai, Andry thought. *A city of hammered gold and amethyst, nestled on the green banks of the Nkon.*

The homeland he had never seen took shape, his mother's stories a song in his head. But it could not last. The rain fell cold, reality impossible to ignore. Knighthood was three or four years off. *A lifetime*, Andry knew. *And there is so much else to consider. My position in Ascal, my future, my honor.* His heart sank. *Knights are not free to roam as they will. They must protect the weak, aid the helpless, and above all serve their country and queen. Not sightsee.*

And there is Mother to think of, frail as she has become.

Andry forced a smile. "When all this is done," he echoed, waving as Okran went down the hill, his steps light on the dampening grass.

Have faith in the gods.

In the foothills of the great mountains of Allward, surrounded by heroes and immortals, Andry certainly felt the gods around him. Who else could have set a squire on such a path, the son of a foreign noblewoman and a low knight? Heir to no castles, blood to no king.

I will not be that boy tomorrow. When all this is done.

At the edge of the clearing, the immortal prince of Iona joined Cortael. His Elder senses were keenly focused on the forest. Even from the hill, Andry saw the grim set of his jaw.

"I can hear them," he said, the words like a whipcrack. "Half a mile on. Only two, as expected."

"We should take our precautions with a wizard," Bress called out. The ax over his shoulder flashed a smile against the sky.

The immortals of Sirandel turned to stare at him as if facing a child.

"We are the precautions, Bull Rider," Arberin said softly, his voice accented by his unfathomable language.

The mercenary pursed his lips.

"The Red is a meddling trickster, nothing more," Cortael called without turning. "Ring the temple; keep your formation." The Corblood was a born leader, well accustomed to command. "Taristan will try to slip through us and tear open a crossing before we can stop him."

"He will fail," Dom rumbled, drawing his greatsword from its sheath.

Okran thumped the butt of his spear on the ground in agreement, while the North cousins rattled their shields. Sir Grandel drew himself up, his jaw hard, his shoulder squared. The immortals fell in, their bows and blades in hand. The Companions were ready.

The skies finally opened, the cold, steady rain turning to downpour. Andry shivered as the wet worked down his spine, needling through the gaps in his clothing.

Cortael raised the Spindleblade to the road. Rain spattered the sword, obscuring the ancient design of the steel. Water ran down his face, but he was as stone, weathering the storm. Andry knew Cortael was mortal, but he seemed ageless in that instant. A piece of a realm lost, glimpsed only for a moment, as if through the crack in a closing door.

"Companions of the Realm," Cortael said, his voice carrying.

Thunder rolled somewhere up the mountains. *The gods of the Ward are watching*, Andry thought. He felt their eyes.

The rain doubled its onslaught, falling in sheets, turning the grass to mud.

Cortael did not waver. "That bell has not tolled for a thousand years," he said. "No one has set foot inside that temple or passed through the Spindle since. My brother intends to be the first. He will not. He will fail. What evil intent drove him here *ends* here."

The sword flashed, reflecting a pulse of lightning. Cortael tightened his grip.

"There is power in Corblood and Spindleblade, enough to cut the Spindles through. It is our duty to stop my brother from this ruin, to save the realm, to save the Ward." Cortael looked at the Companions in turn. Andry shivered when his gaze brushed over him. "Today, we fight for tomorrow."

Cortael's resolve did not quell the rising fear in Andry Trelland, but it gave him strength. Even if his duty was only to watch and wash away the blood, he would not flinch. He would serve the Companions and the Ward in whatever way he could. Even a squire could be strong.

"That bell has not tolled for a thousand years," Cortael said again. He looked like a soldier, not a prince. A mortal man without a bloodline, only a duty. "It will not toll for a thousand more."

Thunder sounded again, closer now.

And the bell tolled.

The Companions startled as one.

"Hold your ground," Dom said. Wind tore at the golden curtain of his hair. "This is the Red's doing. An illusion!"

The bell was both hollow and full, a call and a warning. Andry tasted its wrath and its sorrow. It seemed to echo backward and forward through the centuries, through the realms. Some part of Andry told him to put as much distance between himself and the bell as he could. But his feet stayed rooted, fists clenched. *I will not flinch.*

Sir Grandel bared his teeth and slapped his hand against his chest, steel ringing on steel. "With me!" he shouted, the old battle cry of the Lionguard. The Norths answered in kind.

Andry felt it in his chest.

From the hill, Andry glimpsed two figures walking steadily up the path, fading between the raindrops. The one called the Red was aptly named, swathed in a cloak the color of freshly spilled blood. He was hooded, but Andry could see his face. *The wizard.* He was young, clean-shaven, with pale white skin and hair like wheat. His eyes looked red, even from a distance. They quivered as he took in the Companions, scanning them all from head to toe. His mouth moved without sound, lips forming words no one could hear.

The other man stood not in armor but worn leathers and a cloak the color of mud. He was a rogue, the shadow to his brother's sun. His helmet obscured his face, but it didn't hide the curls of dark red hair beneath.

His blade, twin to Cortael's own, was still in its sheath, jeweled with red and purple, a sunset between his fingers. *The sword stealer.*

So this is supposed to be the ruin of the realm, Andry thought, bewildered.

Cortael kept his sword raised. "You are a fool, Taristan."

The bell tolled again, rolling back in the tower.

The other son of Old Cor stood quietly, listening to the temple bell. Then he smiled, his white-toothed grin evident even beneath his helmet.

"How long's it been, Brother?"

Cortael was unmoved.

"Since birth," Taristan finally offered, answering for him. "I bet you had a good time of it, growing up in Iona. Spindleblessed from your first heartbeat." Though Taristan's manner was light, his tone near jovial, the squire saw an edge to him. It was like watching a feral dog size up a trained hound. "And to your last."

"I wish I could say it was a pleasure to meet you, Brother," Cortael said.

At his side, Dom glowered. "Return what you have taken, thief."

With quick fingers, Taristan half drew the blade at his side, revealing inches of the sword. Even in the rain, the steel gleamed, the etched lines a spiderweb.

He twitched a smirk. "You're welcome to try and take it back if you want, Domacridhan." The Elder's full name fell off his tongue awkwardly, not worth his effort. He wiggled the sword in its sheath, taunting them all. "If you're anything like the vaults of your kin, you'll fail. And who are you to keep my birthright from me? Even if I am the younger, the spare, it's only fair we each hold a blade of our ancestors, of our lost realm."

"This will end in ruin," Cortael growled. "Surrender and I will not have to kill you."

Taristan slid a foot, moving with the grace of a dancer, not a warrior. Cortael shifted to match, extending the blade to his brother's throat.

"The Elders raised you as you are, Cortael," he said. "A warrior, a scholar, a lord of men and immortals both. The heir to rebuild an empire long since lost. All to do exactly what I have done: Bring the Spindles back into crossing. Rejoin the realms. Allow their people to return to a home they have not seen in centuries." He glanced at Dom. "Am I wrong, Elder?"

"To tear a Spindle open is to put all the realms in danger. You would destroy the world for your own ends," Dom growled, his steady manner fading.

Taristan stepped, squelching in the mud. "Destruction for some. Glory for others."

The mantle of the Elder's stillness fell away with the ease of a discarded cloak. "*Monster*," Dom raged, his own sword suddenly raised.

Taristan grinned again, taunting.

He's enjoying this, Andry realized with disgust.

Dom snarled. "You cannot force a Spindle. The consequences—"

"Save your breath," Cortael said. "His fate is chosen."

Taristan halted in his tracks.

"*My* fate is chosen?" he hissed, his voice turning soft and dangerous, a blade beneath silk. Rage gathered in him as the storm gathered above.

On the hill, Andry felt his heartbeat quicken and his breath come fast.

"They *took* you and *trained* you and *told* you that you were something special, an emperor returned, Corblood and Spindleborn," Taristan seethed. "The last of an ancient bloodline, meant for greatness. Old Cor was yours to claim and conquer, yours to rule. What a glorious destiny for the firstborn son of the parents we never knew."

With a snarl, he raised both hands to his helmet and ripped it away, revealing his face.

Andry let out a gasp, mouth ajar.

The two brothers stared, mirror images of each other.

Twins.

Though Taristan was ragged where Cortael was regal, Andry could barely tell them apart. They had the same fine face, piercing eyes, stern jaw, thin lips, high brow, and strange, distant way of all those of Spindleblood. Separate from the other mortals, alike only to each other.

Cortael recoiled, stricken. "Taristan," he said, his voice nearly swallowed by the rain.

The sword stealer drew his own Spindleblade, unsheathing it in a long, slow motion. It sang in harmony with the bell, a high breath to a deep bellow.

"Every dream you ever had was given. Every path you ever walked already decided," Taristan said. Rain lashed the blade. "*Your* fate was chosen the day we were born, Cortael. Not mine."

"So what do you choose now, Brother?"

Taristan raised his chin. "I choose the life I should have lived."

The infernal bell tolled again, deeper this time.

"You gave me the chance to surrender." Taristan's lip curled. "I'm afraid I can't do the same. Ronin?"

The wizard raised his hands, white as snow, palms outstretched.

The Sirandels moved faster than Andry thought possible, three arrows leaping from the string. They aimed true, for the heart, the throat, the eye. But inches from Ronin's face, the arrows burned away. More arrows flew, faster than Andry thought possible. Again the arrows flamed beneath the red glare, little more than smoke in the rain.

Cortael raised his sword high, meaning to cut Ronin in half.

Taristan was quicker, parrying the blow with the clang of steel on steel. "What you learned in a palace," he hissed, their identical faces close, "I learned better in the mud."

The wizard's palms came together, and there was the grate of stone, another curl of thunder, and the hiss of liquid on something hot, like oil sizzling in a pan. Terror bled through Andry as he looked to the temple, once empty, but no longer. The doors swung outward, pushed by a dozen white hands streaked in ash and soot. Their skin split and cracked, showing bone beneath, or oozing red wounds. Andry could not see their faces, and for that he was grateful. He could scarcely imagine the horror of them. A hot light pulsed from within the temple, so bright as to be blinding, as the shadows spilled from the doorway and raced across the clearing.

The Companions turned toward the commotion, faces dropping in shock.

"The Ashlands," Rowanna of Sirandel gasped. Her golden eyes widened with the same fear Andry felt in himself, though he had no idea what she meant. For a moment her focus shifted from the temple to the horses up the hill. It was not difficult to guess her mind.

She wanted to run.

Below, Cortael growled in Taristan's face, their blades locked together. "The *Spindle?*"

The other twin leered. "Already torn, the crossing already made." He moved in a flash of speed, bringing his elbow across Cortael's face with a crack. The great lord spun, falling, his broken nose gushing a torrent of scarlet blood. "What sort of *idiot* do you think I am?"

Dom leapt, roaring an Elder battle cry. He moved in a graceful arc, until the wizard raised a hand and brushed him aside with barely a touch, tossing him into the mud some yards away.

The foul, living corpses of the Spindle forced their way from the temple in the dozens, tumbling over each other. Some were already broken, crawling on shattered limbs rattling in greasy black armor. They were like mortal men but not, twisted from the inside out. Most clutched battle-worn weapons: rusted iron swords and notched axes, cracked daggers, splintered spears. Broken but still sharp, still lethal. Arrows peppered the horde, the Sirandels felling the first wave like wheat before the scythe. They could be killed, but their numbers only grew. They carried an unmistakable odor of smoke and burned flesh, and a hot wind blew from inside the temple, from the Spindle, bringing with it clouds of ash.

Andry could not move, could not breathe. He could only stare as the corpses fell upon the Companions, a scarred and bloody army of a lost realm. *Were they living? Were they dead?* Andry could not say. But they kept an odd circle around Taristan and Cortael. As if commanded to let the brothers fight.

Okran's spear danced, skewering throats as he moved in agile arcs. The Gallish knights formed a well-practiced triangle, fighting hard, their swords stained in black and red. Surim and Nour were but blurs through the fray, shortsword and daggers dancing. They left destruction in their wake, cutting a path through the bodies as they surged. The creatures screamed and fought, their voices inhuman, screeching and frayed, their vocal cords shredded. Andry could hardly distinguish faces—they were bleached beyond recognition, scalps bare and skin the color of bone, scarred

red or painted in dripping oil. Flaking with ash, they looked like wood burned white, scorched from the inside out.

The plan was two against twelve, Andry thought, petrified. *But no, it's twelve against dozens. Hundreds.*

The horses snorted and tugged at their ropes. They smelled the danger, the blood, and most of all the Spindle hissing within the temple. It filled their bones with lightning terror.

Taristan and Cortael circled each other, Cortael's armor half painted in mud. Blood ran down his chin and over his antlered breastplate. Their blades came together, striking true. Cortael was skill and force, where Taristan was an alley cat, always moving, shifting on his toes, sword in one hand, dagger in the other, using both in equal measure. He smashed; he dodged; he used the mud and the rain to his advantage. He grinned and sneered, spitting blood in his brother's face. He slammed his blade down on his brother's shoulder, his light plate and ring mail. Cortael grimaced in pain but seized his brother around the middle. The twins toppled together, rolling through the muck.

Andry watched without blinking, frozen to the spot. *What can I do? What can I do?* His hands shook; his body trembled. *Draw a sword, damn you. Fight. It's your duty. You want to be a knight, and knights are not afraid. A knight would not stand and watch. A knight would charge down this hill and into the chaos, shield and sword ready.*

Below the hill, the mud turned red.

And a knight would die doing it.

Arberin screamed first.

A corpse grabbed his red braid, climbing on his back. Another followed. And another, and another, until the sheer weight of bodies brought the Elder to the ground. Their blades were many. White steel, black iron, pitted and old. But sharp enough.

His flesh gave easily.

Rowanna and Marigon fought their way to their kin. They reached a body still bleeding, his immortal life ended.

Sir Grandel and the Norths were losing ground, their triangle tightening with each passing second. Swords danced; shields bashed; gauntlets cracked on flesh. Bodies piled around them, white limbs and decapitated heads. Edgar tripped first, falling as if through water, slowly, the end already realized. Until Sir Grandel seized him by the cloak, pulling him back upright.

"With me!" he shouted over the din. In the training yards of the palace, it meant *keep up, be strong, push harder.* Today it simply meant *stay alive.*

The Bull Rider roared, his ax wheeling, cutting throats with every pass. Red and black streaked his armor, blood and oil. But the mercenary could not keep up his pace. Andry wanted to scream when the horned helm of Bress the Bull Rider disappeared beneath the corpse tide.

The seconds felt like hours, and every death a lifetime.

Rowanna fell next, half submerged in a puddle, an ax in her spine.

A hammer blow caved in Raymon North's breastplate. The wet rasp of his dying breath rattled even over the battlefield. Edgar bent over him, his sword forgotten as he cradled his cousin's head. Despite Sir Grandel's best efforts, the creatures fell upon the kneeling knight with knives and teeth.

Andry had known the Norths since he was a boy. He'd never thought he'd watch them die—and die so poorly.

Sir Grandel was heavy, difficult to pull down, though the creatures tried. He looked up from the clearing, locking eyes with Andry, still on the rise. Andry watched his own hands move, gesturing without thought, beckoning for his lord to abandon the battle. *With me. Stay alive.* In another time, Sir Grandel would have scolded him for cowardice.

Now he obeyed, and he ran.

So did Andry, his sword suddenly in his fist. His body moved faster than his mind, his feet sliding over the mud. *I am squire to Sir Grandel Tyr, a knight of the Lionguard. This is my duty. I must help him.* All other thoughts faded, all fear forgotten. *I must be brave.*

"With me!" Andry howled.

Sir Grandel climbed, but the creatures followed, tearing at his limbs, pulling him backward. He raised a gauntleted hand, fingers splayed. Not reaching, not begging. Not asking for aid or protection. His eyes went wide.

"RUN, TRELLAND!" the knight bellowed. "RUN!"

Sir Grandel Tyr's last command struck Andry through. He froze, looking into the red maw of the carnage below.

A corpse tore the knight's sword away. He fought on, but the mud sucked at his boots and he slid, pitching forward against the slope, fingers clawing at the wet grass.

Tears pricked Andry's eyes. "With me," he whispered, his voice a flower dying in frost.

He could not watch as one sword fell, and then another. The world spotted before him, black dots spreading to eat up his vision.

The smell of blood and rot and ash consumed everything. *I must run*, he thought, his legs like water.

"Move," Andry hissed to himself, forcing a step back. He felt his father watching, and Sir Grandel too. Knights dead in battle, knights who had done their duty and not forsaken their honor. The sort of knight he would never be. Andry sheathed his sword, his fingers meeting the reins of his horse.

Nour was dead upon the temple steps, their long, lithe limbs splayed across the marble. They were lovely even in death. Marigon wept openly over Rowanna's body but still fought with deadly rhythm. She howled, tossing her hair, not a fox but a wolf with red fur. Surim and Dom were still alive, trying to fight their way to Cortael.

Okran's spear broke at his feet, but he was not without shield and sword. The white armor of Kasa turned crimson, the Eagle painted with a fresh kill.

Andry untied his reins, hands shaking. Then he turned to Okran's horse. The squire set his jaw, willing his fingers into motion. They were numb with fear, clumsy, as he loosed the knight's horse. *I can do this, at least.*

Cortael and Taristan fought in the eye of a bloody hurricane. The mud churned beneath their feet, torn up like a tournament ground. Cortael looked the same as his brother now, ragged and worn, far from a prince or an emperor. Both panted in exhaustion, swaying on their feet, each blow coming a little slower, a little weaker.

Ronin stood before the temple doors, the air swirling with ashes. He kept his arms spread, palms raised, in worship to no god

Andry knew. He tipped his head and smiled up at the bell tower. It tolled in answer, as if a bell could do such a thing.

The Spindleblades met as lightning veined, each blade aglow for a moment, purple-white and blazing.

One of the horses screamed and reared, snapping the rope line. They all bolted, and Andry cursed. Leather slid through his fingers. Andry squeezed and braced himself, expecting to be dragged down the hill. Instead Dom's white stallion whinnied, caught in his hands.

A cry, shouted in Kasan, broke Andry's heart anew. Okran fell, his body skewered with blades. He died looking skyward, searching for the eagle, the wings that would take him home.

Across the clearing, Marigon lost a hand to an ax, and then her head.

Surim and Dom roared, unable to reach her, islands in the bloody sea. The waves closed around Surim first. He whistled for his horse, but the steppe pony was already in the fray, fighting to his side. She was torn apart before she could reach him. It was Surim's ending too.

Andry had no voice left, no thought even to pray.

In the circle, Cortael screamed his rage, his blows coming fierce again. With a swing of his sword, he knocked away Taristan's dagger, the blade falling deep into the mud. With another, he dismantled Taristan's guard and drove the Spindleblade deep into his brother's chest.

Andry froze, one foot in the stirrup, not daring to hope.

The corpse army stopped too, bloody jaws agape. On the steps, Ronin's hands dropped, his scarlet eyes wide.

Taristan fell to his knees, the blade protruding from his body.

He gaped in shock. Above him, Cortael watched without joy or triumph, his face still but for the rain washing him clean.

"You did this to yourself, Brother," he said slowly. "But still I ask your forgiveness."

His twin choked, the words difficult to form.

"It's—it's not your fault you were born first. It's not—not your fault you were chosen," Taristan stammered, staring at his wound. When he looked up, his black eyes were hard, resolute. "But you continue to underestimate me, and for that, you are to blame."

With a sneer, he drew the sword from his own chest, the blade slick and red.

Andry could not believe his eyes.

"Those bells have not tolled for the gods in a thousand years," Taristan said, rising back to his feet, a Spindleblade in each hand. All around him, the creatures made strange sounds, like chittering insect laughter. "And they do not toll for your gods today. They toll for mine. For Him. For What Waits."

Cortael toppled back on his heels, terrified. He raised a hand between them, undefended, at the nonexistent mercy of a forgotten brother. "You will destroy the Ward for a crown!"

"A king of ashes is still a king," Taristan crowed.

In the bog of bodies, Dom struggled, battering his way to his friend.

He won't make it, Andry knew, his vision swimming. *He is too far, still too far.*

Taristan stabbed Cortael's Spindleblade into the mud at his side, favoring his own sword. Cortael could do nothing to stop him as he raised it. There was nowhere to turn, nowhere to run. His face crumpled, a prince reduced to a beggar.

"Brother—"

The blade struck him true, shearing through plate armor and mail into Cortael's heart. The heir to Old Cor fell to his knees, head lolling on his shoulders.

Taristan used one booted foot to draw the sword from Cortael's chest, letting his body slump. "And a dead man is still dead," he hissed, sneering over the corpse.

He raised his weapon again, ready to hack his brother's body to pieces.

But his sword met another, a blade of Iona in the hand of the last Companion alive.

"Leave him," Dom snarled, furious as a tiger. He shoved Taristan back with ease.

The Elder planted himself between Taristan and his friend's body, feet set for another fight though he was torn apart, surrounded, and already beaten. Cortael's sword, bloody and useless, still stood upright in the mud, a gravestone waiting for them both.

Taristan laughed openly, amused. "The stories say your kind are brave, noble, greatness made flesh. They should say you are stupid too."

Dom's lips twitched, betraying a smile of his own. His eyes, the Elder eyes of an immortal realm, were shockingly green. They shifted for an instant, looking up the hill, to the squire planted firmly in the saddle of a white stallion.

Andry's heart surged, his jaw set in grim resolve. He nodded, only once.

The Elder whistled, high and true. The horse exploded,

charging down the hill. Not into the battle, but around it, past the creatures, the bodies, the Companions fallen and dead.

Moving with the speed only an immortal could claim, Dom lunged for Cortael's sword, vaulting head over feet to draw the blade from the mud. He threw it as he rolled upright, using all his momentum to hurl the blade like a javelin, up and over the scarred heads of the Spindle army. It sailed, an arrow from the string. One last gasp of victory against defeat entire.

Taristan roared as the blade and the stallion raced each other.

Andry's world narrowed to the flash of steel as it landed in the slick grass ahead. He felt the horse beneath him, all muscle and fear. The squire was trained to ride, trained to fight in the saddle. He slung himself sideways, thighs gripping hard, brown fingers reaching.

The Spindleblade felt cold in his hand.

The army screamed but the stallion did not break stride. Andry's pulse rammed in time with the hooves pounding beneath him, an earthquake rattling up in his chest. His mind blurred, a haze as each fallen Companion flashed before him, their endings irrevocably carved into his memory. No songs would be sung of them. No great stories told.

It was too much. All his thoughts splintered and re-formed, melting into one.

We have failed.

1

THE SMUGGLER'S DAUGHTER
Corayne

There was clear sight for miles. A good day for the end of a voyage.

And a good day to begin one.

Corayne loved the coast of Siscaria this time of year, in the mornings of early summer. No spring storms, no crackling thunderheads, no winter fog. No splendor of color, no beauty. No illusions. Nothing but the empty blue horizon of the Long Sea.

Her leather satchel bounced at her hip, her ledger safe inside. The book of charts and lists was worth its weight in gold, especially today. She eagerly walked the ancient Cor road along the cliffs, following the flat, paved stones into Lemarta. She knew the way like she knew her mother's own face. Sand-colored and wind-carved, not worn by the sun but gilded by it. The Long Sea crashed fifty feet below, kicking up spray in rhythm with the tide. Olive and cypress trees grew over the hills, and the wind blew kindly, smelling of salt and oranges.

A good day, she thought again, turning her face to the sun.

Her guardian, Kastio, walked at her side, his body weathered by decades on the waves. Gray-haired with furious black eyebrows, the old Siscarian sailor was darkly tanned from fingertips to toes. He walked at an odd pace, suffering from old knees and permanent sea legs.

"Any more dreams?" he asked, glancing at his charge sidelong. His vivid blue eyes searched her face with the focus of an eagle.

Corayne shook her head, blinking tired eyes. "Just excited," she offered, forcing a thin smile to placate him. "You know I barely sleep before the ship returns."

The old sailor was easily thrown off.

He doesn't need to know about my dreams, nor does anyone. He would certainly tell Mother, who would make it all the more unbearable with her concern.

But they still come every night. And, somehow, they're getting worse.

White hands, shadowed faces. Something moving in the dark.

The memory of the dream chilled her even in broad daylight, and she sped up, as if she could outrun her own mind.

Ships made their way along the Empress Coast toward the Lemartan port. They had to sail up the gullet of the city's natural harbor, in full sight of the road and the watchtowers of Siscaria. Most of the towers were relics of Old Cor, near ruins of storm-washed stone, named for emperors and empresses long gone. They stood out like teeth in a half-empty jaw. The towers still standing were manned by old soldiers or land-bound sailors, men in their twilight.

"What's the count this morning, Reo?" Corayne asked as she passed the Tower of Balliscor. In the window stood its single keeper, a decaying old man.

He waggled a set of wrinkled fingers, his skin worn as old leather. "Only two in beyond the point. Blue-green sails."

Aquamarine sails, she corrected in her head, *marked with the golden mermaid of Tyriot.* "You don't miss a trick, do you?" she said, not breaking stride.

He chuckled weakly. "My hearing might be going, but my eye's sharp as ever."

"Sharp as ever!" Corayne echoed, fighting a smirk.

Indeed two Tyri galleys were past Antero Point, but a third ship crawled through the shallows, in the shadow of the cliffs. Difficult to spot, for those who did not know where to look. Or those paid to look elsewhere.

Corayne left no coin behind for the half-blind watchman of Balliscor, but she dropped the usual bribes at the towers of Macorras and Alcora. *An alliance bought is still an alliance made*, she thought, hearing her mother's voice in her head.

She gave the same to the gatekeeper at the Lemarta walls, though the port city was small, the gate already open, Corayne and Kastio well known. *Or at least my mother is well known, well liked, and well feared in equal measure.*

The gatekeeper took the coin, waving them onto familiar streets overgrown with lilac and orange blossoms. They perfumed the air, hiding the smells of a crowded port, somewhere between small city and bustling town. Lemarta was a bright place, the stone buildings painted in the radiant colors of sunrise and sunset. On a summer morning, the market streets crowded with tradespeople and townsfolk alike.

Corayne offered smiles like her coin: an item to trade. Like always, she felt a barrier between herself and the throng of people, as if she were watching them through glass.

Farmers drove their mules in from the cliffs, carting vegetables, fruits, and grain. Merchants shouted their wares in every language of the Long Sea. Dedicant priests walked in lines, their robes dyed in varying shades to note their orders. The blue-cloaked priests of Meira were always most numerous, praying to the goddess of the waters. Sailors waiting for a tide or a wind already idled in seden courtyards, drinking wine in the sunshine.

A port city was many things, but above all a crossroads. While Lemarta was insignificant in the scheme of the world, she was nothing to sneer at. She was a good place to drop anchor.

But not for me, Corayne thought as she quickened her pace. *Not one second longer.*

A maze of steps took them down to the docks, spitting Corayne and Kastio out onto the stone walkway edging the water. The climbing sun flashed brilliantly off the turquoise shallows. Lemarta stared down at the harbor, hunched against the cliffs like an audience in an amphitheater.

The ships from Tyriot were newly docked, anchored on either side of a longer pier jutting out into deeper water. A mess of crew crowded the galleys and the pier, spilling over the planks. Corayne caught snatches of Tyri and Kasan passed from deck to dock, but most spoke Paramount, the shared language of trade on both sides of the Long Sea. The crews unloaded crates and live animals for a pair of Siscarian harbor officers, who made a great show of taking notes for their tax records and dock duties. Half a dozen soldiers accompanied them, clad in rich purple tunics.

Nothing of spectacular quality or particular interest, Corayne noted, eyeing the haul.

Kastio followed her gaze, squinting out beneath his eyebrows. "Where from?" he asked.

Her smirk bloomed as quickly as an answer. "Salt from the Aegir mines," Corayne said, all confidence. "And I bet you a cup of wine the olive oil is from the Orisi groves."

The old sailor chuckled. "No bet—I've learned my lesson more than once," he replied. "You've a head for this business, none can deny that."

She faltered in her steps, her voice sharpening. "Let's hope so."

Another harbor officer waited at the end of the next pier, though the berth was empty. The soldiers with him looked half-asleep, wholly uninterested. Corayne fixed her lips into her best smile, one hand in her satchel with her fingers closed around the final and heaviest pouch. The weight was a comfort, as good as a knight's shield.

Though she'd done this a dozen times, still her fingers trembled. *A good day to begin a voyage,* she told herself again. *A good day to begin.*

Over the officer's shoulder, a ship came into harbor, sailing out of the cliff shadow. There was no mistaking the galley, its deep purple flag a beacon. Corayne's heartbeat drummed.

"Officer Galeri," she called, Kastio close behind her. Though neither wore fine clothes, clad in light summer tunics, leather leggings, and boots, they walked the pier like royalty. "Always a pleasure to see you."

Galeri inclined his head. The officer was almost three times her age—nearing fifty years old—and spectacularly ugly. Still, Galeri was popular with the women of Lemarta, mostly because his pockets were well lined with bribes.

"*Domiana* Corayne, you know the pleasure is mine," he replied, taking her outstretched hand with a flourish. The pouch passed from her fingers to his, disappearing into his coat. "And good morning to you, *Domo* Kastio," he added, nodding at the old man. Kastio glowered in reply "More of the usual this morning? How fares the *Tempestborn?*"

"She fares well." Corayne grinned truly, looking over the galley as she glided in.

The *Tempestborn* was bigger than the Tyri galleys, longer by half and twice as fine, with a ram better suited to battle than trade just below the waterline. She was a beautiful ship, her hull darkly painted for voyages in colder seas. With the turn of the season, warm-water camouflage would come: sea-green and sand stripes. But for now she was as shadow, flying the wine-dark purple of a Siscarian ship returning home. The crew was in good shape, Corayne knew, watching their oars move in perfect motion as they maneuvered the long, flat ship to the dock.

A silhouette stood at the stern, and warmth spread in Corayne's chest.

She turned back to Galeri sharply, pulling a paper from her ledger, already stamped with the seal of a noble family. "The cargo listing, more of the usual." *For cargo not yet unloaded.* "You'll find accurate counts. Salt and honey, taken on in Aegironos."

Galeri eyed the paper without interest. "Bound for?" he asked, opening his own ledger of notes. Behind him, one of the soldiers took to pissing off the dock.

Corayne wisely ignored him. "Lecorra," she said. The Siscarian capital. Once the center of the known realm, now a shadow of its imperial glory. "To His Excellency, Duke Reccio—"

"That will suffice," Galeri muttered. Noble shipments could not be taxed, and their seals were easy to replicate or steal, for those with the inclination, skill, and daring.

At the end of the pier, ropes were thrown, men leaping with them. Their voices were a tangle of languages: Paramount and Kasan and Treckish and even the lilting Rhashiran tongue. The patchwork of noise wove with the hiss of rope on wood, the splash of an anchor, the slap of a sail. Corayne could barely stand it, ready to jump out of her skin with excitement.

Galeri dropped into a shallow bow, grinning. Two of his teeth were brighter than the rest. *Ivory, bought or bribed.* "Very well, this is settled. We'll stand watch, of course, to observe your shipment for His Excellency."

It was the only invitation Corayne needed. She trotted by the officer and his soldiers, doing her best not to break into a run. In her younger years, she would have, sprinting to the *Tempest-born* with arms outstretched. *But I am seventeen years old, nearly a woman, and the ship's agent besides,* she told herself. *I must act like crew and not a child clutching at skirts.*

Not that I've ever seen my mother wear a skirt.

"Welcome back!" Corayne called, first in Paramount, then in the half-dozen other languages she knew, and the two more she could attempt. Rhashiran was still beyond her grasp, while the Jydi tongue was famously impossible for outsiders.

"You've been practicing," said Ehjer, the first crew member to meet her. He was near seven feet tall, his white skin covered in tattoos and scars hard-won in the snows of the Jyd. She knew the stories of the worst of them—a bear, a skirmish, a lover, a particularly angry moose. *Or perhaps the last two were the same?* she wondered before he embraced her.

"Don't patronize me, Ehjer; I sound *haarblød*," she gasped, struggling to breathe in his grip. He laughed heartily.

The pier crowded with reunion, the planks a mess of crew and crates. Corayne passed through, careful to note any new recruits picked up on the voyage. There were always a few, easy to spot. Most had blistered hands and sunburns, unaccustomed to life on deck. The *Tempestborn* liked to train their own from the waves up.

Mother's rule, like so many others.

Corayne found her where she always did, half perched on the railing.

Meliz an-Amarat was neither tall nor short, but her presence was vast and commanded attention. A good quality for any ship's captain to have. She scanned the dock with a hawk's eye and a dragon's pride, her task yet unfinished though the ship was safely in port. She was not a captain to laze in her cabin or flit off to the nearest seden to drink while the crew did the hard work. Every crate and burlap sack passed beneath her gaze, to be checked off on a mental tally.

"How fare the winds?" Corayne called, watching her mother rule over her galley kingdom.

From the deck, Meliz beamed, her hair free about her shoulders, black as a storm cloud. The faint smile lines around her mouth were well earned.

"Fine, for they bring me home," she said, her voice like honey.

They were words spoken since Corayne was a child, barely old enough to know where her mother was going, when all she could do was wave with one hand and clutch at Kastio with the other. *Not so anymore.*

Corayne felt her smile flag, turning heavy. Her happiness curled at the edges, wearing away with nerves. *Wait for your moment,* she told herself. Promised herself. *Not here, not yet.*

The harbor officer ignored their cargo, mostly unmarked. He would not pry these open on the docks, but leave them be, undisturbed until they were far beyond the care of Captain an-Amarat and the *Tempestborn.* Corayne knew their contents, of course, for it was her job to find places to sell or trade them. It was all in her ledger, buried among false lists and true sea charts.

"Keep those at the end of the pier," she said sharply, gesturing to a set of crates. "An Ibalet ship will dock alongside us before the morning is out, and they need to take their cargo quickly."

"Do they?"

Meliz descended from her sailcloth-and-saltdeck throne, a smile tugging at her lips. She was never far from a smirk or a laugh.

Today she looked wrought in bronze, her skin darkened by the sun while the flush of a successful voyage colored her cheeks. Her mahogany eyes sparkled, made more striking by a line of black along her lids.

"Answer well, Daughter."

Corayne squared her shoulders. She'd grown this last year and could look her mother in the eye now. "The furs will go on to Qaliram."

Meliz blinked, her full, dark brow curving into splendid swoops. There were three tiny scars over her left eye, the lucky cuts of an opponent with poor aim.

She took her daughter by the arm, urging her to walk. "I did not know the Ibalets had need for fox and sable in the Great Sands."

Corayne didn't blame her for the skepticism. Ibal was mostly desert. Fur from the north would certainly not fetch a favorable price. But she had her reasons.

"Their royal court has taken a liking to their mountains," she said lightly, pleased with herself. "And with all that desert blood, well, they're not likely to stay warm without our help. I've made my inquiries; it's all arranged."

"I suppose it won't be terrible to have contacts within the royal family of Ibal." Meliz's voice dropped. "Especially after that *mis-understanding* in the Strait last winter."

A misunderstanding that left three sailors dead and the Tempest-born *near sinking.* Corayne swallowed back the bitter taste of fear and failure. "My thoughts exactly."

Meliz pulled her closer. After nearly two months left behind, Corayne basked in the attention. She brushed her head against her mother's shoulder, wishing she could embrace her properly. But the crew were all around them, busy in their work, dedicated to the ship and her needs, with Galeri observing from the edges, more nosy than official.

"You know you have some of that desert blood," Meliz said. "On my side, of course."

Despite the warmth of her mother's arm, Corayne felt a cold ripple of unease in her belly. "Among others," she muttered. There were many conversations she wanted to have with her mother. *My bloodline is far from one of them.*

Meliz looked over her daughter again. It was a poor subject to return home to, and she navigated away from it. "Very well, what else have you lined up for me?"

Corayne heaved a breath, both relieved and eager to impress. She held her ledger open to show pages cramped with delicate, deliberate writing. "The Madrentines will be at war with Galland soon enough, and they'll pay best for weaponry." She allowed herself a small smile. "Especially Treckish steel without *entanglements*."

The metal was valuable, both for its durability and the close control Trec kept over its export. Meliz shared in her delight.

"All this you learn in Lemarta?" she mused, raising an eyebrow.

"Where else would I learn it?" Corayne said sharply, her skin growing hot. "We're a port city as much as any. Sailors talk."

Sailors talk; travelers talk; merchants and guards and the tower watchmen talk. They talk loudly and often—lying, mostly. Boasting of lands they've never seen or great deeds they'll never accomplish. But the truth is always there, beneath, waiting to be sifted free, specks of gold among sand.

Captain an-Amarat chuckled in her ear, her breath cool. Her mother smelled of the sea; she always smelled of the sea.

"Do any talk to *you*?" she needled, intention clear. She glanced at the old sailor who spent his days guarding her daughter. "Kastio, how fares my daughter with the boys?"

A jolt of embarrassment licked down Corayne's spine. She slapped her ledger shut with both hands and drew away, flushing red. "Mother," she hissed, scandalized.

Meliz only laughed, unbothered and accustomed to her daughter's discomfort.

"Oh, come now. I was your age when I met your father," she said, putting a hand on her generous hip, fingers splayed over her sword belt. "Well, a year older. I was your age when I met the girl *before* your father. . . ."

Corayne stuffed her ledger away, returning the precious pages to her satchel. "All right, that's more than enough. I have a lot of information to keep straight, and this is certainly not worth committing to my memory."

Laughing again, Meliz took her daughter's face in her hands. She stepped with a swaying motion, her heart still aboard the deck of a ship.

Though she loved Meliz, Corayne felt small and young in her grasp. And she hated it.

"You're radiant when you blush," Meliz said, all the truth she could muster in her words.

Such is the way of mothers, to think the sun and the moon of their children. Like the Long Sea on a clear morning, Corayne held no illusions. Meliz an-Amarat was the radiant one, beautiful and magnificent. Lovely as any queen, but Meliz was common-born of the Ward, a smuggler's daughter, a child of the Sea and the Strait and every country they touched. She was made for the waves, the only other thing in this world as fierce and bold as she was.

Not like me. Corayne knew herself, and while she was her mother's daughter, she was not her mother's equal. Their coloring was the same. Golden skin that went bronze in the summer, black hair that shone deep red beneath sunlight. But Corayne had thin lips, a short nose, a graver face than her mother, who smiled like a sunbeam. Her eyes were unremarkable, black all the way through, flat and empty as a starless night. Inscrutable, distant. As Corayne felt apart from the world, her eyes showed it.

It did not bother her, to think such things. *It is good to know your own measure.* Especially in a world where women were as much what they looked like as what they could do. Corayne would never persuade a fleet patrol with a bat of her eyelashes. But the right coin to the right hands, the right pull of the right string—that Corayne could do, and do well.

"You're perfect when you lie," the girl said, kindly pulling away.

"I have lots of practice," Meliz replied. "Of course, I never lie to you."

"You and I both know that is realms away from the truth," Corayne said without accusation. It took all her resolve to keep her face still and measured, unaffected by her mother's life—and the trust they could never truly share. "But I know you have your reasons."

Meliz was good enough not to argue. There was truth in

admitting her lies. "I do," she murmured. "And they are always, *always*, to keep you safe, my dearest girl."

Though the words stuck in her throat, Corayne forced them out anyway, her cheeks flushing with heat. "I need to ask you—" she began.

Only for Galeri's thumping boots to cut her off.

Mother and daughter turned at his approach, false smiles donned with ease.

"Officer Galeri, you honor us with your attention," the captain said, inclining her head politely. Theirs was a pleasant arrangement, and small-minded men were quick to take slights from women, even imagined.

Galeri basked in the glow of Captain an-Amarat. He drew close, closer than he had to Corayne. Meliz did not flinch, well accustomed to the leers of men. Even fresh from a voyage, dressed in salt-eaten clothes, she could turn many eyes.

Corayne swallowed her disgust.

"You came from Aegironos, your daughter told me," Galeri said. He jabbed a thumb back at the crates piling on the dock. Runes marked the wood. "Strange, the Aegir usually don't mark their crates in Jydi wolf scratch."

Sighing inwardly, Corayne began to count the coins left in her satchel and wondered if enough could be swept together to appease Galeri's curiosity.

Her mother's smile only widened. "I thought that odd as well."

Corayne had seen her mother flirt many times. *This is not that.*

Galeri's face fell, the workings of his mind easy to read. His soldiers were few, unready, and mostly useless. Captain an-Amarat had her entire crew behind her, and her own sword at her hip. She could kill him and be off with the current before the officers on the next dock even noticed he was dead. Or he could simply move on with the coin already earned, with more to be earned again after the next voyage. His eyes trembled, just for a second, to pass over Corayne herself. The only thing in the world he could hold over Meliz an-Amarat, should things go ill.

Corayne curled a fist, though she had no clue what to do with it.

"Good to have you back in port, Hell Mel," Galeri forced out, matching her grin. A bead of sweat rolled down his scalp as he stepped aside, bowing to the pair of them.

Meliz watched him go, her teeth bared and lips curled into a frightful smile. Who she was on the waves never stood on land, not for long. Corayne rarely saw that woman, the fierce captain of a fiercer crew, who crossed the waters without regard for law or danger. That woman was not her mother, not Meliz an-Amarat. That was Hell Mel.

That name held little meaning here, in the home port of the *Tempestborn*, where the galley glided in on soft winds with little trouble but curious officers. But on the waters, across the Ward, the ship was aptly named, and so was her captain.

Corayne heard those stories too.

Sailors talk.

And Mother lies.

2

A VOICE LIKE WINTER
Andry

He'd traded away his chain mail for food a week ago. His green-and-gold tunic was little more than a rag, torn and crusted with blood, dirt, and dust from the long journey home. Andry Trelland knelt as best he could without collapsing, every limb trembling with exhaustion. It was well past midnight in the capital, and weeks of riding had more than taken their toll. A stone floor had never looked so inviting.

Only fear of sleep kept his eyes open.

The nightmares wait for me, he thought. *The nightmares and the whispers both.* They had haunted him since the temple, since the slaughter that left him alive and so many heroes dead. *Red hands, white faces, the smell of burning flesh.* He blinked, trying to force away the memory. *And now a voice like winter stabbing me through.*

Two knights of the Lionguard flanked the empty throne, their golden armor glowing with candlelight. Andry knew them both.

Sir Eiros Edverg and Sir Hyle of Gilded Hill. They were compatriots to the knights fallen, whose corpses were somewhere in the foothills, lost to the mud. They stared at him but did not speak, though Andry saw concern on both their faces. He looked at the stone beneath him, tracing the patterns of tile while he waited in blistering silence.

Andry knew the sound of men in armor. They clanked and stamped in their steel, marching toward the throne room from the Queen's own residence. When the door to her apartments swung open, spitting out a diamond formation of knights, Andry clenched his teeth so tightly they nearly shattered. His eyes stung; his heart sank. He braced himself for a fresh wash of pain.

The others died and died poorly. The least you can do is hold your ground.

It was no wonder so many vied for the Queen of Galland's hand in marriage. She was young and beautiful, nineteen years old with fine bones, porcelain skin, ash-brown hair, and the silver-blue eyes of her late father, Konrad III. She had his steel spine too. Even though she seemed small in her robe and nightclothes, without a crown or majestic jewels, her presence was dominating. She peered sharply at Andry between the gaps in her Lionguard, never taking her eyes off him as she sank onto her throne.

Her velvety green robe pooled around her, falling like a beautiful gown. She leaned forward on her elbows, fingers clasped together. She only wore the ring of state, a dark emerald set in gold, rough-cut and hundreds of years old. In the dim light, it seemed black as the creatures' eyes, yawning like an abyss.

"Your Majesty," Andry murmured, bowing his head.

Queen Erida looked him over, her gaze piercing. Her eyes snagged on his tunic, reading the stains like she would a book.

"Squire Trelland, please rise," she said, her voice gentle but echoing in the long, ornate room. Her blue gaze softened as Andry clambered to his feet, shaky on his legs. "The road has not been kind to you. Do you need a moment? A meal, a bath? My doctor can be called."

"No, Your Majesty." Andry glanced down at himself. He felt unclean from head to toe, unfit to stand before the Queen of his country. "The blood is not my own."

The knights shifted, glancing among themselves with wary eyes. Andry could guess as to their thoughts. The blood belonged to their brothers, knights of the Lionguard who would never come home.

Erida did not falter. "Have you seen your mother yet?" she asked, still staring.

The squire shook his head. He looked at his boots, flecked with mud and stinking of horse. "It's late, she'll be sleeping, and she sorely needs whatever rest she can find." He remembered the hacking cough that often woke his mother in the night. "I can wait until morning."

The Queen nodded. "Are you able to tell me what happened to you?" Andry felt the question like the cut of a knife. "And to our dear friends?"

White faces, red hands, black armor, knives dripping blood, ash and smoke and rot—

His mouth worked but no words came, his lips parting and closing. Andry wished to turn and run. His fingers trembled and he tucked them away, folding his hands behind his back in the typical pose of a courtier. He raised his head and set his jaw, trying to be strong.

The least you can do is hold your ground, he thought again, the admonishment searing.

"Leave us," Erida said suddenly, looking around at her flanking knights. The young woman went fierce as the lion on her flag, both hands curled on the arms of her throne. She bore the ring of state like a shield.

The Lionguard did not move, stunned.

Andry felt the same. The Queen went very few places without her sworn knights, guardians to the death. His eyes snapped back and forth, weighing the will of the Queen against the will of her warriors.

Sir Hyle sputtered, his pink face going pinker. "Your Majesty—"

"The boy is traumatized. He doesn't need nine of you looming over him," she answered swiftly, without so much as a blink. Her focus shifted back to the squire, her sharp eyes pressing into him. A sadness pulled at her pale face. "I've known Andry Trelland all his life. He'll be a knight alongside the rest of you in a few years' time. Leaving me with him is the same as leaving me with any of you."

Despite all he had seen and suffered, Andry could not help but feel a swell of pride in his chest, albeit short-lived. *Knights do not fail, and I have certainly done that,* he thought. The Lionguard must have shared the same opinion. They hesitated as one, unmoving in their golden armor and green cloaks.

Erida was undeterred and undeniable. Her ring hand curled

into a fist. "Do as your queen commands," she said, her countenance stony.

This time, Sir Hyle did not argue. Instead he dropped into a short, stilted bow, and with a twist of his gloved fingers beckoned the other confused knights to follow. They tramped from the room, a cacophony of steel and iron and swishing fabric.

Only when the door to her apartments was safely shut behind them did the Queen drop her shoulders, curling inward. She waited another moment, then exhaled a long, slow breath. She seemed to shift back into herself, becoming a woman barely more than a child, not a queen with four years of rule behind her.

For a split second, Andry saw her as she'd been in her youth: a princess born, but still without the burdens of a crown. *She loved sailing,* he remembered. All the children of the palace, noble cousins and page boys and little maidens, used to accompany her out into Mirror Bay. They would pretend to run the boat, practicing their knots and pushing around sails. But not Erida. She would sit at the helm and point, directing the real crew over the water.

Now she directed the country, and she was pointing at him.

"I answered the Elder call," she said in a low, raw voice. Her eyes went oddly bright, shimmering with the candles. One of her hands slipped into her robes and drew back out, clutching a roll of parchment.

Andry swallowed hard. He wanted to burn that infernal piece of paper.

She unfurled it with shaking hands, her eyes blazing over the inked message. At the edge of the page, the ancient seal of Iona was still there, stamped in broken green wax. By now the sight of it turned his stomach, and the memory it brought forth was even worse.

Sir Grandel and the Norths knelt before the Queen on her throne. She was resplendent in her court finery and dazzling crown. Andry knelt with them, some yards behind, the only squire to accompany the knights into the audience chamber. For what purpose, he did not know, but he could guess. The Norths were always a bit more . . . self-sufficient than Sir Grandel, who seemed to want a squire's aid for every task big or small. If the Queen had a command for Sir Grandel Tyr, certainly Andry Trelland would be made to follow on his heels.

The squire kept his head bowed, glimpsing the Queen only from the edges of his vision. She was as green and golden as her knights, with a strange parchment in her hands.

In an instant, Andry saw the seal, the crude image of a stag stamped deep. He racked his memory, sifting through lords and great families, their heraldry well known to even a page boy. But none matched.

"This is a summons," the Queen said, turning the letter over.

On his knees, Sir Edgar blanched. "Who would dare summon the Queen of Galland, the greatest crown upon the Ward? The glory of Old Cor reborn?"

Queen Erida tipped her head. "What do you know of Elders?"

The knights sputtered, exchanging bewildered glances.

Sir Grandel laughed outright, shaking back brown hair flecked with gray. "A story for children, Your Majesty," he chortled. "A fairy tale."

Andry dared to look up. The Queen did not smile, her lips pursed into a grim line.

This was no joke.

"Immortals, my lady," Andry heard himself answer. His voice trembled. "Born of the Spindles, having passed into Allward from another realm. But they were trapped, the doorway to their home closing not long after they arrived. The Elders are stranded in our realm, if they even still exist here at all." Impossible beings, rare as unicorns, never to be glimpsed by my own eyes.

"A fairy tale," Sir Grandel said again, shooting a glare at his squire.

Heat flushed in Andry's cheeks and he dropped his head again. It was not like him to speak out of turn, and he expected a sharp rebuke from both his lord and the Queen.

It never came.

"Stories and tales all have roots in truth, Sir Grandel," the Queen answered coolly. "And I would like to know the truth of this." The letter caught the candlelight of the throne room, aglow. "One who calls herself the Monarch of Iona bids us greeting, and humbly asks for aid."

Sir Grandel scoffed. "Aid? What can this decrepit old witch think to demand of you?"

Andry could hear the smile in Queen Erida's voice. "Care to find out?"

"Would that I had ignored their call, and my own curiosity," she mumbled, still glaring at the page. If she'd had any Spindle magic in her, the letter would have burst into flames long ago.

"How could anyone have known?" Andry whispered. *I certainly did not. Even when they warned of danger and doom for the realm.* It seemed a lifetime ago, though only a few months had passed.

The days flew by in his mind, a blur. *The road to Iona, the great halls of their ancient city, the council of Elders and mortals alike. Then the trail of heroes marching into the wilderness, all of them doomed.*

Andry blinked furiously to clear his eyes and head.

The Queen lowered her eyes, running her thumb over the emerald ring.

"I sent you to them, and into danger," she whispered. "The blame for whatever befell Sir Grandel and the Norths is mine. Do not take this burden onto yourself, Andry." Her voice cracked. "Give it to me."

The moments slid by like leaves in a fast current, but Erida waited with the patience of a stone. Andry fought to speak, the words slow and reluctant in his throat.

"In Iona, the Elders—the Monarch—she told us a sword had been stolen from their vaults," he forced out, the tale spilling from him in a torrent. He tried not to be pulled under. "A Spindleblade, forged in a realm beyond the Ward, imbued with the power of the Spindles themselves. The one who took it, a man named Taristan, is a descendant of Old Cor, with Spindleblood in his own veins. With the blood and the sword together, he could rip open a Spindle long since closed, tear a doorway between our realm and another, to whatever lay beyond."

Queen Erida's eyes widened, the whites like a moon eclipsed by blue.

"He was headed for an ancient Elder temple in the mountains, some miles south of the Gates of Trec. The last known location of a Spindle crossing." Andry gritted his teeth. "Thirteen of us went forth to stop him." The first tear fell, hot and furious on his cheek. "And twelve died."

The throne room echoed with his voice, his rage and sorrow. His loss carried up the columns and into the chandeliers of wrought iron and flickering candles. Andry's fists balled at his sides, his resolve threatening to crumble. But he pushed on, retelling the slaughter of his Companions, the failure of Cortael, the smell of immortal blood, and a burned realm spewing a corpselike army. The red wizard, the sword through Taristan's chest, and his leering white smile. How Sir Grandel stumbled and fell, never to stand again. How the squire could only watch and run away with little more than his own skin.

Andry expected the cold whispers to rise with his memories, but there was only his own voice to fill his head.

"I should have fought," he hissed, glaring at his ruined boots. "It was my duty."

Erida slapped her hand against the throne, the noise jarring and slick as a whipcrack. Andry looked up to find her staring, her nostrils flared.

"You came home. You survived," she said firmly. "And what's more, you've delivered a very important message." With a will, she stood, her robe flowing around her. She stepped lightly, descending from the dais to join Andry on the stones. "I've spent more time studying diplomacy and languages than Spindle lore. But I know my histories. Allward was a realm of crossing once, subject to great magic and terrible monsters, we mortals warring with dangers we must never face again. That cannot come to pass. If what you say is true, if this Taristan can cut open Spindles long dead, then he is very dangerous indeed, and he has an army at his back."

"The likes of which none of us have ever seen," Andry admitted, feeling the pull of their hands again. The creatures of Taristan's army shrieked in his head, their voices like scraping metal and cracking bone. "I know it sounds impossible."

"I have never known you to be a liar, Andry Trelland. Not even when we were children, fibbing to the cooks for extra desserts." She drew a breath and dipped her head. "I am sorry for what you have lost."

Though her junior by two years, Andry was much taller than the Queen. But somehow she was able to look up at him without seeming small.

"They were your own knights, not mine," he said.

"That's not what I meant," the Queen murmured softly, looking him over again. Andry saw the same young girl in her eyes, set apart from the rest of the children. Eager to smile and laugh and play, but isolated too. Forever marked as a princess, without the freedoms of a page boy or a maiden or even a servant child.

The young girl vanished with the tightening of her jaw. "You will speak of this to no one, Squire," she added, turning back to her throne.

Without thinking, Andry followed quickly on her heels, his gut churning. *We were caught off guard. That cannot happen again.* "People must be warned—"

Erida did not falter, her voice stern and unyielding. She knew how to make herself heard.

"The Spindles are myth to most, legends and fairy stories, as vanished as Elders or unicorns or any other great magic born of other realms. To speak of one returned, *torn open*, and a man who would wield it like a spear into our hearts? A man who cannot be harmed at the head of a corpse army?" She glanced at Andry over her shoulder, her gaze like two sapphires. "I am ruler of Galland, but I am a queen, not a king. I must be careful in what I say, and what weapons I give my enemies. I will not give anyone cause to call me weak-minded or mad," she snapped, clearly upset. "I cannot move without proof. Even then, it would cause panic in my capital. And panic in a city of half a million souls will kill more than any army that walks the Ward. I must be careful indeed."

Ascal was a bloated metropolis, sprawling across the many islands in the delta of the Great Lion. The streets were crowded, the markets overrun, the canals dirty, and the bridges prone to collapse. There had been riots after King Konrad died: opposition to a girl assuming his throne. Fires in the slums, floods at the ports. Disease. Bad harvests. Religious upheaval between the dedicant orders. A criminal underbelly thick as smoke. *Nothing compared to what comes*, Andry knew. *Nothing compared to what Taristan can do.*

He gritted his teeth. "I don't understand" was all he could muster, running up against the wall of the Queen's resolve.

It was not to be climbed.

"It isn't for you to understand, Andry," she said, knocking on the door to her apartments. It swung open to show her Lionguard knights waiting in the passage beyond, rigid in their armored rows. "You need only obey."

There was no argument to be had with the Queen of Galland.

Andry bowed at the waist, biting back every retort rising in his throat. "Very well, Your Majesty," he said.

She paused, the knights shifting into formation as she took one last look at the squire. "Thank you for coming home." Her face was bittersweet. "At least your mother won't have another knight to bury."

I'm not a knight. And I never will be.

His heart tightened in his chest. "A small mercy."

"May the gods protect us from whatever comes of this," Erida murmured, turning away.

The door slammed shut, and Andry all but ran from the throne room, eager to tear off his clothes and scrub away the last few weeks. Anger overtook his sorrow long enough to propel him through the passages of the New Palace, his feet guiding him down familiar halls.

The gods had their chance.

Asleep, Lady Valeri Trelland did not look ill. She was tucked in comfortably, a fine silk sleeping cap pulled over her hair. She wore no cares upon her face, the skin around her mouth and eyes relaxed. She seemed younger by decades, still a beauty despite the sickness burrowing in her body. They had similar faces, Andry and his mother. Her skin was darker, a polished ebony, but they shared the same high cheekbones and full lips, and their hair, thick, black, and curly. It was an odd thing for the squire to look into a mirror and see his mother. Odder still to see what she'd been before the sickness came, reaching with wet hands for the candle burning so brightly inside her.

She rattled a breath, and he winced, feeling the raw edge of her pain in his own throat.

Sleep, Mother, he willed, counting the seconds as her chest rose and fell. He braced for a coughing attack, but it never came.

Her bedchamber was hot, the air close, with the firewood piled high in the hearth. Andry sweated in his fresh clothes but did not move from his spot on the wall, wedged between a tapestry and a narrow window.

Even with the fire, he felt the cold, the icy finger of dread running down his spine.

It must be hidden.

The whispers spoke with a voice like winter, brittle and cracking. They were a woman, a man, a child, a crone. Impossible to pin down. He shivered as they returned, rising to a howl inside his head.

It is hidden! he wanted to shout, his jaw clenched tight. The cold played along his ribs.

It must not be spoken of.

His teeth gnashed. *I said nothing of it. Not to anyone. Not even the Queen,* he answered. It felt like madness. It could *be* madness, born of slaughter and sorrow.

The voices had first come on the road home, with the Elder stallion beneath him and the Spindleblade lashed to his saddle. He nearly fell from the horse but pushed on, trying to outrun what was already in his head. No matter how far or how fast he rode, they never left him behind.

There was laughter and sadness in the whispers, both in equal measure. *This you are bidden,* they hissed, letting the words carry over him. *Keep it hidden.*

Andry wanted to brush the voices away but remained pressed against the wall. He would not break his silent vigil, keeping watch over his ailing mother.

And the Spindleblade concealed beneath her bed, a secret to all but Andry Trelland.

3

BETWEEN THE DRAGON AND THE UNICORN
Corayne

After two glasses of wine, Corayne's head felt light. Her mind spun, already dreaming of lands beyond Lemarta. The palisade cities of the Jyd, raider country. Nkona and the Bay of Marvels. Almasad, the grand port of Ibal, home to the largest fleet in the realm. She shook her head and nudged her cup away, sliding it over a familiar, greasy table in the corner of the Sea Queen. The seden bar was named long before the time of Captain an-Amarat, but everyone liked to pretend it was named for her.

Meliz looked the part, sprawled in the corner with her back to the wall and her smile to the room. The candlelight gleamed in her hair, crowning her with rubies. Kastio sat by the door to the street, surrounded by sailors and townspeople alike. With the captain returned, he had no cause to nanny Corayne. He swayed, his lightning-blue eyes lidded, a half-empty glass in hand. The crew were well into their cups of wine and flagons of ale. Their voices filled the common room, their bronzed and sunburned bodies crammed into the narrow space. Most needed a wash. Corayne didn't mind. Stinking sailors were better than another lonely evening.

She studied them. The *Tempestborn* picked up two new recruits on the voyage. White-faced twins from the Jyd, barely older than she, but tall and broad, of raider blood.

Two gained, four lost, Corayne thought. Faces swam before her eyes, crew she would never see again.

Four dead.

She heaved a breath, the wine turning to courage in her belly. "Mother—"

"Put out the word I'm looking for oarsmen," Meliz interrupted, swirling her glass.

Her demand caught Corayne off guard. She blinked, confused. "We've at least two weeks before we need to prepare for another run, and we can do that shorthanded if need be."

Short sails in easy water, running light and quick routes along the coast. Corayne knew the voyages of the *Tempestborn* too well and planned around them as best she could. *The summer runs are without much danger. Good to learn on.*

Meliz's grin slid, a mask coming undone. "Strong backs, good rhythm, no fuss."

"For what destination? For when?" Changes in schedule meant mistakes, greater risk. And it threw her own plans into disarray.

"Are you *my* mother now?" Meliz teased, but her voice was sharp. "Just make sure they're good recruits. I've no need for wide-eyed imbeciles looking for an adventure, chasing a Spindle story or a fairy tale or plain old glory on the Long Sea."

Corayne flushed. Her voice dropped. "Where are you going, Mother?"

"They have a tendency to die, and die disappointed," Meliz muttered, pulling at her wine.

"Since when have you minded losing crew?" Corayne snapped, half to herself. The words tasted bitter in her mouth, unfair and unwise. She wanted to call them back as soon as they passed her lips.

"I always mind, Corayne," Meliz said coldly.

"Where are you going?"

"The winds look to be favorable."

"The winds will still be favorable in a month's time."

Meliz looked to the windows, in the direction of the Sea, and Corayne felt lost.

"The *Jaiah* of Rhashir has finally died, leaving sixteen sons to war for his throne. Some say he died of his age or illness. Some say he was murdered. Either way, the conflict makes things easier for us. It is a good opportunity," Meliz said firmly and quickly. As if the words needed only be spoken to become true.

A map ate up Corayne's vision in a weathered swirl of blue, green, and yellow. She saw it clearly in her head, the familiar sea lanes and coasts, rivers and mountains, borders and kingdoms. All places she had never seen but still knew, had heard of but never set foot in. Miles flew past, racing from Lemarta to the Tiger Gulf, the Allforest, the Crown of Snow—the great wonders of distant lands. She tried to picture Jirhali, the great capital of Rhashir, a city of pale green sandstone and burnished copper. Corayne's imagination failed her.

"It's near four thousand miles to their shores, as the crow flies," she breathed, opening her eyes. There was only the map. Her mother was already far away, well beyond her reach. "With a good wind, favorable current, no storms, no *trouble* . . . you'll be gone for months at best." Her voice caught. "If you return at all."

A dangerous voyage, far from what we planned.

Meliz did not move. "It is a good opportunity. Have the ship prepared. We leave in three days."

So soon, Corayne cursed, her fingers curling on the tabletop. "I must ask—"

"Don't," Meliz said without blinking, raising her glass to her lips again.

An angry spark flared in Corayne's chest, chasing off her fear. "In winter you said—"

"I made no promises in winter."

Her word was so terribly final, like the closing of a door.

Corayne clenched her jaw, using all her will to keep her hands on the table and not slap the wine from her mother's grasp. Something roared in her ears, drowning out all sound but her mother and the refusal.

You knew what she would say, she thought. *You knew and you prepared. You're ready to earn this.*

"I'm a year older than you were when you went to sea." Corayne willed herself to look part of the crew. Determined, confident, capable. All things she was to so many people. *So many but for Mother.*

Meliz clenched her jaw. "It wasn't my choice then."

Corayne's reply was quick, the arrow already nocked and aimed. "I'm more use on the water. I'll hear more; I can bargain; I can guide. Think of what the *Tempestborn* was before I started helping. Aimless, disorganized, barely scraping by, dumping half your cargo for want of a buyer," Corayne said, trying her best not to beg. Her mother did not move, did not blink, did not even seem to listen. "I know the charts almost as well as Kireem or Scirilla. I can *help*, especially on a voyage so long and so far away."

You sound stupid. You sound like a child pleading for a favorite toy. Be reasonable. Be logical. She knows your value; she knows and cannot deny it. Corayne took a breath, quieting her thoughts even as she spoke aloud.

"With me on board your profits will triple, at the very least." Corayne clenched her fist on the tabletop. "I guarantee you that. And I won't even take payment."

There was more to say: more lists to rattle off, more hard truths her mother would not be able to brush aside. But Meliz only stared.

"My decision is made, Corayne. Not even the gods can change it," the captain said, her voice shifting. Corayne heard some begging in her too. "My love, you don't know what you're asking for."

Corayne narrowed her black eyes. "Oh, I think I do."

Something crumbled in Meliz, like a wall tumbling down.

"I'm good at my job, Mother," Corayne said, stony. "And my job is to listen, to think, to connect and anticipate. You think the people here don't talk about you and your crew?" She pointed with her chin to the rest of the room, carrying on in their loud manner. "About what you do out there on the open water?"

Meliz leaned forward so quickly Corayne nearly fell from her seat.

"We're criminals, yes," the captain hissed. "We move around crown laws. We transport what others won't or can't. That's what smuggling is. There's a danger to it. You've known that your entire life." The explanation was expected too, another lie of Meliz an-Amarat. "My operation is dangerous, that's true," the woman pushed on. "I'm at risk every time we set sail; so is every person in this room. And I will not risk you with the rest of us."

"The Jydi recruits. They survived, didn't they?" Corayne asked, her tone flat and detached. At the bar, the pale-skinned twins looked as jumpy as rabbits in a snare.

Meliz scowled. "They joined up in Gidastern. Fled some gods-forsaken clan war."

More lies. She fixed her mother with a dark stare, hoping to see through her. Hoping Meliz knew she was seen through.

"They survived whatever ship you found in the Watchful Sea, whatever ship you attacked, emptied, and sank," she said.

"For once that isn't true," Meliz snapped back, near to spitting. "You with all your charts and your lists. That doesn't mean you know what the world is really like. The Jydi aren't raiding. Something is *wrong* in the Watchful. Those boys were running, and I gave them a place to go."

LIES, Corayne thought, feeling each one like a knife.

"You are a smuggler," she answered, banging her hand on the table. "You've broken the laws of every kingdom from here to Rhashira's Mouth. And you are a *pirate*, Captain an-Amarat. You are feared across the Ward for what you do to the ships you hunt and devour." Corayne pushed forward so that they were nearly nose to nose over the table. Meliz's mask was gone, her easy grin abandoned. "Don't bother with shame. I know what you are, Mother, what you have to be. I've known for a long time. And I've been part of this, whether you believe it or not, *all my life.*"

Across the seden, a glass shattered, followed by a roar of laughter. Neither mother nor daughter flinched. A canyon yawned between them, filled only with silence and longing.

"I need this." Corayne's voice broke, bowed by the weight of desperation. "I need to leave. I can't stay here any longer. It feels like the world is growing over me." She reached for her mother's hands, but Meliz pulled her fingers away. "It's like being buried alive, Mama."

The captain stood, her wine in hand. Her stillness was unfamiliar. And foreboding. Calm waters before a storm. Corayne steeled herself, preparing for more lies and excuses.

The captain did not bother with either.

"My answer will always be no."

Be reasonable, Corayne chided herself, even as she jumped out of her chair, fists clenched. The pirate captain didn't move, her stare unbroken and unamused.

Despair bubbled beneath Corayne's skin. She felt like a crashing wave, rolling over with foam as she broke upon the shore. *Be reasonable*, she thought again, though the voice was smaller, more distant. She dug her nails into her palms, using the sting to stay anchored.

"You don't get to make my decisions for me," she said with great restraint. "I'm not asking for permission. If you won't take me on, I'll find a captain who will. Who sees my *value*."

"You will do no such thing." Meliz shattered her wineglass across the floor. Her eyes lit from within, threatening to burn the world down. She took her daughter by the collar, and not gently. The crew took little notice.

"Look around," she snarled in her ear.

Corayne kept still, unable to move, shocked by her mother.

"This is my crew. They're killers, every single one of them. *Look* at us, Corayne."

Swallowing around the lump in her throat, she did as told.

The crew of the *Tempestborn* were a family, of sorts. Alike in their scarred hands, sun-damaged skin, bleached hair, corded muscles. Similar as brother to sister, despite their varying origins. They drank and fought and schemed as one, beneath a single flag, united before the mast and her mother's command. Corayne saw them as she'd always known them to be: loud, drunk, loyal. But the warning echoed. *They're killers, every single one of them.*

Nothing changed, and yet nothing was the same as before.

Her vision swam, and she saw them as the world did, as they were on the water. Not family, not friends. She felt like prey in a den of predators. A knife glinted on Ehjer's hip, as long as his forearm. *How many throats has it claimed?* The big Jydi bruiser held hands with their navigator, golden Kireem, who was missing an eye. He lost it to gods-knew-what. Everywhere she looked, Corayne saw familiar faces, and yet they were unknown to her, distant and dangerous. Symeon, young and beautiful, his skin like smooth black stone, an ax balanced at his feet. Brigitt, a roaring lion tattooed up her porcelain neck. Gharira, bronze-skinned and bronze-maned, who wore chain mail everywhere, even at sea. And on and on. They dripped with scars and weaponry, hardened to the Ward and the waters. She did not know them, not really.

How many ships, how many crews, how many left dead in my mother's wake? She wanted to ask. She wanted to never know. *But you knew this—you knew what they were,* Corayne told herself. *This is what Mother wants, to frighten you away, to keep you onshore, alone in a quiet place at the edge of the world. A doll on a shelf, with only the fear of gathering dust.* She bit her lip, forcing herself to remain steady and staring. The room was filled with beasts wearing human skin, their claws made of steel. If Corayne looked hard enough, she might see the blood all over their hands. As well as her own.

"Killers all," Meliz said again, her grip unyielding. "So am I. You are *not*."

Corayne drew a shuddering breath, her eyes stinging. She blamed the smoky air.

"You think you carry no illusions, Corayne, but you are still blinded by many. Be rid of them. See us for what we are, and what you cannot be." Meliz stared intently, her gaze intensified by the rim of dark color drawn around her eyes. Her voice softened. "You don't have the spine for it, my dearest love. You stay."

Never had Corayne felt so alone, so distant from the only family she knew. *You don't have the spine. You don't belong.* When Meliz let go of her collar, she felt as if she were falling, dragged away by an unseen tide. It was cold and cruel, and so unfair. Her blood flamed.

"At least my father was good enough to only abandon me once," Corayne said coolly, her teeth bared. With a will, she stepped away from Meliz. "You've done it a thousand times."

* * *

Only when she reached the cliffs did Corayne allow herself to break. She circled, eyeing the horizon in every direction. Over the water. Behind the hills, gnarled by cypress groves and the old Cor road. She wanted nothing more than the edges of the world she knew, the cage her mother would never let her escape. The Long Sea, normally a friend, became a torment, its waves endless beneath the starlight.

Even now, she casts me aside. Even when she knows how terrible this feels.

I thought she of all people would understand.

But Meliz could not, would not, did not.

Corayne knew why, in her marrow—she was different, she was not the same, she was separate from the rest. Unworthy, unwanted.

Adrift.

And there was a reason. Something she could not change.

"No spine," Corayne spat, kicking the dirt road beneath her boots.

The stars winked overhead, reliable and sure. The constellations were old companions through many solitary nights. Corayne was a smuggler's daughter, a *pirate's* daughter. She knew the stars as well as anyone and named them quickly. It soothed her.

The Great Dragon looked down on the Siscarian coast, its jaws threatening to devour the brilliant North Star. Back along the cliffs, Lemarta glittered like a constellation of her own, clustered around her harbor, beckoning Corayne to return. Instead she kept walking, until the old white cottage appeared on the hillside.

Stupid to mention my father. Now, on top of everything else, Mother will want to talk and talk and talk about the man we barely knew, telling me nothing of use, only upsetting both of us.

Corayne liked to have a plan, an agenda, a list of objectives. She had none now. It set her teeth on edge.

Lemarta is not terrible, she thought, listing absolutes. *My lot is not horrible. My mother loves me*—she knew that in her bones. *I am lucky. Allward is wide, filled with danger and risk. Famine, war, disease, all kinds of hardship. None of it touches me here.*

This is a good place, she told herself, looking back to the harbor. *I should be content.*

And yet I cannot be. Something in me will not take root.

On the horizon, the Unicorn rose, twinkling with stars. It battled the Dragon every year, each chasing the other through the centuries. Dragons were long dead, but there were tales of unicorns still hidden across the Ward, deep in the guarded enclaves of the legendary Elders, or racing through distant steppes and sand dunes. Corayne did not believe those stories, but it was good to wonder. *And if I stay here, how will I ever know for sure?*

Two shadows on the road jolted her out of her misery. With a start, Corayne realized she was not alone on the cliff.

The travelers were almost upon her, their footsteps impossibly silent, softer than the wind in the grass. Both were hooded and cloaked, black against the night. One was small and lean, with a weaving stride. The other, far larger, made no noise at all. Strange, for someone of such great size.

Corayne set her feet. They were already too close for her to run, even if she wanted to. It would do her no good to turn her back now. She thought of the knife in her boot. It had never been used, but it was a small comfort.

"Good evening," she muttered, standing aside so they could pass.

Instead they halted, standing shoulder to shoulder. Or shoulder to chest, rather. One towered over the other, standing at least six and a half feet high. At this distance, Corayne could tell he was a man, broad and well built. He held himself like a warrior, his posture rigid. The shape of a sword poked out beneath his cloak. His hood kept most of his face obscured, but there was a scar she could see, even in the blue darkness. It dragged at one side of his pale jaw, ragged, wet, and . . . *still healing.*

Corayne's stomach turned. *No spine* echoed in her head.

"The port is behind you, friends," she said. "This way's the road to Tyriot."

"I do not seek anything in Lemarta," the man answered from beneath his hood.

Fear clawed inside her. She moved before the man, stepping back, but he stepped forward to meet her, his motions too smooth, too quick. The other figure remained still, like a snake coiled at the roadside, waiting to strike.

"You keep away!" Corayne snapped, drawing the dagger from her boot. She waved it between the travelers.

To her dismay, the man lunged forward, and Corayne tightened her grip, willing herself to fight. But she couldn't move an inch. *No spine* roared, and she braced herself for a blow.

Instead the man sank to a knee before her, his sword suddenly in hand, the tip of the gilded blade pointed to the dirt. Corayne eyed the silver hilt and good steel. He bowed his head and pushed back his hood, revealing a golden curtain of blond hair and a beautiful face half ruined with scarred flesh. A strange design edged his cloak, antlers worked in silver thread.

"I beg your forgiveness and your mercy, Corayne an-Amarat," he said softly. His eyes glinted green, but he was unable to hold her gaze.

Corayne blinked, her eyes darting between the travelers. She was torn between fear and bewilderment.

Finally the smaller person sneered, revealing the lower half of a woman's face. She crossed her arms over her chest. Each finger was tattooed with a black line stretching from knuckle to nail. The pattern was familiar, but Corayne could not place it.

"Did you intend to frighten the girl to death, or are you simply incapable of interacting with mortals properly?" the woman drawled, her glare leveled at the man's back.

Mortals. Corayne's head spun.

He gritted his teeth. "I must beg your forgiveness again. Killing you is not my intent."

"Well, that's good," Corayne sputtered. Her hand dropped, the dagger useless at her side. "Who are you?"

Even as she spoke, her mind supplied the answer, remembering corners of a children's tale or a sailor's story. *Immortal. He's an Elder. Born of the dead Spindles, ageless and without flaw. Children of a lost realm.*

She had never seen one before. Even her *mother* had never seen one before.

The immortal tipped his face up so that the stars illuminated him fully. Something had cut—no, *torn*—the left side of his face, ripping ragged lines from cheek to neck. Her eyes lingered, and he recoiled beneath her scrutiny.

He is ashamed, Corayne knew. Somehow it made her less afraid.

"Who *are* you?" she asked again.

The Elder sucked in a heavy breath.

"My name is Domacridhan of Iona, nephew to the Monarch herself, blood of Glorian Lost. I am the last of your father's Companions, and I seek your aid."

Corayne's mouth dropped open, shock pulsing through her. "What?"

"I have a story to tell you, my lady," he murmured. "If you would hear me tell it."

4

IMMORTAL COWARD
Domacridhan

The horse was dying beneath him, foam blowing from her mouth. Her shoulder was scarlet, caked in blood. *My blood*, he knew. The wounds had barely closed despite the long days. He tried not to think about his face, clawed and cut open by those *things*, those abominations. An army of *something*, from a realm he could barely fathom. He still felt their fingers, broken nails and exposed bone beneath rusty armor. They were far behind him now, hundreds of miles away. But Domacridhan looked back, emerald eyes wide.

How he'd escaped, finding one of the Companions' horses, he could not say. It was a blur of noise and color and smell, a ruin of memory. So the days passed as he raced on, one kingdom bleeding into another, hills into farm and forest and hills again, until the ground turned familiar. He cut through the mountains of the Monadhrion and the Monadhrian, the Star and the Sun, to the hidden glen. It stretched, filled with mist and yew trees, divided by the winding silver ribbon of the River Avanar. He knew this land as its son and prince.

Calidon.

Iona.

Home.

Not long, he told himself, willing the horse to last. *Not long.*

He could hear the horse's heartbeat, thunderous and failing. He kicked her again.

It is her heart or your own.

Mist peeled back to reveal the Vederan city of Iona on a stony ridge, perched where the Avanar met Lochlara, the Lake of the Dawn. Rain and snow stained the castle city gray and brown, but it remained magnificent through the ages. It was home to thousands of immortals, hundreds of them Glorianborn, older than Iona herself. Tíarma, the palace, stood proudly at the knife-edge of the ridge, with only cliffs below.

The mossy walls of the city were well defended. Stoic bowmen stood the length of the ramparts, near indistinguishable in their forest greens. They knew him on sight, their vision perfect even at a distance.

A prince of Iona returned, bloody and alone.

The mare carried him up the ridge and through the gates, galloping as far as the Monarch's palace. Dom leapt from her back when she fell to the ground. Her breath came heavy and slow, and then not at all. He flinched as her heart beat its last.

The guards flanked their prince without a word. Most were golden-haired and green-eyed, their faces stark white in the mist, their leather armor embossed with the crest of Iona. The great stag was everywhere—in wall carvings, in statues, on the tunics and armor of his fellow Ionians. It loomed over all things, proud and distant, eyes all-seeing.

My failure laid bare before it, he thought.

Ashamed, Dom entered the palace of Tíarma, passing beneath the yawning oak doors. Someone pressed a cloth into his hand, and he took it, wiping at the dried blood on his face. His wounds bit and stung, some splitting open again. He ignored the pain in the immortal way.

But he could not ignore the feel of his own torn flesh.

I must look like a monster.

After five hundred years living within Tíarma, Dom knew it well. He strode rapidly past halls and archways branching off to different wings of the palace and fortress. The feasting hall, the rose garden at the center of the palace, the battlements, and living quarters. They all blurred in his mind's eye.

Only once had he wept upon these stones. The day he became an orphan and ward to the Monarch.

He did his best not to weep a second time.

Cortael, my friend, I have failed you. I have failed Allward, failed Iona. And failed Glorian too. Failed all things I hold dear.

He reached the throne room too soon. The doors were twice his height, carved from ash and oak, intricately made by immortal hands. The sigils of the many enclaves intertwined through the wood, fluid as water. There was Ghishan's stoic tiger; the black panther of Barasa; a wheeling hawk for Tarima; Hizir's lithe stallion with Sirandel's clever fox underfoot; a Syrene ram crowned in spiral horns; Kovalinn's great bear on its hind legs, the sand wolf of Salahae, and Tirakrion's shark bearing rows of daggered teeth. Twin stags reared over them all, chests thrust forward, their antlers impossibly large. Dom had left these doors weeks ago, Cortael at his side, his stern face pulled in resolve, his heart still beating.

I wish I could go back. I wish I could warn them. His teeth ground, bone on bone. *I wish I believed as mortals do and felt their spirits here with me.*

But the immortal Vedera did not believe in ghosts, and Dom was no exception. When the guards pushed open the doors, he entered the great hall alone, with nothing and no one but his grief.

It was a long walk to the throne, over green marble polished to a mirror shine. Columns rose on either side of the floor, framing alcoves and statues to the gods of Glorian. But their deities were far away, beyond the reach of any immortal left on the Ward. Any prayers whispered in this realm went unanswered, as they had for a thousand years.

And still Dom prayed.

His aunt and her council waited at the far end of the hall, seated on a raised platform. The two men, Cieran and Toracal, served as the Monarch's voice and the Monarch's fist. Scholar and warrior. While Cieran's hair was long and ashen silver, Toracal kept his own short, braided at the temples in twists of bronze and gray. They wore robes of dark green and silver over fine silk clothing. Not even Toracal bothered with armor.

The last councillor was Dom's own blood: his cousin, Princess Ridha, who was to be the Monarch's successor. She was her mother's opposite, dark-haired and dark-eyed, with broad shoulders and strong bones. Like always, she kept a sword at her side.

The Monarch herself sat quietly, clad in a loose gray gown, the edges embroidered with jeweled flowers. Despite the chill of the throne room, she didn't bother with furs or a mantle. Most monarchs of the enclaves favored crowns, and her own was simple, little more than quartz pins set in her blond hair. Her eyes were luminous, near to pearl, and so far away. She had seen the light of strange stars and remembered Glorian Lost.

The living branch of an ash tree lay across her knees, its green leaves washed silver by the white light of morning. Such was tradition.

Her inscrutable gaze followed Dom as he approached, his head bowed, unable to look at her fully. *She sees through me*, he thought, *as she has done my entire life.*

He knelt before her throne though his muscles ached in protest. Even a Veder was not immune to pain, in the body or the heart.

"I will not ask how they died. I can see it weighs heavy on you, Nephew," said Isibel, Monarch of Iona.

Dom's voice broke. "I have failed, my lady."

"You *live*," Ridha bit out through clenched teeth, sorrow written all over her face.

I live where others have fallen, for no reason I can understand. The Companions of the Realm wavered before him, some already fading in his memory. But not the Vedera, and certainly not Cortael, who he had known all the mortal's life.

Great heroes lost to slaughter, while Domacridhan walks on.

Toracal leaned forward in his seat, blue eyes searching the

prince. He had trained Dom to the sword and the bow, centuries before, a gruff soldier then and now. Dom braced for interrogation.

"What of the Spindle?" he demanded, his voice echoing.

It was like being stabbed and beaten again. Dom weathered the shame. "Torn open before we arrived, the gate thrown wide. It was a trap."

Toracal sucked in a breath. "And what came forth?"

"An army the likes of which I've never seen." *Burned and broken, but still living. If they could be called alive.* Their hands tore him anew, clawing him to ribbons, shredding his Companions all around him. "They were flesh and blood, near to mankind but—"

"They were not of this realm," Cieran offered, his eyes grave. He was searching for a memory or scrap of forgotten knowledge. His gaze darkened. Whatever he found, he did not like.

The Monarch raised her gray gaze. "The Spindle opened to the Ashlands: a realm burned and broken, full of pain and fury," she said. Behind her, Cieran and Toracal exchanged cold glances, their pale cheeks going white. "It fell out of crossing before the other Spindles, when the realm beyond cracked, its Spindles torn apart. What remains there are beings half-alive, driven mad by torment. Little more than beasts, mortals unmade, splintered and burned to the bone."

"It is as we feared," Dom murmured, gritting his teeth against an even more horrible truth. "This is not the work of Taristan of Old Cor. He's only a servant, a tool of someone else." His breath caught. "This is Asunder. This is Him. This is What Waits."

Even the names felt evil in his mouth, corrupted and poisoned, unfit to be spoken aloud. The others reacted strongly, Cieran and Toracal going wide-eyed while Ridha's mouth dropped open in shock. *They think I've gone mad.*

"What Waits cannot cross to a realm unbroken," the Monarch said softly, her voice placating. But her eyes shone with fear.

"Then He will try to break it," Dom spat. "He means to conquer us."

The Monarch drew back on her throne. The ash branch trembled in her quivering hands.

"What Waits, the Torn King of Asunder, the Devil of the Abyss, the God Between the Stars, the Red Darkness." She drew in a ragged breath. Each one of his names sent a chill through the throne room. "He is a demon, with no love but destruction, no nature but the abyss."

With a will, Dom forced himself to his feet. His mind spun, imagining more Spindles torn, more armies, more blood and slaughter spreading across Allward. But he felt resolve too.

"The warriors of this realm, of the Vedera, can still push back the Ashlander creatures and Asunder too, and whatever else comes forth," he said, raising his chin. "But we must act now. Cieran, send word to the other enclaves. Toracal, Ridha, your warriors—"

Isibel pursed her lips.

Dom fell silent.

"The Army of Asunder is of little consequence," she said, looking at her daughter. "What Waits means to *devour.*" Her eyes softened, the world narrowing to her only child. "The Spindles are crossings, but they are also great walls between the realms. Find enough of them, tear them open, and they *will* crash together. It's how He took the Ashlands. Destroyed its boundaries, uprooted the foundations of the realm itself." Her grip tightened on the branch, knuckles bone-white. "Think of it. The Ward and the Ashlands, destroyed and enslaved to the will of What Waits."

Ridha put a hand to her sword. "This will not come to pass."

"I'm afraid it will," her mother answered.

Heat flared in Dom despite the chill of the hall. "Throw down the branch and take up the sword," he demanded. "You must send out word to the enclaves, to the mortal kingdoms. Summon them all."

Cieran heaved a breath. "And do what?"

Desperate, Dom felt his teeth snap together in a near snarl. "Destroy the corpse army. Close the Spindle. Put Taristan in the ground. Throw What Waits back to His hell. *End* this."

Isibel rose gracefully from her throne, her eyes dancing over Dom's wounds. He froze as she crossed the floor to him, one hand outstretched. Her finger traced a gash from hairline to jaw; it tore through one side of his mouth and sliced his brow in half. It was a miracle he had not lost an eye.

"It is not like us to bleed," she whispered, stricken.

Domacridhan of Iona went cold. For the first time in his life, he felt hatred for his own. It was so much worse than he knew.

"You're afraid," he said dully, glaring at her in accusation. "You're terrified."

She didn't flinch. "We are already beaten, my dear. And I will not send my people to die. You will find no monarch who will."

Gods damn you, he thought. Both fists clenched at his side. "We die if we do nothing. We are of the Ward as much as any other."

"You know we are not," Isibel said sadly, shaking her head. "Glorian waits."

Dom found himself envying mortals. It was their way to rage and snap and curse, to lose control of themselves and retreat to raw emotion. He wished to do the same.

"Glorian is *lost* to us," he forced out.

His aunt reached out again, but Dom shifted away from her touch like a petulant child.

He squared his body to the winged statue of Baleir. The warrior god was supposed to grant courage. *Grant some to these immortal cowards*, he cursed.

"The balance of Spindles is delicate. Our way back was lost to us, its location destroyed, and so we are doomed to remain here for our long eternity." She pressed on, undeterred. "But as Taristan hunts his Spindles, tearing what he can, the boundaries will weaken. Spindles will cross back into existence, both new and old. I wish it were not so, but Allward will crumble, and her Spindles will burn. If we can find the realm of the Crossroads—or even Glorian herself—we can go *home*."

Dom whirled in shock. "And abandon the Ward."

"Allward is already lost." Her face hardened, unyielding as stone. "You have not seen Glorian. I do not expect you to understand," she said heavily, returning to her throne.

Dom saw his own frustration in Ridha's eyes, but the princess remained silent, her hands knitted together. She moved her head slowly, an inch to either side. Her message was clear.

Don't.

He ignored her. His control unwound.

"I understand the Companions were slaughtered in vain." He wiped a hand across his face, scraping blood from his skin to the stone, spattering the green marble with crimson stars. "And I understand you are a coward, my lady."

Toracal rose, his teeth bared, but the Monarch waved him down. She needed no one to defend her in her own hall. "I am sorry you think so," she said gently.

Voices and memories roared in Dom's head, fighting to be heard. Cortael's dying breath, his eyes empty. The Vedera already fallen. Taristan's face, the red wizard, the Army of Asunder. The taste of his own blood. And then, further—tales of Glorian, the legendary heroes who journeyed to the Ward, those courageous, noble men and women. Their greatness, their victories. Their strength above all others upon the realm. *All lies. All nothing. All lost.*

The floor seemed to move, the marble rippling like a green sea as he stalked from the throne, from the Monarch, from all hope he'd had for the world and himself. His only thoughts were of Cortael's twin and cutting the wretched smile from his face. *I should have ended it at the temple. Ended him or me. At least then I would have saved myself from this disaster and disappointment.*

Isibel called after him, a thousand years of rule in her voice. And some desperation too. "What will you do, Domacridhan, son of my beloved sister? Have you Corblood in your veins? Have you the Spindleblade?"

Dom kept silent, but for the slap of his boots on stone.

"Then you are already defeated!" she called. "We all are. We must leave this realm to its downfall."

The prince of Iona did not falter or look back.

"Better men and women than me died for nothing," he said. "It's only fair I do the same."

Later, Princess Ridha found him in the Tíarma stables. He blundered fiercely through his labors, mucking out stalls and scattering hay, a pitchfork in his fist.

It was easy to lose himself in such a mundane activity, even one that smelled so horrible. He hadn't bothered to change his clothes, still wearing his ruined tunic and leather pants. Even his boots had mud on them from the temple, and perhaps some gore too. His hair had come undone, blond strands sticking to the bloody half of his face. A wineskin hung from his belt, drained dry. Dom felt as wretched as he looked, and he looked truly wretched.

He sensed Ridha's judgment without turning to her, so he did not bother. With a grunt, he stabbed a bale of hay and tossed it easily into the stall before him. It exploded against the stone wall. In the corner, a stallion blinked, unamused.

"You always did know when to keep your mouth shut, Cousin," he sneered, thrusting the pitchfork again. He imagined the next bale was Taristan's body, the tines running him through.

"I believe you missed that lesson," she replied. "Just like the one on tact."

Dom bit his lip, tasting blood again. "I'm a soldier, Ridha. I don't have the luxury of tact."

"And what do I look like?"

Sighing, he turned to face the closest thing he had to a sibling.

Gone was her gown. The sword still hung at her side, but the rest of the princess was changed, having traded silk for steel and jeweled locks for tightly wound braids. She rested her hands on her sword belt, letting him look. A green cloak of Iona poured over one shoulder, shadowing her mail, breastplate, and greaves. Ridha was the heir to the enclave, the Monarch's successor, and she had been taught to fight as well as any other. Better, usually. Her armor was expertly made, well fitted to her form, emblazoned with antlers, the steel tinted green. It gleamed in the dusty light of the stables.

The smallest bit of hope sparked in Dom's chest. His first instinct was to smother it.

"Where are you going?" he asked, wary.

"You heard my mother: she won't send her people to die, and neither will any other monarch," she said, adjusting her gauntlets. Her thin smile took on an edge of mischief. "I thought it best I make sure she's right."

The spark grew in leaps. The pitchfork fell from his hands, and Dom moved to embrace his cousin. "Ridha—"

She ducked his arm, her steps light and agile even in full armor. "Don't touch me—you stink."

Dom didn't mind the jab in the slightest. She could have said anything to him, asked anything of him, a dangerous thing to know. *I would dance naked through the streets of Iona or marry a mortal woman if it meant she would help me.* But Ridha demanded nothing in return. In his heart, Dom knew she never would.

"I'll ride to Sirandel first," the princess said. She set a quick pace down the aisle, and Dom was forced to follow. With a practiced eye, she noted the horses, surveying each stall for a steed fast enough to suit her needs. "They lost three of their own to those monsters. And the foxes can be so hot-blooded. Something about the red hair."

Eager, the prince crossed to the tack wall and heaved a saddle onto his shoulder. The fine oiled leather gleamed. "I'll start with Salahae. The sand wolves do not run from a fight."

Ridha snatched the saddle from him. "Leave the enclaves to me. I don't trust your powers of persuasion."

"You're mad if you think I'm staying here," he said, moving to bar her way. Again she dodged. At the far end of the aisle, the stable hands gathered to watch their bickering. Dom could hear their whispers, but he gave them little thought.

"I didn't say that," Ridha said in a chiding voice. "Raising an army to fight the Spindles is one thing—impossible, perhaps. Closing them is another entirely, but it's something we must do if we have any hope of maintaining Allward."

Her search ended at a familiar stall, where her mother's own mount stood waiting. The horse was coal black, bred for speed in the deserts of Ibal. A sand mare. A rare flash of greed gleamed in Ridha's eye before she turned back to her cousin. She took his hand.

"You need Corblood and Spindleblade."

A young face rose up before him, his eyes kind and warm, a green-and-gold tunic cast over his coat of mail. *The squire. Andry Trelland. A son of Ascal.*

"The blade I can find," Dom said grimly. *I hope.*

Ridha's dark brow furrowed. "How? There were only two in

the vault, and Taristan has them both. The other enclaves have none—"

"The blade I can find," he said again, his voice deep with resolve.

Ridha searched him a moment, then nodded slowly. Dom could only pray she was right to put faith in him.

"But the blood," he sighed, leaning back against the wall. The Veder scrubbed a hand down his face, forgetting his wounds for the first time since leaving the temple. He did not forget long. His face stung and he cursed lightly. "Cortael was the last of his line. The others, *if* there are others . . . we have no means of tracking them. It will take months, *years*, to find another branch of that tree. The sons and daughters of Old Cor are all but spent."

"Sons and daughters," Ridha mused, her lips twisting in the echo of a smirk. She stepped into the sand mare's stall, running a hand down the slope of the creature's back. It whickered at her in greeting. "Their numbers are few, that is correct. But Cortael's line ended? There are things he did not tell even you, Cousin."

In spite of the circumstances, Dom loosed a rare grin. "Oh, believe me, I know about your tryst with the mortal. So does half of Iona."

"I'm not the only woman, Veder or mortal, to have lain with Cortael of Old Cor." She laughed, though the sound was hollow. Cortael's death was not only Dom's to bear. He could see that clearly: the weight of loss hanging oddly about her shoulders, like an ill-fitted suit of armor. She was not accustomed to it. Most Vedera weren't. Most Vedera did not know what it was to die or to lose the ones they loved to death.

He jumped when her hand touched the unmarked side of his face. Ridha's fingers were cool and gentle, despite the calluses born of centuries. He felt another pang of sorrow, not for his plight, but for his cousin, who would be riding the Ward alone.

"Take heart, Domacridhan," she said, misreading his woe. "The Vedera are not the only ones who trace the lines of Old Cor."

Ridha had always been quicker than he in the library, beneath the tutelage of scholars and diplomats alike. He stared into her dark eyes for long seconds before the wave of realization crashed over him. He wrinkled his nose in disgust, feeling his stomach churn at what she was implying.

"That's idiotic," he crowed.

She held firm, her back to the mare. "Well, then it's a good thing we aren't idiots. Or at least I'm not."

"I won't do it." He shook his golden head. "I don't trust them."

Her eyelids fluttered in exasperation.

"We didn't know about Taristan, and look where that left us," she muttered through gritted teeth. "You can search every scroll in the library, you can crack Cieran's own head open and pour through the contents, but you won't find another Corblood in time. And you won't find Cortael's child. He made sure of that."

Dom's stomach churned again.

"A child," he forced out in disbelief. *A bastard*, he realized. *Cortael was unwed—or was he? Is there more I did not know about my friend? More he did not see fit to tell me, either for abundance of shame or lack of trust?* Though the mortal was dead and gone, left to rot, he felt a new wave of sadness, and bitter anger too.

"None of that—we don't have time for your brooding," Ridha said sharply.

He pulled a painful scowl. "I don't brood."

"You brood for *years*," she snapped. "Cortael was working his way through the wine cellar when he told me. And it happened when he was little more than a child himself."

"I wish I had known." Again, Dom wanted to believe in ghosts.

Ridha bit her lip. "You remember how he—was," she said, struggling to name him dead. "A man who thought himself a Veder and did all he could to convince the rest of us. It was not in him to admit such mortal mistakes. He wanted to be like us so terribly."

Indeed, Dom did remember. Even as a boy, Cortael set against his own nature. He would try to ignore wounds or cold or hunger. Refuse to sleep, because Vedera often did not have the need. He spoke Vederian as well as any in the enclave. So much so that he'd once told Dom he dreamed in their language and not his own. *We were brothers, mortality aside. But for his blood, his cursed blood, which was his ending.*

"That's all I know." Ridha laid a hand on his arm, drawing him out of his memories. "But rest assured, *they* will know more."

Like a child scolded into eating something good for him, Dom acquiesced. "Very well. I'll do it." *Already I tire at the prospect of such an endeavor.*

She angled an eyebrow, examining him as she would a century adolescent taking his first turn in the training yards. "Do you have any idea where to start?"

Dom drew himself up to his full, menacing height. His bulk

filled the stall door. "I think I can track down a single assassin and beat an answer out of him well enough, thank you."

"Good, but perhaps visit a healer first," she said, picking at his shirt in disgust. Then she sniffed for good measure. "And have a bath."

He replied with a wry smile, allowing her to attend to the sand mare. Ridha had her saddled and ready in what felt like a blink of an eye. Too quick for Dom's taste, even now. He watched his cousin through it all, and she stared back, determined beyond measure. He did not ask if she was riding off on her mother's secret orders, despite the proclamation in the throne room. Or if this was disobedience, if not betrayal. He did not want to know either way.

"Ride well, Cousin," he said. All the horrors of the world, all he had seen just days before, rose up in his mind, their hands and jaws reaching for dear Ridha. *She will not fall as the others did. I won't lose another*, he promised himself.

But you won't be with her, his own voice answered. It shuddered through him.

Either Ridha did not notice or was good enough to ignore his fear. She swung herself onto the antlered saddle with ease, the sand mare shifting beneath her, eager to run.

"I always do," she answered, her dark eyes bright with the prospect of her journey. And their great purpose.

Again Dom wished he could express himself as mortals did. Embrace his cousin, tell her how much her belief and action meant. Emotion rose up in his throat, threatening to strangle him dead. "Thank you" was all he managed.

Her response was as sharp as her sword. He expected nothing

less. "Don't thank me for doing what is right. Even if it is quite stupid."

Dom bowed his head and stepped out of the stall, leaving the way clear for her.

But she paused, one foot in the stirrup, her eyes on the horse's neck. Her gaze wavered. "I did not realize he had a twin," she murmured, almost inaudible. "I did not know—my mother separated them."

"Nor did I," Domacridhan answered. Like Ridha, he scrambled for some understanding but found none. "Nor did he, until that monster appeared out of the mist."

"I'm sure she thought it was the right thing to do. Raise one, protect one. Create only a single heir to Old Cor. Leave no room for conflict. For the Ward."

Though Dom nodded, he could not agree. Not in his heart. She did it for herself, for Glorian. And no other.

With a steel will, Ridha leapt into the saddle. She looked down on him, a picture of a fierce warrior proud and true. "Ecthaid be with you." The god of the road, of journeys, of things lost and found.

He nodded up at her. "And Baleir with you."

On Baleir's wings, she rode west.

After changing his clothes and scrubbing the muck from his body, Domacridhan of Iona rode south. No one stopped him, and no one bid him farewell.

5

THE STORM'S BARGAIN
Sorasa

Her sword was back at the harborside inn, hidden beneath a loose floorboard with the rest of her gear. She only needed her dagger, the bronze edge dim in the dark bedroom of a merchant king. She stood patiently over him, counting his breaths. He slept fitfully, jowled like a fat dog, his breath rattling through yellowed teeth. His wife dozed on the bed beside him, a dark-haired beauty, barely more than a child. Sorasa guessed her to be sixteen. Probably the merchant's third or fourth bride.

I am doing you a favor, girl.

Then she slit his throat, the well-fed blade cutting with ease.

His mouth gurgled and she covered it with one hand, turning him onto his side so the blood did not wash over his wife and wake her. When he finished the familiar process of bleeding to death, she removed his left ear and his left index finger, tossing both on the floor. Such was the mark of Sorasa Sarn, for those who knew to look. This kill was hers and no other's.

The merchant's young wife slept on, undisturbed.

The steady drip of blood was louder than Sorasa's footsteps as she retreated to the balcony, unfurled her whip, and swung across the courtyard to the wall beyond.

She crouched against the pale pink stone, using her hands to steady her balance. The fruit trees of the garden hid her well, and she gave her eyes time to adjust to the midday light. The merchant's guards were slow in the heat, making their rounds on the other side of the courtyard. She took the opportunity to drop to the empty alley below. It offered little shadow.

The sun was high and merciless. It was a dry summer on the Long Sea, unseasonably so, and dust clouded even the wealthiest streets of Byllskos. The capital of Tyriot, usually cooled by sea breezes, burned in the heat. But the weather bothered Sorasa little. Her life had begun in the sands of Ibal, and her mother was of the Allforest, a woman of Rhashir. Sorasa's blood was born for the dry cruelty of the desert or the cloying hot air of a jungle. *These men know nothing of the sun*, she thought as she walked the alleys, winding her way toward the docks.

She kept her steps measured and well timed. The blue waters of the Tyri Straits flashed between gaps in the walls, every home looking down on the famed port. Only the Sea Prince's palace rose higher, its pink towers and red-tile roofs like a burst of Cor roses.

Sorasa glanced at the great harbor of Tyriot, the famous docks reaching out into the Straits like the arms of an octopus. A trade galley would take her forth, leaving behind no trace of Sorasa Sarn.

No trace I have not chosen to leave, she thought, her lips curling with satisfaction.

A shadow, she descended into the temple district, weaving along domed shrines and godly towers. Dedicant priests walked their noon rounds, followed by peasants and sailors, their hands outstretched for blessings from the gods of Allward.

The villa was well behind her when the alarm went up, a strangled cry of guards calling for the city watchmen. Somewhere among the villas, a trumpet sounded. Sorasa grinned as it was drowned out by the tolling bell of Meira's Hand, a looming tower ruled by the goddess of the seas. Sailors begged her mercy, fishermen her bounty.

Sorasa begged for nothing but the bell and the crowd. Both surged, as good as a wall between her and the corpse in his bed.

The crowd moved in a current, most following Meira's blue priests down the main thoroughfare that cut Byllskos in two. They would hit the port soon, and on a market day no less.

An easy chaos to get lost in, Sorasa thought. *All precisely to plan.*

She navigated with sure footing, unaffected by the crowd and its stink. Byllskos was a bustling city, but a village compared to Almasad and Qaliram in Ibal, where Sorasa had spent the majority of her thirty years upon the Ward. She ached now for the baked stone streets and vibrant markets as far as the eye could see, for patterned silk, a sky like turquoise, the smell of fragrant blossoms and spice bazaars, the grand temple of sacred Lasreen, and the shade of the Palm Way. But all paled next to the memory of the sandstone citadel on the sea cliffs, with the hidden gate and the tearing salt wind, the only home she had ever known, her place since childhood.

She felt the shift of air over her a split second before a hand clamped down, its grip tight on the muscle between her neck and shoulder. Fingers squeezed and pinched, sending a jolt of pain through her body.

Sorasa dropped and twisted out of the well-known maneuver, one she had mastered years ago. Teeth bared, she glared up at her would-be attacker.

He did not attack.

"Garion," she bit out. Around them, the parade of godly followers thinned.

Like her, the man was hooded, but Sorasa did not need to see his face clearly to know him. Garion was taller than she, his skin white even in shadow. Still a lock of mud-brown hair fell into his dark eyes, as it had when he was a boy. Where her clothes were plain, dyed in earthen colors easy for an eye to slide over, his own tunic and cloak were garish. Scarlet and embroidered silver were impossible to ignore. He sneered at her coldly.

"I did not take you for a thief, Sarn," he hissed in Ibalet. Though he'd learned it young, it was not his mother tongue, and it still sounded odd in his mouth.

Sorasa waved him off. The black tattoos on her fingers matched his own.

"Perhaps that moral compass of yours needs adjusting," she replied. "I stole a man's life from you, and it's the stealing that has you concerned?"

Garion pursed his lips. "By the Spindles, Sorasa," he cursed. "There are rules. A guild contract is given to one and one alone."

Such tenets were inked in her deeper than any tattoo or scar. Sorasa wanted to roll her eyes, but she had long since learned to school her expressions and hide emotion.

Instead she turned on her heel, setting off at a trot. "Jealousy doesn't become you."

He followed swiftly, as expected. It reminded her of different days. But those days were long ago, and she curled one hand in a fist, the other close to the dagger at her hip. Should he draw, she would be ready.

"Jealous? Hardly," Garion said through clenched teeth. The pair wove deftly through the gathering crowd as they caught up to Meira's faithful. "You have been named and inked. No amount of blood will rewrite what has already been written."

The long tattoo down her ribs suddenly itched, the last marking not a year old. Unlike the many others, blessings and trophies, it had been given against her will.

"Thank you for telling me what I already know," she said, throwing Garion a glance meant to wither a man to the root. "Go back to the citadel. Pace your cage until another easy kill lands in your lap. And I'll steal that one from you too."

Though her face remained still, Sorasa laughed inwardly. She would not mention that she already knew of his next contract and exactly how she would beat him to it.

"Have caution, Sarn," he said. She heard a tremor of regret in him. *He was always terrible at hiding his intentions. Such is the way with men.* "Lord Mercury—"

Sorasa kept walking, her cheeks warm. She feared few upon the Ward. Lord Mercury topped a very short list.

"Go home, Garion," she snapped, her voice sharp enough to draw blood. She sorely wished to be rid of her once friend and ally. This road was easier walked alone.

He ran a hand over his head, pulling back his hood in frustration. Sweat beaded on his pale brow, and there was a fresh sunburn across his cheeks. *A northern boy, even now*, Sorasa thought. Decades in the desert could not change his flesh.

"This is a warning," he said grimly, drawing aside his cloak. At his belt, a dagger like her own glinted, with a hilt of black leather over worn bronze. He had a sword too, far too close to his hand for her liking. She lamented her own, hidden in a dingy room.

Half a mile to the inn, she thought. *You're faster than he is.*

Her hand strayed, fingers closing around familiar leather. It felt like an extension of her own body.

"Would you like to do this here?" She tipped her head to the crowd of priests and worshippers. "I know you don't mind, but I prefer not to have an audience."

Garion's eyes trailed from her face to the dagger, weighing them both. She read his body keenly. He was lean as she remembered. The sword at his hip was thin, a light blade of good steel. He was not a brawler like some they'd trained with. No, Garion was an elegant swordsman, the assassin you wanted on display, to duel in the street. To send a message. Not so with Sorasa: a knife in shadow, a poison on the rim of a cup. Her muscles tightened as her mind spun through her options, lightning quick. *Back of the knee. Cut the muscle, then the throat as he falls. Run before he hits the dirt.*

She knew Garion read her in the same way. They stared for a moment longer, half coiled, two snakes with their fangs bared.

Garion blinked first. He eased backward, his palms open. The cloud of tension between them lifted. "You should disappear, Sarn," he said.

She raised her chin, angling her head to the hot sun overhead. The shade of her hood retreated, revealing her face. Her black-rimmed eyes caught the sunlight and flashed like liquid copper. *Tiger's eyes*, the others used to say when she was young. Garion's gaze felt like fingers on her skin. She let him see the long year written in her flesh. Bruise-like circles beneath her eyes, sharper cheekbones, a dark brow drawn tight. A jaw set at a hard, unmoving edge. Sorasa had been a predator since childhood. She'd never looked it more.

His throat bobbed as he stepped back. "Few of us get the chance to walk away."

"Few want the chance, Garion," she said, raising a hand in farewell.

The crowd swallowed him whole.

I'll never get the smell of this place out of my clothes, she thought dully as she left the piss-soaked inn behind. Her pack hung at her side, the sword and whip at either hip, both well hidden beneath her old traveling cloak. Today it carried an odd scent, of salt and cattle and garden fruit, all of it overwhelmed by the smell of fish. She longed for the days when she could rely on a small, quiet, and clean room at the citadel, with cool stone walls, a high window, and the silence of ages to keep her company. Not so here.

All the better, she knew. *Discord is a better shield than steel.*

Sailors, merchants, beggars, and travelers alike crowded the streets of the port, slowing her down. The braying of animals and the stampede of pounding hooves doubled the usual chaos. The herds of the surrounding countries were in season, and the market yards around the port had been converted to paddocks, holding thousands of snorting, tossing, sweating bulls and cows, all ready to be bought and traded throughout the Long Sea.

She thought of the guards and watchmen up the hill, still searching the streets for a cutthroat. Checking the face of every man and boy who set foot in the district.

With a smile, she threw back her hood, revealing a set of four intertwined black braids. Her spine tingled at walking the streets so exposed, but she reveled at the feel of the sun on her face.

For the second time that day, someone grabbed her shoulder.

Again she dropped and twisted, expecting Garion, a foolish sailor, or a sharp-eyed guard. But the maneuver did not break the man's grip, nor did a well-placed jab to his stomach. His flesh was stone beneath her hand, and not for armor or chain mail. Her assailant towered over her, seemingly twice her size, with the bearing of one who knew how to fight.

You are certainly not Garion.

Sorasa reacted as she had been trained to, one hand going to the clasp at her neck, the other into a pouch at her belt. With a flick of her hand, a puff of stinging blue smoke exploded at her feet, and the cloak fell from her shoulders.

She kept her eyes shut and held her breath as she bolted down the street. The man coughed violently behind her, her cloak hanging loose in his hand.

He shouted something in a language she did not know, a rarity.

Blood surged as her heartbeat quickened. Her instincts served her well, as had her few days learning Byllskos for the contract. The city unfurled in her mind, and she flew down an alley branching off the main port, only to turn hard onto the next busy street. Sorasa schooled her breathing, keeping it in time with her sprint. After checking ahead, assessing her steps, she dared look back.

For a moment, she thought a bull had escaped its pen.

A cloud of dust and clinging blue smoke followed the man as he ran, arms pumping, a dark green cloak flying out behind him like a flag. The sun glinted off his golden hair. He was no watchman of Byllskos or villa guard. She saw that even from a distance.

Another joined the list of people Sorasa feared.

Men and women alike stumbled away as she vaulted between them, throwing a few to the ground. She ran, her right fist prickling with pain from striking her pursuer. She looked back again and a bolt of shock ran down her spine. Though she had a head start and great speed, he was gaining on her quickly.

An idea snapped together in her head. For the first time since she'd set foot in Byllskos, a bead of sweat trickled down her neck.

This is a warning, Garion had said. The first rumble of thunder before a storm.

Was this man the lightning? Lord Mercury's final punishment?

Not if I can help it.

Sorasa turned again, sharply agile as she swung herself into another alley crowded with less reputable vendors, their wares stolen or useless. She dodged, a dancer in the disarray, leaping over bowls of half-rotten fruit, through hanging sheets of fabric, around haggling men and women. All of it closed behind her, undisturbed by her quick and skillful passing. Sorasa half hoped the crowd would hide her, if not slow her pursuer down.

It did neither.

He pummeled his way through, stalls collapsing in his wake. A few women swatted at him, but their blows glanced off his broad chest and shoulders. To Sorasa's surprise, he only blinked at them, bewildered. His confusion didn't last.

Through the crowded alley, his eyes found hers, and she caught a flash of teeth as he clenched his jaw.

Adrenaline snapped through her, a delicious feeling. Despite her fear, Sorasa felt her heart sing in anticipation. It had been a year since her last true fight.

She scrambled up a stack of crates, jumping from stall to stall, balancing on poles and planks, ignoring the shouts of the tradesmen below. Her size was an advantage and she used it well.

But he lunged up the crates like an animal, following her path down to the splinter.

"Shit," she cursed. *A person that large shouldn't be able to hop around so easily.*

Sorasa leapt again, landing precariously on a pole. It swayed beneath her. Below, a man selling bruised fruit shouted and shook a fist. She ignored him, cursing Lord Mercury and whatever he had done to ensure Sorasa Sarn died painfully.

With a flip of her hand, she drew up her hood again, covering her hair. The other assassin was only a stall away now, perched with one foot on a narrow plank, the other braced against the alley wall. In another place, he would look comical. Now he was only terrifying. He glowered at her, eyes green with fury. At this distance, Sorasa could see his short beard was as golden as his hair hanging loose. He didn't look a day over thirty years old.

But one side of his face was scarred, as if clawed to pieces. *By what?* she wondered, her stomach churning.

The sword and dagger hung at her side, begging for her attention like children pulling at their mother's hands. Instead her fingers strayed for the coiled bullwhip, all leather and rage.

"I would like to speak to you," her pursuer ground out in Paramount, the common language stilted and oddly formal for their circumstance. She tried and failed to place his accent.

While her heartbeat still surged, he showed no signs of exertion. Not even a single hair out of place.

"You're speaking to me now," she replied, adjusting her balance, both feet set beneath her. Her toes wiggled in anticipation. The whip loosed, trailing like a venomous snake.

Below them, the fruit vendor continued to yell in Tyri, but no one else stopped to watch. The Byllskos alleys were filled with fools. Two more were of little consequence.

The man did not blink, watching every tick of her muscles. "I would prefer to converse elsewhere."

She shrugged and tightened her grip on the plaited handle of the whip, slipping the wrist loop into place. "That's a shame."

The man stretched out his hand, the palm as big as a dinner plate, the pale skin crossed with calluses and training scars. *Won at the citadel, though I have never seen him before. Is he some pet of*

Mercury's trained in isolation, a dragon to unleash on any of us who cross his will?

"I'm not here to harm you," he said.

Sorasa scoffed low at the back of her throat. "I've heard that before."

He curled his fingers into a fist. "But I will if I must."

The wind stirred his cloak, revealing the heavy longsword at his hip. He was not a swordsman like Garion. The terrible blade was not meant for performance.

It would also be difficult to draw in such a precarious position, all but useless even for the most skilled swordsmen of the Ward.

Sorasa bared her teeth in a grim smile. "Try me, then."

"Very well."

Despite her decades of training, honing her body to the razor's edge, Mercury's dog was somehow faster. His reflexes, his reactions, his instincts. He was a storm. Her only recourse was to anticipate and predict, to move first.

The whip curled around a washing line as she jumped, before his feet left the plank. He leapt forward, intending to catch her around the middle. But instead of jumping over him, she swung around, using the whip and her own momentum to kick off the alley wall. The change in angle was enough to miss him by inches, leaving him to land hard on her perch.

The pole cracked through, splintering under his weight. The fruit vendor shrieked as a six-and-a-half-foot assassin crashed through his stall and crushed a pile of spotty oranges.

Sorasa cut the washing line, clutching the whip as she fell into the alley. With a practiced tumble, she absorbed the brunt of the fall and popped to her feet, a pile of clothes fluttering around her. She grabbed a patched aquamarine cloak from the heap and threw it around her shoulders.

When she looked back, peering around her new hood, she saw a blond head above the crowd, trying to shoulder his way through. The crowd pushed back, rallying against him. The vendor even pelted him with ruined oranges. He hardly noticed, scanning the alley like a hound picking up a scent.

Sorasa did not give him the chance and slipped back onto the main road, her pace even and unbothered. Just another body on the streets of Byllskos.

The cattle auctions continued in earnest, drawing a heavy throng of people and animals alike as traders stopped to observe. She traded the stolen cloak for a long, stained vest and hat from a farmer's cart. Both hid her face and weapons well, though she looked worse than a peasant. *Smell worse too*, she thought with a curl of her lip.

One of her first and best lessons at the Guild concerned no weapon. No blade or poison. No disguises. No language. She excelled in those, of course. They were as necessary as rain and sunshine to a field of wheat. But the most important element, the most vital to fulfilling a contract, was opportunity.

It was not luck that Sorasa caught the merchant king asleep, his guards distant and slow. She chose that moment. And she would choose again here. Mercury's assassin would not be so easily left behind. He would be on her again in a few minutes' time, if he wasn't following already. She did not breathe a sigh of relief as she walked. She did not uncoil or drop her guard. Sorasa Sarn was not so foolish.

Her heartbeat slowed, her muscles recovered, and her head cleared.

Opportunity lay ahead.

With a smile, she approached a pen of black bulls. They gleamed with sweat, packed tight like barrels in the hold of a trade galley. They could scarcely move even to swat off the biting flies. They were next to the auction paddock, ready to trample round and round for the traders. Slowly, she leaned up alongside their gate, one that opened to the dirt square. The lock was simple, a wooden draw bar. She glanced at it and removed her hat, baring her face for all the street to see.

The trap is baited.

One hand darted into her pack and she pulled out a peach, biting greedily into its oversweet flesh.

He was not difficult to spot. The assassin towered over most of the market crowd. He was taller even than Garion, and paler besides. She guessed him to be of the far north—Calidon, or perhaps the Jyd. He had the look of a snowborn raider, with his white face, giant frame, and golden hair.

He barreled on with singular focus, his great strides closing the distance between them.

Savoring the taste of fruit, she tossed the peach and slid the lock, throwing open the gate to the bulls' pen. A nearby man grabbed her arm, but she broke his hold without thought, sending him howling into the dirt with a mouthful of missing teeth.

Ten feet away, the assassin's eyes widened.

Sorasa cracked her whip over the pen.

The herd burst forth, heavy as a thundercloud, with hooves and horns like striking lightning. On and on they poured, the great flanks and shoulders jostling against their fence, threatening to break loose. They rolled toward him in a black tide, bucking and frothing mad with every crack of the whip. *Opportunity*, she thought, satisfied.

She expected him to run. Or dodge. Or simply be trampled, his bones shattered beneath a hundred pounding hooves.

Instead the assassin set his feet and put out his hands. It was a truly ridiculous sight, but Sorasa's breath caught in her teeth.

His hands closed around the horns of the first bull, his knuckles turning white, heels digging into the dirt. He tossed the beast with a grunt, sending it sprawling onto its side. Its head lolled, the neck snapped. Sorasa gaped as the rest of the herd broke around him, a wave around a pillar in the sea. He stood firm and unafraid. His eyes never left her, alive with green fire.

Elder, her brain screamed in realization.

Immortal.

She ran as she had never run before. Through alleys, over rooftops, between walls so tight even the sun could not reach the ground. Cloak after cloak fell from her shoulders, in all colors. Anything to confuse him, to slow him down, to steal another second out of his hands.

She circled, trying for the docks, but he was always there, keeping her from her ship, from *any* ship. Her pouch of tricks was nearly empty, leaving blue, white, and green smoke trailing the streets of Byllskos. She dared not try the black.

Unyielding, unbeatable. The few things she knew of the Elders came rushing back from a lesson learned long ago. *Unbelievable beings born of a lost realm.*

Her body burned with exertion. Her nails tore on brick and wood; her fingers bristled with splinters. She felt little pain, most of it trained out of her. Adrenaline and fear ate the rest. She climbed; she leapt; she tumbled and spun. Fruit carts and barrels of wine exploded in her wake. Dedicant priests cursed her as she parted their ranks. She even debated sprinting back to the villa of the murdered merchant, to the guards and watchmen, who would make a fine shield between herself and the immortal monster.

None of the guild had ever killed an immortal. None had been foolish enough to try. Few had even seen them. *How did Lord Mercury manage to wrangle one into his service?*

She racked her memory for anything that could be of use. Whispers heard about the Elder kind, their strengths, their weaknesses. In the Guild, the masters and mistresses were not so concerned with folk of legend, nor creatures of Spindles lost. No one ever took out a contract on a dragon. Guild assassins did not cross paths with the immortal ghosts still haunting the Ward.

Until Mercury somehow sends one to kill me, she sneered to herself.

She was faster, smaller; she knew the city. But those things only bought her minutes.

And her minutes were quickly spent.

He fell on her too quickly, unstoppable as a rockslide. She

loosed her sword before he could, slicing with a backhanded blow. The next strike met steel, his longsword bracing against her own.

Again she wished for Garion, if only to shove him into harm's way.

But I am alone. It's the road I've chosen.

He was immovable, his blade locked with hers at the hilt. It was all she could do to hold him off, arms and legs screaming beneath the pressure. She had no logical hope of overpowering him and did not try. When he opened his mouth to speak, she spat in his face.

"By the Spindles—" he cursed, dropping back in disgust. He had the manners and idiocy to wipe the spittle away.

She kicked a spray of dust into his eyes and pounced, winding herself around his torso until she was on his back. Her dagger rose, aiming for the spot where neck met shoulder, to pierce muscle and vein. *To kill and kill quickly.* One arm locked over his throat, squeezing tightly. Sorasa could not count how many men she had choked this way.

To her delight, she could feel him gasp for air. *Even immortals need to breathe.*

He moved as she stabbed, the strike glancing. Blood welled up at his shoulder, but not enough.

He seized her by the collar and pulled her free, throwing her off with ease. She landed hard against an alley wall. She bled too, her face scraped raw by brick. Out in the streets, the whistles and trumpets of watchmen echoed. Between a stampede and a dead man, they had their hands more than full.

"We've caused some trouble, you and I," Sorasa gasped out, her eyes on the street. Her entire body howled in pain.

The alley echoed around them. The Elder sneered and checked the blood at his shoulder. "This is foolish," he said, gritting his teeth. There was blood in his mouth too.

Sorasa's pride flared. She gulped for air.

"I promise I will not harm you." Again, the Elder reached out. "Come, Mortal."

Death was a welcome friend to Sorasa Sarn. She and the goddess Lasreen had passed many years bound, hand in hand. One followed the other like night follows dusk. Sorasa had never felt her so close before.

Lord Mercury rose in her mind, white and terrible, his teeth sharp, his eyes distant. It was so like him, to give her a death this way. A death she could not outrun or outfox.

It was good Sorasa did not believe in absolutes. There was only opportunity, and opportunity could always be found.

"Come, Mortal," the Elder said again. His fingers twitched.

"No," she said, laughing as she bolted one last time.

Her sword lay forgotten in the dirt.

She landed in the chair hard, one foot propped on the taverna table. The other jittered on the floor, shaking with nervous energy. *I look a wreck*, she thought, noting the way the barmaid hesitated. She was covered in dirt and blood, one of her braids undone, hair spilling over her shoulder in a black curtain. A cut on her lip oozed. She licked away the blood. With a manic grin, Sorasa held up two fingers and the maid scurried to serve.

Sorasa was not the only patron of the port taverna who looked run through. There were a few battered men who she suspected had met her bulls. The rest were sailors half-dead in their ale. She recognized Ibalet sailors of the Storm Fleet, disheveled in their dark-blue sailing silks. They noticed her too and twitched fingers in hello, greeting a sister of Ibal.

She did not return the gesture.

Two tankards were set down in front of her a moment before the door opened, spilling light through the dark barroom. The sailors winced or cursed, but the immortal ignored them. He stood for a moment, framed in sunshine, his shadow stretching over her.

She did not move as he crossed the taverna and sat.

Without a word, she pushed the pewter tankard across the pitted table. He stared at the sloshing cup of ale, perplexed. Then, with oddly stilted motions, he took a gulp.

Sorasa kept still, her face blank. Her pulse thrummed in her ears.

The Elder glanced down at the tankard, staring into its golden depths. His brow furrowed. Then he drank again, draining it dry. For a second, Sorasa felt a burst of unseen triumph. It faded as he stared at her, unblinking. His pupils went wide in the dim light, black eating up the green.

"Did you know the Vedera are immune to nearly all poisons?" he said slowly.

The Vedera. She tucked the strange world into her mind and exhaled the last of her hope. "What a waste of arsenic."

Part of her whispered to grab for her dagger, her whip, the last powders in her pouch. Another poison, another cut, another opportunity. For any and all things that might save her, even now.

VICTORIA AVEYARD

She felt as if a hole had opened beneath her feet.

I must choose to jump or fall.

Her body ached. She took a deep draft of piss-water ale and wished it were *ibari* liquor. To die with the bittersweet bite of home on her lips. *For I will die here, at his hand, and at Mercury's,* she thought. It was almost a relief to admit.

The Elder searched her face, his eyes snaring on the tattoos crawling up her neck. Sorasa let him look. He did not know each tattoo as she did, its meaning and weight within the Guild.

"Three times you've tried to kill me today," he muttered, as if astonished.

She drank again. "I'd say this all counts a single attempt."

"Then you came close to succeeding thrice."

"*Thrice,*" she sneered back, mocking his tone. *As if we're in a royal court, not a shitbucket bar.* "Well, what now, Elder? How will you do it?"

He blinked, digesting her words, simple as they were. She thought of a child at the Guild, struggling through a lesson they did not understand. He clenched his jaw and sat back in his chair. Sorasa half expected it to collapse under his bulk. Slowly, he put both palms to the table, a display of peace. *He treats me like a spooked animal,* she thought, tasting fury.

"I told you before, it is not my objective to harm you."

He reached to his side, throwing back his cloak. She braced herself for the song of a sword unsheathed. Instead he pulled forth a familiar blade.

Her own.

The sword was thin and well balanced, a double-edged ribbon

of steel with hammered bronze at the hilt. It had been forged in the citadel armory, born of the Guild as she was. There was no insignia, no sigil, no jewels, no carved words. Hardly a treasure. It served her well.

She took it with sure hands, careful not to pull her eyes from the Elder in front of her.

"I have little concern for your well-being, for good or ill," he said.

With the sword back in her possession, Sorasa felt oddly light. "Is that what you tell all the mortal girls, or just me?"

Something crossed his face, like a shadow or a darkness. "I do not speak to many mortals," he forced out.

"I can tell."

The barmaid produced another tankard for each of them, nearly spilling the flat ale. She glanced between the assassin and the immortal, a lamb between wolves. Sorasa waved her off with a silver penny.

He startled at the sight of the coin and drew out his own purse, thunking it on the table. Sorasa snapped to attention, all thoughts of ale and death pushed to the side. Though the purse was small, it burst with gold, winking yellow within the leather. The weak light of the bar played over the coins.

"I want information. I'm willing to pay," the Elder said sharply, drawing out a piece of hammered gold. The coin was perfectly round, marked with a stag. It was not money of any kingdom Sorasa knew, but gold was gold. "Will these do?"

To her shock, Sorasa heard apprehension in the Elder's voice. She nearly laughed aloud as realization dawned on her. *He has no idea what he's doing. He's not an assassin, for Lord Mercury or any other. No matter how strong he might be. This Spindleborn fool is just lucky a street beggar hasn't swindled him by now.*

Opportunity sang in her blood, more familiar than any mother she ever had. With her hands on the table, Sorasa mirrored his posture, leaning forward. She took the coin.

"How can I set a price if I don't know what you're asking?" she said. *The gold is crude but fine, from a pure vein. Bright yellow. A rare sort.*

The Elder did not hesitate. "I'm looking for Corblood mortals, descendants of the old empire. I'm told the Amhara know them, or can find them."

Her face was a mask as she began counting coins from the purse. He watched but did not stop her as one, two, three coins slid out onto the table. Neither bothered to hide the money. They were the most dangerous things in the taverna—in all the city, perhaps.

The Amhara. Her throat tightened, but her face remained a mask. She bit one of the coins, judging the give of the metal. He wrinkled his nose.

"The sons and daughters of Old Cor are few and far-flung," she said around the coin. "Even the Amhara are losing track."

"I seek one in particular."

Sorasa drew another three coins from the purse.

"A child."

Another coin.

"The bastard of Prince Cortael and an unknown woman."

Another.

"He's no prince of any kingdom in living memory," she replied.

The name is familiar enough. Another mortal descended from the old empire, from the Spindles and a realm forgotten. A prince in name only, and to very few. Still, there have been contracts taken before. All failed. She eyed the Elder warrior again. *And now I see why.*

Smirking, she neatly piled the coins. "Mortal living memory, of course."

A rare anger flared in the Elder. "I care not for your ignorance of the ages. Can you help me or not?"

This time she plunged her hand into the purse, grabbing at coins.

The Elder scowled.

It isn't the gold he cares about, she thought, watching his face. *Something else feeds his anger.*

"The father is dead," he ground out. His voice was oddly strangled. *Ah,* she thought. *He grieves for the fallen.* "You'll face no trouble from him."

"It's not her father you should worry about," she muttered. *It's the pirate.*

"A daughter," the Elder breathed. As if he had accomplished something, weaseling such little information from her. He reached for the purse. "Very well, Assassin. That's more than enough in payment."

"Like you know," she scoffed. "I can find the girl for you. And I've settled on a price."

"Good," he said with an eager, desperate grin.

Mortal or immortal, it did not matter. Sorasa read him all the same. His smile had a child's innocence, despite the centuries he had seen. Sorasa despaired of it.

At least he would be useful.

The smile disappeared when she named her price.

But still he agreed.

6

IN THE BLOOD
Corayne

The tale of the Elder and the assassin crashed in an impossible wave.

Corayne broke it into pieces while he spoke, as she did with her lists and calculations. To weigh what he said without being dazzled or intimidated by mention of enclaves and distant cities, ridiculous deeds and Spindle magic. Until it all made some sort of sense in her head. Her conclusions sharpened in her mind, each one more preposterous than the last.

The father I've never known is dead. A portal is torn to another realm. The Ward is in grave danger. And for some reason, these two lunatics think I can do something about it.

Half of her felt afraid. The rest laughed.

She looked over the strange pair, her jaw locked tight. Domacridhan still knelt, his golden head bowed, while Sorasa paced back and forth, barring the road back to port. Corayne sorely wished

Kastio had accompanied her home. Or, better yet, her mother. *She would not tolerate this nonsense, not from anyone.* Not even an Elder, ageless and unfathomable. Not even one of the Amhara assassins, near to legend in their skill.

But Kastio is not here. Mother is not there. There's only me.

Her heart pounded wildly in her chest, but Corayne kept her body still and her face blank.

"We agreed to terms, Sorasa and I," Domacridhan said, bringing an end to his story. He raised his head and stared at Corayne in desperation, enough to make her skin itch. "And she led me here, to Lemarta. To *you*, the only person who can help us, and save the world entire."

Corayne blinked at both of them in turn. The immortal and the assassin blinked back.

"Good evening to you both. Safe journey," she said neatly. Her fingers trembled as she turned on her heel, setting off toward the cottage.

But the Elder was already moving, following Corayne up the overgrown pathway. He made no noise at all as he caught her on the front step.

She glared up at him stubbornly, using anger to hide her unease. *Better to show anger than fear or doubt.*

The ruined half of his face stood out sharply, illuminated by the moon cresting over the hills.

The Elder felt the light and turned his head, hiding his scars. "Perhaps you did not understand—"

Her voice hardened. "I'm mortal, not stupid."

"I did not say you were stupid," he said quickly.

Her hand found the latch of the cottage door, wrenching it open. "My answer, to whatever idiotic question you hope to ask, is *no*."

With two fingers and little effort, he pushed the door shut. Like his scars, his eyes caught the moon.

"The Ward will fall if you do not save her."

The edge in his voice was not unfamiliar. Corayne heard it in Lemarta all the time. Failed merchants bargaining over their meager goods. A destitute drunk pleading for another ale at the tavern. A would-be sailor begging for room on a ship, to find his fortunes on another horizon. This was not want, but need. Hunger driven by fear.

"The Ward falls," she murmured, her hand still on the latch, "because of a man with a magic sword and the villain from a children's story? 'What Waits'?" Corayne shook her head, barking a laugh. "You should head back to Lemarta and find yourself a fool who believes in that kind of thing."

From the road, the assassin laughed. "For what it's worth, I don't believe him either."

His teeth bared, Dom threw a scowl over his shoulder. "I do not expect mortals to believe what we Vedera know to be true, the ancient dangers of a history too long for you to perceive. The Torn King will consume this realm if given the chance. What Waits is waiting no longer." He put a broad, white hand over his breast, clasping it to his heart. A fine silver ring winked on his finger. "I swear on Iona, my lady,"

Corayne's grip tightened on the latch, but she did not open

it again. Something else tugged at her, a deeper pull keeping her rooted. "I'm not a lady," she spat.

To her dismay, Dom's eyes filled with emerald sorrow. The Elder looked on her with pity, with regret. Corayne wanted to slap both from his face.

"I do not know what your mother has told you, young one," he began, hesitant. Her blood flared at the mention of her mother. "But you are. Your father was—"

A haze of red crossed Corayne's vision and the smooth metal of the door latch fell from her grasp. Instead her hand rose, finger pointed, until she found herself jabbing the Elder in the chest, tapping harshly against the stone firmness of his flesh. His eyes widened, bewildered as a new kitten.

"I know exactly who my father was," she snapped, all concern for herself or her temper lost. "He was Cortael, a son of Old Cor, one of the ancient line. His ancestors were Spindleborn, children of a lost realm. There was Spindleblood in his veins, Corblood—as there is in mine."

Spindleblood, Spindleborn. She had never said those words aloud, only heard them from her mother, only known them in her bones and heart and the distant longing that lived inside her. Saying them now, his name, his birthright, what he was and what that made her—it felt wrong. A betrayal of herself, and especially of her mother. The only parent she knew, the only parent with any say in who she would become. *But it is in me, whether I want it or not.* Her breath hitched and heat rose in her cheeks, a stark contrast to the cool air.

"*None* of that makes me his daughter," she seethed. "Let alone a lady."

Or a princess or a fairy queen or any other hero in a story for children and fools.

"I did not realize you knew so much of him." The sadness in Dom's eyes was matched only by his growing frustration. Again, Corayne wished to tear both emotions away. She wanted neither from this stranger on her doorstep.

I've known since I had the sense to know. At least Mother was good enough not to lie about him, she thought, and she meant it.

"I have no use for illusions and false hopes. Your friend was both," she said. And it was the truth, a bitter one she had lived with all her days. "Well, go on. Hand over the gold and be gone from my door."

Dom furrowed his brow. "Gold?" Again he looked to Sorasa, this time in confusion. "You mortals are always asking for coin."

The woman scoffed low in her throat. "We mortals live in the real world." She did not move from her place on the path, keeping long yards between them. "Clearly the man sent money for his bastard," Sorasa explained slowly.

The Elder flushed and scowled in equal measure. "I have nothing of his to give you, my lady."

Corayne only shrugged.

But the assassin gave her pause. She shivered as the woman narrowed her eyes, already dark with a lining of black powder. Sorasa glanced back at Lemarta, to the lights of town and the port. They gleamed gold on the water, outlining the dark silhouettes of boats at anchor. The *Tempestborn* was one of them, a leviathan among the fishing ships.

"No wonder Captain an-Amarat has the finest hunter on the Long Sea," the assassin mused. "She had Cor gold keeping her afloat."

Fear curled around Corayne again. "You know my mother?"

"I know her reputation," she answered. "It is quite terrible."

"Then I can bring you to her. Both of you," Corayne said quickly, an offer as much as a threat. "She knew your prince better than I ever did. She met him, at least. She can help you more than I." *Help you leave this place and never return.*

Dom shook his head. "It's you we need."

"'We'?" Sorasa muttered under her breath.

The Elder ignored her. "It's in your blood, Corayne, whether you know it or not," he said.

Perhaps his mind is as dense as his body, Corayne thought with annoyance. "I'm not interested in you, your quest, or my father's failure. I want none of it," she hissed.

Finally he was silent, and there was no sound but the waves on the sea and the wind in the hills. Dom's gaze went to his own feet. Perhaps it was a trick of the moonlight, but his luminous eyes seemed wet.

Despite her frustration, Corayne softened. She could almost taste the misery rolling off him. "I am sorry for your loss," she added gently. Reluctant, she touched his arm.

He sagged beneath her fingers, coming undone. *Do immortals know how to mourn?* Corayne wondered. She looked at Dom again, a mountainous figure, his neck bowed in pained surrender. *I don't think they do.*

"I am sorry," she said again, dragging her gaze to Sorasa.

The woman waved a hand, her face blank as she watched the road. "I am not involved in these dramatics."

This time, Dom did not stop Corayne from unlatching the door. It yawned open, and darkness spilled from the cottage. He stood resolute and thoughtful, watching as she took a step forward.

"You say you want nothing to do with us, with your father," he said in a low, rough voice. "But don't act like *this* is what you want either."

In spite of herself, Corayne froze on the threshold. She stared ahead, into the shadows of the familiar old cottage. Out of the corner of her eye, she saw Dom raise his hood, his scarred face and emerald eyes retreating into shadow.

"Your blood is born of the Spindles, of distant realms and lost stars. You want the horizon, Corayne of Old Cor. You want it in your bones," he said, turning back down the path to join the assassin on the road. "And she's never going to let you take it."

Corayne drew in a sharp breath, a dozen retorts rising to her lips. They died quickly, cut apart by a difficult truth.

"Your father was the same."

No spine.

The two words caught her like the smack of a wave, pulling her under.

But Corayne refused to drown. And she refused to be caged a second longer, a bird meant to fly, not rot on a cliff with nothing but the wind for company.

She looked back to them, only for a moment. Dom turned and met her gaze, his face filled with luminous, aching hope. Corayne felt it too, the hope she thought had died with her mother's refusal. It bloomed anew, raw and sharp, bleeding at its edges, but stubbornly alive.

"Give me three days," she snapped, slamming the door.

The third day came.

At the kitchen table, Corayne busied herself with arrangements, her face a mask. Dark shadows ringed her eyes, testament to another night of poor sleep. Between her half-remembered dreams and hurried preparations for her mother's voyage, she hardly slept at all.

She stared at her wrinkled and scribbled-over map of the known Ward, using her ledger and compass to keep it anchored. The Long Sea bisected the realm across the middle, in a winding ribbon of blue water that stretched between the northern and southern continents. To the west, it emptied into the Nocturan Ocean, to the southeast, the Auroran. Night and dawn, framing the edges of the known world.

Her inky fingers trailed along the Mountains of the Ward, the soldier line dividing the green fields of Galland from the northern lands and the steppe. Her eyes found a cluster of hills near the Green Lion, the river barely a scribble. It was otherwise unmarked, but she knew—she had been *told*—of a forgotten temple there. *A temple and a Spindle, both torn apart. An impossible thing to believe.* She pressed her finger to the spot, staring at the mark on the map where her father had died.

Where, perhaps, the realm had begun to crumble.

As if I really even believe that.

Meliz woke noisily, clattering around her bedroom on still-rolling sea legs before banging into the central room of the cottage. She fluttered around the kitchen without much purpose, checking the cupboards, adjusting the curtains, poking at the copper pot in the hearth.

Like a child begging for attention, Corayne thought.

She refused to give her the satisfaction and double-checked her papers.

"Kastio is late," Meliz said abruptly, grabbing the pot from the fire. It sloshed with water and sliced lemons, still hot from the burning coals. She poured herself a cup before adding a dash of bright orange powdered root. A rare import from Rhashir, and worth its weight in gold.

She must have truly outdone herself last night to need such a cure this morning.

Corayne eyed the cup as her mother gulped it down. "He has a few minutes," she replied, glancing out the window at the tiny shack built up against the cottage. It had been Kastio's home for more than a decade.

"You stay close to him while I'm gone." Meliz drained the drink. "The roads are dangerous these days, even here," she continued with a smack of her lips. "Jydi longboats disappearing, summer storms off Sapphire Bay." She shook her head. "The realm feels twisted."

Even in our forgotten corner of the world. There had been word of strange doings all over, both good and bad for business.

Coincidence—or chaos unfolding?

"Everything is done," Corayne forced out, folding her papers away. After three days of hard work and too much coin spent, the *Tempestborn* was watered, provisioned, and ready for the long voyage to Rhashir. She procured passage papers through the Strait and the Ibalet navy guarding it. She sent letters to the allies of Hell Mel throughout the Long Sea, and promised gold to those who might be an obstacle. All was finished.

All but one more thing.

"Take me with you," Corayne blurted out, grasping at one last hope.

Take me with you or lose me, she wanted to say. *Lose me to whatever road I've put myself upon.*

Most of the time, Meliz an-Amarat had summer eyes, warm eyes. Mahogany flecked with amber and bronze. But now her eyes were cold and dark, still water beneath falling snow.

And her voice was icy steel.

"I will not."

The road into Lemarta unfurled. Dawn had barely begun, tinging the waters of the Long Sea pink and gold. Meliz walked slightly ahead, leaving Kastio and Corayne to lag along behind. The old man yawned away the last clingings of sleep, his knees creaking. Corayne donned her usual loose shirt and breeches with soft leather boots, worn by the years. It was warm outside, and she needed no cloak or coat, but one dangled from her shoulders anyway. The gloves were already in its deep pockets, tucked away, unused since winter.

She forced down breakfast as they walked, angrily biting into a flatbread greasy with butter, garlic, and tomato jam. Her long black braid hung over one shoulder, thick as sailing rope. Her eyes were wide, focused. She wanted to remember this day.

It will be my last in the only home I've ever known.

Sunlight crept into the harbor, too quickly for Corayne's liking. It was another clear day, with steady wind and currents. *A good day to begin a voyage.* The cloudless blue heaven broke Corayne's heart.

Captain an-Amarat walked the pier to the *Tempestborn*, her hands loose and empty, her back to the port, her face to the waves. Her long, battered coat hung off her bountiful frame, slashed at each side to show leggings and boots. Her clothes were crusted in salt, the veterans of a hundred journeys across the waters of the Ward. There was gray hair at her temples, only a few strands, gleaming like spun silver. She wore no hat and squinted into the sunrise. She looked as she always did before a voyage. Completely free, without weight. Without responsibility. With no allegiance to anyone but the sea.

It was a hard thing to see in a parent. For Corayne, it was a familiar sight.

She reached her mother's side too soon. Part of her wanted to jump right off the dock and into the water. Instead she steadied herself.

Meliz turned to look at her daughter sidelong. Her face was smooth, her skin golden, bronzed by the sun. "I'll be back in a few months, just like you said. With enough coin and treasure to keep us for a hundred years."

"We have that now," Corayne bit out.

She knew the count of gold buried in the cottage garden, sitting in the vaults of a capital bank, and scattered elsewhere throughout the Long Sea. Coin from her mother's plunder, coin from her father's shame. Money was not what sent the *Tempestborn* to the water, not anymore.

"There's no end to what you want, to what you do. You enjoy the life you've chosen, and you won't give it up for anyone. Not even for me."

It was not an accusation, but a statement of fact.

Meliz clenched her jaw. "That doesn't mean it's a life I want for you."

"You don't get to decide where I end up, or what I want," Corayne said. All her lists, all her reasons evaporated, leaving behind a single truth. She heaved a breath. "You know I'm not the same as you." *You don't have the spine.* "And you're right, but not the way you think. In my heart, in my blood—there's something in me that can't sit still." *Spindleblood, Corblood. Whether I want it or not.* "You know what that is."

Her mother's eyes flashed and she blew out a long, frustrated sigh. "*Now* you want to talk about your father?" she scoffed, throwing up her hands.

Her mother was not the same. There was no Spindleblood in her veins. She could not understand. But she was a restless kind too. She knew what it was to ache for change and distance, to look forward and never behind.

"It's a few months only. I promise you that," Meliz finally said, and a door slammed shut inside Corayne. A bridge collapsed. A rainstorm broke. A thread unwound.

And another doorway yawned open.

"Farewell," Corayne forced through gritted teeth, tears stinging her eyes.

Meliz already had her in hand, pulling her daughter tight to her chest. Into the cage of her arms. "Farewell, my girl," she said, pressing a kiss to her temple. "Keep your feet on the shore and your face to the sea."

Corayne inhaled deeply, taking one last gasp of her mother. "How fare the winds?" she whispered into her coat.

Her mother breathed the smallest sigh. "Fine, for they carry me home."

The *Tempestborn* disappeared over the horizon, her sails eaten by the sun. Corayne continued to watch, one hand raised to shade her eyes. Heat rose with the day, and a bead of sweat rolled down her neck, disappearing beneath the collar of her long cloak. She worried her lip between her teeth.

"Kastio," she said sharply.

At her side, the old sailor turned his head. "Eh?"

She gestured to the city streets winding up the hill. Already Lemarta clamored with noise. "I hear Doma Martia has just received a few good barrels of Tyri red."

"Seems a bit early for sampling Martia's wine," Kastio replied. "Even for me."

The coin was cold in her hand, winking silver between her fingers. Enough to buy many strong glasses. Corayne held the penny out to her guardian.

"You must tell me how it is."

Kastio glared at the money but put out his hand all the same. "This is a bribe."

She smiled weakly. "Just a few hours, please. I need to be alone."

Once, the old man had been an officer in the Siscarian navy, an oarsman before that, and a ship's boy long ago, though Corayne could hardly picture him without gray hair and wrinkles. She remembered his stories. Great battles on the sea, the wars with Galland and Tyriot. How bright the stars seemed in the middle of the water. How endless the world felt when the land fell away. All things she wanted and more.

He studied her for a long moment, enough to make Corayne nervous. No matter how old or drunk he might be, Kastio was no fool. He was charged to guard her for a reason.

"She was wrong not to take you, Corrie," he murmured, giving her shoulder a squeeze.

Corayne only stared as he walked off with his toddling gait. She tracked him through the blossoming crowd at the dock edge, then winding his way up to the Sea Queen and Martia's wine cellar. Only when he disappeared around a corner did she exhale, surveying the port.

No ship that will take me, no captain who will cross my mule-stubborn mother. The dock planks passed beneath her feet, echoing with heavy footsteps. The cloak felt heavy around her shoulders, far out of season. Perfect for travel.

She leaves me no choice but one.

The wood planks turned to stone as she stepped off the docks onto the long plaza lining the wharf. Corayne raised her eyes to search, scanning the familiar faces of Lemarta as they went about their lives. Her heartbeat rose in her chest, beating a wild rhythm.

Corayne an-Amarat liked plans. And her first had sailed away without so much as a backward glance. Luckily, she had another.

The sudden voice at her ear was lovely, a soft hiss.

"Three days," a woman whispered.

Corayne did not flinch, turning to face Sorasa Sarn. Behind her, in a shadowed alcove at the edge of the square, she caught a flash of gold and green.

"Three days," Corayne replied.

The assassin was not hooded today. For the first time, Corayne looked on her fully. She ran her eyes over Sorasa's lean frame, agile even beneath her light, sand-colored cloak. The Amhara could not be older than thirty, with jet-black hair and skin like glowing topaz, golden and rich. Though she was clothed from neck to wrist, Corayne noted the tattoos she could see—the lines on her fingers, the snake behind her ear, the unmistakable wing of an eagle and sting of a scorpion peeking out at her neck. Each was an artistry, a masterwork of ink, a testament to her skill and her Amhara training. They drew her eye more than Sorasa's dagger or sword.

Sorasa sniffed. "There'll be time for examination later, Spindlerot. We don't want to keep the immortal annoyance waiting, do we?" She jabbed a thumb over her shoulder. In the alcove, Dom shifted his broad form.

"Certainly not," Corayne said. "Are you going to call me Spindlerot the entire time or just today?"

"I'm still deciding."

The assassin set a sharp pace across the square, and Corayne followed neatly on her heels. She tried to keep her steps even, to walk instead of run. Still her heart thrummed, with both nerves and joy. *Kastio will know I ran. Mother will be away for months. And even if she learns I'm gone, she'll never turn back. Not for me.*

"It's good she left you behind," Sorasa murmured, taking her by surprise. "You're better off this way."

A jolt went through Corayne. "Why's that?"

"Rhashiran civil wars are boring," Sorasa drawled.

Corayne blanched, following her into the shadowed corners of the market.

The darkness did little to hide how out of place Dom looked in sunny, bronzed Siscaria. He bowed low, sweeping back his green cloak embroidered with antlers. The sword at his hip looked even more foolish than he did. Too big, too cumbersome, nothing like the light sabers or knives most sailors favored.

"My lady Corayne," he said. She pulled a face. "My apologies," he added quickly.

"I've met you twice and I've already lost count of how many times you've apologized to me, Domacridhan of Iona," Corayne said, crossing her arms over her chest. Out of the corner of her eye, she saw Sorasa's lips twitch.

Dom kept silent. She could see the urge to apologize again written all over his magnificent face.

"Well," Corayne sighed. "You said you need me to save the realm."

He raised his eyes to hers. "I do."

Half of Corayne thought this stupid; the other half, impossible. But both sides were also in agreement. *This is the best way out of here. To the horizon and beyond it. To whoever I am, in my bones.*

"So how do we . . . save the realm?" she said. It sounded ridiculous out loud.

Dom smiled truly. His grin was a force to be reckoned with, white and wide, his teeth unsettlingly straight. Corayne wondered if all Elders were so offensively handsome. It felt unnatural.

"Two things are needed to tear a Spindle, and the same are needed to close it," he said, holding up a pair of long fingers. "Spindleblood—and a Spindleblade."

"I guess I'm the blood." Corayne glanced down at herself, from her worn cloak to her old boots. She certainly did not look like *whatever* she was supposed to be. "Where's the blade?"

Dom did not hesitate.

"The Royal Court of Ascal."

7

THE QUEEN OF LIONS
Erida

The list of names never stopped growing. Erida wished she could burn it up or rip it apart, but she sat quietly instead, cursing every suitor asking for her hand. *It's to be expected,* she told herself. She was nineteen years old, wealthy, beautiful, well bred, educated, and skilled in all the talents of a proper noblewoman. *Not that any of my accomplishments mean much of anything. It's the crown they want, the crown that draws hopeful proposals. Not my striking blue eyes or sharp wit. I could be a tree stump for all they care.*

The Queen of Galland had ruled for four years, since her coronation at fifteen. She was well accustomed to her duties and the expectations that came with her throne. *But it does not make them any easier,* she thought, adjusting herself in her seat.

Though it had been only an hour in the council chamber, she was already sore, her back kept ramrod straight by an ornately carved chair and the tight lacing of her green velvet gown. The low ceiling of the round tower room did not help matters either, pushing down the oppressive heat of afternoon. At least today her head was bare; she did not have to suffer the weight of heavy gold or silver. Her ash-brown hair lay unbound, falling in waves over pale white shoulders. Behind her stood two knights of the Lionguard, in their ceremonial golden armor and bright green capes. How they stood the heat, she did not know.

Erida always held Crown Council in one of the high towers of the keep, the fortress heart of the New Palace, even in high summer. It was a round room, stern and gray like a grizzled old guard. The windows of the chamber were thrown wide to catch the breeze off the water. The palace was an island in the delta of the Great Lion, surrounded on all sides by river channels and canals. Gates kept the water around the palace clear, but the rest of the delta was jammed with galleys, trade cogs, merchant ships, barges, and ships of the fleet, all coming and going throughout the sprawling capital.

Her councillors listened in rapt attention, seated around their table with Erida at its head. Lord Ardath stood, leaning heavily as he read another letter aloud with a laborious wheeze. He paused every few moments to hack into a handkerchief. The old man lived perched on the cliff edge of death, and had done so for a decade. Erida didn't bother to fear for his health anymore.

"And so, I am humbled—" He gasped and coughed again. Erida winced, feeling her own throat twinge. "To offer Your Majesty my hand in marriage, to join our lives and futures together. I pray you accept my proposal. May they sing of us from the Gates to the Garden. Yours unto death, Oscovko Trecovik, Lord of the Borders,

Blood Prince of Trec . . . and so on with all the other titles that muddy troll likes to trumpet," Ardath finished, dropping the letter onto the council table.

An apt description, Erida thought. She had met Prince Oscovko only once, and that was enough. *Covered in shit after passing out in a military camp latrine ditch*. If he was handsome, she could not tell under the layers of fetid grime and wine stink.

Lord Thornwall picked up the letter quickly. He was a small man, thin and shorter than Erida herself, with graying hair and a red beard as furious as the armies he commanded. Even in the council chamber, he insisted on wearing armor, as if a skirmish might break out at the table. He squinted at the untidy scrawl of the letter, then at the seal and signature.

From her seat, Erida could easily see the mark of the crowned white wolf, the sigil of the Treckish royal family. She could also see the varied misspellings and cross-outs marring the page, as well as several inky fingerprints.

"Written in the Prince's own hand," Erida surmised, twisting her lips.

"Indeed it is," Thornwall said gruffly.

He slid the letter to Lady Harrsing, a veteran of many years in the royal court. She sneered at it, deepening the lines on her face. Bella Harrsing was just as old as Ardath, though far better preserved.

At least she can breathe without losing a lung.

"Don't even bother putting his name on the list," she said, refusing to touch the paper.

Across the table, the fortress of a man named Lord Derrick

scoffed. "You champion that *infant* still learning his letters in Sapphire Bay but won't consider a king's son on our own doorstep?"

Lady Harrsing eyed him, and his flushed, round cheeks, with distaste. "I'd wager Andaliz an-Amsir knows his letters better than this pestering oaf, or *you*, my lord. And he is a prince too, of a nation far more *useful*."

Their bickering was endless and familiar. Though it felt like putting a spike through her own skull, Erida let Harrsing and Derrick carry on like rival siblings. *The longer they argue, the longer I can draw out this distasteful process of selling myself like a prize cow,* she thought. *And the more time I have to think.*

It had been weeks since Andry Trelland had returned to Ascal alone, speaking of Spindle doom and a conqueror from nowhere. *Taristan of Old Cor. The blood and blade of Spindles, with a rabid army hidden in the mountains, horrific beasts under his will.*

She sat in silence, her face still and unreadable. Like a scale, she weighed the squire's words, as she had every morning and every evening since. *Did Trelland speak the truth? Is there a devil on the horizon, meant to swallow us whole?*

She could not know for sure.

The lie is the right choice, the better option. For me and my kingdom.

Harrsing and Derrick continued their sniping, weighing their chosen candidates for marriage. Truthfully, Erida despaired of both Oscovko and the Ibalet princeling, as she did every other name on that wretched list.

Lord Konegin remained as silent as the Queen, sprawled in his chair at her right hand. He was a cousin to Erida's father, and he too had the piercing blue eyes and thoughtful manner of the royal line. *The ambition too*, Erida thought. While the rest sat on the Crown Council to advise the Queen, hand-selected for their value, she'd chosen Konegin to keep an eye on a potential usurper to the throne.

He watched Harrsing and Derrick as one would a game of rackets played down in the garden. His eyes moved between them while they volleyed jabs back and forth. With his blond hair, striking glare, and strong, bearded jaw, Konegin looked too much like Erida's father. He even dressed like him, done up in simple but fine green silk, with a gold-and-silver chain hung from shoulder to shoulder, wrought lions roaring its length. It made her heart ache for a man four years gone.

"Put the name on the list," Konegin eventually said, his voice flat and final.

Derrick shut his mouth at once, an action Erida did not miss. But Harrsing drew herself up to argue, a foolish endeavor where Konegin was concerned.

Erida reluctantly cut her off. "Do as my cousin says."

Dutiful Ardath dipped his quill in a pot of ink and scratched the Prince of Trec's name onto the long parchment that would decide her fate. She felt every letter carved into her skin.

"But we must have a care for his position," she added sternly.

"He is a second son, yes, but this would secure our northern border," Thornwall began. He was never without his battle maps and was quick to point to the Gates of Trec, a gap in the Mountains of the Ward that cut the northern continent in two.

Erida resisted the urge to tell her military commander that she knew geography better than he did. Instead she stood and walked slowly to the massive, magnificent, painstakingly made map of Allward hung on the wall. It filled her vision, and she stood close enough so that all she could see was Galland, her birthright and her destiny. She looked over the familiar rivers and cities, their detail exquisite in the curved painting. Ascal itself stood at the center, her wall of yellow stone picked out in real gold leaf and chips of amber. Even the trees of the great forests of the Ward were drawn. It was the work of a master cartographer and master artist both, using swirls of paint and flecks of stone to create the realm of Allward.

"Our army is five times the size of their own, by a conservative count. If the butchers of Trec wish to try the Gates, let them. But I will not wed myself to a kingdom that needs me more than I need it. And, you'll notice," she said, reaching up to trace her fingers along the map, "Trec has quite an unfortunate border of its own. Wedged between the glory of Galland and the wolves of the Jyd, not to mention the Temur emperor." She pointed to each nation in turn, gesturing from the frozen wastes to the western steppe.

Thornwall leaned back in his seat, looking thoughtful. "Bhur has not conquered in two decades. The Temurijon lies quiet and flourishing. His armies maintain the borders already drawn, nothing more."

For now. The peace held across the west by the might of Temurijon was near legendary, stretching for decades. *Bought in blood*, Erida knew. *But such is the price of peace and prosperity.*

"The Emperor will not live forever, and I am far younger than he is," she replied, returning to her chair. "I'm not willing to gamble on his sons, who might hunger for conquest as their father did in his youth. And I will not form an alliance that will send my soldiers across the mountains to fight and die for another throne, to save Treckish throats from Temur blades."

Harrsing raised her chin. The apple-sized emerald at her neck gleamed. Along with being a shrewd counsellor, Lady Harrsing was the wealthiest woman in Galland. After the Queen, of course. "Well said, Your Majesty."

"Indeed, you see better than most of my generals," Thornwall said. His gaze lingered on the smaller map still in hand. "Though I admit, I have wished to test the knights of Galland against the Temurijon's Countless. What a war that would be." His tone was wistful, almost dreamlike.

"What a war," Erida echoed.

She saw it in her mind as clear as day. The Countless, the great army of the Temurijon steppes and Emperor Bhur, had never been defeated in battle. And none had tried them in decades. She wondered if the horse archers were still formidable, if Gallish steel and Gallish castles could weather such a storm if it came to break. And what kind of empire could rise from such a clash. *With myself at its head, alone without equal. Without need for any other.*

"Our armies are prepared to fight and defeat any kingdom upon the Ward," Konegin said sharply. "And any conflict with the Temurijon would be long in coming. It does us no use to dwell on it now. We have a different task close at hand."

"You are good to keep us on track, Cousin," Erida muttered, feeling the opposite. He offered a false smile in return. "Keep

Oscovko in contention. Are there any names to add? Or to remove?" She did her best not to sound hopeful.

"Duke Reccio of Siscaria has offered his son and sent a portrait of his likeness," Ardath wheezed. "I know you'd prefer not to wed so close a cousin, but I've had it put with the others. A Jydi clan leader also sent a bear pelt and her letter of intention." He drew out a battered page from his folio and passed it to the Queen.

"*Her?*" Lord Thornwall balked.

Erida took it in stride. While the lower peoples of most kingdoms were free to wed as they chose, man or woman, between or neither, a ruling queen was bound by the possibility of children. "She would not be the first. And the Jyd don't birth their heirs, they choose them. I cannot say the same." The letter was not parchment but treated skin. *Animal, I hope.* There were only three words on it, poked in. *You, me, together.*

"I see we're using the word *letter* lightly," she muttered before putting it aside. A low chuckle passed around the table. "Have the pelt sent to my residence in the Castlewood, and a letter of thanks sent to the Jyd."

"The Crown Prince of Madrence, at least, has given up his hopes," Harrsing offered. She put a hand to her necklace. Her skin was paper thin, near translucent, showing blue veins beneath. "Orleon weds a Siscarian princess at the turn of the month. We can cross him off."

The small victory was bittersweet. Erida grit her teeth, loath to say what she must. "Can I not dangle myself a bit longer? I'd like to give our soldiers enough time to rally along the Madrentine border. As soon as the pretense of marriage is gone, we begin our push to the ocean. And I'd rather not fight both Madrence and Siscaria if I don't have to."

"I can try." Harrsing bowed her head. "I'll send word of your . . . renewed interest to the court at Partepalas."

Thornwall scratched his beard. "I'll do the same and alert our encampments near Rouleine."

"Good," Erida said. The Third Legion was already nearby, stationed among the forts and castles of the tumultuous border. *Twenty thousand men will be ready to fight before the autumn sets in.* "How long will they need?"

"The First Legion dispatched from the capital forts two weeks ago." The old soldier leaned back in his chair and blew out a breath, counting out the days on his fingers. "Riding hard, on the Cor roads, without incident, I'd say the knights and cavalry would arrive in less than four weeks' time. The infantry—swords, pikes, archers, and whatever peasant we press into picking up an ax— another two months."

The Queen nodded. "Then buy us three, Bella."

"Yes, Your Majesty."

"I'd rather be bait than a prize," Erida said. *If I am to be dangled on a hook, I'd like to do so under my own terms, for my own ends.* "Well, if there are no more suitors to discuss . . ."

"There are plenty," Konegin ground out.

Talk of war always emboldened her, and Erida put a hand down on the table. She leaned toward her older cousin, careful to keep her temper in check. *Though women have more right to anger than men.*

"And none who tempt me, or Galland," she told him. To her

delight, he drew back in his seat. "If I am to marry, I will do it for the good of my crown. To strengthen my throne instead of selling it. We are the successors to Old Cor, the rightful empire, the glory of the Ward. Find me a husband worthy of that destiny, of my father's and grandfather's dream. Find me a champion."

A high bar to clear. Impossible, perhaps. And that was her aim. Set a target so small none could hit it. If the Crown Council guessed as to Erida's true intentions, they did not say so or show it. They would not call their queen a liar, young as she was. *Nor am I lying*, she thought. *If such a man exists, I will marry him, and wield him like the sword I cannot carry. To carve out an empire like the days of old, from one edge of the map to the other, uniting all beneath the Lion. Beneath me.*

"There are the funerals to see to," Ardath said softly, drawing Erida back from her musings. "Though we've had no word yet. It's possible they never find the bodies."

Erida nodded. She'd selected the riders herself, from the ranks of the Lionguard. To look for the corpses of Tyr and the Norths. *And the army of ruin, should it exist at all.*

"Body or not, they shall be buried in honor, with all the glory they earned in life. Sir Grandel, Sir Raymon, and Sir Edgar will long be in our memories," she said, and it was the truth. The knights had guarded her since the coronation, and her father before. While she would not weep over their loss, she was upset to lose them still.

Konegin nodded in agreement, but his eyes were sharp. "What of the squire?"

The mention of Andry Trelland sent lightning through the

Queen, down her spine and into her fingers. *If what he said comes to pass, if what he saw in the hills was real, if a Spindle is torn, if the stories and fairy tales are true . . .*

But Erida forced an uninterested shrug. "I'm sure another knight will take him on. He's a fine young man; it should be no trouble to find a place for him."

"He said nothing of his plans when he returned? Bloody and alone in the middle of the night?" Konegin pressed. Now it was his turn to lean over the table. "Again, I ask, what did he tell you?"

Though every instinct of etiquette told her to sit back, to make herself small, to smile demurely and placate her cousin with her feminine gentility, Erida did not. Her hand curled into a fist, the grand ring of state difficult to ignore. The rough-cut emerald gleamed sharply.

"Andry Trelland's words were for my ears and mine alone," she said. After weeks of questioning, she could recite it in her sleep. "Rambling, mostly. The boy was traumatized by the slaughter of his lord and the others. But the specifics are known. I've told you as much."

"Killed by a horde of Jydi raiders, yes. All butchered but for the squire." The lie had been an easy one to reach for, and an easy one to believe. "Seeking what we do not know, accompanied by a band of warriors without name, for a purpose we cannot fathom," Konegin barked, slapping down a hand.

Harrsing jumped in her seat.

"Some decrepit Elder, some Spindlerotten witch calls and you send three knights without question, without even consulting us, without even telling us why. And now we must fill their empty graves!" The lord ran a hand through his hair, setting the golden strands on end.

Erida watched him collect himself with a shrewd eye.

"Your Majesty," he added softly, an afterthought as much as a warning.

The Queen held her tongue. She felt fire in her throat, and it would not do to loose it here, kindling that could turn into a blaze.

Lady Harrsing was good enough to speak in her queen's stead. "We have not heard nor seen the Elders in a generation," she said primly. "Tell me, my lord, would you not have done the same? Would you not have sent men to answer a monarch's summons?"

Erida narrowed her eyes, knowing her cousin well enough to guess.

He would have gone himself. Taken a retinue of knights and his own men-at-arms, a wagon of gifts, a parade of servants, and a pair of heralds to shout his titles and his bloodline. Make way for Lord Rian Konegin, grandson of Konrad the Great, King of Galland. *He would have been a spectacle for commons and immortals alike, as close to an emperor of Old Cor as he could make himself,* Erida thought. Her jaw clenched. *And if I were not chained to this throne, I would have done it too.*

Konegin was undeterred. He glanced at Derrick and Thornwall, looking for support. "I'd like to summon the squire and hear his story for myself."

After four years of rule, Queen Erida was as skilled an actress as any of the pantomime players on the stages of the Ascal streets. Her strength flagged as she bowed inward, her shoulders drooping as she shut her eyes. She passed a hand over her face.

"Trelland's agony is my burden to bear, Lord Konegin. Mine alone," she said wearily. "That is the cost of the crown."

A crown you will never claim.

It was enough to placate even Konegin, who retreated like a shattered army.

Erida dropped her hand, and her mask of sympathy. Her face turned cold as she stood from the table, dismissing them with her action.

"Konegin still has not presented his son as a suitor."

Only Harrsing stayed behind. Even Erida's Lionguard had retreated to the hallway, giving their queen a private audience with the old woman. The two stood by the largest window, watching the river as it carried on to Mirror Bay. Green freshwater swirled with darker salt. On the far bank, the famed Garden of Ascal stretched along its island, its trees and flowers manicured to perfection. Despite the heat, nobles and the wealthy merchants of the capital strolled the lawns and paths of the Garden, their shrieking children in tow.

Erida contemplated the greenery across the water. She'd played there as a child, surrounded by a circle of knights. As the only heir of the king, her life was more precious than any treasure. *I never even skinned my knees. There was always someone to catch me.*

With a sigh, she turned to face her advisor. The usual headache thrummed at her temples.

"Because Konegin wants to take my country by force instead of marriage. He'd rather sit the throne himself than put a grandchild upon it peacefully," she said, as if it were the most obvious thing in the world. "He'll only push Herry at me when he has no other choice."

Heralt Konegin, the Prince of Toads. An apt nickname for Erida's mean, squat, and croaking cousin, who did little but drink and stare, fog-eyed. Her stomach twisted at the thought of having such a person foisted upon her.

"There are still suitable partners," Harrsing said, gently guiding Erida away from the window. The Queen allowed herself to be led. "Easy to control, rich in land, gold, armies. Good men who will protect you and your throne."

Protect me. Erida wanted to retch. *There is no man upon the Ward who would not take my crown if he could, nor one who is worth the risk of losing it.*

"I decide who is suitable, Bella. And so far, I have seen none," she said. Though the old woman returned her to the table, it was Harrsing who leaned heavily on the Queen's arm. While her health was certainly better than Ardath's, there was no denying the age that weighed on Bella. Erida winced at the thought of losing her, and she forced a smile instead. "No, not even your Ibalet princeling," she said, winking at the old woman. "Who you so often forget to mention is your *grandson*."

Harrsing shrugged with a wry smile. "I just assume it's common knowledge."

"Indeed," Erida mused.

The map wall of the council chamber flashed with light rippling off the river. It seemed to dance, the lines of rivers and coasts and kingdoms bending and changing. Erida watched and, for a moment, saw no kingdoms at all. None but her own, in every corner of the Ward. She stopped before the painting, her face raised.

"Before his death, my father made his wishes known," she said. "They are easy to remember. There were only two."

Harrsing bowed her head. "Erida of Galland chooses her own husband. None shall be forced upon her."

Again Erida ached in her chest, and wished her father were still alive. His decrees held weight, even in death, but they would not protect her forever. And while Erida was queen, she was a woman first, in the eyes of most. *Untrustworthy, unfit, too weak to rule. History gorges itself on women raised high and then brought low by men grasping for their power. I will not be one of them. I will not lose what my father gave me.*

I will make it greater.

On the map, the golden city of Ascal gleamed.

"My father also said Galland is the glory of the Ward, Old Cor reborn, an empire to be remade." The old Cor roads, straight and true, were stark against the map, inlaid with precious stones. They bound the great cities of the Ward, spreading over the old borders. "I do not intend to disappoint him."

Harrsing grinned in approval. "The Crown Council is with you."

Until they aren't, Erida knew. *Until they find someone else they'd rather stand behind.* Even Bella Harrsing, who had known her since birth, who had served her father before her—even she would abandon Erida if the need came. If a better opportunity presented itself.

"That poor squire," Harrsing carried on, pulling them away from the map and the council table. "I can't get him out of my mind. Having to watch his lords be slaughtered by those northern animals."

A sour taste filled Erida's mouth. Usually Harrsing was far less obvious in her needling. *Who has the boy been speaking to?*

"A tragedy, to be sure," Erida said demurely, her eyes downcast.

Heroes murdered, Spindles torn, a madman with an army. The entire realm in danger. Erida mulled over his harried ranting again. *Truth or madness?* Still she could not say.

In the hall, the Lionguard waited, as did Erida's ladies and handmaidens. All rose to her pleasure, ready to serve their young queen. In their many-colored gowns and flowing skirts, they looked like a school of fish moving as one. Toward food. Away from a predator. Both.

"Send word to Lady Trelland and her son," Erida said to her maidens. "I would like to visit them and pay my respects for our lost knights."

Harrsing nudged her shoulder. "After the petitions."

"Of course." Erida sighed, already tired.

Would that I could do away with this entire tradition, useless as it is. Petitions day meant hours upon the throne, hearing the complaints and demands of nobles, merchants, soldiers, and peasants alike. Mostly it meant keeping her eyes open, deflecting their troubles as best she could.

"How many present themselves as suitors?" she asked wearily, looping her arm into the old woman's. The record currently stood at twelve in a day.

"Only one. I'm told he's quite fetching."

Erida scoffed low in her throat, unamused. "Tell me something of use."

All thoughts of Andry Trelland faded, eclipsed by the demands of a crown.

"Well, let's get on with it."

8

UNDER THE BLUE STAR
Andry

The water steamed, hot over the fire in their small parlor. He could have called for servants to bring tea from the kitchens, but Andry preferred to make it himself. He knew what Lady Valeri preferred, and it was best served piping hot. Their apartments, lovely as they were, were far from the sprawling palace kitchens. Besides, Andry liked to watch the water and wait. It gave him something to think about besides blood and slaughter. Besides the cold, crackling whispers waiting in the corners of his mind.

He stared into the pot over the fire, the surface of the water rippling with slow bubbles. Herbs swirled with an inner current, peaceful and predictable. Andry tried to lose himself in the pattern. Even so, the cries of fallen heroes found him. He wrenched his gaze to the fire, willing their screams away. But the coals cracked and burned, split with flame and ash.

White hands, red eyes, skin like charred wood.

"*Ambara-garay*," said a weak voice. *Have faith in the gods*. His mother put a hand on his shoulder and Andry turned, pulled from his waking nightmare.

She hovered over him, her smile thin but bright. Without thought, Andry took her fingers and kissed them. He jumped to stand.

"Sit, Mama," he urged, all but lifting her into his chair by the hearth.

Valeri Trelland did not argue. She was a tall woman, but wispy, and she curled into herself when she took the seat. Andry tucked her shawl around her narrow shoulders, focused on keeping her covered and comfortable. Despite her illness, the cold that seemed to live in her chest, Lady Valeri was still striking in her beauty. She was not called the jewel of her kin for no reason. Andry saw it even on her worst days, the way a light seemed to glow in her skin, like a dark garnet filled with sunshine. Her hair was short now, braided tightly to her head, the ends set with gold rings. Her eyes seemed larger in her drawn face. They were the rare green of young wheat, hesitant to give over to gold. Andry envied her eyes. His own were a muddy brown. *My father's*. But the rest of him looked like Valeri, with his black hair and high cheekbones.

"Here you are," he said, preparing her cup of tea with sure, quick movements. *Lemon, cinnamon, clove, sweetsalt, honey*. The bounty of summer in the Gallish capital, when all the Ward seemed to cross from Rhashir to the Jydi snows.

Valeri took the cup and breathed in, smiling. The wet rattle in her chest loosened. Andry pulled another chair to the fire and sat, content to watch her sip her tea.

Andry and his family had never lived in a house of their own. His father had been a knight in the king's service, his mother a lady to the old queen and then Erida. His home was these rooms, generously given to them to use even after his father was long dead and his mother too sick to serve. Sometimes he wondered if the Queen's administrators had simply forgotten them. The New Palace of Ascal was a monstrous place, walled onto its own island, a city unto itself, where thousands lived and worked at the Queen's pleasure. It would be easy to overlook a squire and his ailing mother. Before, when he'd served Sir Grandel, Andry slept in the barracks or the Lionguard quarters, close at hand should his lord have need of him. *Not anymore.* He did not lament leaving the narrow cot in a room crowded with boys of varying ages and odors. But the circumstances by which he had returned to tend his mother were a price he wished he did not have to pay.

The palace around them was two hundred years old, built of pale gray and yellow stone. They lived in the east wing, a long hall of apartments broken by courtyards, with the majority of the Queen's courtiers. Their own were at the base of a tower, rounded slightly, its windows like narrowed eyes. Colorful tapestries decorated their walls, scenes of hunts and jousts and battles and feasts. They used to make Andry excited, eager to begin his life as a knight. Now the bright threads were dull, their scenes false.

There is no blood, he thought, his eyes lingering on a woven depiction of the Battle of the Lanterns. In it, the armored legions of Galland fell upon the cities of Larsia, their great green-and-gold flag held high. Though swords and spears glinted in silver thread, they were clean, and the Larsians fell to their knees in surrender.

We were never even given the chance. There was no mercy in that army, or that man. Andry squeezed his eyes shut and turned away even as the cursed image of Taristan rose in his mind. *Corblood in his veins, a Spindleblade in his fist. Made of stone, made of flame, made of mortal flesh. Red blood, black armor, white hands, white ash, white-hot pain and anger and loss—*

"How go your petitions?"

Andry blinked furiously, clearing his head. The hot sting in his eyes faded with his mother's voice. "Sorry—what?"

She put a frail hand on his. Firelight danced on his mother's face, brightening already brilliant eyes.

"Your petitions, *madero*," Valeri said gently. *My dear.* "You have been petitioning lords and knights for service. You told me so last week."

"Oh, y-yes," Andry stuttered, finding his voice. He braced himself for another inquisition. "Yes, indeed, I've been asking around the barracks and the court. Sent some letters off as well," he added, the half-truth tasting rotten. It was against the code of knights to lie, but with his mother in such a state, with such *things* still spilling forth on the horizon, finding another man to squire for was far from his mind. *I have written letters, yes, but not seeking patronage.*

Valeri drained her cup. "Anything promising?"

Quickly, Andry stood to prepare his mother another draft. He put his back to her so she would not see the falsehoods written on his face. *I am no good at lying.*

"A few," he said, stirring honey. "Lord Konegin's son just gained a knighthood and would be in need of a squire."

"If memory serves, that boy is in need of far more," Valeri muttered, giggling to herself.

Andry turned back to her with a wry smile. "Drink," he said, nudging the cup into her hands. "The doctor is due to visit today. The Queen's own."

A strange look crossed Valeri's face but quickly disappeared. "Oh, that isn't necessary," she sighed. "She need not fuss over me."

Andry felt a twist of annoyance. He gently pushed the tea back to her mouth. Even as she swallowed, Andry heard the roughness in her throat. He braced himself for another coughing fit, but it never came. A stillness washed over her, and she fixed him with an odd stare.

"He's university trained in Ibal," he explained. The northern continent was not known for its skills in medicine. "Dr. Bahi isn't another one of the foolish Gallish bloodletters or superstitious moon healers—"

Valeri waved a hand, suddenly sharp. Her eyes bored into his. "Why is the Queen of Galland bothering over me?"

"You were companion to her mother," he offered, and almost winced. *I'm not bending the truth so much as breaking it in half.* "You knew her as a girl. Erida is a compassionate young woman."

"You know the histories better than I do. Have you ever known a king or queen of Galland to be compassionate?" Valeri answered. Her eyes darted to the tapestries on the walls, to the sword and shield of his father, still hung on the stone. A great long scratch divided the shield in two, scarring the heraldry of Trelland's blue star. It had not been earned in the training yard. "Was this shadow of the old empire forged from compassion, or from blood?"

Andry really did wince. The last thing he needed was to think of his father, broken on some field in Madrence, spent like an old coin. "Mother, please."

But she stood, trembling, and Andry could not force her back down. The fire crackled at her back, turning her edges to ruby and gold.

"I came to the Royal Court of Ascal as a foreign bride, set apart from almost everyone around me by my skin and my voice. I have not remained here in high esteem by being foolish, and I will not see my son made a fool," she said. Her hands met his cheeks, turning his face up to look at her. "What does Erida want from you?"

The breath caught in Andry's throat. He hesitated, reluctant to put such a burden on an already burdened woman. Valeri stared down at him, the hearthfire in her eyes, and she was young again, vibrant, beautiful, impossible to deny.

Queen Erida had visited only a week ago, to pay her respects. And to quietly, carefully, and expertly try to pry from him any more details about the slaughter of the Companions. There was little more to say that did not concern a certain sword. And the whispers were clear as a bell.

Say nothing of the sword. Or face the ending of the world.

"She's seen me twice now, and both times I told her as much as I've told you," Andry said, his shoulders still raised in tension. He tried to force some of his mother's own strength into himself. It felt as impossible as coaxing wet coals into flame. "What I saw in the mountains. What happened to Sir Grandel and the rest. The Spindle torn open, the army, Taristan and his wizard." Her gaze narrowed. Andry ignored the sensation of being looked through, being read. "I told her of the Ward's doom."

"And she didn't believe you." It was not a question.

"I don't know. I can't say. Certainly she did not move to act." He shook his head. "And so she spun the story of Jydi raiders, told the court it was an ambush. Everything she's asked of me I've already given."

Valeri's grip on her son tightened.

"Does that include the sword you've hidden beneath my bed?" she murmured.

Andry jolted, looking to the door leading into her bedchamber. He grit his teeth, braced for the rush of whispers. But they never came.

With a soft pat, Valeri drew him back to her. "I am not foolish, *madero*."

He clenched his jaw and took her hands. On shaking legs, Andry rose up, until he stood over her, taller by far. Whatever fear he felt in himself, curled deep in his belly, he saw reflected in her. He did not know what was worse to bear.

"I didn't tell her about the Spindleblade. I didn't tell anyone," he swore, his voice low.

She huffed a dry scoff. "Not even me."

Slowly, Andry pulled Valeri's hands away, but kept her fingers in his own. They were so thin and small, wasting like the rest of her.

"It belonged to Cortael of Old Cor, the mortal of Spindleblood, a descendant of the empire fallen. He died in the mud with the rest of them, and the sword . . . it's the only thing I managed to save."

"It's a fine blade, I'm sure," she bit out. "But why haven't you given it to Erida? Or back to the Elders?"

The squire could only shake his head, barely able to answer. The truth sounded foolish, even in his own mind. But Valeri was undeniable, her eyes like two moons.

"Something in me, a voice I do not know, tells me I shouldn't. That I have to wait. Does that make any sense at all?"

Valeri looked to the fire, watching the flames for a long moment. Her breath wheezed. "Perhaps it is the gods of the Ward, the gods of Kasa, speaking to you so," she finally said. "Or it is simply your own good instinct."

But the voice is not my own.

"I dream of it every night," he said, voice flat. He'd built a wall inside himself, trying to keep the memories at bay. "That sword, the red steel. Sir Grandel and the Norths. All of them slaughtered, even the Elders, immortal as they were. Everything fell before that army, before that man. I see it every time I close my eyes." Andry dropped her fingers and ran a hand over his own face. A numbness stole over him. "Did Father talk of battle like this? I can't remember."

I was only six years old when he died, lost in a fight that meant nothing, for little more than a bend in the river, another glimmer in Galland's crown.

Valeri did not hesitate to shake her head. "Never like this," she said quickly, looking to the shield on the wall. "Never like this."

Andry followed her gaze. The blue star with the scratch down the middle was as familiar as his own two hands. It was the emblem of his father and his father alone, earned not by a long bloodline but by loyalty to the crown, devotion to the dead king, and the ultimate sacrifice on a distant field. He knew the star better than his father's face, which he only carried in flashes. A merry smile, a swoop of auburn hair, long arms always reaching to scoop him up or pull his mother close. Sir Tedros Trelland was as mist in his memories, fleeting and impossible to hold.

His grave is empty too, his body never recovered from the mud of the field. It will be only bones now, if anything at all.

"Do you believe me?" Andry whispered, to his mother and the shield. The blue star seemed to glare. "Do you believe what I saw? What I heard?" He took a shaky breath. "What I *still* hear?"

Valeri took him firmly by the shoulders. She looked up at her son, wide-eyed.

"I do."

Her faith settled around him like a suit of armor.

"Then we need to make arrangements." He stepped out of her hands with a will. *More arrangements, for some are already made.* His letters were on the road and the sail, traveling by courier and boat. Most were bound for Kasa. One had already received a reply. "And you need to be ready to travel."

Valeri's face fell. Andry wished he could tear the sickness right out of her chest.

"*Madero*, you know I can't—"

"I won't hear it, Mama." Already he saw her hacking coughs on the deck of the ship as they fled, putting the Long Sea between themselves and a Spindleborn army. "We go together, or not at all."

There was no fear in Valeri Trelland, a lady born of Kin

Kiane. She flattened her palm against her chest to steady her own breathing.

"Then we go."

The Hill of Heroes basked in the sunlight, green and gold as the Gallish flag. It was another island in the river delta, walled like the palace. Countless tombs and headstones marched in endless rows: knights and great lords fallen for Galland. The graves of the kings crowned the Hill, marked by statues and flowering trees. The capital of Ascal was home to more than half a million people, but one would never know it from these still, green lawns.

Andry saw the Hill's shadow every morning from the training yards of the New Palace, the silhouettes of the stones like fingers against the sky. They reached for him now, white marble and black granite, their grip unbreakable. *With me,* they hissed in a thousand weaving voices. *With me,* Sir Grandel moaned, dying again.

His breath came hard and fast as he walked, his pulse thrumming in his ears. Sweat dripped through his short-cropped hair. He tried to think not of Sir Grandel's corpse, but of his tombstone. It was already waiting, flanked by headstones for the Norths, surrounded by a forest of graves for dead knights. The funeral would be a large affair, with even the Queen in attendance. It had somehow taken weeks to plan, though the coffins would be empty.

He passed through the gates of the cemetery with the rest of the squires, wellborn boys in service to the great knights of the kingdom. The knights themselves were all on horseback, in gleaming armor with cloaks of all colors. Behind the squires came the pages, some as young as seven, dressed in light summer tunics to match their knights. Andry glanced back to see a pair shoving each other silently. In jest or rivalry, he did not know. Most squires grew out of that sort of thing.

Most.

An elbow dug into Andry's ribs. He barely felt it. There was far more to think about—getting his mother out of Ascal, the festering army at the border, the empty graves ahead, the sword hidden, the Spindle torn, the whispers that greeted him every morning.

"I'm talking to you, Trelland," someone said harshly. The elbow struck again.

Andry clenched his jaw. He did not need to look to know it was Davel Monne, who the boys all called Lemon for his name, his yellow hair, and especially his sour disposition. Like the rest of the squires, Lemon's hair was cut short, but it sprouted like horrible weeds.

"I deserve to know what happened, same as you," Lemon hissed, his pale face spotted with freckles. His red surcoat flapped in the breeze, the falcon sigil of the North family worked in eye-catching silver. Andry's own was gray quartered with sky blue for Sir Grandel. "I was Sir Edgar's squire. It's my right to know."

Andry kept silent. Even stupid Lemon knew the story being passed through the halls of the palace, the falsehoods born of the Queen: Jydi raiders, a slaughter in the hills of the border. Other rumors were being woven too. The most popular was a Treckish ambush meant to look like the Jydi, soldiers disguised in furs with axes instead of swords.

"You have the right to be *quiet*, Lemon," he said. "Show some respect to our lords."

Lemon bared his teeth. They were yellow as his hair. "There's our Andry, too good for the rest of us."

He didn't flinch. It was a familiar gibe, easy to ignore, following him from his earliest days as a page. *And a compliment, even if Lemon is too stupid to know it.*

"Is that why you're still alive? Too good for the Jydi wolves to howl over?" Though Lemon was a head shorter than Andry, he was far broader and used his bulk well. He shouldered his way past, knocking Andry aside. His voice rose, loud enough for the other squires to hear. "You wouldn't see me on the Hill, with my lord dead and me still walking the Ward. That's for certain. Can't imagine the shame of it."

Andry flushed darker than Lemon's surcoat. Lemon did not miss it, leering at him, goading him to respond.

I feel that shame every day! he wanted to shout back. But he kept silent, his teeth locked tight, his feet still marching in time with the rest. *He's never seen true battle. None of the squires have,* Andry knew, glancing around at his fellows. Though they marched together, the others felt so far away. *They don't know what it's like.*

Lemon glared, dagger-eyed.

He's only jealous. I rode with the knights while he stayed behind. The envy goes both ways.

Again Lemon knocked his shoulder, and again Andry did nothing.

There are worse things in this world than you, Davel Monne, and they're coming for us all.

The procession reached the sector of the Hill reserved for knights of the Lionguard, who spent their lives protecting the royal family of Galland: Sir Tibald Brock. Sir Otton of the Castlewood. Sir Konrada Kain, the only woman to serve in the Lionguard, who fell defending her king at the Battle of the Lanterns. Andry wondered if their ghosts would be here to welcome their brothers and guide them into the realm of the gods.

But the ghosts of Sir Grandel and the Norths are far away, if they even exist at all.

A pavilion looked over the grave sites, its chairs empty, shaded by a canopy of green silk. The Queen and her own entourage had not yet arrived.

While the knights dismounted, their squires moved in a flurry to grab reins and tend horses, allowing the lords to line up in their ranks. The pages kept out of the way, shunted to one side. Of the squires, only Andry, Lemon, and Sir Raymon's boy, Karl Daspold, had no one to serve. Karl was as kind as Lemon was cruel and kept himself between the two. A dog trailed at his heels, a shaggy yellow hound. It looked up with baleful eyes, waiting for a master who would not return.

Three wagons brought up the empty caskets, each hung with silk. Red with the silver falcon for the Norths, gray and sky blue check for Sir Grandel. A detachment from the palace garrison escorted each wagon as it was wheeled into place aside the pavilion. Even before the arrival of the Queen, Andry guessed there were near a hundred men and boys gathered to pay respects. *Sir Grandel would have liked that*, he knew. Sir Grandel had flourished under attention.

The Queen arrived with a somber call of trumpets. Andry glanced over her entourage—Lord Konegin and his trollish son were easy to recognize, and Lord Thornwall was known even to the pages. As the supreme commander of Galland's great army, he lived in a grand set of rooms in the palace barracks and visited the yards often. Knights and squires alike bloodied each other hoping for his attention.

Right now, Andry only wanted to be forgotten and overlooked. He lowered his eyes, praying the rest of the great lords and ladies passed without paying him any mind.

But it was impossible to ignore the Queen herself. When she dismounted her horse, everyone knelt. Andry glanced up through his lashes, glimpsing Erida of Galland. His jaw clenched again, this time with frustration.

The Lionguard surrounded her, their armor like the sun, their cloaks catching the warm breeze. Andry saw the faces of Sir Grandel and the Norths beneath every helm, their eyes unfocused, dark, dead. *As all will be if we don't do something.*

Light bounced off the steel, bathing the Queen with a heavenly glow. Her gown was cloud gray, the royal color of mourning in Galland. It gave her pale skin a moonlit pallor. A red jewel hung from her neck, a ruby bright as new fire. As she looked over her knights, her piercing blue gaze snagged on Andry, and she held his stare for a long moment.

Despite the summer heat, Andry felt a cold finger trail down his spine. He dipped his head again, until all he could see were his own feet and the grass between them. The blades rippled like the sea. Andry pictured his mother on a ship, her face turned southeast.

We will go to my mother's family. There is a ship from Ascal to Nkonabo. She'll be safe with Kin Kiane, and from there I can return north.

Andry Trelland had ridden to Iona before, and he remembered the way to the immortal city. *Up the river, past granite cliffs and the yew forest, deep in the glen.* He swallowed, terrified of what must be done. To leave his mother, ill and alone, while he returned to the place that doomed the rest? It felt like the height of stupidity.

But what else can I do? he thought, his stomach twisting.

I can tell the Elders what befell us in the hills, what comes from the temple. Certainly they will defend what Erida will not.

And they will know what to do with the Spindleblade.

The service began, but Andry heard little of it. The whispers rose once more, too familiar, his only constant since the slaughter at the temple. In spite of himself, he watched Erida again. The whispers sharpened.

Say nothing; keep your distance, they said, howling with too many voices, all brittle as ice. *Shadow the sword; hide its brilliance.*

The summer wind blew cold, catching the flags of Galland. The Lion seemed to leap in the sky. At the pavilion, the Queen and her ladies clutched at their gowns. Andry shivered down to his toes.

Spindleblood and Spindleblade.

This time, the voices were as one: an old woman, rasping like a knife through silk. It almost sent Andry back to his knees. Shock kicked him in the gut, but he could not react, not here before a hundred eyes. Before the Queen, still watching him with her sapphire stare.

Even while willing the voice away, his hands fisted at his sides, Andry strained to remember it. But the voice was like smoke, twisting through his fingers, impossible to grasp. Disappearing in one breath of wind while flaring in another.

It curled again, seemingly all around him.

A new hand comes, the alliance made.

9

CHILDREN OF CROSSING
Domacridhan

Domacridhan saw so much of Cortael in her. Beneath her mother's influence there was Corblood in her veins, as vital to Corayne's being as roots to a tree. And just as tangled. She struggled with it, grappling with what she could not understand.

Cortael was the same, in his youth, Dom thought, remembering his friend when he was a boy. *Restless and searching, hungry for a place to belong but hesitant to drop anchor.* Such was the way of Old Cor: humans born of travel and crossing, conquest and voyage from one realm to the next. It was in their bones and blood, in their steel, in their souls.

And she does not understand, for there was no one to tell her.

He watched as Corayne haggled at the Lemarta stables, negotiating for three horses. The trader was eager to see them both gone—his eyes darted to Dom standing at her shoulder, and to the sword hanging at his side. Dom kept still under his scrutiny, trying not to draw more attention than need be.

She easily bargained the trader down to half his price, handing over a purse for reins.

There were two stallions and a mare, fully tacked with filled saddlebags, all common bays with brown bodies and black manes. Dom thought of the fine horse that died beneath him in Iona. It was like comparing a hawk to sparrows, but he did not complain. The horses would serve their purpose, and their destination was only a few days' ride away.

Corayne smirked as they walked, leading the horses from the stables clustered against the western gate of Lemarta. Their shadows were short beneath them, the sun high in the sky.

"I don't suppose I could convince you to work with me when this is all done?" she said.

There was laughter in her voice, but he could not fathom why.

"I do not follow," he said, the words stilted.

She shrugged. "Merchants are easier to bargain with when they're terrified, and you seem to terrify them."

Dom felt strangely self-conscious. "I'm terrifying?" he blanched, glancing over himself.

Well, there's the sword, and my daggers, and my knives, and the bow and my quiver, but that isn't much, he thought, taking stock of his weaponry. He looked from his polished leather boots to his finely made breeches and tunic, and then his belt, his cloak, and the embossed bracers laced from his palms to elbows. Everything he wore bore the antlers, worked in muted colors, green and gray and golden brown, like the misty glens of Iona. His fine steel and mail, his master-woven silks and surcoats, lay forgotten at Tiarma.

I look like a pauper, not a prince.

She looks even worse.

Corayne's loose tunic frayed at the hem, there were stains no washing could remove on her breeches, and her boots cracked at the knee, wrinkled like a mortal's aging skin. She had stuffed her dark blue cloak away, not needing it in the heat. She bore no weapons but an old dagger, and her eyes seemed oddly open, as if they could drink in every step forward. He knew she was young, barely more than a child, but she still seemed so small and weak alongside him. Most mortals did.

"Oh," he offered. Again he glanced down, trying to comprehend himself through a mortal's eyes. It felt impossible, like translating between two unknown languages. "That was not my intent."

Those words are becoming uncomfortably familiar.

Corayne didn't mind. "Well, keep it up. That scowl will serve us well on the road."

"I do not scowl," Dom said, scowling. He tested the corners of his mouth, pulling his lips into what he hoped was a less foreboding expression. "Do you expect trouble?"

The west road out of Lemarta wound further inland, with the cypress forest thickening up the hills. Dom could see clearly for miles over the cliffs and the Long Sea. Even the *Tempestborn* did not escape his gaze, a black speck with purple sails moving merrily into deeper water. If there was any danger ahead, he would sense it a long way off. But he had little concern this far south, in the sleepy lands of Siscaria. It had been long centuries since Old Cor had ruled these shores.

"I don't suppose bandits will bother you much," Corayne admitted. She watched not the water but the road as it wove away from the cliffs, pale pink stones giving over to a packed earth track, rutted by cart and carriage wheels.

Dom could not imagine what fool of a bandit would try his blade, but then mortals weren't terribly intelligent to begin with. "Because I am intimidating?"

She nodded, pleased. Her eyes were still black, even in the sun of high noon.

She has Cortael's eyes.

"Even when you aren't trying."

"So why can I not simply intimidate a ship's captain to deliver us to Ascal directly?" he mused, looking back at Lemarta. Fishing boats bobbed like jewels among the shoals. "Why bother riding to the Siscarian capital at all?"

Scoffing, Corayne eased her mare to a stop. "Because, frightening as you might be, my mother is more feared in these waters." With a sigh, she hoisted herself up into the saddle. Mortals were graceless beings, but she was particularly clumsy in this.

She is not well accustomed to traveling on horseback, Dom realized, his gut twisting. *It will make the journey all the slower.*

"We'll take our chances in Lecorra," Corayne said, gathering the reins in one hand. "The capital port is ten times the size of this harbor." She looked back over her shoulder, glaring at Lemarta. "And I'm not known there as I am here."

Sarn's voice was a hiss. "I prefer horses to boats anyway."

"By the Spindles," Corayne cursed, startling as Sorasa stalked out of the tree line.

Dom was not so affected. He knew Sarn was following them all the way from the city gate, where she'd split off to "avoid problems" with the soldiers guarding the city. It felt silly to him. The assassin scaled the walls and kept to the shadows where, Dom had to assume, no mortals could see her. To his eye, she stood out sharply among the leaves and tree trunks, as obvious as a second sun in the sky. At least she moved well in the woods, stepping lightly instead of crashing through the undergrowth with the usual mortal grace of a broken-legged cow. Her silence was her best quality. *Perhaps her only good one.*

"You needn't come if it's such an inconvenience," Dom said, both sets of reins still clasped firmly in his hands. "I've found Lady Corayne. Our quest is our own. You'll have payment when it is finished; on this I give my word."

Beneath her hood, Sorasa curled her full lips.

That is a scowl, Dom thought.

"I learned long ago not to trust the promises of men. Even immortal ones," she said. "I have an investment to protect, and I intend to see it through. The deal was to Ascal. I'll give you no reason to go back on our bargain."

Dom wanted no more deadweight to slow their progress, not to mention threat to their lives. Sorasa Sarn was worse than a mercenary, bought at the highest price, with no allegiance or care for Corayne or the Ward. It would be best to leave her behind. *Better yet, to kill her where she stands. The realm would not mourn the loss of an assassin. And the day will come when it is my head or hers, if we are not dead already.*

She stared back at him, her vibrant copper eyes pinning him in place. He held his ground and her gaze. He did not doubt she knew his mind.

"Very well," Dom snapped, breaking first. He tossed the reins in her direction.

She caught them and swung into the saddle, at ease on horseback. She sneered at the stallion beneath her, looking over its flanks with the air of a butcher inspecting a bad cut of meat.

"You'll lead, Sarn. I presume you know the way to Lecorra." Dom hardly liked calling the Amhara assassin by anything other than what she was, but it felt rude to do so now.

To his surprise, she did not argue, and maneuvered her horse onto the road with a twitch of her heels. *At least horsemanship is well taught in the Amhara Guild.* Corayne fell in behind her, giving her mare a few tentative kicks to get her moving at a decent trot. With a sigh, Dom brought up the rear of their strange company, a mismatched trio the likes of which the Ward had never seen.

This is how all our troubles began. A line of horses on the road, a quest ahead, with Allward hanging in the balance. He shoved the grief away and leveled his eyes on the girl riding ahead of him. Her body swayed in time with the horse, finding a rhythm. From this angle he could not see her eyes, nor her father's stern face. She was black-haired and small, as far from Cortael as a person could be. *She will not share her father's fate.* That was a promise, to the Ward, to Glorian Lost, to Corayne—and to himself.

But then she turned her head to look out to the Long Sea. The sun put her features in silhouette, and there he was again, a ghost Dom could not believe in. *Cortael.* He was in her eyes, in the way she raised her face to the wind and searched the horizon. There was movement in her always, constant as the waves and the stars wheeling through the sky.

Dom bowed his head. He tried to think of his cousin Ridha, riding through the enclaves. Of Taristan and his horrendous wizard, their army spewing from a Spindle. His aunt, cowering in her great halls. Anything but Cortael's gray corpse, skewered alongside his daughter.

It did not work.

By nightfall, they were so far inland Dom could barely hear the waves. *At least Sarn isn't a nuisance,* he thought. The assassin rode on in blissful silence, never turning back, never lowering her hood. Occasionally her hand darted into one of her many hidden pouches or pockets, and then he could hear her crunching on something, perhaps nuts or seeds. *A good meal for a mortal traveling light and fast,* Dom knew. Corayne dipped a hand into her saddlebags in the same manner, helping herself to a dinner of flatbread, a smear of cheese, and thin, cured meats. She was also well prepared for their journey.

Dom felt no such urge to eat. The Vedera did not hunger so often.

Nor did they need half as much sleep as mortals.

Soon Corayne drooped in the saddle, her breath slowing to a deep and steady rhythm. With a nudge, Dom urged his horse alongside hers, ready to catch her should she fall from the saddle.

Once or twice her lids fluttered, her eyes twitching through a dream.

"We should make camp so she can rest properly," Sarn muttered, her voice barely a whisper to mortal ears. "The horses too."

Dom frowned, pulling at the scarred side of his face. It stung. "She's resting now. The horses we can push," he said. "Or is it you who would prefer to stop? I confess, I have no intention of keeping you upright too."

"Touch me and I'll cut your hands off," she said dryly, keeping her face to the road.

"You mortals have such a different sense of humor than we do."

She threw a dark look over her shoulder, one he recognized from Byllskos. When she nearly put a blade through his shoulder. When she loosed a herd of half-mad bulls on him.

"I will be requiring my hands for the time being," he whispered back.

Corayne snuffled in her sleep, her full weight balancing on his arm. In the weak light, with her hood raised, Dom saw her father in her face. He thought of Cortael at seventeen, back in Iona, when he insisted he needed only as much rest as an immortal. In the following weeks, he wavered between menacing his tutors and falling asleep in the training yard, a sword still in hand. It fell to Dom to wake him, because he weathered the ensuing outbursts best.

The memory turned bitter. The boy he taught was a man dead. A seed that grew and died in full bloom. Thinking of him was like picking at a barely healed scab, scraping dried blood away to bleed anew.

"We'll stop before that rise," he said sharply, pointing to a hill hunching black against the deep blue night. *Will that shut your viper mouth?*

"We'll stop at the top," she shot back. The bitter ache of memory gave way to frustration. "I'm not getting caught on the low ground."

"You won't be caught by anything," Dom whispered in annoyance.

But the edge of his mind itched with doubt. *Certainly no one will pursue us. The cursed mortal and his red priest do not know of Corayne, nor can they scour the Ward looking for every branch of the Corblood tree.* He glanced at the cypress forest, reading the shadows. *I hope.*

"I'll keep watch," he said.

Her bright eyes flared again, flame in the starlight.

"That isn't a comfort to me."

On that we can agree.

Again Dom thought he ought to forsake an oath just this once and leave Sorasa Sarn dead in a ditch.

To the north, the Corteth Mountains were a jagged dark haze, even to his eye. Snow clung only to the highest peaks this deep into summer. The Corteth, the Teeth of Cor, were dozens of miles away, on the other side of the Impera, the Emperor's River. It wove through the valley, making its way west to Lecorra and the Long Sea. They would reach it soon and cross the river from which Old Cor had sprung. Dom did not know what legends the mortals kept or if there was even a grain of truth left in their histories, but in

Iona, things were more certain. The Corborn mortals of another realm had first come to Allward somewhere in this golden valley, stepping through a Spindle to build their empire.

Trees grew over the rise, good camouflage from the road below. There was no campfire—Sarn would not allow it—but the air was warm enough. The Amhara slept strangely, her back propped up against the roots of a tree, her face forward, so she might only need to open her eyes to spot Dom at the far side of their meager camp. She did just that every twenty minutes, eyes glowing like hot coals before they closed again. Dom shook his head at her every time.

Corayne lay between them, tucked under her cloak. She'd woken just long enough to tumble out of the saddle and find a soft patch of grass.

With both his companions asleep, Dom finally allowed himself something to eat, if only to pass the time. It did not take long for a rabbit to pick its way into their circle, nose twitching and eyes bright. Dom made no noise as he snapped its neck and skinned it clean with a few quick cuts of his knife. With no fire, he made do and consumed it raw, eating the liver last.

Slowly, Corayne raised her head, her eyes wide and fascinated.

"Won't that make you sick?" she whispered.

He wiped his fingers off on the rabbit's fur. "We do not get sick," he answered.

Corayne sat up slowly, her cloak pooling around her. "You don't sleep either," she said, resting her chin on a hand. Dom felt like a plant being studied, or a page of riddles deciphered. It was not unpleasant, somehow. Her curiosity was innocent.

"We sleep, but not often," he replied. "We don't need it as much as mortals do."

"And you don't age."

"After a fashion."

He thought of Toracal, with his streaks of gray hair, earned over thousands of years. His aunt, with the lines on her brow, at the corners of her eyes, around her mouth, on her hands. *The Vedera are called immortal by those who can not fathom a life of so many millennia, stretched beyond the mortal ability to measure. Death avoids us, but it is not a stranger.*

There was steel in the world, blades that could cut and kill them. Immortality seemed far less certain after seeing so many of his own die before the temple, their blood indistinguishable from that of any low mortal walking the Ward. *And my scars are proof enough of our vulnerability, small as it may be.*

"It's a good thing there aren't very many of you," Corayne said in a low voice.

Dom startled, not in confusion, but surprise. "I beg your pardon?"

She brushed a lock of hair out of her eyes. "Or else your kind would have conquered the world." Her answer was blunt.

"That is a very mortal impulse to have," Dom said, and meant it. Conquest over the men of the Ward seemed foolish to him, even at his young age. Mortals rose and fell like summer wheat. Kingdoms were born and died. Those he'd known in his first century were dust now, barely shadows in his long memory. *Why bother reaching out a hand for what could disappear before you grasp it?*

Even so, there were histories of the Vedera too, records of

immortals who fought alongside or against the men of the Ward. For glory, for sport, for nothing at all. Dom could not imagine it for himself or his people now. They defended their homes on rare occasion, but nothing more. *Cowards they are now, hiding in their enclaves. Ready to let this world crumble around them.*

Corayne stared with her keen gaze. She had a way of prodding without words.

"My people are focused on finding a way home," he offered. "But the way was lost to us, the Spindle closed, and even its location destroyed long ago."

"Destroyed?" she asked, cocking her head.

"The ground my people first arrived on is now at the bottom of the Long Sea, swallowed by the waves," he answered softly, trying to see a place he had never been. "Every day we hope for another doorway, another Spindle. A way back to Glorian."

The last cobwebs of sleep seemed to lift from Corayne, and she leaned closer, sharp with interest. Her tangled braid fell over one shoulder, gleaming almost blue in the starlight.

"Your realm must be magnificent," she said.

"I suppose." Dom shrugged again. "I am Wardborn, still young among my people, still learning the realm we live in now. And what I know of my own realm comes from others."

He felt the familiar lick of regret that came every time he thought of the realm he did not know, the home he might never see. It was tinged with sour, green envy of all those who did know Glorian and could remember its stars.

"They are whole while I am not."

"We have that in common, I guess," Corayne said softly. She

drew up her knees and wrapped her arms around herself, though the air was still warm, even for mortals.

Dom narrowed his eyes. He felt worlds apart from her, separated by a pane of glass. "How so?".

She dropped her gaze to the grass. "I only know my father, his blood, what we come from, what we were born as, from what others tell me." Her fingers picked at a leaf nervously. "And they've told me very little."

She's interrogating me, Dom realized, looking Corayne over.

The curious gleam had not left her eyes. There was hunger too, a thirst for answers she could not get elsewhere, and a strong will to find them. Dom was reminded of scholars back in the enclave, combing their archives for some scroll or tome, for word of Spindles, for any whisper of Glorian Lost. *But I am not a shelf of books eager to be picked through.*

She ran her hands through the grass like a child. It was a good act.

This wound will never heal if you keep cutting it open, he warned himself. But somehow Dom wanted to. He wanted to remember Cortael and give Corayne something to remember too.

Do not, he thought. *Shut the door on those decades, and let them turn to dust as the centuries pass. Such is the Vedera way, our only defense against years of memory.*

"You're Spindleblood. Corblood," he said flatly, if only to give her *something.* "Your ancestors were travelers of another realm, mortal as the men of the Ward, but set apart. Some say the Cors were born of the Spindles themselves, not another realm. But your kind fell with Old Cor, your bloodlines dwindling through the centuries." Her eyes shone in the starlight, egging him on. "It makes you restless; it makes you ambitious; it gives you a *want* so deep you can hardly name it."

Her black gaze seemed to deepen. He could smell the eagerness on her.

"I said the same to your father, decades ago." The wound opened again, a tear through his heart. Dom winced against it, carrying on. "When he raged in his way, frustrated, a mortal boy among living statues, who could not make his flesh into stone no matter how hard he tried." His breath caught. "I am sorry you had to grow up with no one who knew your blood, what it demanded. What it makes you," he said quietly.

This time, she did not scold him for the apology. Instead her face turned hard, and her eyes were shuttered windows. Whatever she looked for, she could not find.

"And what of my father, raised by immortals, who could not even fathom what it is to live in mortal flesh?" she said. "If you pity me, you must pity him too."

The sting burrowed deep, a needle of white-hot pain. Dom flinched and looked away. He heard Corayne stand, her feet rustling the grass like a rough wind.

"Elders don't sleep, don't eat, don't age," she bit out, standing. "But you bleed. Can you love? Did you teach my father to? Because he did not love me."

"There is not a creature in any realm who cannot love," Dom answered hotly. His ancient temper flared and guttered. It filled him; it hollowed him out. Anger was still foreign and corrosive in his body. Without knowing it, he crossed the grassy hill, until he stood over Corayne, tall as a mountain.

She held her ground.

"And I certainly loved your father," he said. "Like a brother, like a son. I was there for his first steps, his first tooth, his first words, screaming as they were. The first drop of blood to fall." Inside he roared, seeing it all over again. "And the last."

Corayne's mouth pressed to nothing; her questions finally failed her. Over her shoulder, Sarn's open eyes were two burning candles.

"Go back to sleep, my lady," he whispered, turning his broad back on Corayne.

She was happy to oblige, settling down with a very mortal huff. She stilled quickly, eyes firmly shut, but Dom could hear her heart beating rapidly, her breath uneven. Across the clearing, Sarn's heart thumped a steady, slow beat. Her eyes did not close.

He was tempted to sneer at her, but an odd smell stopped him cold.

Smoke.

He stilled, head raised to the air. There was smoke, somewhere close, its scent curling around him in a phantom wind. He could not see it, but he could smell and taste the acrid burn. It was not woodsmoke, nor a brush fire. Nothing common.

But it was not unfamiliar.

This was the charring of flesh, hands cracked to bone, skin flaking to ash.

Terror lashed down his spine.

Sarn was already on her feet, her hood torn away, her body coiling with tension. She glared at him, reading the fear as it crossed his face.

"Corayne, get up. Sarn, the horses," he barked, already at Corayne's side. He took her by the shoulders, pulling her upright before she could open her eyes.

The Amhara made for the animals without argument, but froze at the tree line. The sword at her side sang free of its sheath. Her grip adjusted and she raised the blade high overhead, the steel like a bird of prey poised to strike from the sky.

Dom could hear the horses, undisturbed in their sleep, as if nothing were amiss. The smell of burned flesh only deepened, until Corayne clapped a hand over her nose, her eyes watering.

"What is it?" she said, her voice shaking. Dom did not answer, but moved in front of her, one hand still on her arm.

Sarn took measured steps backward, careful to keep her footing with her sword still raised. Her focus locked ahead, on the shadows wavering beneath knotted cypress. Dom did not need to stand in her place to know what she saw.

It was only a question of how many.

Corayne bit back a gasp of fear as he pulled his own sword free, its keen edges cutting the air. He wished for armor, but leather would have to do, for as long as it could.

How did he find us? How could he know? Dom cursed, searching the trees for the scarlet-robed wizard and Taristan himself. In Dom's mind, he was still painted in Cortael's blood, laughing as it bubbled over his lips, with the Spindleblade in hand, more taunting than any smile.

The corpses, the corrupted creatures of the Ashlands and Asunder, wove up the hill in their lumbering steps. White faces leached of color, burned to the bone, their lips torn and cracking, their armor black and greasy with oil, like chicken fresh from the skillet. At the sight of their weapons—rusty knives and broken swords, notched axes and splintered shields—Dom nearly fell to his knees. By the grace of Baleir alone did he remain standing, though every piece of him wished to crumble. Corayne's arm felt cold in his hand. They could run, but without the horses they might be driven into an ambush at the foot of the hill.

The first came through the trees with a lipless smile, leering at Sarn and her sword. It plodded on twisted limbs, undeterred in its path. The Amhara moved in time, keeping her distance as she retreated across the clearing, her eyes wide and unblinking. Twin spots of color rose in her cheeks, the only evidence of her own fear. Still her heart beat slowly, as if she were only sleeping.

Six more followed, with other shapes wavering through the trees. They smelled like a pile of burned bodies, like a rotten inferno.

"Elder," she hissed through gritted teeth. "Can they be killed?"

Despite all, Dom felt the tug of a grim smile.

"Yes, they can."

Sarn stopped moving, her feet set.

"Good."

All lethal grace, she moved in a killing arc, her sword cutting the air in two as she drew a slanting path.

Dom narrowed his focus to the corpses and Corayne, keeping

both at the edge of his perception. With the girl behind him and the creatures ahead, he took lunging steps, his sword twisted in both hands, flashing with the weight of starlight. He drove through the first creature, hefting his blade like a woodsman's ax. It cut the corpse in half, severing the body at the waist with the ease of steel through water.

Were they always so frail? he thought, turning on his heel to chop down another.

Despite her training as an assassin, Sarn stumbled next to him, nearly losing her balance as her sword passed through an Ashlander. She bit out a cry of bewilderment, stopping to watch the corpse soldier.

Dom did the same, and hardly believed his eyes.

Instead of cutting the Ashlander from shoulder to hip, cleaving through flesh, her sword moved as if through mist. The edges of the creature curled from the blade in wisps of white, black, and a shock of ghostly blue. The rest faded like the smoke of a snuffed candle, trailing into nothing.

Sarn did not react, her focus snapping to the next Ashlander, and the next, still coming through the trees. They were faster now, lunging, spurred to action by her strike. She never lost her balance again.

Dom balked, looking back at the two he had already dispatched. But instead of bodies, there was only smoke curling on the ground, disappearing into the grass.

Corayne gaped, slack-jawed, at the sight.

One roared a tortured scream, the voice inhuman, and Dom

reacted with blurring speed, raising his sword to parry a cursed blow. Instead his blade passed through the ruined iron of corpse armor, and another Ashlander gave over to nothing.

The others did the same, fleeing before every strike. Their own weapons turned to dust against steel, until there was nothing in the clearing but the trio and the drifting smell of flame.

In the trees, the horses continued to doze.

Dom spun in a circle, searching for more. Searching for the trick. He expected Taristan to fall on them, expected the wizard to rain lightning. He thought he heard the bell again, tolling for the temple and the fallen. But there was nothing but the breeze in the cypress. His breath came hard and heavy, not from exertion, but from pure bewilderment.

Corayne fell bodily to the ground, her face bone white.

Before Dom could reach her, Sarn blocked his path. The scorpion on her neck looked poised to strike.

"What the *fuck* was that?" she growled.

The world wheeled around him.

Dom opened his mouth to answer, and vomited rabbit liver in reply.

10

JYDI CHARMS
Corayne

She blinked, the air warm again, her blood running hot, the grass smooth between her fingers. The fear was paralyzing, and she searched against the darkness, hunting for another walking corpse.

This is your fate.

The strange voice rang her skull like a bell. Corayne winced as the words cracked and splintered, flowed and coiled. It was human but not, something more, something less. And so *cold*, leaving her skin prickling.

It does not wait, the voice continued, fading without echo, barely leaving behind a memory.

The white-faced demons were gone too. The smell of smoke and burned flesh disappeared with their forms.

A dream. They're getting worse, she thought, her lips parting. She gulped down a bracing breath of air. *I was asleep, and I dreamed of those creatures, red and terrible, broken and hungry.*

But there was Dom, doubled over, spitting into the grass. He wiped his mouth with the back of his hand, his face nearly as white as the creatures. Sorasa grimaced at him, disgusted, her sword in hand, her body still tensed to fight. She glanced at Corayne and her gaze was hard.

Not a dream.

"Calm yourself," the assassin said sharply. "Breathe slowly through your nose, then out through your mouth. You too," she added, rapping Dom with the flat of her sword. He glared and spat again.

Corayne did as she was told, sucking in air.

Not a dream.

The leaping sensation in her gut began to ebb, leaving behind cold truth.

Not a dream.

"That's what came from the Spindle," Corayne said aloud. With a will, she pushed herself to her feet, her legs quivering beneath her. "That's what you fought at the temple. With my father."

Dom straightened. "It is as I said before." His face turned more grim, if that was even possible. "They are of the Ashlands, a burned realm, cracked with Asunder, consumed by the hell of What Waits. They serve Him, and they serve your uncle, Taristan."

Sorasa stepped around him, inspecting her blade in the dim light. The steel was clean. Her lips twisted.

"I assume they did not turn to wisps of smoke at your temple," she said, casting a dirty glance over the Elder. "Or else I have sorely overestimated you."

"They certainly did not," he growled, pointing a finger at his scarred face.

Corayne tried not to think of such wounds being made, carved through his marble flesh with hungry ease. She felt them on her own skin. Knives and nails, tearing her apart. Her mouth filled with a sour taste and she was nearly sick herself.

"Those were a vision, or shades, maybe. A projection of what comes from the Spindle," Dom muttered without much confidence. "The work of Taristan's wizard, perhaps, or What Waits himself. They must know you live." His free hand closed into a fist. "They must be searching for you."

Corayne swallowed around her terror. And the strange new truth. *All the Elder spoke of—the Spindle, my murderous uncle, the corpse army—they do exist. And they're hunting me.*

"We should keep moving," she said through clenched teeth. She started picking up her meager things, if only for a distraction. "Harmless or not, if those things can find us once, they can find us again. And it's only a matter of time until the real thing catches up."

"At least someone here has some sense," Sorasa muttered, stalking off to the horses.

The Elder opened his mouth to argue, but Corayne did not give him the chance. It was difficult enough trying to save the realm without the two of them at each other's throats.

"I dreamed of them," she said quickly, her cloak over one arm. "Even before you found me in Lemarta."

Dom sneered at Sorasa's shadow in the trees, but turned away, his face clearing. Some color returned to his cheeks. "The Ashlanders?"

Instead of a chill, Corayne felt a streak of cloying warmth, like a summer day gone to rot. It settled around her throat. She swallowed against the odd sensation.

"White faces, burned skin," she whispered, trying to remember the dreams that had plagued her for weeks. It felt odd speaking of them aloud. "And something more. I couldn't see, but I could feel . . . it. A presence watching me," she said. "A red shadow, hunting, waiting."

"What Waits," Dom murmured. "You dream of Him."

She felt the heat again. "I thought this was a dream too."

"Your uncle's army is not a dream, or even a nightmare." Dom returned his sword to its sheath. "They are very real. And they will devour the Ward if given the opportunity."

In the shadows of the trees, Sorasa slowed in her work untying the horses. She glanced back into the clearing. Corayne was reminded of a wolf in the forest, invisible but for its gleaming eyes.

"This is a Spindlerotten contract," the assassin hissed, pulling the first horse loose. Though Dom bristled again, Corayne knew better than to react, for she knew her mother.

Meliz an-Amarat was just the same, complaining about difficult journeys or complicated jobs to undertake. She loved them all the more for it. The danger, the risk. The opportunity to prove herself a thousand times over. Corayne guessed Sorasa saw a chance here. After all, saving the entire realm had to count for something, even among assassins. Not to mention whatever payment an Elder prince could afford.

The first horse nosed across the clearing at a sleepy pace, drawn to Dom's hand by either Elder grace or simple memory. Sorasa led the other two, her hood drawn up again. Only the hard set of her mouth could be seen, her jaw clenched against whatever else she wanted to say. Corayne took the reins of her mare, trying to ignore the sensation of both hot and cold, What Waits and what whispered, pulling at her insides. Who they could possibly be, she did not know.

I suppose I might die before I find out.

Corayne exhaled an easy breath. She felt better on the deck of a ship. She understood planks and sails better than horses. And the galley, still in port, offered up a fine view.

She leaned against the wooden rail, taking in the ancient city of Lecorra. It was a smudge of sun-dipped color, made hazy by summer heat. It sprang from the northern bank of the Impera River, fanning out like half a sunburst, with farms and fields stretching beyond the walls. The Siscarian royal villa and the temples sat on the single hill, surrounded by a green island of poplar and cypress. The ancient ruins of Cor were easy to spot in the city, their walls and columns bleached white, unmistakable against the gold, pink, butter yellow, and brick-red tiles of newer construction. The statues and temples still towered, pale and broken against the sky. It was as if the rest of the city were moss growing in the skeleton of a giant. Corayne drank it down, savoring even the shadow of Old Cor. Her body hummed in reply, calling out to something long since gone.

I can feel my ancestors here, distant as they are, she marveled, finally able to name the sensation. *I can feel the shadows of what once was.*

The port held dozens of galleys, cogs, balingers, fishing boats, and war ships. Sails flew in a rainbow of color, flags flapping for every kingdom of the Long Sea and beyond. Corayne spotted a Jydi longboat flying a peace flag anchored next to a triple-decked Rhashiran war galley, not to mention a dozen ships of the Ibalet navy. They controlled the Strait of the Ward, racing back and forth across the narrowest point of the Long Sea, collecting tolls from all who wished to pass. She named the many flags and ships as she named the stars. It was a comfort, to list and understand, when there was so much she could no longer quantify.

The ships make sense when nothing else does.

The *Tempestborn* would be halfway through the Long Sea by now, but still Corayne looked for her mother. *Does she know I'm gone? Will Kastio get word to her that I've run off? Will she turn back to find me?* The thought filled her with dread. But another fear bubbled up inside, corrosive as rust on a blade: *What if she doesn't?*

Her knuckles turned white on the rail. She could not say which would be worse.

The Impera flowed below, the water flashing silver to reflect a sky white with heat.

Around her, the crew of the galley bustled, preparing to set sail for Ascal, shouting in a tangle of languages Corayne knew well enough. They were decent, not so skilled as her mother's crew, but fine enough for a passenger ship. If she shut her eyes, she could pretend this was the *Tempestborn*, that her mother was at the helm, the port of Lemarta looking down on them. Corayne would go back to shore soon, to wave the others off on their journey while she remained anchored, doomed to wait.

But her eyes were open. Those days were gone.

She felt the wind on her teeth before she realized she was smiling. Despite her fears and the sword hanging over them, her body went loose. *This is what freedom feels like.*

"You look like a horse who's jumped the pen," Sorasa said, her voice flat.

The Amhara stood at the rail a few feet away, somehow both watchful and uninterested. Even with her hood thrown back, her face was unreadable, impassive as stone. But the rest of her told an easy tale, from her gloved hands to her clothes laced tight up her throat. Her cloak hid her sword, and her knives were tucked away. Every inch of inked skin was covered, and her black hair was unbound, curling after so long in a braid. Her eyes were lined again, heavy with black powder and a single stripe of gold. She seemed a simple Ibalet woman, unremarkable but for her copper eyes, easy to overlook on a ship of travelers.

Corayne tried her best to tuck away her excitement, and her nerves as well. To slip behind a mask as easily as Sorasa could. She forced a shrug. "I want to see this," she replied, indicating the city of Lecorra. "While I can."

A bit of Sorasa's mask slipped and something crossed her face. Not fear, but close to it. A wariness, a cat with fur on end, a charge in the air before a lightning storm. The Amhara had seen the Ashlanders plain as the rest of them, whether she wanted to admit it or not. It had set her on edge.

Corayne felt it too, beneath every breath. The Ashlanders, What Waits, her uncle hunting. She did not know Taristan's face, but in her mind their eyes were the same, his and her own. An empty black, hungry and consuming.

"Have you ever seen anything like . . . *them?*" Corayne murmured. A woman raised in the Amhara Guild, a killer born, certainly knew more of the world than a pirate's daughter bound to shore.

The assassin returned Corayne's stare, her eyes hard again. "I've seen many things that would terrify most," she replied. "Monsters and men. Mostly men."

Corayne remembered her on the hilltop outside Lemarta, how she'd looked in the darkness when the creatures went up in smoke. The danger was gone, had never even existed in the first place. And yet Sorasa was afraid.

"So that's a no," Corayne scoffed.

"You are a long way from your safe harbor, Corayne an-Amarat." Sorasa's breath was cool, her eyes narrowing to slits. Corayne felt seen through and hated it. "With only farther to go."

Corayne clenched her teeth and turned away from the city. She glanced at Sorasa's neck again, remembering the scorpion, black as oil, its hooked stinger raised to strike. *Was the tattoo a prize earned or a punishment endured?* Corayne fought the urge to ask.

"You're a long way from home too, Sorasa."

The sun glowed in Sorasa's hair, illuminating each bend of black. With the sky bright and her hood lowered, Corayne could see old scars on her exposed skin. Small cuts, long healed, from the nick of a blade or a fist. They spoke of many hard years in a place Corayne would never see. Her curiosity flared, not to be sated. It was annoying at best, like facing a puzzle she could not solve.

The assassin shifted. "Perhaps you should check on Dom.

Make sure he hasn't rotted down below, or been sick again," she said, gesturing toward the hold. The Elder was not so adept at disguise and so would spend their journey to Ascal in a glorified cabinet below deck.

Instead Corayne curled her fingers on the railing, gripping the wood. She stood firm, refusing to be chased away.

"I don't like the way he looks at me," she muttered. "He sees my father. He sees death. He sees failure." Corayne felt her shoulders bow with the weight of a person she had never known.

Sorasa glared at the sky. If there was one thing Corayne knew, the assassin hated the immortal. "I'd guess a Spindlerotten Elder isn't used to such things."

"I think he sees my uncle too," Corayne added, shoving out the words, hoping to cast out her guilt with them. Her cheeks flared with heat. "I didn't know I looked so much like them."

The assassin didn't answer, looking her over. *Looking for the face of a fallen prince and a rising monster.*

"I don't belong anywhere," Corayne said, her voice failing.

To her surprise, Sorasa cracked a smile. "There are plenty of people like that," she said. "And nowhere is still a somewhere."

"That's foolish."

"Well, if you don't belong to a place, perhaps we belong to each other? We who belong nowhere?" Sorasa offered. Her copper eyes glimmered, dancing with the light off the river.

Despite the ugly feeling in the pit of her stomach, Corayne found herself smiling too. "Perhaps," she echoed.

"I never knew my parents," Sorasa pressed on. "I only know where they came from. Couldn't tell you their names, who they were, if they are living or dead." She spoke evenly, without emotion or attachment. It was a statement of fact, nothing more. Not even a secret worth keeping.

Corayne bobbed her head. She felt the key in the lock. She need only turn it to open a door into Sorasa, the Amhara, their ways. "The Guild is your family?" she asked, drawing closer.

A corner of Sorasa's mouth lifted, her smirk turning cruel. She muttered something under her breath, in Ibalet so fast and violent Corayne could not translate it, before switching to clear, daggered Paramount.

"They are not," she growled.

The key shattered.

Neither spoke again until the ship was moving, the bright waters of the Impera carrying them out of the city. Lecorra gave over to the walls and outskirts, then farmland, then forest and scrabbly hills. A few towns clustered on the riverbank, with clay tile roofs and sleepy streets. Corayne turned her face forward, to watch every new curve of land as it came into view. Sorasa did not move from her side but did not bother to hide her annoyance at such a task.

On the deck, other travelers knotted in their groups. Most were merchant bands, along with a pair of Siscarian couriers in a duke's livery, and a performing troupe that was very bad at juggling. They clustered, eager to stay out of the hold, where the row benches stank. Corayne thought of Dom, cooped up in a minuscule cabin, his shoulders brushing either wall as he suffered the odors below.

The other travelers weren't of much interest to her, not while the ship raced toward the open sea. But Sorasa watched them intently, weighing each person on board as she would a prize pig. Corayne glanced at the assassin occasionally, trying to glean anything, always coming up short.

Near dusk, Sorasa straightened, pushing up from the rail, her eyes on another passenger.

An old crone approached from the opposite side of the deck, her footsteps uneven as the boat moved beneath her. Her hair was wild and gray, braided in places, set with feathers, yellowed bone, and dried lavender. She held out a basket, smiling with gapped teeth, crowing in Jydi. Corayne only understood a few words, and that was enough.

"*Pyrta gaeres. Khyrma. Velja.*"

Pretty girls. Charms. Wishes.

She was a peddler of empty promises, selling bits of trash she called tricks or spells. A polished river stone, some useless herbs tied with human hair. *Nonsense.*

"*Jys kiva,*" Corayne replied in the woman's language, her pronunciation poor. But the message was clear enough. *No interest.*

The crone only grinned wider as she came closer, undeterred. Her fingers were so knobbled by age and use they looked like broken branches. "No price, no price," she said, switching to accented Paramount. "A gift from the ice." The basket rattled in her hands.

Sorasa moved between the crone and Corayne like an older sister shielding her sibling from a swindler. "No need, *Gaeda*," Sorasa said. *Grandmother.* Her tone was oddly soft, drawing little attention from the rest of the ship. "Back to your bench."

The crone did not stop smiling, her face split with wrinkles, her skin pale and spotted. Everything but her eyes seemed bleached of color. They were a luminous blue, like the heart of a lightning bolt. Corayne stared, feeling a brush of something familiar at the back of her mind. But she could not catch it, the sensation always slipping from her grasp.

"It's fine, Sorasa," she muttered, putting out her hand to the old woman.

The Jydi dipped her head and grabbed a twist of blue-gray twigs from her basket. They were tied with twine and catgut, trailing with beads that could be bone or pearl. "Gods bless you, Spindles keep you," she prayed, extending the gift.

Sorasa took it before Corayne could, holding the twigs between her gloved thumb and forefinger. She sniffed at it, drawing in a shallow breath. Then she touched her tongue to the wood. After a moment, she nodded. "Gods bless," she said, waving the crone away.

This time the old Jydi did not argue, and shuffled off, her basket tucked close. She moved down the deck, bestowing similar bits of nothing to the other travelers.

"It isn't poisoned," Sorasa said, tossing the twigs at Corayne's chest.

She caught them shakily and looked at the twist of garbage in disbelief. "I doubt a decrepit old woman is trying to poison me."

"Old women have more cause to kill than most."

Corayne turned the twigs over in her hands, quirking a smile. "Is guard duty part of your contract?"

The assassin returned to the railing, leaning back on her

elbows. She tipped her face to the setting sun, enjoying the glow. "I was tasked to find you and get you to Ascal alive."

Alive. Again, Corayne felt a chill that had nothing to do with temperature. *I am marked somehow. There is something in my blood that blesses and dooms me.*

"And the payment?" she asked, if only to have something to say. "I certainly hope you set a very high price for an Elder prince."

"I certainly did."

How much? Corayne wanted to ask. Instead she gritted her teeth and closed her fist around the Jydi charm. The beads dangled. They were not pearl, she realized, looking at them up close, but human finger bone, each one carved into a skull.

Some days later, Dom gasped free of the tiny cabin. To Corayne's surprise, he looked pristine despite nearly a week cloistered in with sweating oarsmen, stale air, bad water, and little food. He sucked down a breath of fresh air and raised his hood, joining Corayne at the rail.

Meanwhile, Corayne felt dirty and slightly sick, her stomach still roiling from the waves of the open sea, though they were in the calm waters of Mirror Bay by now. Clearly her mother had not passed on her sea legs or strong stomach. But Corayne forgot her pains quickly.

Twilight fell softly, the sky fading from pink to purple over the water. The lights of Ascal loomed on the horizon, a constellation coming to life.

The great capital of Galland straddled the river delta, sprawled across the many islands at the mouth of the Great Lion. Bridges and gates strung across the waterways like necklaces set with torch jewels, their lights rippling where fresh water met salt. Corayne tried not to gape.

"It's huge," she gasped. "It's bigger than I thought a city could be."

Dom nodded at her side. "Indeed." He glared out from beneath his hood, his face pulled once more into his now-distinct scowl. Ascal was no wonder to him, but an obstacle to be surmounted. Something to be feared. And that made Corayne afraid too.

"This was a Cor city too, once," she added, feeling the truth of it in her skin. There were ruins beneath Ascal, the bones of an empire a thousand years dead. "How do I know that?"

She expected the Elder to have an answer, but words failed him, his face drawn.

Sorasa gave them both an odd look, then gestured to the shore. "It was destroyed and rebuilt a dozen times, in a dozen places. What was once Lascalla is now Ascal, capital of Galland, the great successor to Old Cor." She spat in the water. "Or so they like to think."

Temple domes and cathedral spires clawed against the waning sunset, ripping bloody streaks through the sky. The storied walls of Ascal, yellow in sunlight, gold at dawn and dusk, held in the bloated city like a belt. Smoke rose from the slums, a thousand plumes from a thousand hearths. Corayne squinted, searching the roofs and streets for what could be the palace, but found nothing. *It must be buried deep in the city, guarded and walled again.* Her stomach dropped at the thought of navigating their way to the palace, let alone getting inside.

Boats and ships of every flag skittered over the water, ants in a row, making for the teeming port of Ascal. The bridges and water gates forced all but the smallest vessels to use the same avenue. Their own ship fell in line, and the jaws of the city opened to them.

The assassin wrinkled her nose. "Brace yourself for the smell."

They sailed past a great fortress for the city garrison, big as a lord's castle, with stout towers and guarded ramparts. The green banners of Galland flew from its walls, the golden lion proud and massive. Corayne stared openly at the stone towers on either side of the delta channel. Both spat out gigantic chains that sank into the water, looping under the sea traffic and over the riverbed. She knew the chains could be raised, effectively cutting off the port and city within if need be. She could not help but think of Taristan's army, the soldiers of Asunder, crawling over the chains like skittering white spiders.

"Those are the Lion's Teeth," Sorasa murmured, pointing at the towers guarding the river. Corayne leaned close, eager to hear more. "All must pass through except the navy of Galland, bound for Fleethaven." She waggled her fingers at another island in the river mouth, then at a canal. "That goes to Tiber Island, for merchants and traders."

Tiber. The god of gold. Corayne knew him intimately. Her mother's crew sent prayers to him before every voyage.

"And what about us?" she asked, watching the city grow.

Sorasa pursed her lips. "Wayfarer's Port. It's first place anyone journeying by water arrives in Ascal," she said. "Always crowded with weary travelers, pilgrims, runaways, and anyone else seeking their fortune in the capital. In short, a mess."

The smell hit hard, falling in a stinking curtain. Manure, spoiled meat, bad water, rotten fruit, sweat, butcher blood, sewage of all kinds. Oversweet perfume, spilled wine, beer gone stale. Smoke, salt, the rare brush of a fresh breeze like a gasp of air to a man drowning. And, beneath it all, the incessant cling of *damp*, so deep Corayne wondered if the entire city had gone to rot. She pressed her sleeve to her nose, breathing in the familiar scent of home still holding to her cloak. Oranges, cypress, the Long Sea, her mother's precious rose oil. For a second, her eyes stung with sharp, unshed tears.

"Where is the palace?" she asked, blinking away the sting. "I assume we can't just walk up to the gates and ask to speak with a squire."

The crew began their work in the sails, while the oarsmen below slowed their pace. The drumbeat keeping their time boomed like a heart.

"No, I doubt we can," Dom said, taking an experimental breath. His face pulled in revulsion. "I've never smelled anything so foul," he mumbled. Corayne had to agree.

"You're an Elder prince," Sorasa scoffed. She tied off her hair in a neat braid, careful to let it hang so her neck was still covered. "If anyone can knock on a palace gate, it's you."

Dom shook his head. "I did not suffer a week below deck to be spotted now. Taristan knows Andry Trelland escaped with the sword, and a squire of Galland is easy to track home. They could be watching the palace and the Queen." He spat the words out like a poison. On the rail, his fingers curled.

He wants to wring Taristan's neck, Corayne knew.

She shoved her own hands into her pockets and bit her lip. "He could have the sword already," she said softly. Her fingers brushed the Jydi charm, useless and dusty, the beads smooth and cool. It slowed her thrumming pulse. "And all this is for nothing."

Dom frowned. "We can't think like that, Corayne."

Banking on hope without sense is a certain path to failure. "Well, I do."

"The alternative is to accept the realm is doomed," he replied, forceful. "I will not."

Torches flared in his eyes, reflected from the docks jutting out on either side of the river. Their own berth was near, cleared and waiting on the north bank of the waterway.

Again Corayne saw white faces, skin worn to bone, blood, and black armor. The silhouette of a man with her own eyes. Even now she could not believe it. *I stand on a ship that is not my mother's, in a kingdom not my own, chasing a quest the man who abandoned me could not fulfill.* The last week caught up with her in a blur. It did not seem real. It did not make sense. Not like the stars or her charts and lists. This did not balance. Her nerves prickled.

Adjusting his green cloak, Dom fixed Sorasa with a challenging glare. His sword, bow, and quiver were hidden, giving him a hulking shape. "So, assassin of the Amhara, legend of the shadows, quick with tongue and blade, what do you suggest we do now?"

"I suggest you bribe a guard at the kitchen gate like everyone else," Sorasa said.

Dom grumbled in annoyance. "Less conspicuous?"

The Amhara did not answer, eyes on the dock. Her thoughts were elsewhere—in a tavern, a gambling hall, a brothel, with friend in Ascal. Though Corayne doubted Sorasa Sarn tolerated friendship. *Or she's looking forward to getting rid of us. Her job is nearly done. We need only set foot on the dock and she'll be gone. She didn't agree to anything else.*

With a sigh, Corayne nudged Dom in the side. It was like being a ship's agent again, haggling a price between two opposing sides. *If both sides despised each other, and one didn't quite grasp the concept of currency to begin with.* An exhausting proposition.

"You're going to have to give her more money," Corayne explained, "if you want her to get us into the Queen's palace."

"I've paid quite enough," the Elder snapped. Corayne elbowed him again, shoving against the granite wall of his abdomen. He didn't seem to notice. "We'll find our own way."

"Fine," Corayne huffed. Then she put her hand to the Amhara, palm out in a gesture of goodwill. "I suppose this is goodbye, Sorasa Sarn."

Sorasa eyed her fingers with distaste.

Just as Corayne suspected. She pulled her hand back, her voice sharpening, meant to sting. "Enjoy watching us blunder our way toward what could be the end of Allward, for the sake of your pride and few more coins to rub together while the realm crumbles."

A hiss rattled past Sorasa's bared teeth, her eyes dancing in the torchlight. The ship bumped into its berth with the groan of wood and snap of rope. The Amhara swayed gracefully as the deck bobbed beneath them. Again her mask slipped. Corayne saw anger. The useful kind.

"Well, when you put it that way," she finally snarled, shoving off the rail.

Corayne grabbed Dom's arm and pulled him along by his cloak, like a dog on a leash. They shouldered through the crowd together, nearly losing Sorasa in the scrum. Her face flashed ahead of them, rigid with frustration. She slowed, letting the other travelers break around her.

"Keep up," she snapped, before muttering more Ibalet under her breath.

Corayne smirked. She'd grown up with sailors. She was no stranger to foul language.

"I am not a meddling monkey," Corayne answered.

Sorasa startled. Even she could not hide her flush. "You speak Ibalet?"

"Don't worry, I won't tell Dom what you called him."

Behind them, Dom huffed along, his boots calamitous on the docks. "I do not care for a murderer's opinion," he said, a clear lie.

Corayne suspected he would care very much. After all, Sorasa had called him a stupid, stubborn ass. *Although*, she thought, *my translation might not be accurate.*

The Ibalet words for stupid *and* handsome *are quite similar.*

11

THE ASSASSIN'S BURDEN
Sorasa

She did not think herself a woman of conscience. Whatever morals she'd been born with had not come with her past the gates of the citadel. No Amhara could be made with such weights. And yet she felt the pull of something unfamiliar and sharp, tugging her off her path, like a hook in the gills of a fish. Sorasa wanted to rip it out, flesh and blood be damned. Be off with the current, to wherever opportunity might lead. Instead she found herself grinding her teeth in Wayfarer's Port, assaulted on all sides by stink and noise, with two very persistent hooks buried deep. She dragged them along the streets against her better instincts. *Certainly the Cor girl and the Elder can find their way to the New Palace without dying. Or, if they die, so be it.*

But Corayne's words gnawed at her. *The end of Allward.*

Those specters of another realm had certainly felt like it, fleeting as they'd been. Sorasa had seen men gutted, burned, crushed, poisoned, and devoured, in all states of death and decay. Killed for contract, practice, sport, or Mercury's favor. Assassinations disguised as cult rituals or gruesome accidents. Corpses dismembered, scattered, or dissolved in lye. Bodies wrung out by torture or deprivation. She'd witnessed all and done most. But there was nothing, not from the snows of the Jyd to the jungles of Rhashir, that rattled her so much. This memory refused to be forgotten, the taste and smell of it sharp in her mind. Blood, rot, iron. And *heat* like she could not understand. For a woman born in the sands, that was the most unsettling piece of all.

She swallowed hard. *There will be no Amhara Guild left if the realm shatters. This is just good logic. Simple business. A means to an end.*

There were other routes onto the island that was the New Palace, walls and gates and bridges be damned. If the Elder did not want to be seen, despite all his preening, then Sorasa would make it so. She adjusted her cloak into something shapeless, a bland form of nameless color, smudged between sand and gray smoke in the torchlight. As a woman with a good face and a body carved by years of training, she was more likely to be noted on city streets. Sorasa had no intention of being noticed, let alone remembered by any guard in the street.

If we can even make it out of the port, she thought bitterly. *Between the gawking girl and the sentient tombstone, it will be a wonder if we get there by midnight.*

And Corayne did gawk, her mouth slack as she drank the city in. If not for Dom, she would have been a fine target for pickpockets and beggars. The Elder, hooded behind her, was a sentinel none would trifle with. Except, of course, the drunks, the brawlers, and the drunken brawlers. They clustered outside the dock taverns and free houses, half in shadow, waving flagons and shouting at the Elder in a spray of languages.

Dom faltered, his lips pursed beneath his hood. "I believe those men are asking to fight me," he said, confused.

"I can't blame them," Sorasa muttered under her breath.

"Why would they want to do that?" the Elder asked. "I'm twice their size."

He scrutinized the taverns again, looking over rat-faced men in greasy clothing. They looked back, jeering, showing yellow teeth if they had teeth at all.

Sorasa waved him on with a tug of her gloved fingers. "Boys do stupid things to feel like men, no matter how old they are."

Inns and taverns sprouted like weeds all over Wayfarer's, its streets narrow and overcrowded. Most people left the port quickly, creating a steady tide into the city. Sorasa kept them deep in that current, snug within a group of robed pilgrims more slack-jawed than Corayne. She breathed a sigh of relief when they escaped the jostling island and crossed the Moonbridge, named for its smooth, half-circle arch over the Fifth Canal.

Corayne's gaze snagged and she slowed to stare at the monstrous Fleethaven, just as intimidating as the navy it harbored. It was dug into the next island, with a long channel leading to an interior circle. There were berths for each ship of the fleet, stalled like a horses in a stable.

"It's a cothon," Sorasa said, shoving the girl along. "And not much to look at. A shadow to the war ports of Almasad and Jirhali, a bad copy."

Both flashed in her mind, the cities of Ibal and Rhashir thick with heat haze and palm shade. Where Galland could dock twenty warships at a turn, the others could hold a hundred with ease. The streets of Almasad went gold in her memory, glittering like they never had before. Sorasa forced another breath, the air sour with the beer stink of the northern capital. It was like a bucket of cold water.

"Such is the way of Galland. Everything stolen well and poorly remade," she added, keeping her grip on Corayne's arm. "If you insist on stopping to look at every cobblestone and corner ditch, I'm going to make Dom carry you."

The city unfurled, dark and spattered with flickering lights like globs of red and gold paint. They bled on the waters, dancing in the wake of boats, ferries, and little skiffs rowing the canals. Sorasa got her bearings as they walked, resetting the points of her internal compass. Corayne tromped at her side, doing her best to gawk and walk at the same time.

"The Konrada," Sorasa said, gesturing to the tower before Corayne could ask. It spiked up from the center of Ascal, black against the stars, windows glowing from within as if fire burned deep in her spine. "A cathedral to every god of the Ward, all twenty, built by Konrad the Great."

Behind her, Dom did his best to smile. The look seemed foreign on his face. "For someone who hates traveling companions, you make a talented guide."

His steady voice and superior tone split Sorasa's head. "The tower is open inside, two hundred feet from dome to floor," she continued, glaring at him. "Do you know what happens to a man's skull when he falls that distance?"

The Elder soured. "Is that a threat, Sarn?"

"Just sharing happy memories," Sorasa replied. "I have many in this city."

Next to him, Corayne's eyes nearly rolled out of her head.

They tried to avoid the main streets, sticking to alleys. The avenues connected the bridges like veins through a body and would have been easier, but more obvious. Even at night, market stalls and performer pavilions crowed, fountains choked with people washing clothes and filling buckets. Carts wheeled; dedicant priests walked in their rows; dogs nosed for scraps while cats shrieked. The city garrison patrolled, lanterns raised and faces slack beneath their helmets. Children laughed or wept around every corner.

Where Corayne gaped, Dom glowered in disgust. Sorasa could not help but agree. *Ascal is a foul place*, she cursed, stepping over a black puddle. Between the bridges, the stinking canals, and the many hundreds of thousands of people who lived within the walls, the capital was an experiment in how not to plan a city. Everything was infinitely more chaotic than any city of the south or west.

But chaos makes ease, she knew. *In a crowd, on a street, in a city's foundations.*

They rejoined a grand avenue to cross the Bridge of Faith, its length set with great iron torches like spears. In daylight it would be rammed rail to rail with pilgrims seeking the Konrada and the blessings of the gods. Now it was all but empty, scattered with a few errant priests mumbling to themselves or preaching to beggars.

They stepped off Faith and onto the plaza, wide and round. Sorasa fought the familiar urge to run. She felt exposed, a hawk reduced to a mouse in the field. The cathedral tower loomed, watching over them with proud indifference.

Though she despised Ascal, even Sorasa could not help but admit the city was grand in every sense of the word, for better or worse. Such was the way of the northern kings, who saw themselves as emperors, burdened and blessed to rule from every corner of the horizon.

The New Palace was no exception, a giant hunched beyond the cathedral.

Corayne breathed a sigh, the gasping sort. Not in awe, but in fear. "I had a picture of it in my head," she murmured as they walked. "What I thought the palace would look like."

"And it came nowhere close," Sorasa answered. *I know the feeling*, she thought, remembering the first time she saw the sprawling palace. *The great seat of the Gallish kings, the fist of this land.* It stole her breath then. It almost did now.

The palace rose at the city's heart, walled on its own island, its towers and keeps a soft gray that flickered gold under the flaming braziers upon the ramparts. Galland's lion snarled from a hundred green banners, streaming like emerald tears. Gargoyles and spires clawed the sky from the rooftops. Torches flared on the ramparts of a dozen towers. Lights pulsed behind gleaming windows of stained glass. There was another cathedral on the palace grounds, the Syrekom, monstrous in size, with a rose window like a gigantic jeweled eye. Parts of the palace were brand-new, the stone almost white, the architecture flamboyant and daring, a stark contrast to the rest. The gate was a mouth of iron, jaws wide at the end of the Bridge of Valor.

Two dozen knights lined Valor, armed with spears, their helms donned. They wore green silk over their armor, each embroidered with a roaring lion. At night they looked inhuman, unfeeling, in service to their queen and country.

"That is too many guards to bribe," Dom said dryly from beneath his hood.

"I don't plan to use a bridge," Sorasa replied with equal bite.

"Do you intend to swim in that . . . *substance?*" he said, sneering at the fetid canals.

Before she could spit a retort at the Elder, Corayne did it for her. "Clearly there's some kind of tunnel," she said softly. Her eyes darted to the Konrada, then the palace. "There's more below us. In the Old Cor ruins."

"Yes," Sorasa replied stiffly.

She glanced at the girl, looking her over again. In Lemarta, Corayne had seemed unremarkable, another daughter of the Long Sea, with a sun-kissed face and salt-tangled hair. *Smart, curious. Restless, maybe, but what girl of seventeen is not?* There'd been only a flicker of something in her. It burned now, a candle catching light. And Sorasa could not say what it meant.

"There used to be a stadium here, where the Cors raced their chariots on sand, or staged navy battles on the flooded grounds," Sorasa explained in a low voice. "Only a sliver remains, at the east end of the palace. But the foundation, below us—below the canals, even—it's a maze of tunnels, some decades old, some two thousand. Many burned when the Old Palace fell; others have collapsed or flooded since the days of Old Cor. But not all."

Corayne narrowed her eyes at the Konrada again, looking to its roots rather than its pinnacle. The wall dedicated to Immor faced them head on. The great god of time and memory held the moon and sun in his hands at equal height, with the stars like a halo behind his head. In his chest was a rose window, burning with blue and green light. A doorway arched between his feet, one of twenty, spilling the sound of evening worship.

Sorasa beckoned them both toward the cathedral, a smile on her lips. "The Konrada vaults hold nothing of value anymore, but they do go deep."

"That will suffice," Dom said grimly.

Corayne could only nod. Her eyes went wide again, and she seemed once more the girl in Lemarta, not the daughter of a dead prince, with the realm's fate laid between her hands.

"I think the tunnels smell worse than the streets," Corayne said, her voice muffled. She drew her shirt up over her nose and mouth, leaving only her black eyes visible. She glared at the walls and the dirt floor, searching for faults. Her eyes seemed to eat the meager light.

Dom's growl echoed. "I did not realize that was even possible. And yet here we are."

"Funny, the Elder legends don't mention how *fussy* your kind is," Sorasa snapped, though she had to agree. The tunnel air was somehow both sour and stale. The canal ran above them, and clearly the walls were perpetually wet, covered in moss that gleamed by the weak light of her torch.

The Elder muttered a retort in his own language. It echoed down the tunnel, passing away into the blackness. The Konrada vaults were behind them now, occupied only by a gray priest who would regain consciousness sometime around dawn.

The memories came with each step. Her first contract behind the walls of the New Palace was fifteen years ago, the last only four. Both ended with men dead in their chambers, missing ears and fingers, contracts fulfilled and messages relayed. She took no pride in them nor satisfaction. Duty was done for its own sake—at least, it was then.

Beneath Ascal, in the chilling damp, Sorasa had never felt farther from the Amhara and the citadel. She chewed her cheek, the air cold through her clothing, like a touch of sickness.

After a long while, the tunnel began to slope upward. Dom brushed the back of his hand over the wall, feeling the stone. "We're out from under the river," he said, his knuckles coming away dry. "We must be under the palace now."

"Oh, good," Corayne said. Her voice held the edge of panic. "Now I can stop worrying about being drowned and focus entirely on being crushed."

A rare chuckle passed through Sorasa's teeth. "It's not so bad," she replied. "Protect your skull and ribs. You'll be all right."

The girl blinked at her. "You're a very strange person, Sorasa Sarn."

"It's a strange world out there," Sorasa said. Her eyes met Dom's as he brought up the rear of their trio. He fell into his constant scowl. "And growing stranger by the second."

The Elder opened his grim mouth but stopped himself, squinting, his immortal eyes seeing farther than her own could. There was something in the darkness.

Corayne glanced at him, worrying out of her skin. "What is it?" she hissed, dropping her voice. One hand stole to her boot, where she kept a small and useless knife.

Someone should teach her how to use that, Sorasa thought, noting the girl's poor grip.

Dom only raised his chin. "You'll see."

The gate came, barring the passage. It was good, old iron, with no lock and no hinges, welded into plates on either side of the tunnel. This was meant to stop anyone who stumbled this way, from either direction.

"Is this new?" Corayne offered, searching for answers as was her way. "Or do you have a trick around it?"

"I'd wager this is near two hundred years old," Sorasa sighed, eyeing the ironwork. "And yes, I have a trick. He is quite large and quite annoying," she added, looking pointedly at Dom.

He sneered down at her. The torchlight turned his golden hair to fire and cast shadows along the sharp lines of his stern face. Darkness pooled in his scars.

"*I'm* annoying?" His green eyes burned like the embers. "*You* brought us to a locked gate."

Sorasa looked over his broad hands and wide-set shoulders with a sniff of indifference. She remembered the bull in Byllskos, tossed and toppled by the immortal.

"I brought you to a locked gate about to be knocked open. There's a difference," she said.

The Elder pursed his lips and looked back at the iron bars. His brow furrowed deeply, his body unmoving.

"What, afraid of a few bruises?" Sorasa prodded.

He made a noise low in his throat, somewhere between a growl and a huff.

There were a few bruises.

12

THE LAST CARD PLAYED
Erida

The Queen knew why her future husband demanded roses for the morning. Scarlet, crimson, ruby, red as the sun at the first light of dawn. Red was the color of the old empire, and roses bloomed in its shadow, red ghosts to remember ruins gone. They grew all over Ascal, especially in the gardens of the New Palace. They did the same in Lecorra, the once capital, and in the old cities of the provinces from Kasa to the Gates of Trec, where Corblood once ruled. Erida had to admit, she craved roses too, and she thought of ways to wear them in her hair for the ceremony. *Bound with silver, braided, pinned. Woven into a crown, perhaps.*

Her maids busied themselves in her apartments, laying out gowns for the morning in the grand solar. They would be working well into the night, inspecting every square inch of silk and brocade for flaw while the seamstresses looked on, worrying their hands. Every other servant who could be spared from the preparations or the feast hunted roses. She watched them through the windows, picking through the gardens by torchlight, shears in hand.

Erida's gown for the ceremony would be cloth of gold trimmed in green, with a cream veil over her crown, as was Gallish tradition. But tonight she favored crimson, to please her future consort. The color felt odd, but not unwelcome. Erida looked down as she walked, her skirts flowing, the silk reflecting the lights of the long hall. Her fingers twitched, winking with the emerald ring of state. It was not a long walk from the residence to the great hall. She could do it in her sleep, every turn and stair etched in her memory.

Tonight it felt both endless and far too short.

My ladies are nervous, she knew. They trailed at a distance, letting Erida walk alone. Like all but the Crown Council, they did not know who she had chosen to wed, or why. Erida counted no confidantes among their number. It was too dangerous to share secrets with her ladies-in-waiting, let alone befriend any one of them. Three were daughters of Gallish nobles, and the other two came from the courts of Larsia and Sardos. Their allegiances were elsewhere, to ambitious fathers or distant kings.

Not to me. There are no companions for ruling queens. The weight on my shoulders is far different, and far more. My mind is my own and no one else's.

She folded her hands together, falling into her well-practiced air of calm, though she was anything but. Her pulse quickened with fear and anticipation. She would present her consort tonight and marry him in the morning. It had been announced only a few days ago, and the court had not ceased its buzzing ever since. Only the council knew her choice, and they were sworn to secrecy. To her surprise, they seemed to have kept their oath, even Konegin.

For that, at least, Erida could be thankful.

Yet her heart pounded. *He is the best choice, the only choice. And he could still be my ruin, a jailor with a rogue smile, a king in all but name, holding my jeweled leash.* It was a risk she had to take.

Lord Konegin aimed to catch her by surprise, but Erida expected him to find her before her entrance. She was not disappointed.

"My lord," she said as he approached, moving to cut off her train of ladies and guards.

He was nearly alone, accompanied only by a pair of knights sworn to his service. Where her own wore green with gold, his two armored men wore tunics of gold with green, the lion roaring and reversed. Konegin himself favored emerald from the rich leather of his boots to his brocade mantle fastened with a jeweled pin beneath his throat.

His bow was pitiful, barely a jerk of his golden head. "Your Majesty," he said. His chain of office winked at his neck. "I'm glad to have found you before all this begins."

As if you were not crouched around the corner like a hound waiting for scraps, Erida thought, forcing her smile.

"Indeed, it has already begun if my seneschal is true," she replied, waving a hand to the stout little man who oversaw the palace and its doings. He cowered behind her ladies. Very few members of the royal court cared to step between the Queen and her cousin, for no amount of gold nor glory. "The barrels are flowing free, and I believe the wine is being passed by now. From Siscaria tonight, isn't it, Cuthberg? Now that the Madrentines are bothering us at the border again."

"Y-yes, Your Majesty. Siscarian red and a Nironese vintage from Sapphire Bay for your table," the seneschal answered in a halting voice, though the Queen had little true interest.

She held her cousin's piercing gaze as she held her smile. Forcefully, with all her focus.

"I must confess, I wish I saw more of your betrothed," he said, fishing poorly. "I've barely been able to speak to him."

Erida waved a hand, dismissive. "He spends most of his time in the archives, both in the New Palace and in the Konrada vaults." It was the truth, easy to tell.

Konegin quirked a blond eyebrow. "A student of history?"

"After a fashion. He wants to know all he can of Galland before he joins me on her throne."

The lord curled his lip with distaste.

"Cousin, I understand your misgivings." She spoke as kindly she could. Konegin was a scale to balance. He needed to know her worth, her power as queen, but not feel threatened by it, lest he be spurred to action. "Please know I hold your counsel in the highest regard."

Konegin pursed his lips, his beard closing over his mouth. "And yet you ignore it so easily, if you allow me to advise you at all."

"You have not been ignored." *Only men can speak all day long and still think themselves silent.* "But the choice is my own. You swore an oath to my father to see that through."

"I did," he answered sharply. "And I regret it."

A spark of anger flared in Erida's chest. Any word spoken against her father was a word against the crown, the kingdom, against the blood in her own veins. She wanted to throw him in the stocks for even daring it. *But what good would that do?* she warned herself. *His son is pathetic, but his lands are many, his reach long. There are many more loyal to Konegin than they are to me. It is better to wait, to fortify myself, to grow strong before trying the snake pit.*

Erida kept walking, her pace slow as to not be rude. But enough to keep her party moving, the feast close on the horizon. *Balance.*

Konegin fell in next to her.

"You think him too lowborn for me, I know that," she said evenly. For not the first time, Erida wished she had inherited her father's height so she could look her cousin in the eye. "I see that. But trust me when I say I'm thinking of Galland, of the crown, of our country, in every second I live and breathe. He is the right choice for all of us, for what we can *become.*"

Konegin scoffed. "I believe in flesh and blood, in what is real, Erida."

Ahead, a door loomed. *Sanctuary.* The passage, the great hall, the future. Freedom from loathsome cousins and false betrothals, from dreams unrealized and impossible.

"So do I," Erida replied. *More than you know.* "But, Cousin, you've spent all these years sitting my council, naysaying every name upon my list. Blood princes of Kasa, Ibal, Rhashir, Trec, every kingdom upon the Ward. The wealthiest heirs of Galland, the great princes of Tyriot. Men of means and power. You've never favored any of them, nor supplied a name yourself." She surveyed him with a stern eye. "Suggest a suitor, Cousin, if you have one. Or accept who I have chosen, for the good of us all."

Lord Konegin turned sour. He chewed his thin lips, resisting as long as he could. This was a corner he had long avoided, a card he didn't want to play yet. *But your hand is forced. Lay it down and let me see,* Erida thought, almost greedy. She felt victory in her teeth.

"My son is unwed," he ground out.

The Prince of Toads, Lord Troll, a thirty-year-old boy with his father's temper, his mother's weak constitution, and a walrus's gut. I'd just as soon marry a corpse. It would smell better.

Even so, it was a consideration. If only to keep the crown from her cousin's head. *I would not be the first woman to wed for spite.*

"Your son is a valued member of my family, a beloved cousin as you are." Both the Queen and the lord nearly laughed at the bold, bare-naked lie. They shared a smirk, like adversaries smiling over crossed blades. "I would think he has an embarrassment of princesses and wealthy heiresses clamoring for his hand." *To their detriment, poor women.*

"He does indeed," the lord said, offering nothing else. "But Heralt would put them aside to serve Galland, to serve our noble and majestic blood."

Ahead, her knights flanked the double oak doors, and then wrenched them open to show a passage of antechambers. They were all dark wood, lacquered and polished, carved to intricate perfection. Each archway was the mouth of a lion, fanged and snarling. Erida imagined them snapping shut as she passed, barring Konegin's way. *Or biting him in two.*

"It's good he doesn't have to make such a sacrifice," she said as she stepped into the passage. Her knights pressed in, their armor jangling in the closer quarters. All of them were broad and muscular, chosen for their strength and skill. Not to mention their tact. Shoulder to shoulder, the knights kept formation, effectively pushing her cousin away.

Lord Rian Konegin settled back on his heels, his cloak spilling over one shoulder. Framed by the doorway, by the passing flutter of her ladies, he seemed a rock in the sea, unmoving as the waves crashed all around. The Queen turned away, satisfied with her own performance. *The sea will conquer even mountains, given the time. And you will grow old long before I do, your power dying as mine blooms.*

Her voice was light, musical, girlish, a costume as much as her scarlet gown.

"Enjoy the feast, Cousin."

13

THE NOOSE
Corayne

Dom brushed dust and dirt from his cloak, cleaning himself off after the debacle with the tunnel gate. *Even though his appearance should be far, far down his list of priorities,* Corayne thought, watching him rework the braid at the back of his head, gathering half his hair into a severely neat plait as he walked the now-dry tunnel. *At least he's effective.* The cracked gate far behind them was testament of that.

Though it felt like an eternity, winding through the heavy darkness, barely twenty more minutes passed before Sorasa's torch illuminated the bottom of a spiraling staircase.

"Finally," Corayne said. She drank in a gasp of fresher air, tasting the difference.

Dom glared at the steps. "You first, Sarn," he growled low in his throat.

The assassin sneered, ascending the steps. "An immortal Elder, hiding behind a woman and a child. How noble."

He didn't rise to her needling, but a muscle feathered in his cheek.

"I'm seventeen, hardly a child," Corayne muttered under her breath, frowning at the stairs.

Her legs were still sore from their days in the saddle. Just the prospect of the climb already had her thighs burning. And burn they did, after only a few minutes' time. Her breath echoed, growing heavier by the second. Though she had run the cliffs of Lemarta since she was a child, mounting the steps of the port town without blinking an eye, this felt infinitely more difficult.

She tried counting the steps, to pass the time and to keep her nerves level. *Every step brings us closer to the palace above, to a sword that might not be there, to a queen who might not listen.* Marching into the black unknown was like carrying a log across her shoulders. It weighted down every step, even the easy ones.

"You said your squire is a lady's son," Sorasa said, her voice echoing down "He'll be in the east wing, where the courtiers keep their apartments."

Corayne tried to check her labored breathing. She gulped down wet air. "Is that far?"

"Not particularly."

That isn't an answer.

"You'll go first. You can pass for a kitchen maid," Sorasa added, looking over her shoulder. Without breaking stride, she ran her eyes over Corayne's clothing. "Ask for his rooms. Simple."

Corayne looked down at her boots, her leggings, and a tunic dried stiff with salt spray. "I don't look much like a maid."

Sorasa rolled her eyes so strongly Corayne nearly felt it. "You're within the walls already," she sighed. "Just keep your chin up, seem bored, speak plainly. And you're a girl. Harmless. No one will bother looking at you twice."

Suddenly Corayne wished the steps were endless. "I don't know if I can do that."

"It's all right—" Dom began, but Sorasa cut him off with a click of her tongue.

The assassin quickened her pace, as if in punishment for Corayne's fear. "You're the ship's agent for one of the most notorious pirates of the Long Sea, and her daughter besides. I'm sure you've got steel in that spine somewhere."

Heat bloomed in Corayne's cheeks, flaming against the cold, damp air of the stairwell. *No spine*, she heard her mother whisper in her ear. The memory shivered her and emboldened her in equal measure. *I'll show you spine.*

The stairs ended in a wide, flat room, dim but not dark, the ceiling supported by dozens of fat columns. An undercroft of some sort, very different in style from the ancient tunnels below. Sorasa led them through, picking out a path no one else could see, until they reached another set of stairs. Luckily, it was much shorter, and led to a single ancient door.

Now Sorasa was quiet, and put her ear against it.

With the slightest huff, Dom placed his hands on the Amhara's shoulders. She tensed like a predator, a fist balled, one hand drawing her knife, even as he shifted her out of the way. Her eyes went wide, livid, her nostrils flaring as she sucked in a hissing, angry breath.

Dom shot her a look of annoyance before laying his face against the door, his ear pressed up. Corayne nearly laughed aloud. Of course an Elder would hear better than any mortal, even an Amhara. It was simple logic.

That didn't calm Sorasa at all. "I've killed men for less," she growled.

"You're welcome to try," Dom said with disinterest, his focus elsewhere. He listened for a long second while the assassin seethed. "The room and passage beyond are empty. A guard is making his rounds above us, but moving away," he said, drawing back to look down on them. "Perhaps let me do the spying from now on."

Sorasa dropped her torch. It spit embers across the stone. "About time you made yourself useful," she hissed, reaching for the door.

"About time you both shut your mouths," Corayne muttered.

The assassin paused, her teeth bared in a threatening smile. Her copper eyes darted, reflecting the weak light of the torch smoldering at their feet. "Well, I won't burden you with my presence much longer."

Corayne wasn't surprised. An assassin had no place in their quest; her road ended here. But still she felt the pang of loss. "You're gone after we find Trelland."

"In the wind," Sorasa said with a nod. Then she leered at Dom. "Until someone finishes his great task, and upholds his end of our bargain."

The shadows moved over his face, sharpening his features. He seemed old for a moment, as though the long years of immortality were finally catching up to him. "It will be upheld."

"Unless you die," Sorasa said airily, pulling hard on the door.

"Gods willing, if it means never seeing you again," Dom muttered as it opened.

Corayne blinked fiercely in the sudden light, her body tensing. She braced herself for shouting, a guard or a maid, someone to raise the alarm. But Dom had heard truly. There was no one on the other side, just a half-empty storeroom. The air was dry and stale. This room was forgotten, barely used. From this side, the door was unremarkable, old wood threatening to splinter. It had no handle or doorknob Corayne could see.

No one will be coming back this way.

The passage was as empty as the storeroom. Tapestries hung from the walls, and fine rugs carpeted the floor, muffling their footsteps. Most were Gallish-made, by weavers without much skill or artistry. Green and gold, again and again. *Do they ever get sick of those colors?* Corayne wondered, as they passed a woven image of a lion with a squashed face.

She told herself not to be afraid. She walked with an Elder prince, a witness to a great terror. If they were waylaid before finding Andry, they would simply be brought to the Queen first. They could warn her all the same. *Or be thrown directly into the dungeons for trespassing.*

She pushed the thoughts from her mind and focused on trying to look the part of a maid. A servant in the palace would keep her eyes down, not gape at tapestries she saw all day long. *You work in the kitchens, in the kitchen garden specifically.* That would explain the dirt on her hands and knees from their long journey. *You tend the . . . what's in season right now? Tomatoes? Cabbage?* Her mind spun, grasping for a good story to tell. *A courier came in from the stables; he had a letter for Valeri Trelland. Sent me to run it to her.* Though Corayne had spent years negotiating on her mother's behalf, trading stolen cargo and illegal goods, she was never alone in her lies. The *Tempestborn* always had her back.

The Tempestborn *is far away now. I'm on my own.*

Sorasa and Dom navigated well, avoiding the clank of armor that meant guards or knights. It was only a few minutes, but the seconds dragged and Corayne's heartbeat thundered.

"Servants," Dom breathed at her shoulder. "Through the archways."

Corayne's jaw clenched and she felt herself nod. Up ahead, the passage widened, one side scalloped with columns and arches opening onto a flourishing garden of roses. Steeling herself, she walked forward while the others hung back. *You work in the kitchens.*

A pair of women knelt among the roses, filling their baskets with scarlet flowers. Their faces gleamed with sweat, and they wore thick leather gloves to defend against thorns.

"Please tell us Percy sent you to help," one of the women said with a gasp of breath. She wiped her brow with the back of her hand. "We'll be cutting flowers all night at this rate."

Corayne's voice faltered. "I—"

The other maid, older than the first, waved a fistful of roses in her direction. "Hope you brought gloves, dear."

"No, sorry—" Corayne said, speaking around the lump in her

throat. She swallowed, eyeing the two. "I've got a message for Lady Valeri Trelland. A letter, from a courier—"

"Trelland?" The young maid blanched. "Isn't she dead?"

Corayne's stomach plummeted to her feet.

"She's not dead," the other answered, still wagging her roses. "She's just sick is all. Sick the long, slow way. Doesn't leave her chambers much anymore. But she's still kinder than all the rest put together." Then she pointed with the flowers. "Keep on the way you're going. Her quarters are at the bottom of Lady's Tower. Look for the painting of King Makrus."

Corayne bobbed her head in a grateful nod. "Thank you."

The older maid screeched as she moved on. "And tell Percy we need more hands if we're to cut enough flowers by morning!"

"I shall," she replied, though she had no idea who Percy was and even less inclination to seek him out.

The tightness in her chest unwound and she turned back to the passage, only to find Dom and Sorasa waiting idly on the far side of the arches. Both had passed by without the maids, or even Corayne, noticing. Sorasa jabbed her thumb over her shoulder, her lips forming words with no sound. *This way.*

The Lady's Tower was otherwise empty, its occupants asleep or elsewhere, perhaps feasting, perhaps getting into all kinds of court mischief. There was something happening in the morning, if the maids were to be believed.

Corayne had no idea what King Makrus looked like, but Sorasa led the way. Eventually they found a painting of a man more troll than king, with mottled skin and a hulking figure. *Paintings are supposed to make people look better than they were,* Corayne thought, glancing over the dusty portrait. She could not imagine how ugly he must have been in life.

He loomed next to the door to the Trelland apartments, and they closed the last few yards at speed, hurtling forward as if something might stop them at the last moment.

Corayne felt odd, detached from her body, as if she could watch herself from afar. None of this seemed real, even against the dusty smell of the passage, the soft carpet beneath her boots, the stone wall cold against her fingertips. She took a deep breath and blinked, half expecting to wake up in her bed in Lemarta, with Kastio preparing breakfast in the next room. *It's just another dream. My father, my uncle, the Spindle torn, the Elder and the assassin. All of it will disappear, fading in the morning light.*

But the world remained, unmoving, insisting to be seen and felt. Impossible to ignore.

Corayne stared at the door.

Dom stared at the door.

They stared at each other, both hesitant, both frozen. Black eyes met green, iron on emerald. Centuries separated the two of them, but they were alike for a moment, standing on the edge, terrified of the unknown below.

What if the sword is gone?

What if the sword is here?

"Should we knock?" Corayne forced out, her mouth suddenly dry.

"Yes," Dom said hoarsely. "Sarn—" he added, looking over his shoulder.

But there was no one behind him. No woman in unremarkable

clothing, her cloak pulled up tight, a single tattoo bared in the torchlight.

Sorasa Sarn of the Amhara was gone, leaving no trace, as if she'd never existed at all.

Her absence set a fire in Dom, burning away his fear. He rapped his fist on the door. "Ecthaid willing," he hissed, naming a god Corayne did not know, "the tunnels will collapse on her murderous head."

Her stomach twisted as the lock turned. When the door pulled open, she found herself face-to-face with a young man. Her stomach dropped again.

He was tall and muscular, but still coltish, growing into himself. His skin was smooth and perfect as polished amber, glowing warmly. There was only the shadow of a beard, the first attempts of a boy. His black hair was cropped short, for function. Of course he was the squire Andry Trelland, who had survived the slaughter at the temple where so many had died. Corayne didn't know why, but she had pictured him as a man, a warrior like the others. *But he can't be much older than me, no more than seventeen.* At first she found his face kind, with a gentleness to it. But, like Dom, he had something raw beneath his pleasant expression, a wound still torn open that might never heal.

"Yes?" he said plainly, his voice deeper than she expected. Trelland kept the door close to his shoulder, obstructing her view of anything behind him except for flickering firelight. He stared down at her, expectant. She was the only one he could see, his focus absolute and entire.

"You're Andry Trelland," Corayne said softly, all pretense forgotten.

Andry's mouth twitched in amusement. "I am. And you're new to the palace," he added, looking her over with sympathy. He eyed her dirty hands. "Kitchens?"

"Not exactly."

"Squire Trelland." Dom's voice was thunder as he stepped around Corayne, putting her between them. He looked right over her head.

Anything soft or friendly about Andry's face disappeared, a slate wiped clean. His dark eyes widened and he leaned heavily against the door, like his knees might give out.

"My lord Domacridhan," Andry breathed. He ran his eyes over Dom's scarred face, tracing the ripped flesh. "You live."

Dom put a hand to the door, pushing it wide. His brow furrowed.

"For now."

My name is Corayne an-Amarat. My mother is Meliz an-Amarat, captain of the Tempestborn, *lady scourge of the Long Sea. My father was Cortael of Old Cor. And this is his sword.*

The Spindleblade lay sheathed across Andry's knees. Corayne couldn't take her eyes off it as Dom and the squire spoke, trading tales of their journeys after the temple. The dark leather sheath was boiled and oiled twice over, if her eye was true. Good, sturdy, old. But not old the way the sword was old, the steel of it cold even from a distance, humming with a force she could barely feel and hardly name. Andry had not drawn the blade yet. She did not know what it looked like. If there was still blood on it, from her own uncle, who should have died and had not. From her father, his life running red over his hands. The hilt was clean, at least, the cross guard set with winking stones. In the firelight, they flickered between scarlet and purple, like sunset or dawn. The grip was wrapped in black leather, worn to a different hand. There was no gemstone in the pommel, but an etching like a star, or a many-armed sun. The symbol of Old Cor, a light since lost. Forged in another realm, imbued with power she could not understand.

"It's yours," Andry said slowly, and she realized he was staring. He and the Elder had finished, both well up to speed. Without hesitation, the squire lifted the sword and held it out to her. Dom's eyes followed the blade.

Corayne drew back in her chair before the fire, her eyes wide. She was already sweating in the close, warm air of the Trelland apartments. Her breath caught in her throat.

Valeri Trelland leaned forward in her own chair. "It sounds like you'll need it, my dear," she said, her voice placid and slow.

As the maids had said, Valeri was clearly battling a sickness, her body frail, her dark skin drained of warmth. But she sat up straight, her green eyes clear. She was unafraid.

"All right," Corayne bit out, extending her hands.

The sword, finely made and well kept, was lighter than she'd thought it would be. *I've never held a sword before*, she thought idly. *A true sword, not a pirate's long knife or ax. A hero's sword.* Her eyes narrowed. *A dead hero's sword.*

Despite the hot air of the room, the sword was cool to the

touch, as if drawn from a river or ocean, pulled from the night sky between the stars. Her curiosity rose inside her again, hungry jaws wide. Slowly, she slid the blade from the sheath an inch, then another. The etched steel gleamed in the firelight, the design punctuated with markings like writing. For a moment, Corayne thought she might be able to decipher it. *A bit of Ibalet, some Kasan, a Siscarian loop*—but no. The words of Old Cor were lost as the empire, lost as her father. She sheathed the Spindleblade again with a hiss of metal and a sharp pang of sadness.

Her hands closed around the grip. She filled the shadow of a man dead.

"So the Companions of the Realm live on," Andry said, looking from her back to Dom. He set his jaw, and some of the softness of his face melted away. "The quest is not failed, simply unfinished."

By now, Corayne had lost count of how many times Dom's lips had pulled into his scowl. This was certainly the worst one yet.

"That is one perspective," he managed, sounding flustered. "Two of us remain."

"Three," Corayne said, startling even herself. She blinked fiercely. *Be brave, be strong,* she told herself, though she felt miles away from either. She raised her chin, trying to remember her mother's voice, the one she used on the deck of a ship. In control, in command. "There are three now."

Dom watched her intently, a sorrow languishing in his eyes. Corayne didn't know whether to embrace him or slap him out of it. "Very well," he said, his voice low.

As if this wasn't what he wanted, what he asked for, what he sought me out to accomplish. Corayne gritted her teeth. *I'm here because you brought me,* she thought. *You can at least pretend this isn't a death sentence.*

"And more will join us soon," Andry said eagerly, all but leaping from his seat. He began sweeping around the parlor room, his energy vibrant and jarring against the circumstances. "I warned the Queen but she's done nothing. Now, with you, my lord, and you, my lady"—he nodded at them both, still pacing—"she won't have a choice. Queen Erida is fiercely protective of her kingdom. Certainly she won't let it fall into ruin beneath Taristan's feet."

He paused before a shield on the wall. It was old, notched at the edges, the face painted gray with a blue star cut in two by a long slash. The squire stared up at it, as a priest might look upon his icons and altars. With a sinking feeling, Corayne realized she saw no signs of his father in these rooms. She looked at the ruined shield again, and at the boy before it.

We have something in common.

"I'll help you of course," Andry said, tearing himself away from the shield. "I'll bring Mother to Nkonabo, out of harm's way, but I'll return. I swear it."

Again, Dom looked pained, and Corayne felt some of it too. The daughter of Old Cor and the immortal didn't have much choice in the matter, but the squire? *It is a long way to Kasa, and a long way back.*

"You don't have to do that, Andry," Dom said.

"It's my duty," Andry said fiercely. "My lord is fallen. I will avenge him."

"You should stay with your mother." Corayne selfishly regretted the words even as she said them. "Protect her."

Andry went to his mother's chair, standing like a guardian at her side. "And I will. But I'm a Companion. I have a duty to fulfill."

"Very well, my son," Valeri said, her eyes sharp. She put a hand on her son's arm, soothing him a little. "We'll leave this very night. I can be ready and waiting at the city docks by the time you finish with the Queen. All the arrangements are made; we need only send word."

"I'll call for your maid and porter," Andry murmured in reply, kissing her closed fingers. "I'll meet you on the ship before midnight."

"The sooner we're gone to Nkonabo, the sooner you can return," his mother said with a small but pleasant smile.

It seemed to satisfy Andry, but Corayne saw the tightness at the corners of her mouth. The wariness going up behind her spring-colored eyes. No mother would send her child into danger willingly, even if it was their dearest wish. Suddenly it was not Valeri Trelland she saw by the fire, but Meliz an-Amarat, her hair tangled by a salt wind, lips moving without sound.

Take me with you, Corayne wanted to ask again.

I will not echoed.

"You should go to the Queen tonight, right now," Valeri pushed on. She stood from her chair, hesitant on weak knees. "Before everyone gets too swept up in the festivities."

"Festivities?" Dom quirked his head to one side. His scars caught the hearthlight.

Pacing again, Andry searched through cupboards in the parlor. He drew out matching baggage, a pair of satchels packed and latched tight. *Both filled for a long journey*, Corayne saw.

"The Queen is nineteen years old, and has been fielding betrothals ever since she came to the throne four years ago," Andry said with an annoyed sigh. "Fending them off, mostly. But I guess her council has finally worn her down. She's due to announce her husband at court this evening and marry him in ceremony tomorrow morning."

Roses for the ceremony, cut by hand all night long, Corayne remembered the maids in the garden. It would be bare by morning, when Queen Erida married a man she'd been forced to accept. Corayne felt a sting of pity for the young queen. As much pity as a common girl could have for a monarch of the realm.

"Certainly this takes precedence," she said. "And maybe it's an opportunity for a reluctant bride. An excuse to delay a wedding she has no desire to go through with."

Andry grinned at her, his smile like a star. It lit him up. "That could work."

Corayne couldn't help but smile too, riding a rare, unfamiliar blaze of hope.

"The Queen will listen," she said, leaning on the Spindleblade. She used it to push herself to her feet, only to find it was more than half her height in length. "As your queen did not, Dom."

His great limbs unfolded, and Dom stood with grace. He was like a moving statue, slow and deliberate, a harsh contrast to Andry's rabid energy. "Mortals are hot-blooded, quick to anger, quick to fight," he said. "It has been your flaw these centuries past. Perhaps it will be your salvation too."

Corayne chewed the inside of her cheek. *Elders anger too, if you are any measure,* she thought hotly. She wanted nothing more than to scold him. *You are a pot on a slow boil, angry since the moment I met you, trying to grieve with no idea how, seeking revenge without direction. You are a predator with nothing to hunt.*

Instead she glared at the sword, its jewels gleaming.

"I have no idea how I'm going to carry this."

14

THE GREEN KNIGHT
Ridha

Three days she cursed Sirandel, snarling obscenities with every galloping step of her mother's horse. In Paramount, in Low Vederan, the bastard tongue born of centuries on the Ward, and in Pure Vederan, the voice of Glorian, the voice of a realm she had never known. Ridha, princess of Iona, heir to the Monarch, only child of Isibel Beldane and Cadrigan of the Dawn, rode with a fury. The sand mare kept on, bred to endure, but even she began to tire. Ridha did not.

Cowards all, the foxes and the stags, she thought, despairing of her home and the enclave now miles behind her. She cursed the Sirandels' palace of trees and rivers, their forest meadow halls and root vaults. Their city of immortal splendor, hidden deep in the Castlewood, grown as much as it was built. As the daughter of Iona, the Monarch's heir, they feasted and celebrated, her presence cause for great interest. But it did not last. Her tidings were dark, her requests unthinkable. Ride to war, after centuries of peace? Fight the man who could bring them home, even if it meant losing the Ward to What Waits and the jaws of Asunder? Spill Sirandel blood where Iona would not, for a cause so deadly?

Your mother is wise, the Monarch of Sirandel had said, his long face grim. His hair was more gray than red, silvered by time. *We will follow her judgment. Glorian calls.*

Ridha wanted to spit in his face. Instead she nodded, drank the spirits offered, ate the food given, and stole away in the night.

Even the wolves knew to avoid her, slinking away from the deer path as she urged the mare through the forest. She no longer felt the armor slung across her body, gleaming green, worked with antlers and the stag she now lamented. *Is it raining?* she thought after a long moment, breathing in the damp air of the Castlewood. Indeed, water streamed down her face, working through her dark hair with cold, wet fingers. *How long have I been soaked to the skin?*

It was not the Vederan way to feel such things, but a chill stole into her all the same. *And not because of the rain.*

Again she cursed in rage. At herself, mostly.

I sent Domacridhan into the world alone, seeking assassins and Cor heirs, seeking a blade, seeking revenge if not death. She saw her cousin in her head, burning as hot as an iron in the forge. All anger, all grief. He was no philosopher or diplomat, or even clear-headed. *And now, with the fall of the realm on the horizon?* She tightened her grip on the mare's reins, her knuckles white beneath her gauntlets. *Have I sent him to his doom?*

Worse even was the more selfish question:

Have I already failed?

As the trees blurred past, green-leaved and black-trunked in the downpour, a white figure rose. It was fixed but following, unmoving but always keeping pace. The image stung, near blinding, and Ridha shut her eyes, letting the mare choose her path. The figure remained. It was no stranger. Ridha would have known her mother's face anywhere, even in a sending, where all was mist, unreal and real, rippled and distant.

"Come home," Isibel said. "The Sirandels have refused. So will the rest." Most of her was as ashes, the edges of her pale skin and silver-gold hair flaking. The sending was not strong, but Ridha was her own blood. It would not take much will to connect them. "Come home."

The princess galloped on. *I will not.* She set her teeth and her resolve. *Sirandel is only one enclave, and they are not the only immortal warriors upon the Ward. I need only choose, and choose well. If I do not . . .*

Another smiling refusal could be the difference between life and death, for all she loved and knew. Though he had no skill in magic, she saw Domacridhan again, his face torn and bleeding, his eyes filled with the horrors he had witnessed in the foothills.

The Spindle temple was some days northwest, not far by her measure. Cortael's brother could still be there, flanked by his wizard and his army, vomiting out of the torn Spindle. *How many would there be now? Domacridhan suspected that more than a hundred came through in the first minutes, enough to overwhelm them. There could be thousands by now. Many thousands.*

The cold in her deepened, until she felt made of ice instead of bones.

VICTORIA AVEYARD

* * *

The edge of the Castlewood came sooner than she'd expected. But then, it had been decades since she passed this way, and mortals were apt to tear down what they could not tame. The forest dropped away around her, leaving only a barren belt of stumps and root holes. She could hear mills a half league off, churning on the banks of the Great Lion, cutting lumber to be sent downriver to Badentern and eventually the trade port of Ascal. Gallish oak and steelpine were famed across the Ward, fetching high prices in all seasons. Used in everything from water barrels to ship masts to shields. Steelpine was fire-resistant—Spindletouched, some said. Once, this forest had been as riddled with Spindles as with holes in a burrow. They'd left only hollows and clearings, hot springs that varied between water and gnawing acid, flowers that could heal or poison. Mortals with strange eyes and a tremor of magic, running thin in the later centuries. Such was the way of the Spindles, leaving blessings and curses in their wake, memories of the doorways that were and would never be again.

The sand mare was named Nirez, the Ibalet word for a long winter wind that cooled the unforgiving desert. It blew for days on end, signaling the turn of the season and the dawn of the new year in the south. That wind flagged now, and Nirez's fluid gait lost its rhythm. Only a half step off, but Ridha felt the shift.

She was not her cousin. She would not ride the horse to death. Largely because she would never procure another sand mare in these parts, and Gallish ponies were dull, dumb, and fat. She passed many as the field of stumps gave over to farmland and pasture, gold and green as the lion flag. Hedges cut the landscape, lining the gentle hills to separate wheat from barley. It was a blue, clear day, the sun warmer than it was in the thicker forest. Her armor shone like a mirror, and many farmers stopped their work to watch her ride past. Though Ridha was prepared for bandits or highwaymen, her sword ready at her side, there were none to be found. The belly of Galland was a sleepy land, well patrolled and protected by the vast kingdom.

The first village was small but had an inn and a passable stable. It was only noontime, so the yard was near empty when she trotted through, Nirez blowing hard, her black flank foaming with sweat. The stable hands, a boy and girl barely older than ten, were slow to act. They clopped heavily into the yard, their faces freckled and red with heat.

The boy sneered at her, a woman in armor, but the girl gaped, her pale eyes going round.

"It's three pennies to stall your horse," the boy spat, wiping at his nose. "Another one for hay and water, another for grooming."

"My lady—sir," the girl added, jumping into a bow that was more a squat. Ridha guessed she had never bowed in her life.

In reply, she tossed a round silver coin in their direction. The girl snatched and caught it first, turning it over in her grubby hands. She wondered at the image of the stag.

"That's not a penny!" the boy shouted, but Ridha was already walking toward the adjoining inn, her pack and saddlebags slung over one arm. She'd paid more than three times what they'd asked, in coin not diluted by a treasury in a city they would never see.

Though a princess of an immortal enclave, Ridha was no stranger to inns. Unlike most of her kin, she'd seen many in her four centuries upon the Ward, across many corners of the northern continent. Tavernas in Tyriot, the brewhouses of Ascal, Jydi ale lodges, the wine-soaked sedens of Siscaria, Treckish gorzka bars with clear liquor that would blind you if given the chance. She squinted at the faded sign hung over the inn door, unmoving in the still air. The name was worn away.

The interior was dark, the windows narrow and small, a fire barely embers in the hearth. Her immortal eyes swept over the inn quickly, needing no time to adjust. Most of the ground floor was the common room, set with a few tables and a long bar against the far wall. There were stairs to her left, marching up to the few cramped bedrooms, and a door to her right. Someone was snoring behind it—the innkeeper, perhaps. A single maid stood at the bar, most likely his wife. Ridha suspected the boy and girl were her children. They had the same freckled face, sandy hair, and curious disposition.

Two patrons occupied the far corner, tucked between the hearth and the wall, well settled with pewter tankards before them. They had knives at their belts and steel-toed boots, but they were ruddy, beaded with drink sweat, missing hair and teeth. Of little threat.

"What can I do for you . . . *miss?*" the barmaid said. Her eyes roved over Ridha's face and armor. "I've got a room to let, six pennies for the night, seven with board. Ale's more."

This time Ridha was careful to count out the pennies. Flashing silver before children was one thing, but the others were a risk. They might try to rob her, and then she'd have to waste time and energy roughing up farmers. She slid seven pennies across the bar top.

240   REALM BREAKER

"I've paid the stable hands to mind my horse," she added, nodding toward the door.

The barmaid dipped her head. "I'll make sure they do the job. Little imps seem to wander more and more these days. Room's at the top of the stairs, first on the right," she added, gesturing. "I can draw you a bath for a few pennies more."

Though the road had been long, Ridha shook her head. She'd bathed last in Sirandel, in a pond lined with silver, attended by handmaidens with bowls of scented oil and lavender soap. She had no intention of souring the memory with a cramped tub bucket before a weak fire.

The room was narrow, with a sloped ceiling, single window, and a short, hay-stuffed bed. The blanket was threadbare, mouse-eaten at the edges. Ridha heard rodents in the walls, skittering back and forth from the garden to the roof. She didn't plan to sleep that evening. It was Nirez who needed rest, not her. Instead she shucked off her armor and stored it in a chest with her sword and saddlebags. She kept her dagger, tucked beneath her long, charcoal-gray tunic, along with a boot knife, as well as her jewelry: a pendant and the hammered silver ring of Iona on her off-hand thumb.

For a long moment, she considered sitting on the bed and staring at the wall until dawn. It would certainly be just as productive as returning downstairs. But her body drifted, her feet stepping without sound, until she found herself in the common room again. She claimed a table by the hearth, her back against the cool wall, one hand gesturing for a drink.

Bitter ale, thin soup, bread surprisingly good, she thought, taking stock of her meal. She ate and drew with her finger on the table-top, tracing the lines of a map only she could see. *Where can I go next?* she asked herself again, naming the enclaves. They were far-flung, a long journey in every direction, every choice a risk. *Who might help, and who might turn me away?*

In the corner, the men gurgled back and forth, their Gallish accents thick and harsh. Ridha tried not to listen, but as an immortal Vederan, she had no trouble hearing their heartbeats, let alone their conversation.

"Married, or getting married soon," one of the mortal men grumbled quietly. He sucked down the last of his ale, tipping the tankard. Then he belched and smacked his lips. Ridha cut a glare at him, though he didn't notice. "Can't remember which."

His companion was lean, with strong forearms bared to the elbow. A woodcutter. He shook his head. "Come on, Rye, I'm sure we'd know if the Queen was married already. There'd be a 'nouncement. A rider." The woodcutter flapped a hand at the doorway. "I dunno, a lion prancing down the lane to roar the good news."

Rye laughed harshly. "You think the Queen cares to tell us her doings, Pole?"

"We're her subjects—'course she does," Pole said indignantly, puffing out his chest. Ridha felt the corner of her mouth lift. *A mortal monarch barely has time to learn herself. She won't be learning about you anytime soon, Master Pole.*

Rye shared the same opinion. He chuckled again, slapping a hand on his table. "She doesn't even know the name of our village, let alone the people in it."

"I s'pose," Pole muttered begrudgingly, his face flushed. "So to who?"

"Who what?" the other replied. He grabbed for a hunk of bread, dipping it in his soup. He ate like a bear, messy and without regard. Brown water dripped from his graying beard.

Pole sighed. "Who's she marrying?"

"D'ya think I'd know?" Rye said, shrugging. "Or you'd know the name if I said it?"

"I s'pose not," Pole said, embarrassed again. He scratched beneath his felt cap, at a scalp near to balding. "*She* might," he added suddenly, jerking his chin.

Ridha slowly pushed the ale away, freeing her hands.

Rye did not notice, too occupied with his soup. "Who might?"

"Her, the fancy one." Pole dropped his voice to a whisper. She heard him clearly, as if he were shouting across the common room. He even pointed with a knobbled finger. "Came tromping in here like a knight in six feet of armor with a cloak to match."

It took longer than it should have for Rye to follow. But finally he noticed Ridha at her table, her chair braced against the wall, her eyes fixed on her plate. "Oh right," he said, clear he'd forgotten her completely. "Maybe she will."

And then Pole really was shouting across the room, picking a scab on his neck as he did so. "Hey, do you know who the Queen's marrying?" he said, his voice shrill and hard.

Ridha bit back the urge to cover her ears, remove herself, or remove him. *I should have just stayed upstairs and stared at the wall.*

"I beg your pardon?" she said instead, her voice soft from days of disuse.

The men exchanged a very patronizing roll of their eyes. "The Quee-een," Pole said, drawing out the word. *As if I'm completely stupid, even though I'm the one they're asking for information.* "Who's she marrying?"

"Which queen?" Ridha replied, in an equally slow voice. There was a host of queens, mortal and immortal, reigning and consort, this side of the mountains and the Long Sea. Silently, she willed Nirez to recover quickly, so she might be free of this inn.

Rye blinked his mud-brown eyes. His mouth went a little slack and he looked to Pole in confusion. "There's more than one queen?" he hissed under his breath.

Baleir save me.

Pole waved him off. "The Queen of Galland," he said, as if it were the most obvious thing in the world. "Queen Erida."

"I can't say I know much of her." It was the truth. Ridha had not traveled far from Iona in twenty years, never riding west of the Monadhrion. The mortal lands changed so quickly, even in two decades. It was not worth recalling what she remembered of them.

The two men scoffed in unison. Now Pole really did think her stupid, an overly tall woman playing at knighthood in borrowed armor. "She's been queen of this here kingdom for four years yet—you certainly should," he sputtered.

A heartbeat in Elder time, Ridha thought. "I am sorry, but no," she answered, dropping her eyes. "No idea who she might be marrying." *And no interest either.*

The innkeeper's wife bustled out from behind the bar, wiping her hands on her apron. She put herself between Ridha and the men, smiling at them as she cleared their table. It was no small reprieve when she took up the conversation.

"Must be a great prince. Or another king," the woman said, balancing plates. "That's how it works, don't it? That lot always keep to each other. Keep things in the family, so to speak."

While the men blustered between themselves over subjects they had no knowledge of, Ridha sat back in her chair. She felt oddly warm in her skin, though the fire was barely lit, and the room was cool and dim. All this talk of royalty and marriage put her off balance, for she was a princess herself, with a duty to a throne and an enclave like any other royal woman. Elders might live long, seemingly endless years, but there was still a need for heirs. Isibel Beldane and Cadrigan of the Dawn had not wed for love, but for strength, and for a child to keep the enclave when the Monarch could not. *At least I have time, where mortals don't. At least my mother does not force me into choices I don't want to make.* She felt warm again, a cloying heat at her collar. She frowned, fingers pulling at her tunic. *Or does she? Is that not what this is? The rule of another driving me forward, in acquiescence or opposition?*

She gritted her teeth, feeling the now all too familiar surge of anger in her chest. *Cowards,* she thought again. In Sirandel and Iona, where Elder warriors would rather sit and hide than fight. *Dooming us with their fear.*

The flow of ale did not stop. The innkeeper's wife filled the men's tankards with a bright smile, then Ridha's, though she had no intention of drinking any more of the poorly made crop water. Still, she nodded in thanks all the same.

"So how about this proposition of Old Joe's?" Pole was whispering again, raising a hand to hide his mouth. It did nothing to stop Ridha from hearing, though she wished she could not.

"Joeld Bramble is a loon," Rye said, dismissive. "It'll come to nothing. Don't bother."

Pole leaned forward on his elbows, too eager. He glanced around the room warily, as if the walls had suddenly grown ears. "Joeld Bramble has family on the coast. They said the Watchful's been awfully quiet for this time of year. No Jydi, no raids. Not a single longboat spotted since last season."

Ridha kept her eyes low, on the table carved with crude initials and cruder words. But her focus homed in on the men. The marriage of a mortal queen did not interest her, but this was different. Odd. The hairs on her neck stood up.

"So he thinks he can take their place, can he?" Rye sputtered. "In what, a canoe?"

"I'm only saying. If the Jydi raiders aren't raiding, someone else can do it. Make it *seem* like raiders. Smash up a shrine, rob a few churches, maybe take some goats. Disappear back across the Castlewood and none's the wiser." Pole ticked off each step of the poor and foolish plan on his fingers. But it was not the scheme that interested the immortal. She furrowed her brows, trying to think. "Raiders blamed, we come home rich."

Rye remained silent and pressed his lips together, looking over at his companion. Pole grimaced, preparing himself for another rebuke, but it never came. "Maybe Old Joe has an idea," Rye finally murmured, winking an eye.

246

REALM BREAKER

Her chair scraped across the floor, shocking in the quiet. Both men jumped in their seats, looking up at Ridha as she stood. She wagered she was taller than both, in boots or bare feet.

"Does your Old Joe have any idea why the Jydi have stopped raiding?" she said clearly, looking between them. They both gaped; then Rye turned sour, his face crinkling.

"You listening to our private conversation?" he sneered.

Ridha fished out a penny for the ale and left it on the tabletop. "I find it difficult not to."

Pole was less offended. In fact, he seemed enamored by the attention. "No, he didn't say," he replied.

Ridha did not miss him shuffling in his seat, making room for her in the corner, should she feel so inclined. *I'd rather sidle up to a troll than to scabby, bald Pole.*

"Didn't know, you mean," she sighed.

Pole shrugged. "Same thing."

"What's it matter to you, lady knight?" Rye spat, trying to insult her with a compliment.

Though she had little cause to explain, Ridha heard herself do it anyway. Even the barmaid listened, leaning forward as she pretended to clean a glass with a dirty rag.

"Jydi raiders are fine sailors and finer fighters," the Elder said. "Cutthroats, warrior pirates, borne of summer snow and winter storms. They're hard people. If they aren't raiding, there's a reason. A good one."

Even immortals knew the sting of a raider blade, or they had in centuries past. The Jydi were not afraid of the Vederan nor had they forgotten them like the other mortal kingdoms. The lure of their riches was too great. Ridha herself had fought a raiding party with her kin, on the northern shores of Calidon some decades ago. She had not forgotten it.

"I suggest you tell your friend that," she warned, heading for the stairs.

Though the sun was still high outside, with dusk hours away, Ridha shut herself up for the evening, for there was work to do and plans to be laid out.

Her decision was made.

Sometime past midnight, the two men did try to rob her. She sent them both out the open window. Judging by his limping retreat, poor old Pole broke an ankle in the fall. The innkeeper and his wife tried an hour before dawn, though the wife seemed reluctant. Ridha let the blow of his rusty ax glance off her armor before warning him not to harangue travelers, especially women. This time she made sure to close the window before shoving him through it, spilling glass all over the yard below.

At least the children had done their part. Nirez was groomed and watered, well rested and ready for the long road to Kovalinn, the enclave deep in the fjords and mountains of the Jyd. Something was wrong in the north, as it was wrong at the temple.

Perhaps it was already knocking at the door, or beating down their walls.

Ridha of Iona intended to find out.

15

THE PATH CHOSEN
Corayne

Somewhere in the palace, a bell tolled. It was full dark outside, the stars like pinpricks in the windows. Dom slowed in his steps, faltering for the first time since Corayne had met him. She glanced his way, concerned. To her surprise, it was the squire who waved her off.

"He's fine," Andry said, sharing a look with the Elder. "Let's keep moving."

The Spindleblade was a nuisance. It was too long and cumbersome to wear at the hip, at least not without hitting a wall or person every time she turned, so Dom and Andry had rigged her sword belt to lie from shoulder to hip instead. She fastened her blue cloak to hide most of it from passing eyes. The sheath dug into her back, reminding her of the sword with every step. It wasn't so difficult to carry this way, but it would be impossible to draw should she need it. Not that Corayne expected to be dueling any time soon, with the Spindleblade or anything else.

The guards knew Andry and nodded at him as he led their small group through the palace, toward the Queen's feast. The passages became a long hall of vaulted ceilings and soaring columns supporting pointed archways. In the daylight, it would be magnificent; the windows all made of intricate stained glass. Now they were dark, the panes dull as dried blood. Some courtiers milled about the columns—couples, mostly, dancing around each other like circling predators and prey.

At the end of the long hall was a tall oak door bound in iron, cracked ajar, the sounds of music and conversation spilling out. Andry pulled it open, his smooth face set with determination. He met Corayne's eye as he waved her through, offering her the smallest nod.

"She'll listen," he murmured, an assurance to both of them.

For some reason, it calmed her nerves a little, enough to keep a tremor from her hands.

Dom followed, massive and looming, his cloak thrown back to show his fine tunic and broad form. More than a few courtiers eyed him with interest as they entered the great hall, a canyon of marble and glass and candlelight. But any interest the small band conjured was fleeting. Queen Erida's betrothal feast was well into its courses, the servants roving between tables with platters of roast meats and fresh summer vegetables. Dom dodged them all, dogged in his focus, his eyes flying to the curved wall at the far end of the room. Corayne did the same, looking up to a raised dais backed by vaulted windows and lion banners. Chandeliers dangled from the ceiling of the hall in two rows, their iron hoops as wide around as a carriage, hanging from chains of heavy link. There was a high table set with a long green runner embroidered in gold, a parade of silver plates and goblets marching the length of it. A dozen men and women sat in their raised seats, grinning and talking among themselves, most of them fair-skinned and pale-eyed. Even though Corayne had never seen her before, there was no mistaking who was the young queen.

Erida of Galland had been mentioned often in Corayne's ledger. Her fleets patrolled Mirror Bay and the Long Sea like lions over grassland, hunting pirates and smugglers, protecting their waters. But their captains were easy to bribe. Galland was an empire in all but name, fat and sated, its borders far-flung. Its interest lay mostly in growing wealth the easy way: through trade, tariffs, and subjugation. There were the escalating border skirmishes with Madrence, the Jydi raids every summer, but nothing to interrupt their long harvests and the passage of gold. Gallish merchant vessels were bloated, slow, easy prey. Corayne expected their queen to be the same.

She was sorely mistaken.

Erida was young, that much was true, with a lovely, gentle face and skin like a polished pearl. She did not speak to the people flanking her but listened intently as they jabbered in her ears. Her face was as still as the surface of a pond. The crown on her head was gold, as was the rest of her jewelry, set with every kind of gemstone, a rainbow of emerald, ruby, and sapphire. Beneath the chandeliers, her gown flared a deep, visceral blood red, cut in crimson and scarlet, vivid as a still-beating heart. Corayne would have expected more of that Gallish green, but perhaps red was tradition for weddings? Then Queen Erida caught her gaze, her eyes a piercing blue even across the hall. She tipped her head, staring as they approached, her focus darting from Corayne to Dom and then to Andry following close behind.

Erida stood quickly, waving back the knights at the base of the high table.

"Let them pass," she said, her voice light and musical. Giving no cause for concern.

The guards in their golden armor pressed back, allowing the trio enough room to approach. Corayne clenched her teeth, hoping Andry and Dom would do the talking. She didn't want to explain the realm's destruction in front of a feasting crowd.

Andry bowed quickly, nodding at several of the table occupants as well as the Queen's knights, before honoring the Queen herself. "Your Majesty," he said, bending low at the waist.

"Squire Trelland," she answered, inclining her own head. "I'm glad to see you feasting with us again, after so long in your mourning," the Queen said, clasping her hands together. "Will your mother be joining us? Lady Valeri is always welcome at my table."

Lady Valeri is halfway to the city docks by now, if not already on board a ship bound for Kasa, Corayne knew. They had sent her off less than an hour ago, tucked into a wheeled chair with two servants for the long journey.

Andry merely shook her head. "My mother is still not well enough for feasts, I'm afraid. But I have brought two more to your great hall, Your Majesty. You would do well to listen to what they have to say."

She did not hesitate, her courtly smile fixed in place. "Very well."

"Alone," Andry said, "in the privacy of your chambers. If it pleases you," he added hastily, bowing again.

The squire is court-raised, born behind the walls of a palace, Corayne surmised, hopeful. *He knows how to speak to nobles and royalty without losing some semblance of a spine.*

Again, Erida ran her eyes over Corayne and Dom, weighing them both. What she saw in them, Corayne could not say.

"Her Majesty cannot simply abandon her betrothal feast," said the nobleman at her side, his gaze cutting. "Her husband has not even been presented to the court yet."

"It can wait a matter of minutes, Cousin. Squire Trelland has no cause to lie, and I trust his judgment," Erida replied, turning a winning smile on him like a sunbeam. It did not reach her eyes. But the man set down his goblet and opened his mouth to argue.

"This is a matter of great urgency, Your Majesty," Corayne blurted out. She let every ounce of desperation and need rise in her face. And hope too, whatever there was in the corners of her mind. "Your kingdom depends on you. The *realm* depends on you."

"The realm," the Queen echoed, looking at Andry. The squire stared back, his face just as desperate, trying to communicate as much as he could without speaking. Between them, Dom kept his mouth firmly shut, though a vein stood out in his neck. Corayne worried he might explode or simply drag the Queen off if they wasted another minute on court posturing.

Erida perceived.

"Very well," she said, gathering her skirts. "Follow me."

No less than six guards in lion armor followed, peeling off in formation to flank the Queen as she led them away from the high table. There was some murmuring on the dais and through the great hall, but none of it seemed to bother Erida as she walked, her crown high and proud. Corayne could not help but let the hope inside her grow, a flower in sunlight. And yet there was cold in her still, pricking at her fingers and toes, like she'd been out in the winter rains too long. It was an odd sensation, difficult to ignore, begging to be heeded. She shoved her hands in her pockets, hoping to warm her them a little. Her fingers brushed against the charm from the old Jydi woman, bits of twig and polished bone.

They didn't go far, entering a passage behind the dais that led down a shallow stair. Doors branched off on either side, some open to show parlor rooms and dark fireplaces, shelves of books and long couches piled with cushions. Erida brought them to a round room, the base of another tower, its ceiling low and intricately carved. *More lions*, Corayne thought wearily. There were a few chairs, as well as a stout table, but no one bothered to sit.

The guards did not stay. Queen Erida waved them off with a quick brush of her hand and a pointed glance, gesturing to the door. They obeyed, leaving the Queen alone with a squire and two strangers.

She must trust Andry very much, Corayne thought. *Or be more foolish than I thought.*

"Well, you've come to talk about the Spindle," the Queen said sharply. Her face did not change, but her gentleness disappeared.

She was as stone, resolute, her brow sterner than her years suggested. "I've heard the tale twice over from Andry Trelland. I might as well hear it again from you."

Not a fool at all.

Dom raised his chin. "I am Domacridhan, a prince of Iona, what you call an Elder, son of Glorian Lost. Your knights answered the call of my aunt, the Monarch. I bore witness to their slaughter at the Spindle, and I saw the army brought forth from a burned realm," he said quickly, the words coming hard and fast. "All Trelland told you is true, and you will not waste another minute of whatever time we have left. I only hope it is not already too late to stop Taristan of Old Cor."

Corayne winced at the hot accusation in the Elder's words. Though Dom was an immortal prince, Erida was a queen, and they needed her aid more than any other. She braced herself for the inevitable: a denial and a dismissal.

It never came.

Erida nodded at Dom, her hands folded again. A ruby winked on her finger, big as a grape. "And you?" she asked, looking to Corayne with sapphire eyes. "Did you survive as well?"

"I was not there, Your Majesty," Corayne said. The sword was cold against her back, stealing the heat from her flesh. Part of her wanted to rip the Spindleblade off and give it away, to someone better suited to the task of saving the world. To Dom, to Erida, even to Andry.

The rest, the part she did not understand, the part that grew with every passing day, would never let the sword go.

"My father was at the Spindle," she said, trying to look somber for a man she'd never met. Erida's face fell a little. "Cortael of Old Cor. He was of Spindleblood, able to open—and close—any Spindle still in existence."

The Queen looked her over, eyes widening as she took Corayne in. *Does she see the Spindle in me, the tremor of something lost and distant? Do I look as different as I feel?*

"So it's your blood too, then," Erida said finally, steel in her voice. "You can do the same. *You* can fix this."

Corayne could only shrug. "That's the idea."

The tower room was round, made for pacing. The Queen did so slowly, like a philosopher in a library, searching for answers. A flush rose in her pale cheeks. "Taristan has an entire army, and while you three seem capable enough, I doubt you can face it alone."

"We cannot, Your Majesty," Corayne said. She wished she could show her, wished they had more proof than Dom's scarred face and Andry's story. "I've seen only shadows of it, but the shadows were enough."

"So the realm depends on me." Erida raised her chin, standing in profile against the low fire. Corayne thought of kings on a coin, their images worked in copper and gold. "My armies, my soldiers. My blood as much as your own."

"It does" was all Dom said.

Corayne shot him a withering glare, then dared a step forward, her cloak hanging loose around her shoulders. Up close, she and the Queen were of a similar height. But everything else could not have been more different. She was a pirate's daughter and Erida a ruling queen.

"If it helps," Corayne murmured, "one can hardly be expected to marry while fighting a war against hell itself."

The Queen's true smile was a small thing, one corner of her mouth turning upward. She loosed a single, knowing laugh. "I wish that were true," she said sadly, her shoulders drooping in resignation. "But my agreement is made. I'll need to go through with it, for better or worse."

"I'm sorry for doubting you, Andry, and for not acting sooner," Erida added, moving to address the squire. He did not gloat as most men did, and remained still when the Queen took his hands in her own. He looked disconcerted by her touch, as if he wanted to pull away. "Before, I could not believe it—I thought lying to the court was the best option—but with you three standing here . . ." She looked over them again and faltered, showing the girl beneath the crown. Frightened, alone, but brave to a fault. "I see the truth of it now."

"Thank you, Your Majesty," Andry whispered, slowly removing his hands.

She only nodded and clapped her palms together. At the sound, the door to the chamber flew open, her knights still waiting dutifully in the hall. "Well, let's get on with it," she sighed.

They followed her out, a row of strange ducklings behind a stranger duck. Corayne had to stop herself from bouncing as she walked. Though her uncle's army rose before her, with hell behind him, she felt lighter than ever, hopeful—*optimistic*, even. The Queen of Galland would help them fight. The largest army in the north was with them, and certainly more would follow. She had Dom to keep her safe, a queen on her side . . . every step away from Lemarta had been a leap into a life she'd never thought possible. Every moment was danger, excitement, freedom. Every morning brought a new horizon.

If only my mother could see me now, she thought.

"So, Spindleblood. A descendant of Old Cor."

The Queen fell in beside Corayne, the golden knights hemming them in.

She glanced at Erida and felt another burst of relief. "Don't remind me," Corayne muttered, drawing another laugh from the Queen.

"We don't choose what we're born to, Corayne," Erida replied. She touched the crown on her brow. "We can only walk the path put in front of us."

Corayne shook her head. The cold feeling snuck into her fingers again, sharper than before. "I'm not sure why my path had to involve the end of the world."

To her surprise, the Queen of Galland took her hand kindly, giving it a reassuring squeeze. Erida stared at her intently, as if looking into a deep pool.

"At least we're walking it together," she said, dropping her grip. "I believe in you, Corayne. Something about your eyes—I suppose it's your blood. The legacy you carry."

Corayne wished she had a mirror. Wished she could see what the Queen saw in her, what Dom saw in her father. Something in the fathomless black.

"I wouldn't know."

"It could be the sword too. The Spindleblade." Erida's eyes darted, looking to Corayne's hip and then her shoulders. She fixed on her cloak with a knowing smirk. Ahead, the door back to the great hall swung open, bathing them in a wash of noise. "You have it, don't you? I'm told we'll need it."

"I do," Corayne whispered as they walked through, side by side.

She felt Andry and Dom at their backs, and the knights in their golden armor. The army of the Ashlands and the hell of What Waits were far away, barely a wisp of memory. And her uncle was a shadow, a mountain on the horizon that need only be climbed.

We can do this.

Queen Erida ascended the dais with ease, accustomed to the eyes of a hundred courtiers. She raised a hand for silence and they obeyed, their conversations dying to soft murmurs through the cavernous hall. At the high table, her advisors jumped to their feet, allowing her to pass in her bloodred gown. She nodded in turn, wearing her cold court smile.

Corayne and the others stood to the side, with nowhere to sit and nowhere to go without causing a fuss. The knights did the same, at ease in a semicircle around them. Dom clasped his great hands behind his back. Andry stood tall, his eyes narrowed with focus as he watched the Queen settle her audience. His jaw tightened when she opened her mouth.

"My lords and ladies, I thank you for joining me this evening," Erida said, dipping her head gracefully. Her courtiers responded in kind. *They adore her,* Corayne knew. It was easy to see the love the Gallish court held for their young queen. *Will they love her tomorrow, when she sends their children to war against a madman and a devil?*

"I know my betrothal has been long in the making, perhaps

too long for some of you," the Queen continued. Behind her, a few members of her council exchanged knowing smirks and the edges of laughter. Erida took it well in stride. "But with the aid of my illustrious council, I have come to a decision, and upheld the will of my father, King Konrad, who built all you see before you." Erida put out one glittering hand and gestured to the vaulted ceiling, the columns, the great glass arches and rose windows of the hall. "His wish for me, and for Galland, was one we all share. We are Old Cor reborn, the glory of the realm, heirs to an empire we are destined to rebuild. With my husband at my side, I intend to fulfill that destiny."

Among the tables, several courtiers raised their goblets and drank deeply. A few cheered in agreement. Even her cousin, the surly nobleman, banged his fist on the high table.

Corayne felt the thud of it in her chest, like a war drum. Next to her, Andry flinched. There was sweat on his lip, an odd shallowness to his breath. Corayne furrowed her brow and put a hand to his wrist. His skin felt clammy and cold.

"Andry?" she whispered. "It's all right. Your mother needs you, and no one will blame you for leaving to protect her."

The squire drew a shaky breath, his lean chest rising and falling.

"I thought I heard—did she ask you about the Spindleblade?" he whispered.

Corayne frowned, confused. "Yes."

Andry took her hand without breaking his gaze, his eyes never leaving Erida's face. She felt a jolt as his fingers joined with her own. Then his lips pulled back, baring his even white teeth. It was not shame on his face, or regret.

Terror.

"I never told her about the sword," he breathed, sounding dazed.

Hot and cold leapt up inside Corayne, fire and ice, burning fear and frigid shock. She blanched, owl-eyed, unable to move, rooted to the spot. *Never told her about the sword.* It was still there, the length of steel running down her back, tucked beneath her cloak, digging uncomfortably between her shoulder blades. Forged in a lost realm, twin to her blood, the only other thing in the realm that could stop an apocalypse.

I never told her about the sword.

Dom gripped her shoulder, strong and desperate enough to hurt. She met his eyes quietly, slowly, and saw Andry's fear, her own fear, mirrored in the Elder prince. It was worse than on the hilltop, when the corpse shadows advanced, their swords raised, their jaws wide and hungry. *How can this be worse?* Corayne wanted to scream.

But she wasn't stupid.

She knew how.

The knights tightened their formation, boxing them in. There was nowhere to turn, nowhere to run. Corayne heard every clink of their armor, the rasp of their steel, as the Queen basked in the adoration of her court. Her voice rose, high and clear, echoing down the columns and archways. On the opposite side of the dais, a pair of silhouettes appeared, one of them tall and lean, the other swathed in a crimson cloak.

Dom's grasp broke with a huff of pain, and the Elder stumbled to a knee, a dagger poking from his side. His blood ran hot and scarlet, blooming from the wound as a knight stood over him, face stern beneath his helmet. Corayne opened her mouth to scream, only to feel the sharp poke of another dagger at her ribs, begging to slide between her bones. The knight behind her breathed heavily on her neck, close enough to cut her throat if he so desired.

"Keep quiet," he hissed. "Or I'll run you through."

She had a knife in her boot, the sword on her back.

Useless in my hands, Corayne thought, her mind screaming.

She could only stand, gasping through clenched teeth, watching Dom bleed as Erida beckoned to the silhouettes. The first stepped into the light with a roguish smile, a flowing gait, and the proud arrogance of a conqueror.

"It is with great pleasure that I introduce you to my prince consort, my husband, a son of Old Cor, heir to the bloodlines of the ancient empire, and father to the new world before us," Erida said. Her gentle face was angelic. "Prince Taristan of Old Cor."

The court rose to applaud their queen's chosen, the high table already standing and calling their praises. The roar crashed like a wave, beating Corayne down and down and down, drowning her, pinning her, dragging her away from all hope of rescue.

There he is.

Her flesh and blood. Her father's twin. Her monster.

Hair like dark copper, the shadow of a beard, a thin mouth unsuited to smiles. Long nose, a brow like a rod of iron. A handsome face, all things considered: a fine doll for evil strings. Taristan of Old Cor, a Spindleblood prince, a traitor to the realm entire.

He barely acknowledged the court, offering only a single, sharp glance before he looked at the Elder kneeling, the squire, and Corayne.

The yards between them disappeared. His eyes were her own, black and endless, a sky without stars, the deepest part of the ocean. They were not empty: there was something in them, a presence Corayne could barely sense. But she knew it too. She saw it in her dreams. Red and hungry, without form, without mercy.

What Waits.

He stared out from her uncle's eyes, waiting to strike.

The man who followed Taristan could only be the Red. The wizard looked skeletal, white-skinned and blond-haired, with pale red eyes ringed with pink flesh. His mouth opened a little and he inhaled, tasting the air. She felt a clawing heat pull over her, prodding at her exposed skin.

Toasts were called out, goblets raised again, but Corayne heard none of it. She was frozen, caught between the knight's dagger and her uncle's starving glare. He looked ready to eat her whole.

He very well might.

His steps were deliberate and smooth, taking him down the table, one hand extended to his queen's advisors. They touched his rough fingers or kissed his knuckles, pledging allegiance, paying fealty, congratulating him on the good match. Only the Queen's cousin hesitated, waiting a long moment before taking Taristan's hand.

Taristan's eyes never left Corayne's face. A thread ran between them, a rope from his hands to her neck. He pulled himself along it, closer and closer, until Corayne could hardly breathe.

She trembled when he stopped before her, glaring down with menace. Over his shoulder, Erida watched, her head held high. There was no fear in her, no shock. No regret.

Taristan raised his fist and Corayne braced herself for a strike, curling inward.

Instead he gripped her cloak, tearing it away with the easy rip of blue cloth.

Out of the corner of her eye, Corayne saw the sword hilt flash in the light, its jewels aflame. She tried to back away, only to feel the knight's dagger pierce her clothing, nearly breaking the skin. There was nowhere to hide.

"Get away from me," she managed to bite out.

On the floor, still bleeding, Dom seethed. "I'll kill you," he growled at Taristan, one hand pressed to his side. Even though three knights stood above him, hands on their swords, armored to the teeth, Corayne believed he would try.

"So eager to repeat your mistakes, Domacridhan," Taristan said wearily. Then he seized Corayne by the neck, his back obscuring her from the rest of the court. To anyone watching, it would seem he was merely speaking to a few guests, one of them kneeling in reverence. They were too busy in their revels to notice anything amiss. "Shall I kill her in front of you too?"

He smiled into her face. Corayne wanted to spit, to struggle, but found her mouth dry and her mind blank of any options. This was not in her charts or lists. There was no preparing for this moment. They'd thought the Queen might not believe them, but to choose the other side? To choose *him*?

I have no plan for the path in front of me.

"Get away," she said again, her hands balling into fists. While the heat of the Red's power washed over her, her hands and feet remained cold, nearly frozen, the sensation creeping over her wrists and ankles.

Taristan only shook his head, reaching for the sword. His grip tightened on her throat, while his other hand closed around the hilt of the Spindleblade. He grinned when he touched it.

"That doesn't belong to you," he murmured, his breath oddly sweet in her face.

Something broke inside her, snapping clean. A rush of cold pushed away the heat, and with it, Corayne slipped her hand in her pocket. Something tugged her fingers along, guiding them to the Jydi charm, the useless trinket. It felt frozen, hard as ice, the twigs honed to keen points.

She had never been so afraid.

With a will, she looked into Taristan's eyes. She saw flecks of crimson in them, scattered like blood around the iris. They seemed to dance as he gripped the sword, pulling the first inches from the sheath. He was not watching her, but the steel, his lips moving without sound as he read the unfathomable runes on the blade.

The Jydi twigs dragged along his face like a clutch of needles, their bite blue and ferocious, clawing ragged lines down his cheek. He howled, leaping back, and the sword slid back into place. Corayne expected to feel the dagger between her ribs, sliding clean through her organs, but it never came.

Instead the knight behind her let loose a strangled yelp, blood spurting from beneath the golden gorget covering his throat. Dom launched to his feet, striking between the other knights. Andry twisted, managing to break the grip of his captor with a few fluid motions born of both surprise and skill. Together they cut a hole in the Queen's guard, even while the hall exploded in confusion and chaos.

The Queen shouted something; Taristan fought to his feet; the Red swept across the dais like a scarlet cloud of thunder, his hands raised and mouth forming a spell. Corayne nearly fainted in shock, her knees threatening to give out, as someone grabbed her around the middle, dragging her backward.

"Run, gods damn you, *run!*" a woman's voice said, hissing and familiar.

Corayne could barely breathe, but she found the will to move, lunging over the flagstones. The charm was still in her hand, the twigs no longer cold, their broken ends dripping with blood too dark for mortal veins.

Someone shoved her through the door at the side of the dais, urging her onward.

She looked back to see a flood of guards, their swords drawn, cloaks cast aside. *No use running,* Corayne thought dimly. *I might as well just sit down and wait.*

Then there was a noise like a thunderclap, followed by the shrieking scream of flowing chain, iron links sliding through their rings at breakneck speed. One of the many chandeliers of the great hall crashed down, the circle of it crushing a few men in their armor. It was not the last to fall. The chains loosed in succession, like a ripple on a pond, each hoop of iron and flame landing in a cloud of dust, breaking tables and limbs in equal measure. *Boom, boom, boom*—another beat of the war drum. One fell onto the dais, slamming down through the high table, cracking it in two. Corayne looked for a crimson dress, a jeweled crown, a wolf disguised as a queen, but Andry pulled her further into the passage, obstructing her view.

Sorasa Sarn was the last through the door, barring it behind her, shutting out the great hall. Her eyes were wide, manic, as she took them in, looking from Dom's wound to Corayne to Andry's flushed and panting face. The dagger in her hand dripped scarlet.

"Do I have to do everything around here?" she snarled.

16

GOOD BUSINESS
Sorasa

The gold was heavy in its pouch, lashed to her thigh beneath her leggings. The coins lay flat against each other, silent despite their number. Any assassin who could be betrayed by the clink of coin wasn't worth it in the first place, and Sorasa Sarn was worth every piece. The Elder gold would go far indeed, funding travel to any corner of the Ward. *If Galland is going to war with hell, I want to be far away.*

She gritted her teeth, trying to forget the acrid smell of burned flesh and rot and broken realms. *Saving the world is not the work of assassins*, she told herself. *Just move on, Sarn.*

It took no time to pick a lock and find new clothing in an empty apartment. She discarded her cloak and tunic in exchange for a berry-red gown edged in gold and silver thread. It was too loose, but well suited for hiding her sword, daggers, and coiled whip. She kept her leather leggings and boots too, concealed beneath the flowing skirts. With her hair unbound, she could still pass as a ladies' maid, if not a foreign noblewoman visiting from the south. They were easy masks to slip behind, and she wore them well.

She passed the maids with their baskets of roses, crimson in the torchlight. They scuttled by, complaining of thorns and the Queen's wedding.

Tonight, it was not opportunity that called Sorasa Sarn, but grim curiosity.

Even at the citadel, protected by sea cliffs and desert, the Amhara were well informed on the doings of the world. Queen Erida was well known, as were her many rejected suitors. Princes, warlords, rich land barons, and poor heirs. None were worthy of the Gallish queen.

But someone is today.

Sorasa's footsteps slowed, hesitating at a crossing of passages. The great hall was ahead, but the servants' wing was to the left, its hallways narrow and winding, a warren of storerooms, sleeping quarters, kitchens, cellars, a brewery, a buttery, a laundry, and a bakehouse. Not to mention its own gate, dock, and bridge to the rest of the city.

The decision took only a moment.

The residence, great hall, and east wing were newborn, a riot of vaulted archways, soaring stonework, and stained glass completed only in the last decade. They were magnificent, beautiful, and woefully vulnerable, built for style rather than safety. A dozen alcoves and balconies made Sorasa's path even easier. She moved on, chin high before servants and eyes low before guards, her manner shifting from lady to maid and back again in fluid rhythm. As always, she was surprised by how easy it was to pass through a palace unaccosted, without question or even a curious glance.

No wonder so many women served the Guild. *The Amhara has great need for those who can pass unseen, and who is more unseen to men than a woman?*

A long passage ran the southern length of the great hall, connecting the east wing to the keep with a row of lion-faced columns, some stoic, some snarling, each regal as a king. The doorways between the columns to her right were open, flung wide to show the great hall in all its splendor. A knight stood in each, facing outward, eyes dull as Sorasa walked past. Queen Erida's late father had spared no expense in his palace, crowning his high table with a curved wall of windows brilliant as jewels. Green silk and velvet dominated the crowd of courtiers, each in competition to be more verdant than the last. One idiot appeared to be wearing a lion's mane as a collar. By Sorasa's glancing count, more than two hundred nobleborn men and women feasted, shouting toasts to the Queen and her betrothed. He was not on the raised dais yet, if the empty chair by the Queen was any indication. Erida was impossible to ignore at the center of her high table, her gown red as a polished ruby, her face moon white. A marvelously simple target for any inclined to send Galland into a succession crisis.

Not my job, not my problem, Sorasa thought, eyeing the knights again.

She turned a corner, edging along the banquet, half listening to chattering voices. She set to climbing, ascending steps to a gallery above.

It ringed the great hall in a wide balcony, open to below, and was blissfully empty of roving courtiers. The chandeliers, great hoops of iron, hung level with the gallery, on heavy chains strung along the double-vaulted ceiling, the links bolted at each end of the hall.

The feast unfurled below her in all its glory. Pale faces passed from table to table, bending together to whisper or shout, some dancing, some eating, all drinking their fill. Sorasa had seen many royal courts in her years, from Rhashir to Calidon, and though the languages and customs varied, the people were the same, easy to predict. Most would be wondering about the Queen's betrothed too.

Does Mercury know? Sorasa thought, settling into the shadows of the gallery.

He would be back at the citadel, gray hair falling around him, sitting in his old chair, at the center of a thousand threads pulled from every corner of the Ward. Letters and birds and spies, whispers and codes.

The master of the Amhara sees every piece of the great puzzle, while the rest of us blindly feel for edges.

Her lip curled with distaste. Mercury's leash always chafed, even when she enjoyed his favor, hating and loving his attention at the same time.

The minutes flowed like water. She had learned patience in the cells of the citadel, as a child all but vibrating out of her skin with nervous energy. That energy was trained from her quickly, after a night in darkness with nothing but a Rhashiran armory lizard for company. More than ten feet long, with jaws to rival a wolf, the armory was deadly but near blind. Standing still was a child's only defense against being eaten alive. It was nothing to stand still now, with only knights and drunken courtiers to mind.

Indeed, she counted no less than six spilled goblets of wine, three platters smashed, and one old man snoring into his plate of summer greens. The rest chattered and drank, even at the high table. Sorasa recognized the man at the Queen's side as her elder cousin Lord Konegin. *How much would the Queen pay to know that he offered the Amhara a king's ransom to kill her?* she wondered, smirking. *Or that the old woman on her council bought off the contract with enough gold to sink a war galley?*

The hall grew more raucous with every passing course and passed flagon of wine. *Soon her court will be too drunk to remember who she picked.*

A flicker of movement caught her eye, not below, but across, on the other side of the gallery, on the balcony opposite her own. It was shadowed as well, seemingly empty but for two faces at the edge of the light. She squinted and raised a hand, covering the chandeliers, allowing her eyes to adjust for the darkness the figures stood in.

One had the bearing of a soldier, straight-backed and trim, a hand resting on his hip where Sorasa could just see the hilt of a fine sword. His cloak was black, left open to show a doublet of purple velvet patterned like scales. His face was bowed, his focus on the high table, showing only the glint of dark red hair. The other was a priest, hooded in crimson. Judging by his colors, he was a dedicant of Syrek. The god of destruction and creation, conquest and peace. A patron of the kingdom of Galland, whose rulers supposed themselves conquerors and creators.

Neither man took any notice of her, distracted as the rest of the palace by the mystery about to unfold. They filled her with an icy touch of dread and gut instinct. They didn't speak, though the soldier shifted, and his fingers clenched and unclenched on his sword hilt. *Impatient.* Not like the priest, who was a statue in scarlet, his face bone-white beneath his hood.

The dedicant orders serve their gods and their high priests, not kings or queens. He listens for another, gathering word to be passed on, Sorasa surmised, looking over the priest again. *But the soldier? Who does he serve?*

He did not have the bearing of a noble. He was not a knight or a great lord, and no diplomat would spend a feast hidden away. But he wasn't a palace guard either, not in those clothes, without armor or the lion emblazoned on his chest.

She kept her eyes on him as she moved, careful in the shadows, her steps muffled by the rich carpet along the gallery floor. *Perhaps he is a spy,* she thought. *An assassin from the Amhara, or from another guild.* Her eyes dragged over him again. He was tall and lean, with wiry muscles standing out at his neck, the kind earned hard, through necessity. *He could be a simple cutthroat, hired in some gutter. A mad dog set loose.*

Her concentration snapped away at a commotion below, three figures striding between the long banquet tables, set shoulder to shoulder. Two she recognized.

So they found their squire.

The Queen waved her knights off, allowing the three to approach her table. Sorasa wished she could hear their plea, absurd as it would be. *Dom the walking storm cloud, Corayne and her flickering courage.* "*Your Majesty, we need your help to defeat an army of demons led by my mad uncle. Yes, I'm the only one who can stop him. Yes, I'm a seventeen-year-old girl. Yes, I'm perfectly serious.*"

But Erida did not turn them away. Instead the Queen beckoned, her face gentle and open, so they could speak privately of the Ward's fate. *Tell her of the corpses on the hill,* Sorasa thought, remembering her blade as it passed through them. *Tell her of the slaughter. Tell her of your scars, Domacridhan.*

"Domacridhan."

The soldier hissed, the sound carrying down the gallery. His voice was venom.

Sorasa pressed back against a column, folding herself into the shadows.

The soldier was glaring down at the Elder, and then at Corayne, before raising his face to the light. His eyes, black and familiar, seemed to glint red, a trick of the chandeliers.

Bits of thread joined in her mind, weaving a picture and a realization. Reality slotted together like plates in a good suit of armor.

Every instinct Sorasa Sarn had ever earned lit on fire, scorching her with warning.

The first, the strongest, screamed.

RUN.

"Look at his face, Ronin," the soldier murmured to the priest, who did not move. *He is no priest, at least not to any god of the Ward.* "I thought Elders were supposed to heal."

"They do. When cut by weapons of the Ward," Red Ronin replied. The wizard folded his hands into his robes. "But a

Spindleblade? The weapons of the Ashlands, of Asunder, blessed by What Waits? Those wounds are not so easily closed. It's why the Elders remain in their enclaves, cowering, even when the prince survived to tell the tale of us. They see what we can do. They fear *us* more than any mortal army upon the Ward."

Sorasa did not dare another step closer. Her hands worked beneath her skirt, pulling out a small dagger. She cut quietly along the sides of her gown, giving herself more room to move.

Run her instincts howled again. She could already feel the palace closing in, stone and glass, silk and wine. *Fuck the Elder and the girl and the squire. Fuck the Ward.*

"She looks like me," Taristan said sharply. He watched as Corayne disappeared from the hall, following the Queen and her knights through a side door. "Like my brother."

At least Dom is with her, Sorasa thought again, her teeth clenching together. *Six knights against an Elder. Good odds. He's survived worse.* Her heartbeat raced. *Unless he doesn't. And then it's just the squire, a boy. She's as good as dead.*

And the Ward as good as destroyed.

Frustration ate at her fear, warring for dominance. *This was not in the contract,* she snarled to herself, wishing she could scream. Wishing she could flee. *But where? Not home, not even to the citadel. What Waits will devour them both, with Taristan at his side, fists to his fangs.*

"I must say, I'm still shocked she agreed to this."

Taristan's voice grew closer, his steps quiet, but thunderous to Sorasa's ears. He tapped the hilt of his sword, clinking a single ring against the metal like a small, hateful bell.

She sank, bending her knees, shifting her weight to the balls of her feet. *I can sprint for the stairs, vault over the gallery, break my fall on a nobleman's head.* Her options spun.

The Spindlerotten traitor and his pet wizard closed the distance at a steady, almost lazy pace. "Ambition is in her blood," Ronin answered serenely.

His voice took on an odd quality: another layer of sound, as if someone else spoke with him, forming a deeper harmony. It echoed, even when the wizard fell silent.

"It's good we reached her first, before the other could."

"A choice we did not need to make," Taristan scoffed. "I see no witch with my niece."

The wizard's robes hissed over the carpet like a snake. The double voice was gone, leaving only his own. "Even so, we have a strong ally in the Queen of Galland. Corayne of Old Cor will be dead soon, and of no consequence any longer."

Sorasa took her chance, peering around her column with one narrowed eye. The pair stood at another stairwell, the steps leading down into the great hall. Taristan looked back at the chandeliers, light splaying across his hard features. *She does look like him.*

"If she has my brother's blade, we need only take it and lock her away," Taristan said, again tapping his sword. The sheath was silver-and-black leather, the steel hidden while jewels flared at the hilt, red as ticks swollen with blood.

Ronin shrugged. "To die when What Waits comes and sets this world to ash beneath your feet?" he said, guiding Taristan through the arch. "Trust me, my friend, dying now is a mercy to her. As for the Elder, let him live, let him *watch* . . ."

Their cruel laughter echoed with every step down the curling stairwell.

Run run run run.

Sorasa allowed herself five more seconds of fear and indecision. Five only.

Her breath hissed through her nose, coming out hard between her teeth. *One.* Taristan was the Queen's chosen. *Two.* Her army would protect his Spindle, the passage spewing a sea of corpses. *Three.* No kingdom could stand against Taristan and Erida, not alone. *Four.* Sorasa Sarn was no one. There was nothing she could do about the great dealings of the world. *Five.*

She stood and moved quickly, a cat among the columns, before dropping to her knees at the end of the gallery. Below was the high table. Across was the doorway, set ajar, leading off to wherever the Queen and Corayne had gone.

There is something I can do.

The gown tore again as she cut a square from the wine-colored cloth. She'd exhausted her common powders back in Byllskos, but the black remained, tucked at her belt in its triple-wrapped packet, a square smaller than her palm. With careful hands, she tore it open, sprinkling small, dark grains onto the center of torn fabric. The writing on the packet was nearly worn away, the language of Isheida barely recognizable. *Worth five times its weight in gold.*

She made a pouch, tying the corners together tightly, but careful to leave one length of cloth free. She hoped it was long enough. She hoped it was short enough.

Below, she watched two knights emerge ahead of Corayne and the Queen, and then Dom and the lanky squire, flanked by the remaining four knights. Sorasa looked at Dom first, searching his face for any sign of worry, any indication he knew what was coming.

She nearly cursed aloud. *Of course he doesn't.*

"I know my betrothal has been long in the making, perhaps too long for some of you," Queen Erida said below, and her court laughed like hyenas.

There were no candles within reach, not even the chandeliers, so Sorasa made do with a corner of flint and the steel of her dagger, striking them together to produce a spray of sparks.

The cloth caught light, the edge burning.

She did not have time to fear losing a hand or worry about being seen. She thought only of her aim. The weight of the pouch, the flame traveling steadily up the dangling fabric. The thickness of the chain fixed to the wall beyond the balcony rail, a metal plate set deep into the smooth stone. The iron links traveled up at an angle, through the first great ring, then down to a chandelier, and up again. Again, again, again, the chain like a necklace strung with jewels.

She leaned and swung her arm, all her focus in the tips of her fingers as the cloth left her hand. She refused to imagine failure— the flame snuffing out, the powder spilling, the pouch missing its mark. Below, the Queen wheeled in her bloodred gown and she tossed the bundle. It moved in a slow arc, rising as falling until it hit the chain and the wall, tipping, the flaming lead trailing, fabric crumbling to smoke and ash. And then it stuck home, lodged perfectly, wedged between the links of the great chain and the stone wall.

Her steps were light and fast, carrying her back around the horseshoe of the gallery. When the knights tightened their formation, obscuring Dom and Corayne from view, she felt the familiar twist of defeat. *Do they already know? Do they feel the noose around their necks? Corayne must. She's not an idiot.*

Erida's voice echoed up the stairwell, rising to meet Sorasa as she spiraled down. "It is with great pleasure that I introduce you to my prince consort, my husband, a son of Old Cor, heir to the bloodlines of the ancient empire, and father to the new world before us." More applause and congratulations rippled through the great hall, cresting like a wave. "Prince Taristan of Old Cor."

Now, Sorasa thought, bending her will to the pouch lying in wait. As if she were a witch or wizard too, Spindletouched, and not just a mortal woman with a talent for killing things. *Now,* she pleaded, begging to Lasreen the Morning Star, to Syrek, to Immor, to Meira of the Waters, to every god and goddess worshipped upon the Ward.

They did not answer.

She slowed at the bottom of the stairs, easing her pace so as not to be noticed. Her eyes darted, drinking in the scene, hunting for any opportunity, no matter how small. All around, courtiers stood and clapped, calling out to their dear young queen. Sorasa grabbed a silver flagon of wine from the closest table, using it as a shield to move closer to the dais, never blinking.

Dom was on his knees, his fingers uncurling and curling into a shaking fist, as knights held his shoulders. The courtiers could not see that he was wounded, kneeling in pain, not in deference to the Queen or her betrothed. His expression had not changed, his face dour, lips pulled into their usual grimace, but Sorasa saw the tightness in him plain as day. *He is in great pain.* Corayne was equally trapped, a single knight too close to her, a gauntleted fist tucked up against her side, certainly holding a knife. The sunborn daughter of Siscaria was white as a ghost, her eyes wide, staring past the far side of the dais, past the high table, past the Queen.

Sorasa didn't need to look to know who she gaped at.

Taristan stalked across the dais at an easy pace, content in his victory. He leered with a crescent-moon smile as he stood over Corayne and tore her old blue cloak away. The sword on her back mirrored his own, a twin. The other Spindleblade.

The squire did have it—and now Taristan will too.

The Elder hissed something Sorasa could not hear, but she saw the lightning bolt of rage cross his face. Taristan muttered in return, amused, before putting his back to the court, his tall frame blocking Corayne completely.

The dagger tucked against Sorasa's wrist, eager and waiting. Her sword stayed beneath her slashed skirts, too conspicuous to draw yet. *Now now now now,* she prayed, cursing herself for having cut so long a wick. The pouch was still in place, the smallest spark still climbing. Sorasa quickened her pace, coming within feet of the high table, the wine still in hand. The knights didn't notice another maid, even one with torn skirts. *Nearly there.*

A howl split the great hall. Taristan fell back from Corayne, clutching one side of his face, blood welling between his fingers. His wizard bolted forward over the dais, mouth moving fervently, shouting a prayer or a spell or both.

Sorasa heard none of it; the world narrowed in her eyes. It was time to act.

She painted Lionguard armor red.

Wine for the closest, the flagon catching him hard in the chest. It spilled all over him as she pretended to trip, nothing more than a clumsy servant. Her sudden, deliberate weight made him stumble, and she was by him, blade close, focused on the knight above Corayne. His arm drew back, the glint of the knife keen and cold at the girl's ribs. Sorasa's was faster, jabbing between the joints of his armor, finding home in the veins of his neck. He sputtered and fell, grasping his neck, dripping crimson all over himself. It poured hot and wet over Sorasa's hands even as she grabbed for Corayne. The girl was frozen, an odd scrap in her grasp, her legs unmoving, body like lead.

If I have to drag this girl all the way to the docks, I swear to Lasreen . . .

"Run, gods damn you, *run!*" Sorasa snarled, throwing her sideways into a sudden gap in the wall of knights. Three more were sprawled on the floor. Dom stood over them, a dagger protruding from his side, a swath of blood staining his tunic and trousers, dripping to his boots.

Sorasa saw their predicament as an equation, her mind reducing to battle and circumstance, as she had been trained. *Three on the floor, one still stumbling with the wine, this one dead.* She vaulted over the knight choking on his blood, running after Corayne. She hoped Dom and the squire were smart enough to follow. Taristan and Erida's knights certainly would.

The rumble of an explosion set a rare smile to her lips, which widened with the sound of running chain. She paused at the passage door to glimpse the chaos. The chandeliers fell in succession, each one a hammer, splintering tables, sending plates and bodies flying. Courtiers tried to dodge, leaping over each other, while the dais dissolved quickly, the Queen's advisors fleeing in all directions. Taristan fought to his feet, caught in the melee, one side of his face jagged with cuts, while Red Ronin cursed at the vaulted ceiling. The Queen found herself prisoner to her own knights, the Lionguard shielding her from debris.

The Elder passed Sorasa first, his face a white sheet. Then came the squire, Trelland. Sorasa added them to her count.

Four alive.

She drew a long, ragged breath. *Run*, her instincts said, only a whisper now.

It was easy to ignore.

She drew the door shut and barred it with a heavy *thunk* of wood. In the great hall, the chandeliers continued to fall, thunderous. Her own heart beat in time, a steady rhythm. The danger fed something in her, enough to quell any fear for now.

The other three did not share the sentiment. Corayne reached back to check her sword, her fingers shaking horribly, her eyes wide as dinner plates, black ringed by stark white. The Spindleblade was still there like a gash down her back, comical in size compared to her small body. Dom leaned against the wall beside her, his lips in his teeth, one hand testing the dagger still buried in his side. Only the squire seemed to be of any use. He ripped his blue-and-gray coat into rags, holding them against Dom's wound.

"Do I have to do everything around here?" Sorasa said, wiping her dagger clean. The red ending of the knight's life disappeared with a few quick drags. She glanced down the long passage of branching rooms, antechambers of sorts for the Queen and her council.

Corayne looked through her, as if the assassin were nothing at all.

"That door won't hold," she murmured, stepping back. Already someone was banging on the other side. Many someones. It jumped on its hinges, straining against the bar. "She's with him. The Queen is with *him*."

"Thank you. I also have eyes," Sorasa bit out. "Can you run, Elder?"

His left side was painted crimson. He only grimaced. There was blood in his beard too, turning the golden hair red. "It's nothing," he said, and batted Trelland away. "The Vedera heal quickly."

"Don't—" Sorasa began, lunging for him.

But the godsforsaken imbecile of an immortal was well past stopping. He drew out the knife in a single motion and tossed it away, smearing blood across the floor. More sprang from the wound in his ribs, gushing like a fountain, and he faltered, hissing, dropping to a knee.

"Oh," he gasped as he fell.

Corayne caught him, slipping in the puddle of immortal blood. "For Spindles' sake!"

The copper tang was sharp on Sorasa's tongue as she pushed the Elder to the floor.

"I can't imagine living for a thousand years and still being so stupid," she said, tearing his tunic at the wound. "It's almost an accomplishment."

"Five hundred," Dom hissed through gritted teeth, as if it made any difference.

"Immortal or not, you are still very capable of *bleeding* to death."

Somehow, he seemed surprised by the possibility.

Sorasa ignored him so she wouldn't kill him herself. Instead she ripped and ripped his clothing, grabbing for anything that could be a bandage. Trelland offered his rags and she crammed them into the gaping hole, his ribs glossy white between hard red muscles. At least Dom didn't flinch as she plugged him up like a bucket with a leak.

"Any more brilliant ideas, Elder?"

He was on his feet quicker than she would have thought possible, standing over her in his tattered clothes, chest bare to the torchlight of the hall. His skin was like his bones, gleaming and pale.

"Run," he rattled.

"We won't make it back the way we came in. And the kitchen bridge, the Bridge of Valor, the garrison docks . . ." Sorasa faltered, ticking off every path, every escape route she knew. Each one shuttered before her eyes. "I can get myself out of here, but not the rest of you."

"Well, that's helpful," Corayne snapped.

The door banged again as something large and heavy collided with the wood. Probably a table being used as a battering ram. It wouldn't be long until the door fell, or Erida's guards approached from the other side. They had minutes, maybe.

Seconds.

Trelland crossed to the windows, looking out into manicured gardens. Torches leapt up all over as guards were roused and dispatched. A maze stood beyond the green lawns, shadowed in its spirals, a labyrinthine design of hedges. The palace cathedral sneered over it, proud and daunting, a grand wonder. Its columns arched like a rib cage. The squire's face tightened.

"We should try Syrekom," he said in a low voice.

"The cathedral?" Sorasa scoffed. The knight's blood and Dom's dried on her face and hands, crusting over. There was no difference between them, mortal and immortal. They tasted the same. "Claiming sanctuary only works in the stories, Squire. This isn't one of them."

A few knights were in the gardens, their torches bobbing, but none entered the maze. Sorasa tried to remember Syrekom Cathedral beyond it, a monster of gray marble and glass, a crown jewel of Ascal, built to honor their greatest and most terrible god.

"Syrekom," Trelland said again, firmer this time.

His hand twitched, reaching for a sword that was not there. He had no armor, not even a knife that Sorasa could see. Only his trousers and torn coat, a bit short at the wrists. He was still growing, a boy even now, after all he'd seen. *But he does not sound like a boy now.*

"I'll take us through the maze and then . . ." His gaze hooked on Dom's blood. "I hope you can all swim."

Sorasa eyed Dom. His breath came in short, beleaguered gasps. He glared back at her.

"I learned to swim before your bloodline began," he growled, setting off with a stormy glare and a furious pace. She almost expected him to walk straight through a wall. Instead he kicked a door open, leaving it dangling on gold hinges.

Maybe he'll drown, Sorasa thought idly, half a wish.

17

FOR THE REALM
Andry

The New Palace had been a home, a sanctuary, a school, a training yard. Now it was a prison, a hunting ground, an executioner's block.

Andry felt the ax hanging over his head as he led the others into the maze, sprinting as fast as his long legs would carry him. In the barracks, he'd learned to run in armor. It had made him strong in steel, and even faster without it. But he felt bare now, vulnerable. *I don't even have a knife*, he thought in frustration. Not that he could blame himself. How could he have expected Erida to turn on them, on him, on the *Ward*?

But she didn't turn tonight, he told himself. His body shook all over, unmoored as the realization swept him out to sea. *She's already been against us, for gods know how long.*

She's been with him, Lord Cortael's twin. That rogue bastard.

The curse smarted in his head. Andry Trelland didn't care for foul language, even running for his life.

Shouts rose all over the palace grounds, and torches flared through the gardens as the Queen's knights gave chase. But they only existed on the edges of his mind. To Andry, there was only the maze—and his mother.

At Wayfarer's Port by now, he told himself. It felt like a prayer waiting to be answered. *On a ship already, safe with her carers, tucked into her chair. Sails raised, with a captain bound for her home.* His heart tore inside him as he pictured Valeri Trelland at the rail of a ship, waiting for her son. *I should have gone with her. This is no place for me.* The maze pressed in, the rows perfectly manicured, not a leaf out of place. He wanted to burn it all to ashes. *I just need to get off this island. That's all I have to do. Get out of the palace, and get to the docks.* He breathed hard, in through his nose, out through his teeth. *Get off the island. Get to the docks.*

Corayne panted next to him, fighting to keep up. Back in the apartments, she had not seemed so small, but now, with the sword on her back, with the world on her shoulders, Andry thought she might fade into nothing. Only her eyes were unchanged, somehow blacker than the sky above them. She looked back into the maze, trying to see through the hedges as they spiraled. Lord Domacridhan and the Ibalet woman kept up behind them.

A horn blast echoed and Andry flinched. The sound, heavy and proud, sent a shudder through the air.

"What was that?" Corayne asked, breathless. The horn sounded again.

"The palace garrison," he replied, quickening his pace. His jaw set painfully.

He'd never seen the garrison summoned before, not for battle. As a boy, he'd always wished for them to be called forth in their armored splendor, to defend the Queen and her court. *Well, I suppose I'll get to see it now.*

Domacridhan limped, forcing each step, one hand pressed against his ribs. Blood welled between his fingers, black in the dim light. *The last time I saw him, he was being swallowed by corpses,* Andry thought. *He survived the temple—certainly he can survive this.*

The Ibalet woman shoved the Elder onward when he flagged, her teeth bared. "How many in the garrison, Trelland?" she called, her voice sharp with worry.

Though chivalry and etiquette demanded it, Andry doubted asking for the lady's name would be wise under the circumstances. "Two hundred. Enough to withstand a siege."

"I'm flattered," the woman answered.

Two hundred soldiers. Two hundred swords. Two hundred shields. Two hundred men I've known and trained with, seen every day in the barracks. Two hundred oathed and sworn, loyal to the Queen, to Galland, to the Lion. Andry did not doubt their resolve, even the ones he counted as friends. *They'll kill me the same as any other enemy. It's what they were trained for.*

And I would do the same, in their place.

"This way," he hissed, angling his body for what looked like a solid wall of leaves. He slipped easily through the hidden gap in the hedges.

Where the rest of the maze was artistry, with stone pathways and gurgling fountains, this was narrow and scratching, unattended, barely a dirt trail between the towering plants on either side. It was an open secret. Many of the squires, knights, court ladies, and even some royals, brought companions here for a few moments away from prying eyes.

The wind blew cold, sending shivers over Andry's exposed skin. He gritted his teeth, bracing for the voice that came with the cold, the whispers old and young. The voice he could hardly remember and never forget.

The road runs in one direction, dutiful squire, the voice groaned, splintering.

Andry growled low in his throat as the whispers shattered in his head. He staggered, losing speed but fighting onward.

"Are you all right?" he heard Corayne call, but the whispers gobbled her voice up.

Burn the life behind you, save the realm from the fire.

And then the voice was gone again, receding with the wind, falling to nothing as the shouting outside the maze grew. The spire of Syrekom Cathedral rose ahead, its arches taunting. The shouting grew, and flames flickered in the leaves, bleeding through from pathways, closing in.

Corayne still watched him intently, slowing her pace to match. She reached out with a tentative hand. Without thought, Andry took it, her fingers warm in his own.

"It's nothing," he said, his breath coming in uneasy pants. "I'm fine."

There was a moan behind them as Dom faltered again, falling to a knee. The woman growled a curse in her own language.

290   REALM BREAKER

"Keep going!" she called to them before either could break stride.

Corayne turned to look back, but Andry tugged her on. "They'll catch up," he said, his grip tight. *Was that a lie?* he wondered. *Does it even matter anymore?*

The hedge shadows were tall and strange, wavering between starlight and torchlight, white and red. One of them lurched, coming alive. A broad silhouette stumbled out onto the trail, his fine red-and-silver surcoat stained with wine.

"Look at you, Trelland," Lemon crowed, swaying on his feet. He leered, his face ruddy and sweating. A goblet gleamed in his hand. He waved it between Andry and Corayne, spilling dark red liquid. "Bringing a girl down the paths. I didn't know you had it in you!"

Andry dropped Corayne's hand and tried to push her by the other squire. His palm brushed up against the sheath of the Spindleblade. It felt cold as ice.

"Good night, Lemon," he gritted out. *Best to slip around him, leaving him spinning in the dark.* "Enjoy the rest of the feast."

"Have a drink with me, Brother," Lemon slurred. He caught Andry around the neck. "And introduce me to your maiden," he added, putting out his other arm to bar the way. The goblet collided with Corayne's middle, spilling wine on her shirt. His smile widened as he took her in. "Good evening, my lady."

Corayne looked down at her stained clothing, then back to Andry, her eyes snapping to his. Frustration flared in her, hot as coals. *Don't,* he wanted to say. *Just keep moving.*

"Enjoy the feast," she said in a small voice, taking Andry by surprise.

She angled out of Lemon's grip, careful to keep her back to the hedges and the Spindleblade hidden. Luckily, Lemon was too drunk to notice Corayne's lack of ladylike attire, not to mention the sword sheathed over her shoulder.

"All right," Andry muttered, trying to pull free.

The torches closed in. There was only so much time before all hope of escaping was gone.

But Lemon's hand tightened, fingers digging to get a better hold on Andry's collar. He finally noticed the flickering lights and shouts echoing over the gardens. "Who're they lookin' for?" he said, his gaze sharpening. He licked his lips. "They called the garrison, Trell. We should help."

"You do that, Lemon," Andry replied, trying to pry his hand away.

The other squire bristled, his mood shifting. He brought up his other fist.

"There you are, Trelland," Lemon hissed up into Andry's face. His breath stank of wine and onions. "Still think you're better than the rest of us, even with your lord dead and gone. Failed worse than any squire here." The insult dug into him, sharp as a knife. But Lemon wasn't finished. He looked again at Corayne. "You know he got his knight killed, don't you?"

Andry felt his cheeks go red with heat.

She scowled, dropping all pretense, her eyes boring into Lemon's. "He survived, which is more than the knights can say."

Lemon only scoffed, and glared back at Corayne with a curl of his lip, his eyes raking over her. This time Andry watched him notice her ruined braid, her travel-worn clothing, the old leather boots on her feet. "What're you staring at, you ratty bitch?"

Andry's rage was like a thunderbolt. He broke the squire's hold in an instant, taking him by the scruff of his shirt. *"Davel,"* he growled.

Corayne didn't seem to mind such language. She raised her chin, continuing to glower. Her eyes were flat, black and yawning, unsettling to see.

"I'm trying to figure out exactly how long until you piss yourself, Squire," Corayne said in response to Lemon's question.

Lemon sputtered and lunged, but Andry held firm, using his height and sobriety to their full advantage. "That's enough," he said in a low voice. As if Lemon were an animal to be soothed.

It only incensed him further, and Lemon ripped himself away, spitting mad. But he didn't have a chance to speak again. The dagger was a golden mirror at his neck, full of torchlight.

"Yes, quite enough," the woman said, materializing out of the path. Her hand clawed Lemon's straw-like hair, pulling his head backward, exposing more of his throat. He couldn't see her, but the squire went rigid, feeling the blade against his skin.

"Sooner than I thought," Corayne muttered, glancing at the squire's legs.

As much as he wanted to see Lemon grovel, Andry knew better. He stepped forward, reaching out to the Ibalet dagger, a bronze artistry with a hilt like a coiling snake. The woman holding it was calm, her face too still.

"Don't kill him. Please," he said, his voice filled with force. *The last thing we need is more blood spilled.*

The woman's mouth twitched in annoyance. "Remember Trelland's mercy, boy," she breathed, lowering the blade from his throat.

Lemon met Andry's eyes, showing what little remorse he could. "Thank—"

Her fist connected with his jaw, knuckles on bone, snapping his head to the side with crackling force. The squire fell forward in the dirt, out cold.

"Was that necessary?" Andry gaped. Lemon lay flat, a puddle of drool already forming.

The woman sheathed her dagger with a snap. "You wanted him alive."

Andry felt another burst of cold. He swallowed hard, watching the woman's back. Dom joined her from the shadows, still limping. She moved like a predator, all angles. The court of Galland was no stranger to the women of Ibal, but this one was like none he'd ever met before. Her gown was torn to shreds, and there was blood on her hands and face. Not her own, but Dom's. *And some knights too. She killed Sir Welden in the hall*, he thought, remembering the old soldier as he bled to death, his neck cut open. The memory threatened to make him sick.

Corayne fell in next to him, her arm inches from his own. She looked pale in the moonlight, glancing back at Lemon's unconscious body as they ran from it. It didn't seem to unsettle her quite so much.

"Who is she? What the hell are we doing?" Andry muttered.

Corayne huffed out a breath. "I've been asking myself that for a while now."

They burst through another gap in the hedge, nearly careening into a shallow pond of lilies and lazy fish. On the far side, a gateway opened onto a plaza of cut stone, the tiles arranged like sunbeams spilling out from the cathedral. The walls of the New Palace ran up against the sanctuary without gap or flaw. The vaulted windows were dark and looming. Lights like fireflies moved along them, the reflections of torches as the garrison wove through the maze in hot pursuit.

Dom kept pace now, his legs moving furiously without any rhythm. He surged with the Ibalet at his side, her sword unsheathed and gleaming. It was plain but well made, flashing darkly. Still nothing compared to the Spindleblade.

The Syrekom yawned, a mouth of vaulted portals and gargoyles—winged gods and stone kings—looking down with empty eyes. The curved doors were solid oak, locked fast for the evening. It took the Elder only two tries to kick them open, even with his wound. He panted, fading, his skin paler than the moon. On top of everything else, Andry felt a squeeze of fear for Domacridhan's life.

The nave of the cathedral stretched, tall enough to house a forest, its columns marching in double rows to the far wall of windows. They clambered down the aisle bisecting the empty pews. Only a few candles guttered in their stands. Most went dark as they ran past.

"Gods, please don't kill any priests," Andry muttered, glancing toward the Ibalet.

"Wouldn't be my first," she answered neatly.

A red light grew in the glass windows. It flickered and flamed, born of a hundred torches as the Queen's soldiers overtook the palace grounds, surrounding the cathedral.

Andry clambered up the steps to the solid gold altar, where the high priest performed services. Six windows loomed over it, stained-glass portraits of mighty Syrek and his great deeds. After years of worship, Andry knew them all without looking. Each image, of flame, of war, of conquest, of creation, was picked out in red, gold, and green, filled with swords and lions, brilliant in the sunshine, foreboding in the dark. He winced when Dom grabbed a bronze brazier and lobbed it into the closest glass masterpiece.

It shattered with a crone's shriek, spitting glass into the river below.

"Ride the tide; keep under as long as you can," the Ibalet barked, waving Corayne up to the broken window. The woman checked Corayne's sword, tightening the buckles of the belts for her. Again Corayne looked back, finding Andry. This time, he saw fear in her. Only a flash, but enough.

He ducked his chin, giving her the best nod he could muster.

She nodded back, resolute.

Dom was the first to jump through, and Corayne followed with a graceful dive. The Ibalet didn't hesitate, leaping into the dark air, the splash of her body almost soundless in the river below.

Andry stepped up to the jagged edge of the window. The water was relatively clean; most refuse got caught on the water gates that kept boats away from the palace. They wouldn't be swimming through slum garbage. It didn't make jumping any easier. Nor did the thoughts swirling in his mind.

Torchlight filled the windows, and he heard the whipcrack bark of orders outside as the garrison arrived. There was nothing behind him but steel and fire. The Queen was with Taristan, the man who had killed Sir Grandel, Lord Okran, Cortael—his own twin—and all the rest, their bodies left to feed the crows.

They'll torture me. Question me. Punish me for hiding the sword, for helping Corayne. This was obvious. Andry could already see the dungeons of the keep in his mind. *And then they'll name me a traitor and kill me.*

But still he could not jump. It wasn't the fall that frightened him, all twenty feet of it into the rushing black river. The drop could have been two inches or two miles. Either way, it felt like an ending, a gate falling shut. A failure of everything that came before.

My father, dead for the Lion, dead for duty to a crown I've betrayed. He forced a hiss. *A crown that betrayed me, and the realm entire. I've done nothing wrong.*

I've done nothing wrong, he thought again as he dropped through the air. For the first time, he took solace in the words of the whispers.

Burn the life behind you.

The days of Squire Andry Trelland were certainly aflame.

It was his mother's face he saw when he hit the water, suspended for a moment in cold, endless dark. The current pushed him along and he let it, holding his breath beneath the surface.

There was no red heat here, as he'd seen in Taristan back in the hall. No malicious shadow moving behind the black. Only the river, only cool hands pushing him along.

And those damned whispers, which sounded like ice, like winter, solidifying into one voice.

Stand tall and steadfast true.

The darkness comes; your choices grow few.

Andry was a son of Ascal, born and raised in the capital. He knew the canals well, and his skin crawled as they swam. He kept his mouth shut and tried not to think of everything the water carried, from the upriver slums of Doghead to the slaughter yards in the Cowbank. In the dark, he could pretend the river was clean. And in the dark, they were difficult to see, difficult to follow.

The whispers faded, leaving Andry alone in his head. His own voice now pounded in his head. *Get out of the palace. Get to the docks.* With each breath he thought, *Get to the docks.*

He kept close to the others, until the Ibalet woman angled toward shore. They hauled themselves out, one by one, dripping wet on the meager bank, a dirty triangle of mud and sand half covered by an overhang of the street above.

Andry clambered quickly to his feet, as did Corayne. She patted the belts of the Spindleblade, checking the sword as she shook the hair from her eyes. It was still there, safe in its sheath.

"Get up or get hidden," the woman hissed, glaring at Dom still sprawled on the ground. Her gaze burned like two candles. "I doubt even three of us could drag a log like you out of here."

Dom groaned, too weak to respond, but rolled his knees, one

hand braced against the wound. It seemed to be bleeding less, despite all the exertion of swimming.

Andry shot to his side, slipping a hand under the Elder's arm.

"Push through your feet, my lord," the squire whispered, the immortal heavy in his grasp. He was almost as heavy as a knight in armor. "Lean on me."

"Me too," Corayne chirped, taking his other arm. She nearly buckled under his weight.

"Thank you," Dom murmured, sounding surprised, his pale cheeks flushing pink. By their aid or his own weakness, Andry couldn't say. *Probably both.* "Good that my cousin isn't here; she'd never let me hear the end of it."

"I'll be sure to mention it if I ever meet her," Corayne said, grinning through the strain.

Meanwhile, the Ibalet woman pulled off the rest of her torn dress, revealing a wet shift and leggings beneath. Her silhouette was smaller but not slight, every muscle well formed and taut, like a piece of rope wound up on itself. More tattoos showed at her collar and wrists, where her bronze skin was exposed to the air. Andry glimpsed a bird's wing and some Ibalet writing in curling script, a constellation, and a dagger like a half moon, before his stomach twisted and he had to avert his eyes.

"Apologies, my lady," he gritted out, looking at the wet ground.

The Ibalet scoffed out a laugh. "Never seen a woman's body before, Squire?" She sounded amused. "I think it's a bit late to be thinking of your honor."

His face went hot, cheeks flaming. "If I must betray the kingdom to save her, I will do so," he mumbled. *There is no going back, even if I wanted to. No way but forward.*

Upriver, lights blazed, the streets swimming with torches as search parties set out from the New Palace. Andry pictured the cathedral, the knights of the garrison standing at the broken windows, staring into the black abyss of the canal. *The predators to our prey.*

Dom followed Andry's gaze. "They'll be after us soon,"

"They're after us now," the Ibalet spat, ascending the bank with catlike focus. She wore a cowl now, hiding her face with repurposed scraps of her gown.

The squire swallowed hard and tried to think around the chaos in his head. They hobbled slowly up the slope, following the assassin.

"The garrison will fan out," Andry said, eyeing the street. *Get out. Get to the docks.* "They'll link up with the city watch, the other barracks—Queen Erida has an army in this city." He pointed with his free hand, gesturing along the canal as they reached the top. "We're across the waters; there are no more canals or islands. If you move fast enough, you might outrun anyone they've sent to the outer gates." The city spiraled around him, a cobweb of streets and bridges. "You can get out of the city before they lock it up tighter than a rat trap. Keep straight on until you hit the walls. Conqueror's Gate is the biggest, with more traffic, but Godherda has fewer guards. At least it should right now"

Corayne glared around Dom's body, her lips pursed into a grim line like the slash of a dagger. "*We* can get out of the city," she said sharply. "Or do you have some other plans I don't know about, Trelland?"

Andry felt a muscle jump in his cheek. He swallowed hard

and gently stepped away from Dom, careful not to upset his shaky balance. "Just head north," he said, his voice firm.

Corayne's eyes went wide, not in fear but in anger. "Where will you go?"

His answer was all too easy. "I'm not leaving my mother."

"You'll be caught," Dom rumbled, his breathing labored, his face pulling in pain. "And killed, Andry. Caught and killed." His green eyes wavered. "Taristan will not hesitate to end the life of a single boy. Innocent blood does not bother that demonic excuse for a man."

"I know that." Andry remembered all too clearly the way he had looked at Corayne—as if she were an obstacle, an object, something to be swept aside, all for the sword on her back. "But I cannot leave her."

I've failed everyone else. I won't fail the one who matters most.

Corayne was undeterred. "Wayfarer's Port is on the other side of the city."

"I know where it is," he replied, growing impatient.

"But can you make it?" Dom said, forcing a shaky step toward the squire. Corayne moved with him, trembling under his weight.

"Safe journey to you all" was Andry's only reply. He dipped his head, bending into a bow.

Corayne cut him off, her whisper hard and hissing. "You said yourself they'll shut the city." Something sparked in her, like a torch being coaxed into flame. Again she looked to the water, and the city islanded within it, her walls and lights endless. "Captains don't wait to get stuck in closed harbors. That ship will be in Mirror Bay before you can get to the port, and it will have your mother on it."

"Whatever you decide, possible death or certain death, be quick about it," the Ibalet hissed, a shadow on the street.

His feet were already moving, boots smacking hard against the cobblestones. *Get out, get to the docks,* he told himself, the words like a prayer. Anything to drown out Corayne's next burst of reasoning. Valeri Trelland beckoned in his mind, her warm hands pulling him close, her embrace like a blanket.

"You'll die trying," Corayne said, already an echo, already fading.

Andry Trelland had never seen Kasa, but he'd heard enough in his mother's stories. The port of Nkonabo, the city spined with monuments wrought in alabaster and amethyst. The home of his mother's Kin, its verdant garden courtyards, the little pond filled with purple fish. Family he never knew clustered around the gates, waving him inside, welcoming him to a new home.

His pace quickened, his heart racing, as if he could run all the way to Kasa.

But even the grand kingdom beyond the Long Sea is of the Ward. And the Ward is set to burn. Fires leapt up in his mind's eye, engulfing the temples, the towers, the walls, the streets, as corpse soldiers overwhelmed the realm. They crawled over the courtyard, their flames eating the gardens, the water bubbling in the pond, the fish boiling alive. And his mother died with them, screaming in her chair, reaching for a son who could not save her.

Andry wanted to cry, his eyes stinging, his heart torn in two as his boots skidded to a halt. In the distance, the city watch roused to hunt.

There would be no reaching the port. And nowhere on earth his mother would be safe, if the realm fell to ruin.

"Ambara-garay," he whispered, turning around.

Have faith in the gods.

18

TO DIE TRYING
Domacridhan

Dom had not known it was possible to miss the feel of steel between his ribs, but he certainly missed it now. His vision spun as it never had. From pain or blood loss, he did not know; he had never felt the true extent of either. Not in training at Tíarma, not in battles centuries past, not even at the temple, surrounded by an army of hellish Ashlanders, his face a bleeding ruin. This was so much worse. *And I did it to myself,* he cursed.

Corayne kept pace, still under his arm. The edge of her jaw was set like an ax, resolute and sharp, as she maneuvered them both up the bank. Dom braced a hand to the gash between his ribs, fingers sticky with his own blood. The pressure seared but kept him living, and served as a good distraction now.

The farther they walked from the squire, the deeper the ache in his chest became. *At least I won't have to watch him die,* he thought bitterly. But his anguish was short-lived.

Dom heard footsteps, familiar long strides fighting to catch up. He turned to see Squire Trelland following in their shadows, leaving the canals and Wayfarer's Port behind him.

"She'll be all right," Corayne said when she saw him, her voice somber. "And so will you."

Andry did not reply, his face bowed. He was careful and quiet, but the immortal could still hear his tears. He looked as he had at the temple—overcome, dull-eyed, broken by the massacre. And still dutifully trudging forward, without even a flicker of hope to light the way.

They hurried through a market. Whitewashed wattle-and-daub shops and timber-framed homes leered over them, their windows like empty eyes. Dom heard no patrols as Sarn led the way, her shift glaring white in the alleys. It was like following a ghost.

How fast does word travel in a city like this? he wondered, thinking of the gates. At every turn, their journey seemed to face its ending, only to carry on a bit further. *Perhaps Ecthaid has answered my prayers after all, and he protects our road.*

Or we've just been lucky.

The luck held. Godherda Gate arched before them, the ironbound oak shut but not barred, with only a pair of city watchmen on duty to guard the way. As Andry had said, it was small, barely a door in the outer walls of Ascal. Easy to defend, but easy to forget.

Sarn sped up, as did Corayne, pulling Dom along on shambling feet. Andry grabbed his arm once more, taking some of his weight, until he could nearly run. Again his vision swam, black spots growing and shrinking before his eyes.

"Just keep your legs moving, my lord," Andry said, sounding both close and far away.

Bells began to ring somewhere, reverberating in the air and in Dom's skull. He squeezed his eyes shut as they echoed, shrieking. For a moment, he was back at the temple, staring at the white tower and the impossible toll of an ancient bell.

The watchmen shouted something, their voices punctuated by the clank of their armor and the sing of steel drawn loose.

The bells are a command. Their queen calls. Our time is up.

"Bar the gates—they're closing the port—" the first watchman ordered. His words ended in a wet squelch.

Dom opened his eyes to see Sarn cut through the second watchman. Her sword dripped rubies and the gate yawned behind her, a crack between the doors widening with each moment.

It was Corayne who pushed him through, kicking the wood open.

All he could do was move, his energy finally spent, the wound winning the hard battle against his body. *Don't drop*, he told himself, repeating the squire's words. The bells kept screaming, accompanied by a dozen horns all over the city, from every gate and watchtower. He tried to think, tried to remember this part of the realm. What roads lay ahead, what the land beyond Ascal was. But Dom could barely open his eyes, let alone puzzle out a plan.

You'll die trying. Corayne's last plea to Andry hung in his head, ringing like the bells.

That seems to be our only fate, Dom thought, feeling their circumstances rise up like a storm cloud. No allies, no direction.

Nothing but the sword and the teenage girl who could barely wield it. *To die trying.*

He smelled as much as felt the horse as they shoved him on it, laying his great bulk across the saddle like a sack of grain. Dom felt the urge to apologize to it. *Normally I am very good at this*, he thought dimly. The ground moved beneath him, glimpsed through slitted eyes.

The others, he wondered, trying to move his head, but a stern hand kept him steady.

He clung to life as long as he could, until there was only the sound of hoofbeats. The bells and horns faded, and the darkness swallowed him up.

Light danced over his eyelids in rhythm: shadow and sun, shadow and sun. It moved in time with a creak of old wood, the flap of canvas. Or was it wings? *Baleir has wings. The god of courage is with me, I am in his grasp, and he will take me home to Glorian, where only the dead can journey now.*

Indeed, someone *was* holding him, the press of fingers firm against his rib cage and chest. And he could hear heartbeats. *Do gods have beating hearts?*

Pain lanced along his ribs and he hissed, drawing a breath through already-clenched teeth. His eyelids fluttered. The light was blinding, but golden and warm. Something broke the sun, passing in front of it in steady motion. He squinted, trying to make sense of his surroundings. *Certainly the realm of the gods is beyond my comprehension.*

There was a wall, a roof over him, wood beneath, a creaking

wheel outside a window, and the gurgle of a stream below it. Mice skittered somewhere, and cobwebs ruled the corners.

He groaned as a familiar sensation returned, hot and sharp.

"I did not know one could still feel pain after death," he forced out.

The heartbeats flared and he felt another jab. It lessened this time, more sting than stab.

"Just keep still, Dom. She's almost finished."

The voice was weary—annoyed, even. It was not the voice of a god.

Ignoring the advice, he tried to move and nearly succeeded, but for the two pairs of hands holding him down.

"Corayne?" he whispered, hunting for a glimpse of her. He caught pieces. Black hair edged in red light, her hands bare and too small, her knuckles scabbed. She still smelled like the river. And blood. The whole room smelled like blood, overpowering with the sour bite of iron.

"Yes, it's me," she huffed. "It's all of us. It's *only* us."

The world came back into sharper focus. "Where are we?" He looked again to the window full of sunlight, and the churning water wheel feeding the mill. "I thought I was dead."

"If only," said Sarn's poisonous voice.

The sting returned, piercing the skin. A gliding sensation followed, sharp and pulling. With a jolt, Dom realized she was stitching him up, weaving his torn flesh back together. He couldn't see her at all, only feel her deliberate, careful fingers as they worked.

"I've never seen anyone lose so much blood and survive," she said dryly.

Dom tried to sneer at her, but only shifted a little on the rough table. The wood creaked beneath him, groaning against his weight. He realized his shirt was gone entirely, even tatters torn away.

"Where's Andry?" he said suddenly, craning his head. Again, Corayne and Sarn held him down.

"The squire saw the truth of Corayne's words, and good that he did. They were closing the port when we escaped," Sarn said. "He followed us out of the city."

"I remember . . . *some* of that. But where is he now?" Dom answered, frustrated. "I can't hear his heartbeat."

Corayne came around the table, one hand braced against his upper arm. She wasn't terribly strong. "You can hear heartbeats?" she said, sounding impressed. "Since when?"

"Ah, birth?" Dom answered tentatively. He looked over the room again, mostly at the thick layers of dust coating every surface.

Sarn worked another suture. "We're on an abandoned farm, some miles west of Ascal. Trelland is plundering the house while we huddle in this broken-down mill. Or at least that's what he's pretending to do while he frets over his mother." Her disdain was bitterly clear.

This time, Dom didn't let Corayne hold him back. He rose up on his elbows, turning to put himself face-to-face with the assassin. Her cowl was gone, hanging loose around her neck, showing her full lips pressed together so tightly they almost disappeared. Like Corayne, she had dark circles beneath her eyes, and the black powder lining her lids was smeared away. Neither had slept, and mortals were so very dependent on sleep. Even so, the rage in his chest, born of grief and failure, rose up like embers being stoked to flame. *How dare she judge the boy so?* He bared his teeth, fists clenching. She didn't flinch or move her hands from his side. Her needle pulled insistently.

"You are truly without a heart, Amhara," he growled.

She stuck him again. "Thank you."

Dom scowled. "We're too close to the city." The mill suddenly felt stifling, as if it might collapse on them at any moment. "We should still be on the move."

Sarn took the accusation in stride, to his chagrin. "We were a bit limited in how far we could go, thanks to someone's attempt at field surgery."

He tried to knock away her hands, reaching for the needle. "I can do this myself, you know," he snapped. Now that he could see the wound in the daylight, he realized how serious it was. And, he noted begrudgingly, how well the assassin could stitch.

"Somehow I have a hard time believing that," she replied, intolerant.

"Somehow I thought I escaped this nonsense bickering," Corayne finally butted in, pressing her hands to Dom's shoulders. He fell flat with a huff. "I've got the Queen, her army, and my damned uncle to worry about. Let's not add to the list, shall we?"

Dom felt oddly scolded, his cheeks going warm. "I'm not paying you another coin, Sarn. Not a *penny*," he said, trying another tactic. *Without payment, certainly the Amhara will disappear.* "You are free to go and do as you like."

"Well, I'd like to survive the next few years, in a realm that isn't claimed and conquered by a hellscape," Sarn answered smoothly, killing his hopes. "I suppose the best way to do that is to stay with the girl, since you aren't much use."

"And a single assassin is?" Dom spat. She tugged the needle again, harsher than she needed to be. He let her; his body was already healing. The flare of pain faded with every second, and he felt rather smug about it.

Until she lowered her face, her mouth inches from his ribs. He could feel her breath on his skin, ghosting along the ridge of the closed wound. Dom nearly sprang off the table as she bit through the thread, tying off the last of his stitches. Her face was still, impassive, but smirking victory danced in her eyes.

Behind him, Corayne failed to smother a laugh. "I'll take who I can get," she said, patting Dom on the shoulder, "to accomplish what we need to do next."

Her eyes trailed, fixing on the corner. Dom sat up and followed her gaze to see the Spindleblade, propped up and half hidden. A beam of sunlight spilled before it, swirling with motes of dust. Inside the mill, the Spindleblade seemed unremarkable, not even a relic. The jewels of the hilt were dull, the steel dim. Dom remembered it in the vaults of Iona, surrounded by a hundred candles, the reflections dancing. It had sat there for centuries, free from the ravages of time. He remembered it in Cortael's hand, when it was time for him to take the Spindleblade as his own. There was no magic in the steel beyond its tie to the Spindles, but it seemed to bewitch him. The sword was a relic of a world dead, a people all but lost. It spoke to him in ways even Dom could not fathom. He wondered if the blade spoke to Cortael's daughter in the same way. He could not know. She was more difficult for him to read, her eyes always darting, her mind working in furious motion. She changed paths too quickly for him to follow.

"We can't hope to close the Spindle at the temple now," Dom murmured. Gingerly, he stepped off the table, testing his legs. They held, the weakness of his wound fleeing. "Not without an army to fight our way through. He'll have thousands of those specters assembled, many thousands. The wrath of the Ashlands and What Waits gathers." Despite the warm air of the mill, he shuddered, hair raised on his bare arms. "And then there's Taristan himself. I don't know how to kill him." He thought of Cortael, his sword plunging through Taristan's chest. *It did little. It did* nothing. "If he even can be killed."

Corayne's eyes ran the length of the blade again, losing focus. Then she blinked, coming back to herself like someone rising from sleep. She turned her back on the blade and went to the wall, where a few crates were piled, not to mention some stolen saddlebags from the stolen horses outside. After a moment, she produced a dark gray, rough-spun shirt and tossed it at Dom. He pulled it over his head, nose curling at the smell and the touch of the poorly made clothing.

"Let's focus on what we can do, not what we can't," Corayne said. "We've got a Spindleblade. We've got Spindleblood. We've got an immortal prince of Iona who witnessed the tearing of a Spindle and Erida's alliance to my uncle. We've got—all this," she added, gesturing vaguely at Sarn, now leaning against the window. "Certainly there are others who will listen. Other monarchs, Elders, *someone*."

Dom rolled the sleeves of the shirt, which were somehow too long. "I have a cousin, heir to the throne of Iona. She rides the Ward now, seeking aid from the other enclaves. If anyone can rally the Vedera, she can," he said, as much as the thought of Ridha pained him.

Corayne bobbed her head. "Well, that's something."

"It's basically nothing," Sarn muttered from the window.

"It's *something*," Corayne snapped.

The assassin shrugged, unconvinced. She flicked a braid over her shoulder, peering out the window.

Dom could finally hear Andry outside, his footsteps harried as he burst through the door.

The squire was less disheveled than the other two. Even his bruises were not so bad. With his open manner and lanky frame, he could easily pass for a wealthy farmer's son, or a young tradesman traveling the countryside. He had the kind of face people trusted and overlooked.

"Sorasa, you should—" he began, jabbing a thumb over his shoulder. Then he spotted Dom standing and ducked into a quick, practiced bow. "Oh, good to see you awake, my lord."

Sarn curled her lip. "Don't call him that."

Dom ignored her, as he tried to do always. "Thank you, Andry. What is it?"

The wheel churned outside, gears groaning as the stream babbled on. Birds sang in the fields, and the wind was gentle through the leaves. Dom listened hard but could find nothing amiss. After Ascal, the peace of the farm was shocking.

Andry glanced back and forth, one hand braced to keep the

door open. He gestured to the farmhouse, a dilapidated wreck across the lane, half hidden by gnarled apple trees. Abandoned, for years if not a decade.

"I think there's something you should see," he said. "All of you."

19

SO THE BONE TELLS
Corayne

At home, time divided into long portions, weeks or months, to suit trade demands, voyages of the *Tempestborn*, and the change of seasons. The days were a hallway, a clear passage of open doors. In Lemarta that meant days of waiting, plotting around distant storms or political upheaval on some foreign coast. Corayne felt bored more often than not, watching the horizon with her ledger, letters, and reports tucked close. But she had room to maneuver, to think, to plan.

Now Corayne felt like she was back in the hedge maze, running blindly around corners with gods-knew-what waiting on the other side. She could only react and hope to survive. Not exactly ideal.

"What could it be now?" she muttered as they followed Andry out of the mill.

The abandoned farm had a haze to it in the morning light, a

golden mist that softened the hedges and overgrown fields. It was as lovely as a painting. Corayne hated it. *Too quiet, too safe*, she thought, glaring at the rutted lane. Everything felt like a trap. She had strapped the Spindleblade on before they left the mill, and it dug into the newborn welts on her shoulders and waist. That did not improve her mood.

Andry waved them over the threshold of the dilapidated farmhouse. Half of it still had a roof, but it was more cobweb than timber. The rest opened to the sky, like a giant had come along and put his fist through the ceiling. Debris gathered in the corners, and most of the furniture was broken or gone, with only an iron pot half buried in the hearth. Anything else of use piled on the floor, in ordered rows like a regiment of soldiers. *Andry has been busy.*

Sorasa sniffed at the pot, her eyes narrowed. Corayne followed, peering in to see a pile of boiled bones. They seemed to radiate cold, despite the warm sun spilling over the house.

"Animal," Sorasa muttered, her eyes narrowed. "But fresh."

On the other side of the room, Andry stood over a pile of rags, his copper cheeks tinged with red. "I didn't notice her at first," he said hesitantly. "I wasn't quiet, but she didn't stir."

Corayne stiffened, eyeing the rags again. It was difficult to tell what lay beneath. The bone cold seemed to thrum. "Did you say *her?*"

Andry swallowed. "I don't know if she's—"

"She's alive," Dom answered, cocking his head. Apparently he *could* hear a heartbeat, one of the more unsettling things about the Elder warrior. There was a steadily growing list.

He bent to the rags, crouching on his heels, and inhaled deeply, like a dog catching a scent. Gently, he pulled back the first layer, a patchwork blanket in every color of dirt. A head of gray, frizzing hair peeked out between his feet, stuck with twigs, leaves, and beaded braids that made Corayne twinge. Why, she could not say.

She took a step forward, her knees shaky with exhaustion. But a fist closed on her arm, the fingers digging in sharply.

"Wait," Sorasa warned, holding her back.

"Mistress, we're sorry to intrude," Andry said, taking a knee next to the pile. The gray head didn't move. Corayne strained to see her face but Dom and Andry blocked her view.

Dom ran a hand over his blond beard. "She's in a deep sleep. Too deep for a mortal."

"Leave her and we'll be on our way," Sorasa said. "She hasn't seen our faces; she won't be able to aid anyone looking for us."

The Elder bit his lip. "Are you certain of that?"

The assassin shrugged. "Fine, slit her throat."

"Sorasa," Corayne hissed, sucking in a breath.

Andry squared his shoulders. "You'll do no such thing," he barked, and Corayne saw the flash of a knight in him.

Sorasa glanced between them, puzzled. "You're being hunted by the Queen of Galland and a demon king. I don't recommend making it any easier for them."

The sleeping woman sat up quickly, as if she'd never been sleeping at all. Her eyes opened, blue as the most brilliant sky. Her mouth was like a gash, her lips thin, lined by wrinkles from a lifetime of smiling.

"Kill me and Allward is as good as gone," the old woman said cheerfully. Her voice lilted, playful, edged in a familiar accent. The woman's gaze bore into her like a battering ram, a grin jagged on her pale, old face. "Don't gape, *pyrta gaera*; it hasn't been so long."

Corayne clenched her teeth against a cry of shock.

"You," she breathed. *The old woman from the ship, the Jydi peddler. Useless trinkets and silly rhymes.*

Dom rose from his crouch as the woman scrambled to her feet. "You know her?"

"She was on the ship to the capital," Sorasa said, putting her body between Corayne and the Jydi. "She boarded when we put in at Corranport and then got off in Ascal with the rest." Her eyes roved over the old woman. She looked the same as she had on the galley, swaddled in a mismatched shawl and filthy dress. Her feet were bare and black with dirt. "You followed us."

"I don't see how that's possible, Sorasa," Corayne breathed. *From the docks, to the palace, chased out of the city. It doesn't make sense. She would have to know where we were going before we did.* Her hand twitched at her side. Cold prickled in her fingers.

The old woman shook her head, laughing.

"You followed *me*," she crowed, patting down her manic hair. "Or your horses did, good beasts they be." She shuffled toward the pot in the hearth. Her hands were like bird wings, fragile and flapping.

Sorasa pushed Corayne away, backing them both out of the woman's path.

She paid them no attention and upended the pot, spilling

bones across the floor. Rib bones, leg bones, vertebrae, and skulls. Rats, rabbits, birds. All picked clean, white as clouds. She let them fall, observing a pattern the rest couldn't see.

"You're a witch," Andry said, sounding dazed.

She didn't answer, inspecting her mess. The Jydi was lithe for her age, turning and twisting, even dropping to the floor to inspect the spread of bones from every possible angle.

"A witch," Corayne murmured. In her pocket, her fingers closed around a twist of wood. She pulled it loose, the sharp ends black with dried blood.

The Jydi shrugged. "I'm what I am, and that should be." Then she tutted to herself, a liver-spotted hand on her chin as she searched the bones. "I should have done this under a tree."

The charm trembled in Corayne's hand. "Why did you give me this?" she asked, the bone beads dangling from her fingers.

The old Jydi didn't reply, too busy with the floor.

Dom stepped around her, keeping his distance. He was twice her size, if not more. "I think the better question is, *who* are you?"

"Or, perhaps, why are we bothering with this at all?" Sorasa said, her eyes flashing in frustration. She gestured to their horses, tied up across the lane. "We need to keep moving."

"I gave you something?" the woman murmured to Corayne distantly. She finally looked at her, and at the charm still in her hand. Confusion clouded her brilliant eyes.

Corayne clenched her teeth. "Yes, on the ship, *Gaeda*." *Grandmother*. "Do you remember?" She stretched out her arm, holding the charm within reach.

The old woman swooped, snatching it away. The touch of her fingers was like ice, and Corayne flinched.

"It's only branch and string," the Jydi said, inspecting the twigs. "Something and nothing." She ran the beads over in her palms, then licked the bloody ends. The rest of the room grimaced as she tucked it into her dress.

"Sarn is right—we can't stay," Dom huffed. *Desperate enough to agree with Sorasa.* "Erida's soldiers will be searching for us, and for the Spindleblade. We have to keep ahead of them."

Andry picked his way through his neat piles, careful to avoid the bones. "Galland keeps a standing army in Canterweld, half a day's ride north. They'll be out ranging for us by the end of the day, if they aren't already. Ten thousand combing the countryside." He shook his head, despairing of their chances already. He stuffed a sack with cloth for bandages, a ball of string, and, to Corayne's surprise, a dented teakettle. "If the Queen calls a muster . . ."

He stopped mid-sentence when the witch touched his shoulder, her knobbled hand like a white talon.

"Keep him near, *gaera*, he's a good one," she said, patting idly at his back, then his face. Andry made a small noise, his eyes wide. The witch ignored him, pointing two fingers at Dom and Sorasa. "I haven't decided on these two, but better than none."

Sorasa braced bloody hands on her hips. "She's seen our faces and she won't stop rhyming. We need to kill her."

"I don't think that can be the solution to every obstacle," Andry said weakly.

The Amhara was not amused. "It's served us fine this far."

Corayne sorely wished for her charts, or at least a map. "What we *need* is a plan of action. A direction, a heading."

"Staying out of Gallish custody is plan enough," Sorasa replied. "Ride for the closest border, regroup in safety. Not in a crumbling barn ten miles from execution."

The weight of another sleepless night suddenly loomed, heavy and precarious as the collapsed roof. Corayne ran a hand over her brow, trying to think. Everything felt soft-edged and slow, a sleepy warmth battling against the odd, bracing cold.

She bit her lip. "That Spindle isn't going to close itself."

"Spindles," the old woman said lightly, emphasizing the syllables. She toed a rabbit's spine aside and made a noise of triumph. Her smile leered. "So the bone tells."

Even the wind in the fields dropped, going silent. Andry froze over his pack while Dom gripped the collapsed wall, his knuckles white on stone. Slowly, he hung his head. Sorasa did not move, her body too still, her face impassive and neutral. As if she was holding back, fighting to remain calm. Corayne could hardly breathe, feeling like she'd just taken a hammer blow to the chest. The air in her lungs hissed out slowly.

"There's more than one?" she whispered, looking to Dom. He met her eyes with something like shame.

"Already," he murmured. "Already."

Incensed, Sorasa leapt forward, hands free and flexing. She glared into the old woman's eyes, as if she could find something in them. "Why does anyone believe this?" she spat.

The witch swept aside another bone, letting it skitter over Sorasa's feet. Her smile turned brittle.

"Amhara Fallen, Amhara Forsaken, Amhara Broken," the witch said, each word like a knife. Sorasa fell back, flinching as the blow landed home.

"They call you Amhara." The witch looked at each of them in turn, her brilliant eyes flashing. "But you are Osara."

Sorasa collided with the crumbled wall of farmhouse, broken stones coming up to her shoulders. Her eyes flared open and her mouth moved but nothing came. Corayne had no idea what the witch's words meant, but they were enough to steal fire from Sorasa Sarn.

"Sorasa, what is she saying?" Corayne bit out. "What is Osara?"

But the Amhara assassin did not answer. Her nostrils flared and she dropped her gaze, her sunset eyes burning at her feet.

Andry gritted his teeth, his words bringing them back. "There's another Spindle. Another army."

Dom dragged his eyes from Sorasa, now silent and far away. "This was his plan from the beginning. The more Spindles he opens, the weaker the realm becomes, the thinner the boundary between Allward and What Waits. Like destroying columns holding up a dome. Of course he'd tear another before we could strike back."

Corayne heard defeat in him, clear as day. She felt it too, but refused to let it eat her whole. She took the Jydi witch by the arm instead. Her flesh was as cold as her fingers, even through her clothes.

"Do you know where, *Gaeda?*" Corayne asked. It was like grabbing for the chain of an anchor already sinking. Useless. "Where the Spindle is or where it might lead? Is another army already here?"

The Jydi fixed her with a piercing stare, bones littered at her feet. She nudged one without looking. "No. No. *No.*"

"All right," Corayne said, latching on where she could. The chain snagged in her grasp. "Can we hope to fight whatever comes through? Or at least hold it off long enough to do . . . whatever it is I have to do?"

My blood, the blade. Another Spindle. Her stomach flipped. *Another chance.*

"There's only four of us, Corayne," Dom muttered.

"Five," she bit back, still holding on to the witch. "Can we do it?"

The Jydi stared into Corayne for a long moment, as she had stared at the bones.

Can she read the future in me too? Corayne wondered. *Or is this all nonsense, a trick of a peddler? Junk like the charms.* But the twigs had burned cold in her pocket, scratched blue on Taristan's face, made a man who could not be harmed bleed and scream. Corayne wanted them back in her pocket, though she couldn't say why.

"We must be quick," the Jydi finally answered. "Call me Valtik."

Lifting her chin, she snapped her gnarled fingers.

Corayne braced herself for a burst of something extraordinary, but nothing happened, no spell to collect the bones or pack up anything of use. If the witch was truly Spindletouched, her magic was not the kind from any story Corayne had heard. Valtik kicked at the bones again, casting them aside on her way to the crumbled door.

Sorasa stood at the wall, still silent, her lips pursed to nothing. Valtik looked to the assassin as she passed, a finger pointed.

"And we must be seven," she said. "You understand, Forsaken?"

Corayne did not. To her surprise, Sorasa nodded.

Seven.

"I don't understand, and I would like to know what you're talking about," Dom snapped, crossing the room in silence.

Valtik stepped out into the lane. She hummed under her breath, kicking up dirt with her bare feet, like a peasant child enjoying an empty morning.

"I'm speaking to you, Witch," Dom rumbled, his frame filling the open doorway.

She only held up two hands, five fingers raised on one, two raised on the other. *Seven.*

Dom cursed under his breath, in the Elder language unknown to all.

The assassin finally came back to herself, pushing off the wall to join Dom in the doorway. "We rode to Ascal seeking a hammer," she said, arms crossed. "But why use a hammer when a needle will do?"

"I don't know what you're talking about either," Dom bit out.

But the Amhara simply stalked after the Jydi, her braid trailing behind.

Corayne rolled her eyes and shoved Dom out of the ramshackle house. "If Valtik is going to rhyme, you can't start talking in riddles, Sorasa," she said, exasperated. "I refuse to save the realm under these conditions."

If that's even still possible, she thought, gritting her teeth.

Out in the overgrown lane, Dom threw up his massive hands, muttering again, his Elder curses coming in fits and spurts. He shambled toward their horses, tied up next to the mill.

"You'll need to ride with the witch, Corayne," he said, looking apologetic.

"I don't think so," Corayne answered, her eyes locked ahead.

"Well, *I'm* not—" Dom sputtered, then stopped short, following her stare.

Where there had been four horses only minutes ago, five now stood. A gray mare, as unremarkable as the rest, chewed on grass as if nothing were amiss. She even had a saddle and reins. Valtik stood by her, idly stroking the beast's neck.

"They follow me." The witch shrugged, a mad blue gleam in her eyes. "You'll see."

Sorasa was already in the saddle of her own stolen horse, stealing glances at the witch. *Amhara Fallen. Forsaken. Broken. Osara.* The words had hit a nerve in her like nothing else, not even Dom. *But why?*

The sun shone warm overhead, but there was a coldness to the breeze that hissed of winter. Corayne crossed her arms over her chest, fighting the urge to shiver. Andry came up alongside her, his pack over one shoulder. The teakettle clanged in it, heavy and unnecessary.

"Are you planning on inviting Taristan to tea?" she said, eyeing his pack. "That's the first thing I'd pitch overboard if my ship were taking on water."

He felt her scrutiny and shifted, hitching the pack higher. "It's something I can do," he offered. A gentle blush colored his cheeks and he looked away, toward the others. "It's a bit of home."

He wasn't looking at the horses, at the witch, at Dom stomping into the mill. He looked through them. His heart was somewhere else, or at least it wished to be. With his sick mother, somewhere on the water, her face pointed south, with a strong wind at her back.

"It's a safe route to Kasa," Corayne said. It wasn't a lie. The shipping lanes east were clean this time of year, an easy sail for an able captain. "Safer than any road we might travel."

"How would you know?" The sudden sharpness of his voice took her by surprise. Even in the palace, running for his life, he'd been gentle. But then, she barely knew him. It was only last night they had met. *It feels like a lifetime already.*

"I know what it is to think of a ship and wish," she murmured, her heart clenching.

Andry Trelland's eyes melted like butter in a pan. Corayne looked away quickly and fiddled with the belts of the Spindleblade, adjusting it on her back for something to do. Her cheeks felt hot.

"Used to be my job," she added, her voice rough.

Andry bit his lip. "That's what Sorasa meant, when she said you knew ships."

"I know some. One more than the rest." The *Tempestborn* rose up before her, its familiar purple sails and painted hull, a captain with black hair and laughing eyes at the prow. The admission tumbled out, beyond her control. "My mother is a pirate."

She lowered her face, not wanting to see any more judgment or discomfort from Andry Trelland. He'd been through enough already. *Not to mention he's a squire, raised to be an honorable knight. His mother is a lady, nobleborn, beautiful, intelligent, and far kinder than any parent I've ever known.*

"That sounds . . . exciting," he said, taking great care with his choice of words.

"For her." *Not for me. Not for the people she robs or kills.* "It's the first time I've ever said that out loud. The others know. You should too."

"I don't see how that's relevant to anything." Corayne's head snapped up to find Andry staring at her, his faced gold at the edges with summer sunlight. He watched her intently. "What your mother is, or what your father was."

My father. Even though she had seen Taristan, far too close for her liking, his face identical to her father's, she could not see Cortael in her mind. The image wouldn't hold. It was wrong somehow, and she knew why. It didn't matter that she had seen his twin. She would never see Cortael himself. Whatever remained was ash and bone. He was lost to her, without hope of return. A man she didn't want, who hadn't wanted her. And still it cut her to pieces.

"You saw him die. You knew him." *You heard his voice; you saw his face.*

Andry shifted, uncomfortable. "A bit."

"More than me."

Sorasa's shout forced them apart. She stood in the saddle, the cowl back around her neck, a dirty shawl or blanket draped around her shoulders. She could pass for a farmer or a beggar, if no one looked too hard.

"It's three days' ride to Adira," she called. "I'd prefer to do it without a Gallish army on my heels."

"Adira?" Corayne and Andry said in unison, both gaping. But

while Trelland was incredulous—stunned, even—Corayne felt a rare burst of excitement.

Dom seemed to share Andry's trepidation. He launched himself into the saddle, wheeling his horse up alongside Sorasa. He loomed down on her, eyes flashing. "You can't be serious."

"The witch said seven," Sorasa said neatly. "Adira will get us to seven."

"Adira will get us *killed*," Andry sighed, climbing neatly into the saddle.

After a moment of scrambling, Corayne got her foot under her in the stirrup and swung a leg gracelessly over the saddle. Still, she smiled. *Adira*. There was not a sailor aboard her mother's ship who did not have a tale of the Adoring Port, a pilgrimage for all below and beyond the laws of any crown.

"You were at the temple, Trelland," Corayne said, leaning over to eye the squire. "Don't tell me you're afraid of a few drunks and cutthroats."

Sorasa grinned and snapped her reins. "More than a few."

"Gods save us," Andry murmured under his breath.

20

BLEED FOR ME
Erida

"The suitor is next, Your Majesty," Lady Harrsing said in her ear, bending over Erida, who was seated on her throne.

Both sighed in annoyance. The old woman and the Queen had seen a hundred of their like over the years, petitioners noble and peasant, both men and women, rich and poor, handsome, ugly, and everything in between. They had only one thing in common—they were stupid enough to think they could tempt the Queen of Galland.

In most courts, petitions were heard in public, in a throne room or great hall jammed with courtiers feeding their own amusement. Not so in Galland. The petitions chamber was small and comfortable, wood-paneled with tapestries on the walls, one end of the room raised to seat the Queen, her chosen advisors, and her knights of the Lionguard. Today the odious honor fell to Lady Harrsing and six guardians, half of them nearly asleep. There were more knights stationed just outside, in the halls and passageways branching off the throne, should the need arise. Erida guessed they were dozing as well.

She could not blame them. She wanted nothing more than to sleep too, but she had another hour of hearings to suffer through. I can manage another starry-eyed dreamer, she thought, dismissing the Madrentine diplomat in front of her with a wave of her jeweled hand.

He bowed low and left the throne room, clearly dissatisfied. The Queen cared little for the whims of Madrence and forgot him as soon as he disappeared, leaving the space before her dais empty and waiting for the next person brave enough to approach.

Erida blinked, surprised when not one but two men approached the throne. Most petitioners were easy to read, by either the heraldry on their clothing or the set of their faces. Not so with these two. One was some kind of priest, cloaked in scarlet, his hood thrown back to show pale skin and white-blond hair. He walked with his hands folded, hidden in his sleeves. She guessed him to be a dedicant of Syrek, Galland's patron god, though his robes were unfamiliar from any service she'd ever attended.

The other had no heraldry and no immediate look. He was pale with dark red hair—definitely of the northern continent, but she could not place him further. He had come far, if his muddy boots and dirty cloak were anything to be believed. His hands were gloved, but she wagered his nails were dirty. A soldier, she guessed, judging by his gait and the hard set of his jaw, the squaring of his shoulders. Some captain from an outpost, drunk on glory, victorious in an insignificant skirmish somewhere, and now he thinks to conquer me too.

The sword beneath his cloak gave her pause. As he walked, the *folds of his clothing parted, and she glimpsed the wink of jewels. Ruby and amethyst, red and purple.* No simple soldier carries a sword like that, *she thought.*

He did not kneel like the others, and neither did the priest. A cord of tension drew through the room, her knights rousing in their armor.

"Welcome, petitioners," Erida said aloud, looking between them as she recited the words hammered into her skull. "What would you ask of the Lion?"

The man met her gaze slowly, raising his face. Even in the throne room, well lit by many torches and chandeliers, his eyes were dark, black as jet but without its gleam. They seemed to swallow the room. In spite of herself, Erida felt a pull to them.

"I have nothing to ask, and the world to offer. I would give you my hand in marriage, and I would give you the realm entire." He reached out, and even from a distance, she thought she could feel his fingers. "I am Taristan of Old Cor. I carry Spindleblood in my veins, a Spindle-blade in my fist. Take them both."

For a moment, Erida felt fear. Pure terror.

She had heard that name before, from the lips of a squire with blood on his hands.

Her well-practiced mask never wavered, as good as a shield now. She hid behind it, taking even, steady breaths. Only a few seconds passed before her fear melted like iron in the forge.

It took shape again, becoming steel.

Then there was only resolve. A plan.

A choice.

* * *

Thanks to the antics of the Spindleblood mouse, the squire, the lumbering Elder, and *whoever* that woman was, Erida's wedding ceremony had to be moved from the Syrekom. The Queen of Galland couldn't very well be married surrounded by broken glass, with evidence of catastrophe looming over everything. The court would already be talking about the feast for weeks. She didn't need to throw any more kindling on that fire.

Luckily, there was no lack of cathedrals within Ascal. The Konrada was close enough and grand enough for a royal wedding. The Queen had an army of servants at her disposal, not to mention an actual army, and they worked tirelessly through the night to prepare. They hung the spire of the Konrada with new banners, golden as a sunbeam, and scattered roses throughout the sanctuary. They polished marble, cleaned windows, dusted pews, and shooed off the beggars at spearpoint. In the morning, the procession from the palace made for a breathtaking sight. While the court paraded over the Bridge of Valor, the citizens of Ascal crowded along the neighboring canals, craning for a glimpse.

Erida was difficult to miss, alone within a circle of knights, her cream veil trailing a full twenty feet behind her. The bridal crown was a pretty circlet of gold, curling with emerald vines and ruby roses. Taristan followed after her, resplendent in imperial red, a son of Old Cor in image as well as blood. He looked far from the man she'd met in the throne room, his muddy cloak exchanged for silk and brocade. But the soldier's edge remained. No amount of finery could hide his lethal heart.

Ascal cheered for them both. In her mind, Erida cheered too.

He was the promise of empire. The promise of a husband who could give her as much as she gave him. Who held value as much as weakness. High enough to help her, low enough not to control her. A rare thing to find, for a ruling queen.

Despite the *events* of the night before, the ceremony went on without much trouble. The sun still shone; the gods still blessed the union; Lord Konegin did not attempt a coup before the vows were made. No one else dropped a chandelier or six on the court.

All in all, a success, Erida thought, eyeing the glittering crowd within the cathedral tower.

The ceremony ended in the traditional way of Galland, albeit grander than any common wedding across the kingdom. The high priest of the Godly Pantheon presented Prevail, the marriage sword of Erida's family, and held it between them, the hilt like a standing cross. The blade was two hundred years old, too fine for war. It did not know blood. Every king and queen of Galland had married with it in hand, fingers joined together, in defiance of all that would tear them apart. Erida took it with relish, enjoying the feel of its leather grip. *I am the first queen regnant to hold this sword*, she thought, as Taristan's warm hand covered her own. The high priest relinquished it, letting them hold it together. The jewels of the hilt, emeralds and diamonds, glittered beneath the stained glass of the Konrada. The gods themselves watched from their walls. Erida could feel their marble gaze.

She hoped her father was watching too.

"With this sword, you will conquer all that seeks to separate you," the high priest said, a blessing to the couple and a prayer to the mighty Syrek. "Your allegiance is to each other and to the crown."

Erida bowed her head first, dipping her brow to the pommel. "To you, to the crown," she said. They were the last of her vows, the binding words. She expected to feel them like a chain around her neck. Instead there was nothing. Not joy, not fear. Nothing changed in her heart. The line she walked remained straight and true.

"To you, to the crown," Taristan answered, lowering his own face as she straightened.

His black eyes followed her movement. His head was bare, the red of his hair shining darkly without a consort's crown. Taristan had refused even a simple circlet. He had no use for jewels or gold. Though he had spent all night combing the city with the garrison, he did not look like it. Erida saw no circles beneath his eyes, no sharp pull of exhaustion at the edges of his face. There was only the grim shadow of failure, something they shared. *For now.*

And of course the four lines torn down the left side of his face. Starting below the eye, the scratches were not so deep, but they were unmistakable and refusing to fade.

He's still handsome, at least, Erida thought, contemplating his face. The scratches did little to hide his well-boned features, more rugged than beautiful. *Which is more than I can say for most.* And, truly, he was a man. Not a boy playing at swords or an overgrown toddler coddled into adulthood. Taristan of Old Cor walked his own pace, self-assured, single-minded in focus. He was no stranger to blood or ambition. She'd seen it in their first meeting. She'd seen it in their second, the night before. And she saw it now, the third time, as he became her husband, rigid as a statue, determined as stone.

When he stood up again, the deed was done. She braced herself for a wave of regret that never came.

This is the path I've chosen.

She looked him over, her new prince consort. The celebrating, simpering court drowned out all sound from the high priest, who spoke words she did not need to hear. Taristan was not smiling, his lips set like a challenge. She offered no smile of her own. He returned her stare, black eyes meeting blue. He was not unfathomable. His wants were clear, his use obvious. There were things each could take from the other, in equal standing.

He is the right path.

Prevail returned to the high priest but their hands remained joined, as they would all the way back to the New Palace. His skin was hot but not uncomfortable, her palm fitting oddly well in his. Their steps matched as they turned from the altar and led the procession back out of the cathedral, the aisle carpeted in soft green. Taristan did not speak, as taciturn as he'd been in their first two meetings. Of course, the second had been under less than ideal circumstances, with only a few words passed between them at all before the feast went to ruin. And the first meeting had been closer to a military negotiation than a proposal, both sides well armored and clear in intention.

Taristan's red wizard fell into the procession, a scarlet dot at the corner of her vision, just outside the circle of the Lionguard escort. Ronin, he was named. Spindletouched and gangly, he was ill at ease surrounded by people, and spent most days in the archives, hunting the tomes and crumbling parchments for word of Spindles long gone. He did not speak now, but his red hood was lowered, showing a white face and pink-rimmed, darting eyes. He reminded Erida of a hairless rat.

Outside, the summer heat continued to climb, and Erida was glad for the short walk back to the cool shade of her palace.

The canals echoed with the voices of Ascal. Her subjects roared their approval from seemingly every bridge and waterside street, their faces a pink-tinged sea. Erida waved and gestured for Taristan to do the same. Coaxing the love of the commons was always wise, especially when it was easy. And there was nothing the commons loved so much as a wedding, the splendor of a life they could not fathom brought close for a heartbeat. Joy, false as it might be, was difficult to resist.

Erida fed off it, the love of the people for the Queen. It was a comfort as much as a shield. *While they love me, I am safe.*

Taristan's fingers flexed in hers, his grip loosening as they reached the Kingsbridge.

"Wait until we're out of sight," she warned. Her teeth set in an exaggerated smile. "Don't give anyone an excuse to gossip. They'll find enough reason without our help."

He grimaced but tightened his grasp again. There were calluses on his palm and fingertips, patches of skin worn rough by years of swordsmanship. The touch of them shuddered her a little. Taristan of Old Cor had lived hard years, the testament of them in his skin. She tried not to imagine those hands elsewhere, as they would be later. There was no wedding without a bedding, no bond of marriage without a bond of body. *A sword in the church and a sword in the sheets*, as the crude saying went.

"I care little for court opinion," he muttered, almost inaudible.

All thoughts of the bedding and his fine face snapped apart. Erida refused to roll her eyes. *I'll have a lifetime to teach him how wrong he is, but I don't need to start this instant.*

"How lovely that must be," she said dryly.

Erida had never dreamed of her wedding, though her ladies-in-waiting had often asked. She'd made things up to satisfy them. *A cathedral filled with flowers, milk-white horses, Madrentine lace, the marriage sword bright as lightning, a veil as long as a river, gifts from every monarch in every corner of the Ward.* Some of those things had come to pass without much effort.

But what Erida had truly wished for on this day, not even a ruling queen could acquire. Her mother was dead. Her father was dead. Neither Konrad Righand nor Alisandra Reccio had lived to see their daughter crowned or wed. She tried to feel them with her, as she'd felt the gods in the cathedral, but it was like reaching through open air. The usual emptiness remained. It was an old wound, but today it bled anew. It was difficult not to look for them, even when she knew they would not appear.

With the feasting hall in tatters, the ruins of her father's chandeliers smashed all over the floor, the reception took place in the palace gardens, beneath hastily assembled tents, with an armada of servants waving long fans. At least a good breeze blew off the lagoon, through the only gap in the palace walls.

Their table was separate from the rest, isolating the new couple from all but each other. Even Erida's council sat apart, arranged around a long table with Ronin glowering in their midst. She pitied Lady Harrsing, who tried in vain to engage the wizard in talk.

Erida sat, taking her hand from Taristan's. His blood ran too hot for summer. He did not seem to mind the temperature, despite his thick red doublet and the heavy gold chain strung between his shoulders. His cheeks remained pale; there was no sweat on his brow.

A servant offered him a goblet of wine. He took it without drinking, assessing the facets of the crystal cup, letting it catch the light. Taristan of Old Cor was noble in blood but not birth. He was not accustomed to the riches of royalty, nor the expectations.

"Are you going to gawk at me all day?" he said, raising his gaze to match her stare.

She didn't blink, unfazed by the challenge. "Where are you from?"

His answer was quick, stoic. "I am the blood of Old Cor."

Erida resisted the urge to roll her eyes once again. Instead she pulled at her wine, using the seconds to cool her frustration. "I mean, where were you *born*?"

"I don't know," he answered, shrugging without thought. "My parents were either dead or gone by the time I had the sense to look for them." His fingers played over the crystal goblet, looking for flaws. "The Elders took my brother to Iona and made him there. The rest of the world made me."

Thoughtful, Erida tried to listen between his words, to read thoughts as they raced through his mind. But his abyssal eyes were stone blank, as inscrutable as his face.

Taristan nudged the wine away. Unlike most rogues, he did not seem to have a taste for drink. "I spent my days in wandering."

"Even as a boy?" She pictured an orphan growing up harshly, with no money and only his wits, then his fists, to rely upon. *And then his blood, his great lineage, buried like a diamond waiting to be discovered.*

"Corblood do not grow roots," he said sternly. "I dislike this interrogation, Your Majesty."

Erida sipped at her wine before answering.

"I am your ruling queen; I follow my own will." *The agreement is already made, our lines drawn. But I might as well remind him.*

"Do as you like," he said, shrugging. The court glittered before them, eager to eat and drink even in the hot air. But they were as jumpy as rabbits. The events of the night before were not so easily forgotten. "Your will bothers me little, so long as we keep sight of the same goal."

The realm beneath the Lion, an empire of Galland, the Ward in my fist. The glory of Old Cor reborn. In her mind, the map on the wall of the council chamber bloomed with green, like grass in springtime. She could already feel all the world laid out, the hopes of her forefathers realized in a woman's hands. *My father's dream made real.*

She ducked her head to hide a smile, using her hair as a shield from the rest. Conquest was in her blood. It sated her better than any feast.

The first of twenty-one courses—twenty for the gods and one for the kingdom—was brought out quickly. The original plan had called for soup, but in the heat, the kitchens had wisely pivoted to a spread of herbs, cold sauces and spiced jams, cured meats, and thick, white cheeses.

Erida was served first, though she had little appetite.

"The city garrison continues their search," she said in a low voice, poking at her plate. *Quietly, discreetly. Peering into every ditch and sewer looking for Corayne and her Spindle sword. We must give no cause for alarm, to either the commons or the court.* "And we have companies riding out from the fort at Canterweld to comb the countryside. If she can be found, she *will* be found." The scratches on Taristan's face were not as blue as they were yesterday, giving over to purple as bruises took shape. "It's good she attacked you. No one will question us riding her down."

Taristan curdled under her attention, turning his head to hide the wound. "There are other matters to attend to," he ground out. A red sheen flared in his gaze, a trick of the sun filtering through the flapping tents.

This time, Erida did roll her eyes. She wondered if her new husband would be as predictable as most men. In this, it seemed, they were all alike.

"I know my duties, Taristan," she replied coolly, careful to use his name. Not a title, not an endearment. No *my lord* or *Your Highness*, by careful design. *I am king and queen. My rank far outweighs your own, no matter where your blood comes from.* "They will be performed."

Taristan hissed and forcibly drained his goblet, the wine dark on his lips. "I'm not talking about whatever nonsense your court requires after a wedding," he said. "That weighs very little in my mind, when measured against what is to come."

She blinked, surprised, though she did her best not to show it. A queen's hand of cards should not be so easily played.

"And what is to come?" she replied. "You have twenty thousand . . . *men* in the foothills of the Ward Mountains, awaiting orders before a Spindle torn." *Men* being the corpses of a burned realm, every soldier broken and obedient to her new consort, armed to the teeth and then some. They had killed Sir Grandel and the Norths, men she'd known all her life. But their ghosts bothered her little. "They're nothing to sneer at, but no match for the men at my disposal, should I muster the combined might of Galland."

"You know an army of Ashlanders is not all the Spindle gave me." Though the sun was bright, a darkness seemed to pool around Taristan. Erida felt it on her bare skin, a weight like a feather touch.

"Yes, the temple did something to you," she said, tentatively brushing his arm. Her eyes trailed over his chest, where a sword had punched through his heart. To anyone looking, they might have seemed the picture of cautious newlyweds. Instead of wolves sizing each other up. "The Spindle did something to you."

Taristan watched her trailing fingers. He remained as still as the surface of a pond, and just as inscrutable.

Erida swallowed, pulling her hand away. She was glad for their small table, away from the prying eyes and ears of a court that would not understand. To Konegin and the rest, Taristan was a blood match, a son of Old Cor with little more than his dynasty to offer, an inheritance for their children. A stepping-stone to the old empire, a path to be forged by her heirs. A birthright they could claim in conquest. Emperors and empresses reborn. But Erida remembered what Taristan had said in her petitions chamber, when she'd commanded the rest away. When he'd cut his palm and bled and healed before her eyes. When he'd told her of his destiny, and what it could buy them both.

She could not resist the opportunity, then or now.

"And you have another Spindle ripped in the desert, its forgotten realm bleeding through." She threw his own words back at him, the promises made with his proposal. Spindles torn, armies won. At the temple, in the dunes. More would follow, if Taristan and his wizard held up their end of the bargain. "As you said, you gain strength with every Spindle, and therefore so do I. In your body, in your army. So gain it," she whispered.

Her fist clenched on the table, knuckles bright with jeweled rings. She wished for Prevail in her hand, or the Spindleblade sheathed at her husband's hip. For a weapon to match the fire she felt inside.

"Take your sword and bleed for me, and I will bleed for you. Win us the crown our ancestors could only dream of."

He inhaled sharply, returning her scrutiny, and Erida almost felt the breath drawn through his teeth. He was thirty-three years old, fourteen years her senior. In royal circles, that was not so terrible. But he seemed older than his years. Because of the life he had lived or the Corblood in his veins, Erida did not know. *A crown sets you apart*, she knew. She'd felt one all her life, even before it landed on her head. *Perhaps it's the same with him: the weight of destiny never lifting. Until it becomes second nature.*

He continued to stare, black-eyed, a muscle feathering in his jaw. The son of Old Cor, a rogue and a murderer, did not enjoy being ordered around by anyone. *Men never do.*

"A marriage is a promise, and we promised each other the world entire," Erida said hotly, looking away from him with wrenching force. She set to her plate, but it held no taste for the Queen. She wanted nothing more than to be finished with all this nonsense. *I'm better suited to the council chamber than the feasting hall.*

Taristan's laugh was low, and as rough as his hands.

She looked back at him, braced for disdain. Instead Erida saw a sliver of pride.

"The Lion should take you as its sigil," he said, gesturing to the banners all over the tents. Green and gold, roaring true. "You're twice as fierce, and twice as hungry."

"Is that a compliment?"

"It was meant to be," he answered.

At the closest table, still several yards away, the red wizard sat and glared. He ignored the council around him, for all of Harrsing's efforts. Konegin pretended Ronin didn't exist at all, speaking only to his lump of a son. Both were gray-faced in defeat. Erida spared them little mind. Lord Konegin was an obstacle, yes, but small in comparison to the road ahead. And she had an ally against him, a powerful one, who could not be killed by man nor steel.

The wizard drew her eye instead.

"At first I thought Ronin was a priest."

Taristan finished the meat on his plate, leaving the rest undisturbed. "Silent and useless gods do not hold my interest," he muttered.

"In Galland, we pray to Syrek above all. God of war, god of victory, god of conquest, god of life. And, in some scriptures, some teachings, the god of death too. The god of hell and heaven, in equal measure. You need only decide which side to worship and believe in."

She thought of the statues, the idols, the many stained-glass windows and tapestries depicting Syrek and his bleeding sword, his flaming spear, sunlight like a halo around him, smoke and victory in his wake.

"The scriptures say he brought forth Old Cor, ushering your people into Allward from their lost realm." Erida leaned forward. "Perhaps he means to do so again."

Taristan did not hesitate. "Perhaps."

When the servant returned, Erida did not refuse another glass of ruby wine.

"Where does Ronin guide you next?" she asked when he was gone. The drink was cold, at least, a relief in the heat. And it numbed her a little, smoothing her edges after a long night and longer morning.

"He's found some promising leads in the cathedral records, whispers of Spindles through the centuries and further." Erida wanted to ask precisely what but refrained. "We'll head east."

"And what will the next Spindle bring us?" *Invulnerability granted. One army given. And in the desert, the power to rule the seas. What more comes?*

"I don't know until the crossing is made. I could open a door to any realm in existence, known or unknown. To Glorian, the home of the Elders, or the lost realm of my ancestors. To Infyrna's furious blaze, the frozen wastes of Kaldine, Syderion, Drift, Irridas, Tempest," he said, rattling off realms Erida only half-remembered from religious lessons and Spindle tales.

"Even the Crossroads, the door to all doorways." Taristan's voice dropped to a whisper. "Or Asunder herself." He looked to his wizard, holding his red gaze. Something passed between them, a message even Erida could not fathom. "If the girl cannot be found by nightfall, you must set a guard in Ibal, and in the foothills."

A corner of her mouth lifted in a smirk. *Corayne of Old Cor is barely more than a child, a sparrow alone while the hawks circle.* "You're afraid of her getting through burning sands and an army? She barely escaped my *palace*—"

"But escape she did," Taristan bit back. The red sheen was in his eyes again, a glimmer like the edge of a coin. "There's more at play with her, and the others traipsing after her." His face darkened, his black brows swooping together. "Set the guard, Your Majesty."

Dispatching men to the temple, to guard foothills within my own border, will be easy enough. We just need to keep a low profile, direct attention elsewhere. Erida clenched her teeth. *But to send a company to Ibal, a foreign kingdom? Over the Long Sea and into the Great Sands, past their fearsome navy . . . how do I disguise that? How do I even make such an order?*

Taristan held her stare as she thought, watching the scales balance. She wanted to shrink from his attention, to think alone, to plan in her own measured way. But there was no escape from the man beside her. *And there should not be. He is my husband, a choice I made, a path I followed. He is mine to use. I should not hide from him.*

Though no answer came, Erida knew she would will one into being eventually. She nodded slowly and he smiled, cruel as a knife-edge.

"Very well," she said. "You'll leave this evening."

He dipped his head, glancing at Ronin again. The wizard placed his white hands on the table and stood, despite the second course being served around him.

"I'll leave in an hour," Taristan replied, matching the wizard.

Erida watched him stand, her face carefully blank. She was not the only one to see. The eyes of the court rose with her consort, some of them grinning rudely, others whispering. Erida did not like being pushed into a corner, but this was a corner she needed to face.

With a sigh, she rose to her feet as well, leaving the plates and wine abandoned.

"I suppose it's best the court think you eager rather than indifferent," she hissed. He eyed her sharply, confused for a blistering second.

Then she pulled him away, the Lionguard traipsing along at a respectable distance.

"One course of the wedding feast," she muttered, taking his arm with a violent grip. "I believe we've set the record."

The royal residence was oddly quiet. Most of the palace servants, even her handmaidens, had been commandeered for the ceremony and reception. The halls echoed, yawning as Erida walked the well-known steps to her bedchamber. The Lionguard tromped behind, their armor ringing, but they would not follow much longer. The bedding of a ruling queen would have no witnesses. Not even the red wizard, who followed behind the knights with his haunting glare.

It was not so warm within the cool stone of the palace, but she felt heat all the same, creeping up her arm and into her spine. Taristan's palm still pressed against hers, neither of them dropping the charade of a couple. As with the glass at the feast, he looked sharply at everything—the walls, the rugs, the tapestries— drinking in a world he had never known before. All of it was as familiar to Erida as her own face. She tried to see it through the eyes of another. It felt bizarre.

Her solar was as long as a gallery, lit by a wall of windows looking out over the gardens. She could see the tents, big as ship sails, and the lagoon beyond like a green mirror. The knights planted themselves beside the windows in practiced formation. Their path ended here, guarding the door to the Queen's bedchamber. But no further.

Better to get it over with as soon as possible. One less thing to do.

Taristan glanced at Ronin before Erida could, his expression tight. "Be ready to leave."

The wizard didn't argue, and turned in a smooth arc, his red cloak sweeping behind him. He left the long sitting room without a word, disappearing through another doorway, seeking a back stair. *Only a few weeks and he knows the palace as well as my oldest servants.*

It was not often that Queen Erida of Galland opened a door for herself, and she endeavored not to struggle with the thick oak ones leading to her bedchamber. They swung on greased hinges, heavier than she remembered, to reveal what looked like the heart of another cathedral.

Rugs patterned the floor, frames of priceless mirror glass

decorated the walls, and curtains hung the columns and archways. Red flowers bloomed in vases, perfuming the air. A rose window illuminated the chamber, an ancient bed caught in the circle of rainbow light. In winter, curtains could be drawn around it, to insulate against the cold, but they were flung open in summer, the down pillows and brocade silk blankets difficult to ignore. Erida had never seen this room so empty or so still. With a jolt, she realized she had never been alone in her bedchamber, not once in her life.

The door shut with a snap. In spite of herself and the calm she tried to exude, Erida jumped in her skin.

Taristan dropped her hand. "This is of little use," he grumbled, gesturing between them.

Then he shucked off the golden chain between his shoulders. His cloak fell with it, a pool of silk blood. He walked, not to the bed but to the closest window. It looked over the spires of the New Palace, beyond the walls to the river, the canals, the bridges. Ascal splayed out, served up on a plate. He looked eager to devour it whole.

Erida removed her crown with more care, laying it on a dressing table. "To me, yes," she answered, grateful for something to argue. It would make this less strange. "But an heir would cement *your* precarious position here."

He leaned against one of the columns, arms and ankles crossed. "A waste of time. I don't need a child; I need Spindles," he replied. "I'll consider our dynasty when the Ward is won."

The Queen scoffed and set to the pearl buttons marching down the back of her dress. They were difficult, near impossible without her fleet of maids. Taristan let her struggle, never moving from the window.

"You're a rare man," she said, eyeing him over her shoulder. "Unfortunately, Husband, we can only remake the world when we own it. But for now there are rules."

The pearls unfastened, slipping through their loops, until the gown hung off her frame. Erida stepped out from it as nonchalantly as she could, clad only in her underclothes. A fine silk shift, light as a dove's wing, left little to the imagination. Still, Taristan did not move, even when the Queen perched on the edge of the great bed.

"Make no mistake, my cousin Konegin would seize any opportunity to cast you down and annul any marriage of mine he opposes."

"Then kill him," he said dryly, dripping with disinterest.

Erida would be lying if she said she had not considered such a thing, especially in recent days. Konegin had his uses, but they were steadily becoming outweighed by his dangers.

"If only life were that simple," she said, picking at her sheer skirt. *Perhaps if I do away with clothing all together, I might stir him to action and get this over with.* Then another thought seized her, and she snapped up her head, eyes wide as she looked over her consort. "By the gods, are you chaste, Taristan?"

His responding smile was crooked, drawn up to show a single, deep dimple in his cheek. Somehow, the scratches down his face complemented the grin. Those flat black eyes sparked, and Erida fought the urge to break his stare.

"Hardly," he said, a hand straying to the gold clasps of his doublet. "But aren't you? Isn't that one of your *rules*?" He cast a hand around the room, using the other to unfasten the fabric at his throat. Pale skin showed beneath.

Finally, Erida thought, gritting her teeth. She wasn't sure which was more frustrating—her obtuse husband or the rising thud of her own heartbeat.

"Some rules are less important than others, and easier to break, if you know how," she said dismissively. The Queen of Galland was only bound by what the court saw, and it was easier to hide dalliances than a fever or cold, with both men and women. "So get on with it, then."

His doublet hung open, revealing his own underclothes. The neck of his shirt was unlaced, strings hanging. The planes of his bare chest stood out, sculpted like a maiden's dream, well formed by the years. But the smooth skin was scarred in a way Erida had never seen, white lines tracing over his collarbone. As her eyes followed their paths, she realized they were his veins, standing out like roots or branching lightning. He closed the distance between them as she looked, her blue eyes wide and consuming. *Is his whole body like this?* She wondered. *Is this the price the Spindles demand?*

"Is this what you want, Erida of Galland?"

Suddenly he stood over her, glaring down, a lock of dark red hair falling over his forehead. She reached up to remove his doublet, fingers grasping at his collar, but he seized her by both wrists. His skin seared against her own, though his grip was gentle as he pulled her hands away.

"Get on with it," she said again, a whisper this time. A plea as much as a command.

He leaned forward, coming closer. Erida could smell the tang of smoke on his skin, the new embers of flame.

Then he dropped her wrists. "Not like this."

She didn't move when he reached behind her, swiping pillows and blankets to the floor. Silk and fine linens peeled away, spilling off the bed at haphazard angles. He even shifted the mattress for good measure, forcing her to jump to her feet.

"What are you doing?" Erida demanded, looking between him and the ruined bed.

He didn't answer and assessed the blankets. After a long moment, he nodded, satisfied. Then he rounded on the Queen, his focus unbroken, his eyes combing over her hair. His fingers soon followed, loosing her braids, mussing the ash-brown curls until they fell in errant waves, unkempt and out of place. Erida stared at him through it all, speechless, furious. She wanted to slap him away. She wanted to pull him closer, the heat of his fingers a threat and a promise. Taristan kept his lips pursed, his breathing even, his eyes far from her own as he worked. And, finally, he tugged at the shift, lowering one side of the collar, until a white shoulder peeked through, spotted with three small freckles few men had ever seen.

Before she could even flinch, he drew a dagger and cut at his own palm, using the hand to smear a line of blood across the white sheets.

Only when he stepped back, putting a full six feet between them, did he raise his eyes. His palm healed before her eyes, the flesh knitting back together as he wiped the blood away. He scrubbed his other hand through his hair, setting it at ends like her own. Erida glared at him with all the rage and indignation she could muster, her anger volcanic. A tinge of pink spotted high on his cheeks, the only change in his stoic face.

"I'll send word when Ronin gets his bearings," Taristan said, bending into a short, stiff bow. It was the only awkward thing about him, like watching a lion try to joust.

"That's too much blood," Erida said dryly, glaring at the mussed blankets, feeling hot all over. *How dare you*, she thought, running a hand through her ruined hair. She wanted to strangle him.

"Enough to satisfy any stupid lords who dare to ask after our bedsheets."

"There will still be talk," she said through clenched teeth. *If you shrug again, I will kill you, and find someone less infuriating to marry.*

Taristan tossed his doublet away with a curling sneer, leaving only his undershirt tucked into his breeches. He seemed more himself without the trappings of royalty, and he rolled his shoulders, the white veins moving with his muscles.

"Let them talk, Your Majesty," he replied, turning on his heel. It was the closest thing to a farewell he gave, another Spindle already on his mind.

In his wake, the Queen burned. *Not like this*, she thought, playing the words over and over in her mind. It was a puzzle she didn't know how to solve.

21

EYES OPENED
Sorasa

Fleeing on horseback was not the means of escape Sorasa would have chosen. The farmlands of the Great Lion's fertile valley rolled with gentle hills and patchwork fields, offering poor cover in daylight. Their mounts were little more than pack horses, even the strange gray mare the Jydi witch had somehow summoned. There would be no mad gallop for the border. *Not on these stumbling nags*, Sorasa thought, despairing of the stolen horse beneath her. It was no sand mare, a shadow of the horses of her homeland, who moved like wind made flesh.

She led the way again, with Andry on her left. The squire was sharp-eyed, at least, always watching the horizon behind them. He named castles as they loomed, silhouetted on the hills, pointing out the feudal holdings of some lord or lady. Information of little use, mostly, but at least Corayne drank it in, asking questions as the hours passed.

The Cor girl was like a rag in water, soaking up whatever she could of the lands around them. She wore a stolen shawl over her shoulders to hide the Spindleblade on her back. And she had a hat ready, should they pass an errant patrol. Not that Sorasa—or Dom, for that matter—would give a country patrol the opportunity to see Corayne's face. The assassin would sooner kill ten watchmen than risk one breathing a hint of their whereabouts. Her focus strayed from the road to Corayne more often than not. Dom was the same, his eyes never leaving Corayne's shoulders, as if his stare alone could shield her from the dangers of the world.

Valtik didn't seem to notice any of them at all. The witch let her horse meander, keeping pace but weaving away from their track to pick through broken hedges and saddle-high fields of wheat. She sang under her breath, in Jydi and in another language no one could place. Of course the words rhymed. Sorasa shut the song out.

It's difficult enough minding the squire, the Elder, and the apparent hope for the realm. I refuse to waste time or energy minding the witch too.

The farm lanes branched, trailing between hills and streams. Peasant farmers paid them little notice. No one patrolled the lanes, but they were winding, doubling back on themselves. As the hours wore on, the farms grew more sparse, separated by brush and woodlands instead of hedges. The horses slowed, picking their way on tentative legs.

"Our only advantage is speed," Andry said, sitting up in the saddle as they broke through another stand of undergrowth. He urged his horse alongside Sorasa's. "If we get on the Cor road west, we can give the horses rein and make better time."

Sorasa grimaced when Corayne mirrored Andry's motions, maneuvering her horse to her other side. The assassin did not enjoy being hemmed in by anything, let alone teenagers.

"I've always wanted to see a Cor road," Corayne said. She even heaved a wistful sigh.

"I met you on a Cor road, you scheming imp," Sorasa bit back, and Corayne's face fell. "If the Queen of Galland has any sense, she's sent her fastest scouts along the roads in every direction, with orders to look out for a beanpole squire, an immortal troll, and a cloaked girl with a stolen sword and too many questions." Sorasa twitched her heels and her horse jolted out ahead. "If you want to take the roads, fine, but we'll be riding into an easy trap."

Dom's voice was deep behind her. "Certainly you have a plan for whatever enemies we do run into, Sarn," he said dryly.

"Most of them involve throwing you at them," Sorasa shot back. He grumbled in reply.

"No roads, Corayne," she added finally. The girl sank in the saddle, scowling. Sorasa could see a hundred replies fighting up her throat. "Farm lanes and deer paths won't get us to Adira quickly, but they'll get us to Adira alive."

"And once we're there?" Andry reined alongside her again, undeterred. He looked older on horseback, at ease and in control. "You going to sell us to a northern slaver or bet our lives in a game of dice?"

Sorasa wanted to ignore him. Silence was a stone wall few could climb. And the squire's fear of Adira was inconsequential, if not idiotic. But she had a feeling he would pester her all the way to the city gates if need be. She offered a flash of teeth barely cousin to a smile.

"I was sold into slavery before I could walk, Trelland. I don't intend to put anyone else through that, even Lord Domacridhan," she said, jerking her head back at the Elder. It was easy to pretend she didn't see the sudden pull of pity on their faces. Even Dom softened a little, like granite worn by centuries of wind and rain. Sorasa had no use for any of it. "And I doubt any of you would be worth much in the gambling dens. The witch, maybe."

Corayne and Andry exchanged uncertain glances, falling quiet. But before Sorasa could enjoy it, Dom rumbled from the rear of their party.

"You aim to recruit more of your kind in that cesspool," he growled.

Sorasa sucked in a frustrated breath. *How can a few rumors of thievery, murder, and citywide criminal enterprise have everyone in such a twist?*

"Assassins and mercenaries," Dom pushed on. "Bound by coin, not honor or duty."

"Am I still being paid for my services, Elder?" Sorasa snapped, turning in the saddle to face him. Dom's infernal gaze bored into her. "No, the Amhara are not my aim," she said, collecting herself. "One of us is enough. But I do have two others in mind."

"Murderers and thieves, then," she heard Dom mutter.

"Better than a queen already allied against us. Or an Elder monarch too afraid to leave her palace," Sorasa snapped. She listened for his telltale snarl or hiss of frustration. Somehow, he rewarded her with both.

She guided her horse down a stream bank and crossed the rocky shallows. The air was cooler, the light soft. Though her homeland was dominated by the vast beauty of the Great Sands, it was also a country of water. Oasis pools, thousands of miles of bright coast, and the mighty Ziron thundering out of the mountains to dance northeast across the desert, giving life to Qaliram and Almasad before joining the Long Sea. She felt better with the water kissing her boots and the farms fading behind them.

The others followed her into the stream, silent and storm-faced. Andry, afraid of the city ahead. Corayne, afraid of the sword on her back. Dom, afraid of nearly everything.

And I am afraid too. It did no good to ignore fear or doubt.

The borderlands between Galland and Larsia were no wilderness. An hour's ride in any direction would bring them to a farm or castle or village. But for now they threaded a needle. It was right somehow, the path unseen but still felt.

Though the horse beneath her was next to useless, Sorasa patted a hand down her neck.

"Besides," she said, "only one of them can be considered a murderer. Best not to bring it up."

"I can take first watch."

Andry stared down at her. He was both taller and wider than the Amhara assassin. His stance was broad, his brown hands on his hips, his dark eyes black in the dim light of evening. Even in his battered clothing, with no beard and light bruises on his face, he looked the picture of a knight.

She heaved the saddlebags from her horse's back, tucking them over her arms. "Noble of you, Squire," she said, dropping them in a heap. The clearing was good ground to make camp, halfway up a rocky crag, their backs defended by sheer rock, their front obscured by trees. "But I think the Elder can manage."

Corayne stood at the edge of the campsite, looking down into the valley of the Green Lion. Under a black moon and clouded stars, there was only darkness. Her sword laid flat next to her. She rolled her shoulders, working away the ache of carrying it.

"Dom should sleep," Corayne said, glancing at the immortal. He tightened under her suggestion. "Heal up. It isn't every day you lose half the blood in your body."

He scowled, working on a small fire. The kindling glowed. "I doubt it was half."

Sorasa and Corayne rolled their eyes at precisely the same time.

"We'll double," the assassin said, patting the squire on the shoulder. He pursed his lips but didn't argue. "I don't intend to sleep through another corpse vision. Or worse."

The witch returned abruptly, her hair braided with ivy. She grinned toothily at them all as her mount nudged its way in among their tied horses.

"Oh, I wouldn't worry about another sending," Valtik said airily, sitting down in the dirt. Her bare feet splayed out before her, soles black as the sky. "The threads have drawn together, all that is ending."

Dom stood and frowned at her. "A sending?" he breathed, incredulous.

"Care to explain?" Corayne said, looking between them.

"It's Vederan magic, rare even among my kind." Dom paced around the witch so he could face her. She didn't look up from her hands, busy weaving something Sorasa couldn't see. "Vedera of great power can send images, visions, figures. To carry messages, mostly."

Valtik tutted low in her throat and stuffed her weaving up her sleeve. She kept her back to the growing flames. "It isn't just your magic." Then she checked the pouch at her waist, rattling the bones inside. "Keep an eye out for rabbits, boy. I'm low on knuckle-bones. Tragic."

Sorasa wanted to point out the absurdity of calling a five-hundred-year-old immortal being such a thing. *Unless it isn't. Unless he is a boy, to someone like her. A Spindlerotten witch.* She eyed Valtik again, glaring through the shadows. The old woman was as gnarled like a tree root, her eyes unnatural, blue as the heart of a lightning bolt.

"You sent them." Corayne's voice was flat and hard, steely as her face. Her grip on the sword tightened, fingers locking over the leather of the sheath. "The corpses, the ghosts."

I could smell them: they were burned and broken. I could hear the air gasping in their ruined chests. I could feel them, the heat of unending flame. They were as smoke, real and unreal, before my very eyes. Sorasa clenched her jaw, searching Valtik's face for some answer. The old woman did not move.

"*You* sent them," Corayne said again, her teeth gritted. Cold air rippled over them, a brush of winter. "Did you send my dreams too? The nightmares I've had all summer long?"

"Was not I who touched your sleep," the Jydi crowed. "But something red and dark and buried deep."

Corayne felt it now, clawing at her throat. The memory of her nightmares nearly turned sunlight to shadow. She swallowed hard but saw no lie in the old woman.

Then the squire jolted like a startled horse, some realization breaking over him. He circled the witch, incredulous. "I have not heard the whispers since I found you."

"The whispers—what whispers?" Dom's voice stumbled.

Trelland ignored him. "So many voices, and one like winter. One like *yours*." His breath caught. "You've been speaking to me for weeks, telling me what to do. Keep the sword hidden, abandon my mother—"

"How?" Dom sputtered. "Whispers? A sending? They were Taristan's army, the Ashlanders exactly—"

Valtik said nothing, content to watch them flounder. And Sorasa watched her. She crossed her arms, keeping her distance from the Jydi witch, far from the circle of the weak fire.

"I think instead of how, we should be asking why," Sorasa murmured. "Why whisper to Andry Trelland? Why send corpse shadows after us in the night?"

To her surprise, Valtik's head snapped up and her grin was manic, unhinged for a shivering second. The kindling crackled at her back, outlining her hunched figure, leaving her face in shadow, half formed. The light played tricks. Her teeth were too long; she went cat-eyed, pupils like slits in the strange blue. The ivy braids gleamed metallic, slick. Sorasa clenched her jaw, willing herself to see what existed and not what the witch wanted her to see.

"You know why, Forsaken," Valtik said, blinking. She shifted, and the shadows pulled back to show an old woman again.

"Something to guide you. Something to guide them. To open your eyes, after where you've been."

Her muscles tightened, taut as coiled rope. "Stop calling me that, Witch."

"I only call people what they are," Valtik replied with a half-moon smile. She waggled her feet like a child playing before the hearth.

"And what would you call yourself, *Gaeda?*" Corayne said, easing herself to her knees next to the witch. Andry tensed, as if he wanted to pull her back from the old woman. But Corayne was unafraid, looking intently into her eyes.

Valtik put a wrinkled hand to Corayne's cheek.

Corayne didn't flinch, letting the witch stare into her.

"The North Star," the old woman finally said, tweaking her on the nose. Then her hand darted into her long cloak, pulling out the twig-and-bone charm still crusted with dried blood. She pressed it into Corayne's fingers, closing each one over it. "Or bizarre," she added, chuckling.

"I agree with the latter," Dom said.

Corayne leaned back on her heels, whirling to him. "You go to sleep," she said, full of force. He blanched, flushing red over his cheeks and neck. The Elder had probably not been ordered to bed for centuries, if it had even happened at all.

He sputtered, "I am not a mortal infant."

Corayne stood and shrugged, undeterred by his towering height. "We need you healthy, Dom."

"I—oh, very well," he blustered, storming away from the campfire.

Sorasa nearly howled when he lay down in the dirt like a dog, with no cloak, no blanket, no bed of any kind. He simply folded his arms, face to the sky, his eyes dropping shut in an instant. The snore that followed was instantaneous and unbearable.

"Would anyone stop me if I smothered him?" she muttered, scuffing her boot in Dom's direction. "Joking," she snapped, catching sight of Andry and Corayne's disapproval. "Andry, I'll wake you when it's your turn at the watch."

The squire ducked his chin. "All right."

"And you, no sendings, no whispers—" Sorasa added, turning back to the witch. But Valtik was gone, leaving no trace, not even the odd earthen scent that followed her everywhere.

"Oh she's gone again," the assassin sneered, eyeing the darkness. She felt oddly like the darkness was staring back. "Magnificent."

With every passing day, Sorasa bet with herself. Who would break first and succumb to their curiosity? The next afternoon, she thought it would be Dom, when his eyes narrowed on her with his usual furor. But he never spoke. Corayne was an easy guess. The girl had thoughts about everything, from the strength of the wind off Mirror Bay to the growing season in the lowlands. Certainly she would find the spine to question Sorasa Sarn, the Fallen, the Forsaken. And there was Trelland too, not as blatant as the others. But he stole glances all day long, his interest obvious even to the horses. Valtik already knew and wouldn't bother. *She probably spends all day thinking up rhymes*, Sorasa thought, grinding her teeth.

In the end, it was Corayne who summoned the courage. She

362 REALM BREAKER

had the tact to ask a few days later, in the evening, apart from the others, who were busy preparing another meager camp. Andry was off using his foolish kettle, brewing up some tea.

"Osara," Corayne said, letting the word hang in the air.

The sky was clear, and Sorasa lifted her face to the stars. She stared at them instead of Corayne. They had known each other only a few weeks, and sometimes it was easy to forget that the girl had Corblood in her veins, and a pirate for a mother. *Not tonight,* Sorasa thought.

"It's a title given to blooded Amhara exiled from the Guild," she said plainly.

Fallen, Forsaken, Broken. All meant the same, all were uttered with the deepest and most vicious disgust. *Osara,* in her language, which stung worst of all. Lord Mercury had declared it in front of all the Guild, with every eye upon the fresh mark still bleeding on her ribs. Cruder than the rest, only a few lines of stick and poke, given without thought to her pain. She never made a sound while they did it, branding her forever, casting her from the ranks of the Amhara. Even Sorasa admitted the punishment fit the crime.

"I suspected as much," Corayne murmured, dropping her voice. It would not stop the immortal from hearing their conversation. Sorasa only wished he could hear all the times she cursed him in her head. "Dom didn't know, when he found you in Byllskos. When he contracted you to find me."

"I was simply the first Amhara to cross his path, the easiest to find, the only one no longer shielded by the strength of the Guild." She glanced across the clearing, a flat surrounded by thick forest. The border was close, the trees pressing in as they could not in the valley. Sorasa moved into the eaves of the wood and Corayne followed without question. "He doesn't know how money works, or much of the world, for that matter. Of course I took the contract, even if the Guild no longer allows me to."

Corayne narrowed her eyes, and Sorasa braced herself for the inevitable question. The why. The reason for the words cut and inked into her flesh.

But it did not come.

"What are you going to do with the money?"

"What does anyone do with money?"

"Most get old and fat in comfort." Her gaze lingered on the assassin's tattooed fingers. They were crooked, scarred beneath the ink, callused by bow and blade. "I don't think that's what you want."

Her scrutiny rankled. Sorasa gave her a sneer sharp enough to cut flesh. "You think smuggling steel and charting trade routes for a ship you've never sailed on gives you the faintest idea what I want?"

"I think growing up with a pirate for a mother, a woman with all the money she could ever want, a daughter she claims to love, who will never turn from the risk and reward of the sea, gives me some idea," she said coolly, folding her arms. "I know he offered you something more than money. Something more valuable than all the gold in the vaults of Iona. I just couldn't figure out what."

Until now.

"Well, Corayne an-Amarat. Impress me with what you *think* you know," Sorasa hissed. She felt like a lonely traveler facing a mountain lion, spreading her arms wide in an attempt to scare it off. An odd thing for an assassin to feel against a young girl, even one as keen and clear-eyed as Corayne.

"You need a way back in, and you can't buy it, or you would have already."

Sorasa had never met Meliz an-Amarat, Hell Mel, captain of the *Tempestborn*, the furious and fierce mistress of the Long Sea. And if Taristan's face was any indication, her daughter did not take after her mother's line. But her mother was in her all the same, in the set of her voice, the steel resolve, the dogged and unyielding pursuit. For Meliz, that meant treasure, bounty, a profit. For Corayne, it was truth. She hunted it like a hound.

"Assassins love gold," she pressed on. Her eyes took on a distant look as she spoke, sifting through her own thoughts. "But they love blood more. The Amhara Guild is famed for their skill. And what could be more skillful than killing an Elder?"

I asked for gold and he paid it. I set a higher price than any before. All the wealth of Iona, an immortal queen's treasure laid at my feet. He promised it without thought.

And when I asked for his life, for his throat cut by my own hand, in a place of my choosing, before the eyes I wanted . . . he didn't hesitate to promise me that too.

There was no use in denial. Corayne would see through it. She wouldn't push, but she would know. *And what do I care? I've done worse to better, and for less in return.*

One insufferable immortal life is worth the Guild. It is a cost I am happy to pay.

"If you're worrying about Domacridhan's gigantic *head*, don't bother," Sorasa answered. They were closer to the water now,

Mirror Bay only a few miles south. A breeze blew cool through the trees, smelling of rain somewhere far off. She inhaled greedily. Still, the scent of rain was a novelty to her. "The road is long before us."

Corayne's throat bobbed. The stars were in her eyes. "And at the end?"

"If we survive, you mean?" *A rather large if.* "Let's think about that bridge when we cross it."

"I'd like to know that bridge isn't going to be cut in half."

The constellation of the Unicorn shone brightly overhead, said to be a good omen. A sign of luck. Sorasa believed in neither, but it was still a comfort. There were unicorns in her homelands, among the famed Shiran herds of the sand dunes. Black with onyx horns, white with pearl, brown with bronze. She had seen them with her own eyes, more than once. They were gone in most of the north, fading with the years, but the south knew how to protect its wonders. Sorasa longed to see one again, a wonder made of flesh instead of starlight.

She took a step away from Corayne, drawing her stolen coat closer. Summer still ruled, but Sorasa felt a chill sink into her desert blood.

"Ask the witch, if you want the future. 'So the bone tells,'" she chuckled, rolling her eyes.

Corayne's expression soured. "I don't think it works like that."

"If it works at all," Sorasa replied. "She might be Spindlerotten, but she's not exactly helping us along, is she? Or, at least, she only helps when she feels like it."

"I think they prefer the term *Spindletouched.* And she *is* helping."

"Calling us names and speaking in riddles isn't the kind of help we need." Once again, the witch was nowhere in sight. She could be hiding three steps away or three miles, for all Sorasa knew. It was frustrating; it was unnerving. There was no urgency to the old woman, even with all her warnings about the realm and its doom. "She says there's another Spindle torn, fine. Where is it? What is it doing? What are we supposed to face, and how? Does she expect us to ride into hell and fight What Waits ourselves?"

Sorasa jumped when Valtik seemed to melt out of the tree line, a pair of dead rabbits dangling from her belt. "Where's the fun in telling you everything?" she said, not breaking pace. "That's a boring song to sing."

"There are too many curse words, in too many languages, for me to choose only one," Sorasa growled at the witch's silhouette. *Why am I doing this?* She asked herself for the hundredth time.

The corpses loomed in answer, just as terrible. Even though she now knew their origin. That was somehow worse, to think they'd only been sendings, shadows of what the realm truly faced. The many hands of Taristan of Old Cor, who was the hand of What Waits.

After a moment, she realized Corayne was still with her, letting the shadows creep around them. She watched Sorasa as she would the sea, reading a tide. It was disconcerting, to say the least.

"You didn't ask why I was exiled."

Corayne shifted, as if coming unstuck. "I figure that's your business," she muttered, nearly inaudible as she walked away. It was her turn for first watch.

Sorasa tried to remember the last time she'd said thank you to a living person and meant it. *Years, if not decades,* she realized, racking her brain.

Well, no use in breaking the streak now.

22

WORTH THE PAIN
Andry

They crossed the Orsal under the cover of darkness, the gentle river sloshing up to their knees as they rode single file beneath the keen light of a sliver moon. *We are in Larsia now*, Andry knew, feeling the invisible divide pass over them. He expected relief, but it never came. *The Queen of Galland will hunt us no matter where we go, so long as we hold a Spindleblade. So long as Corayne lives*. Andry shivered, but not from the water soaking through his breeches.

She rode next to him, bowing under the weight of the sword. As soon as they were out of the river, she dozed, her head lolling forward on her chest. Andry smiled to himself and marveled at her ability to sleep in the saddle, or on any ground they made camp on. Even with the weight of the realm on her shoulders, Corayne an-Amarat had a talent for sleeping.

But she does not sleep deeply, he thought. Despite the weak light, the shadows beneath her eyes stood out starkly. Her eyes fluttered behind her lids, swept away in some dream.

When they finally made camp by a copse of willow trees, he was glad to take the first watch. Sorasa claimed one tree like a tent, disappearing behind a curtain of leaves, while Dom took another, gesturing for Corayne to follow. Even when she was sleeping, he was never far from Corayne. She yawned, half awake, trudging into the roots.

Any good squire knew how to clean and dry traveling clothes, and Andry Trelland was a very good squire. He spent his watch tending their gear, scrubbing mud from leather, oiling steel, and checking over the horses. He lost himself in chores he used to chafe under, giving his mind something to focus on that wasn't the ending of the realm. When it was time to wake Dom for his turn, the camp was spotless, their saddlebags organized, the horses sleeping soundly with cleaned shoes and gleaming coats.

The willow branches parted, showing two lumps asleep among the roots, tucked into their cloaks. For once, Corayne was still, her face smooth, her mouth slightly parted. Her black hair fanned out around her like a dark halo.

Andry's cheeks warmed against the cool night and he glanced away, turning to the great hulk that was an Elder. To his surprise, Dom was still sleeping. His brow furrowed, his eyelids squeezed shut, and his lips moved without sound, his face pulled in what looked like pain.

"My lord?" Andry whispered, dropping his voice so he could barely hear himself.

The Elder's eyes snapped open, wavering as he took in his

bearings, pulling himself from sleep as one might pull themselves from the sea.

The squire waited, biting his lip with worry. *This is not like him*, he thought, but before he could offer to take a double watch, Dom rose to his feet in silence, throwing the cloak of Iona around his shoulders again. He went without a word, slipping back through the willow branches.

Andry followed. *Well, at least I can sleep now*, he thought, but Dom's behavior gave him pause. Instead of roving the camp, taking the perimeter as he usually did, the leviathan Elder settled onto a rock and stared at his boots. His jaw worked, his gaze far away, his mind clearly somewhere else.

"Was it a bad dream?" the squire heard himself ask. Though exhaustion mounted, pulling at his edges, Andry claimed the boulder next to Dom.

"The Vedera do not dream," he answered with a prim sniff. Andry only stared, an eyebrow raised. "Often."

The squire shrugged. "If you want to talk, if you need someone to speak to—"

"The only thing I need is Taristan's head on a spike," Dom snarled to the stars.

His rage was obvious, but beneath it—*pain*. Andry felt it in himself, the anger and sorrow melding into one, until it held him together as much as it pulled him apart.

"I dream of it too, that day at the temple," he murmured. "I see them die every time I close my eyes."

The Elder said nothing, silent as the stone he sat on. His face went blank, his eyes like shuttered windows. Whatever Dom felt, he wrestled it away where no one else could see. But Andry perceived.

He inched closer.

"Had you ever lost someone, before all this?"

Certainly an immortal has seen things die before, but not so close. Maybe he doesn't know how to grieve, or understand death at all. Perhaps he's never had to.

The silence stretched like a blanket, Dom's face still empty. Andry waited. He had learned patience as a page boy, an easy lesson in the halls of the New Palace. It was nothing to call on it now, when his friend needed it.

Finally the Elder roused, his eyes gleamed, oddly wet.

"I was a child when my parents were taken from me, called home to Glorian by the Elder gods," he said slowly, each word a battle. "Some three hundred years ago. The last dragon upon the Ward was terrorizing the Calidonian coast. They rode from Iona, seeking glory." His voice broke, his massive hands knitted together. "They never found it."

Andry swallowed hard.

"My father died when I was a boy too," he forced out. The pain had been dulled by the years, its edge long lost. But still his father's absence was an ache, a hole he would never fill. "It was nothing as exciting as a dragon. Just a petty border skirmish. Men dead on both sides, for no real reason."

The squire looked up to find the Elder staring, studying him as he would an opponent.

"Cortael's death feels . . . different," Dom said, searching for the right words. "Worse."

Andry dropped his head again, nodding furiously. "Because we were there. Because we lived while the rest didn't."

Sir Grandel and the Norths rose up before him, their faces white in death, their armor rusted, their bodies going to rot. Lord Okran appeared too, the shadow of Kasa's eagle passing over him. Andry squeezed his eyes shut to block out the images, only to find them staring behind his eyes. Inescapable.

"We survived, and some part of us regrets it. It doesn't make sense, that I live while they are in the ground," he forced out, eyes stinging. "A living squire, and so many dead knights."

Dom's voice rumbled, low in his throat, choked with emotion he did not know how to feel. "If I could, I'd make you a knight right here. You've certainly earned it by now."

Another figure joined the dead warriors in Andry's mind: a knight of Galland with an easy smile and a blue-starred shield. *Father*, Andry thought, calling for someone who would never answer. *I can't even remember his voice.*

He forced himself to look at Dom again, letting reality chase the visions away. He stared at the Elder, green as the forest, gray as stone.

"I don't think that's a path I can walk anymore," he muttered. It felt like letting go of an anchor and drifting out to sea. Unbound but without direction, free but on treacherous ground. "The Battle of the Lanterns was fought on this land," he said suddenly, looking back and forth along the willows crowding the riverbank. "Galland and Larsia, warring for a barren border."

"I don't know much of your recent histories," Dom answered, sounding apologetic.

Andry nearly laughed. *The Battle of the Lanterns was a century ago.* "My mother had a tapestry of it in our parlor. The great legions. Galland standing golden and triumphant over the Larsian surrender. I used to stare at it, try to see my own face among the knights, the Lion across my chest, a victory in my hands." He saw the woven image in his mind, the colors too bright, the soldiers of Galland suddenly hateful, their visages sharp and menacing. "Now I stand against them. Everything I've ever known, everything I've ever wanted. It's gone."

"I feel the same," Dom said, to Andry's surprise. "Let someone else be a prince of Iona. I want no part of that place, a haven for cowards and selfish fools." The Elder sucked in a breath, chest rising and falling. He glanced at the willow where their great hope slept, small beneath her cloak. "Cortael never told me about Corayne."

Andry followed his gaze. "To keep her safe?"

Dom shook his head. "I think he was ashamed."

The squire felt his teeth gnash together, both in anger and to bite back a curse. *I will not insult a dead man.* "Then he never knew her," he replied instead, eyes still leveled on the willow. A wind rustled the branches, revealing Corayne nestled among the roots. *Brilliant, brave Corayne.* "No parent could be ashamed of a daughter like that."

"Indeed," Dom answered, his voice oddly thick.

"It's all right to miss him though. It's all right to feel this hole." The advice was as much for himself as it was for Dom.

As before, the Elder sniffed, turning to stone. "Sorrow is a mortal endeavor. I have no use for it." He jumped up from the boulder, his face wiped clean of any emotion.

Andry joined him, standing with a shake of his head. "Sorrow touches us all, Lord Domacridhan, whether we believe in it or not. It doesn't matter what you call the thing ripping you apart. It will still devour you if given the chance."

"And how do I defend against such a thing, Squire?" the Elder demanded, his voice rising. Luckily, Corayne did not stir. "How do I fight what I cannot face?"

In the training yard, the knights would bash their gauntlets, clutch hands, pull each other up after a particularly nasty blow. Without thinking, Andry raised his own fingers, palm open, an offer as much as a plea.

"With me," he said. "Together."

Dom did his very best not to crush the squire's fingers as they locked hands.

"It's your turn for watch," Andry muttered, wincing under the strength of Dom's grips.

But it was worth the pain.

23

BELOW THE PRIEST'S HAND
Corayne

Corayne had heard stories of Adira from nearly every member of her mother's crew, her mother included. The card tables, the concubines and brothels, the night markets hawking goods from all over the Ward, stolen or otherwise. Real dragon scales, ancient and crusty, in the curio shops. Spindletouched mages brewing up tonics and poison outside taverns. Thieves' gangs and pirate crews outfitting their companies. The crown of Treccoras, the last Cor emperor, had been won in a game of dice in the House of Luck and Fortune, then immediately lost to the marshes. But the history was there too; she'd heard it mostly from Kastio. When moved to talk, he spoke of distant years, centuries long since passed, as if he were reciting from the pages of a university tome, or had an impossibly long memory.

It had been Piradorant once, truly the Adoring Port, beneath the ancient empire. The small city and surrounding territory had sworn allegiance to Old Cor long before her armies arrived. There was no conquest. She was a willing bride, and the Cors treated her as such. Her walls were gilded, her streets wealthy. She blossomed, a flower basking in the light of a doting sun. But the empire fell, night came, and the world moved on in its shadow. The stumbling kingdom of Larsia grew and eventually chafed with the might of neighboring Galland. The Larsians fought to defend their border from encroachment. The city now called Adira filled the cracks between.

Wedged between warring kingdoms, often cut off by battle or blockade, Adira survived through less than honorable means. Pirate ships regularly ran Gallish blockades to feed the hungry city. Cutthroats and rogues slipped around entrenched armies. Within the walls, the city rotted like an apple. The King of Larsia did not have the strength to wrest it back from the criminals who controlled it, and Galland would not bother. The Gallish kings cared for glittering capitals and vast expanses of rich land. Not a fortress slum on a marshy peninsula, its streets bristling with rusty knives and gutter rats. Adira adapted to the world as it was, becoming what it needed to be.

The peninsula had a gray-green look as they approached from the north, a spit of land shoved out into the Bay alongside the mouth of the Orsal. The river flowed through marshland, belching silt into the bluer salt water. Adira sat at the peninsula's head, the city walled in by a crown of mossy stone and wooden palisade. A stone causeway zigzagged over the marshes, through the worst of the mud, with no less than six drawbridges, all of them pulled up. It was a Cor-built wonder, like the roads, aqueducts, and amphitheaters within the old borders. There would be no assaulting Adira from land, not by any army upon the Ward.

As they rode onto the causeway, Corayne caught sight of the docks before the mist closed it. The sails of a dozen ships crowded the harbor like needles in a pincushion. Pirates and smugglers all. Not a single flag of a lawful kingdom. Corayne smiled as she had in Lecorra, drawn to this place, rooted in it somehow. But this time it wasn't the Spindletouched echoes of Cortael she felt. This was the land of her mother, of Hell Mel.

Andry balanced her obvious excitement with naked fear. His eyes locked on the first drawbridge, drawn up against the sky like a flat hand ready to fall and crush them all. The squire of a noble court had no place here. He already stuck out like a sore thumb, even next to Dom. And that was a very high mark to clear.

"Hey, no worries," Corayne murmured to him, drawing her horse in close. She bent, the sword digging into her back. "Half the stories aren't even true. No one's going to boil your face off and sell your skull."

The reins cracked in his fists. His eyes widened. "I never heard that one before."

The first drawbridge fell without so much as a word from any of them, not even a bribe from Dom or a threat from Sorasa. On the other side, two bridge wardens stood, toothless and gray-faced, silent as they rode on. Corayne thought a bit of face boiling might improve their appearance.

"Draw your hoods," Sorasa said, pulling her cowl into place. She arranged the shawl around her shoulders so the daggers in her belt and the sword at her side would be easy to wield.

Dom did the same, stone-faced, sweeping the green cloak of Iona back from his left hip. He seemed a bit lighter these days. *The road must agree with him*, Corayne thought. The mist closed in, nearly obscuring Valtik as she plodded along at the rear. On her gray horse in her gray clothes, she was a shadow as much as the bridge wardens, a ghost of the marsh. Even her lurid eyes were veiled, gone to gray like the rest of the world.

Corayne felt like a horse blinkered. There was only the causeway and the muffling silence of the mist. The land around Adira existed in some eerie in-between, part of no kingdom, separated by a narrow barrier of mud.

At the second bridge, the wardens had bows ready, arrows quivered at their hips. Corayne suspected there were more hiding in the wetlands.

"You lost?" one asked, his voice lisping over his broken teeth. His cheeks were pockmarked.

"Not yet," Sorasa answered.

The bridge fell.

Such was the way at every turn: wardens shouted challenges and Sorasa answered. Corayne couldn't tell if it was a code or not. She memorized the responses all the same. *You lost? Not yet. What's your business? Same as yours. Who do you know in the city? Too many to name. Are you going to make trouble? Most likely.* In truth, it was probably the combination of a tattooed Amhara and a hulking mountain of a man with a sword to match his glowering face that opened the bridges. The rest of them were inconsequential. Even Valtik kept her mouth shut, following in off-putting silence.

The final bridge dropped without a challenge, connecting the causeway to the city hill. The mist lifted while they climbed, and the world came back into sharper focus. A shantytown bunched around the gate and walls, loosely organized, as the city spilled out of its own boundaries. It had the look of a slum but none of the despair.

Adira was bigger up close, hunched on the rise, thrust out of the haze, with clear sight in all directions: over the marsh and the foggy causeway, over the flat waters of Mirror Bay. The border was not far but felt a thousand miles away. *Taristan and Erida cannot touch us here.* As the smell and sounds of the city intensified, Corayne felt something like an embrace. She sucked down a breath of fresh salt air, raising her face to the sun. This was one of the most dangerous corners of the Ward. *And the safest place we can be.*

"All those bridges, and they leave the gates open," Andry said, eyeing the city wall.

Indeed, the gates were flung wide, flanked only by a pair of wardens. They leaned on old spears, more for show than for function. Corayne smirked. "I suppose after six bridges, the marsh, and whoever else watched our approach, they have no reason to keep the gates shut all day long."

The wardens were dressed in leather and rough-spun cloth. Like the bridge guardians, they wore no uniform or color to unite them in their work. They watched, silent but sharp.

Sorasa said nothing to either of them, urging her horse onward. She only pulled down her cowl, exposing her face as she rode first through the gate. Maybe it was a trick of the shifting light, but Corayne thought she saw the assassin's shoulders droop, releasing some tension. A criminal haven was a lullaby to a contracted killer.

Andry retreated into his hood, showing only the hard set of his jaw. Despite his unease, he seemed less a squire and more a traveler, weary but unafraid. Still, his fingers twisted on the reins. Corayne was struck by the very odd impulse to grab his hand. She blinked, startled, and pushed it away. Warmth flushed in her face, and she willed her cheeks not to turn red.

The wall wasn't thick, barely as wide as three men abreast. Corayne passed through quickly. She couldn't help but notice murder holes pocking the ceiling. Her skin crawled at the thought of a man pouring hot oil down on her.

"At least it doesn't smell as awful as Ascal," Dom grumbled as he cleared the gate, one hand resting on his sword. Valtik followed close behind.

The square inside the gate was oddly quiet, but then it was still daylight. Corayne assumed that most of Adira's residents would be sleeping off the night before, and the ones who weren't were well past noticing a few more riders on the streets.

Sorasa nudged her horse east, past a headless statue, its hands raised in supplication. Someone had draped their laundry from its fingers.

"I didn't know there could be so many places to drink," Andry whispered to Corayne, leaning close as they passed a stretch of taverns, each one more cramped than the last. Unlike Dom and Sorasa, he was still unarmed. The best he had was the kettle, still thunking softly in his saddlebags.

"Want to peel off?" she replied. The square became a spider-web of streets, quieter than the gate. An old man weakly advertised games of chance from a balcony while a woman squawked at him to stop talking. "I doubt Sorasa would mind."

He laughed, meeting her stare. Up close, his eyes were dark stones flecked with amber.

"I think Dom and Sorasa would rather tie us up and drag us than let us explore," he said, jabbing a thumb over his shoulder. The Elder rode close behind, his glare leveled on Corayne's back. *I might as well be tied up already.* "Not that I want to."

"Oh, come on, Squire Trelland." Corayne smiled and leaned further, one hand gripping the pommel of her saddle for balance. She cut a glance at the street. It felt like a vein, thrumming with life she couldn't see. Two men stumbled out of a dice house, trying to fight and missing every blow. They reminded her so much of the *Tempestborn* crew her heart ached. "Aren't you curious?"

Andry watched the pair. "I've seen drunks before, thank you."

A pair of knights a bit tipsy on the Queen's vintage are not drunks, Corayne thought.

"There's more to do here than drink," she replied.

Andry nodded. "And I hope we get it over with quickly."

"Maybe not too quickly," Corayne shot back. He glanced at her, an eyebrow raised in question. She bit her lip, chewing the moment. "It's nice to see you worry about something that isn't the end of the world," she finally said, almost too softly for mortal ears.

Beneath his hood, Andry smiled, his face brightening.

"Likewise, Corayne."

"The laws of Adira are simple." Sorasa's voice was as gentle as a whipcrack, snapping over them both. She turned in the saddle,

382 REALM BREAKER

directing her horse with only her knees and the grip of her leather-sheathed thighs. "There are none," she concluded, matter-of-fact.

Corayne got the sense her warning was mostly for Dom, who barely understood a proper mortal city, let alone one run and ruled by outlaws. And for Andry, who gaped at their surroundings.

"Kill a man in the street if you like, but know you can be killed just as easily. Cut a purse and be prepared for a cut in return. There are no guards, no city watch. Only the wardens on the bridges, walls, and gates. And their objective isn't to protect you; it's to protect Adira." Sorasa waved her fingers, gesturing back the way they'd come. Like she said, there were no more wardens to be seen, a stark contrast to every other city Corayne had passed through. "Nothing and no one else. Anything can be taken, from every direction. Keep your eyes up. Don't lose sight of me." Then she reached, tugging on the bridle of Corayne's horse, so that the mare huffed and drew in close. Sorasa met Corayne's eyes with a stare to bore through steel. "Don't wander off."

"Wouldn't dream of it," Corayne answered like a child accused. *I can't exactly explore with the Spindleblade between my shoulders, balancing the salvation of the Ward with its impending doom.*

"Good," Sorasa cut back. "And before you start in on your questions, we're headed to the Priest's Hand."

Andry blanched. "There are priests here?"

Sorasa grinned. "Not the kind you're used to, Squire."

The Priest's Hand was a church, or had been sometime in the last two centuries. Now it was a marketplace, the pews long since removed to make room for stalls. Smoke wafted overhead, trapped by the domed roof of a former shrine to Tiber, the god of trade and craftsmen. His face was painted on the walls, wearing his usual crown of coins. Corayne knew him well.

There was little order to the place. The smell of muddy soup wafted from a cook stand, while a Tyri sailor with gold teeth displayed a cage of beady-eyed ravens. A man sold animal bones next to twin sisters praying over glittering lengths of jewels and beads. There were cloth merchants, fishmongers, fruit vendors, and stalls with no obvious purpose but to sell bits of junk. Stolen goods, Corayne knew, eyeing the displays as they passed. She saw her charts again, weaving the lines of trade through the Long Sea. She smirked at the telltale oily sheen of Treckish steel at a workman's table, though Trec kept a tight fist on their mines and craftsmen. She wanted to linger, but Sorasa drew them through the church as if they were all tied together. Only Valtik halted. Naturally, she went to a spread of ribs, spines, and femurs, pawing through them with a slack grin. She even tested a few, tossing them between her hands and over the ground like a gambler playing at dice.

Perhaps that was the idea. *So far, my fate seems like a bad turn of luck.*

Dom kept close at her back. For once, he wasn't so out of place. While the streets were quiet, the Priest's Hand was busy, and many Adirans were as large as Domacridhan. Bruisers, bandits, pit fighters, sailors with sun-damaged cheeks. Lean thieves and beautiful courtesans from all over the Ward wove among them. A man with diamond-pale, glowing skin even winked at

Dom, blowing him a kiss with a beckoning hand.

Corayne stopped searching stalls and began searching faces, hoping to spot whoever Sorasa intended to recruit to their quest. She nearly halted before an Ibalet man, his look similar to Sorasa's, with a belt of daggers and eyes like a falcon. But Sorasa passed him by without a second glance. Soon the long walk through the church was finished, and they stood before the abandoned altar. Instead of a droning priest reciting godly scripture, a pair of dogs lounged around it, panting with slobbering smiles.

"Are they here? Have we missed them?" Corayne said, looking back down the church. A few eyes trailed them, watching carefully. The two most obvious were a pair of men in long gray robes, their boots new leather. They had the look of a religious order, even if there was no religion under this roof. "We're being followed," Corayne said flatly.

"*I'm* being followed," Sorasa replied with a sigh. She even waved a hand in their direction. "They're nothing. The Twilight Brothers are a joke."

Andry's jaw dropped. He looked from Sorasa to the robed men, not bothering to drop his voice. "The Twilight Brothers? They're killers, assassins—"

"And what am I? A milkmaid?" Sorasa smirked, once at Andry and then at the Brothers. They sneered, turning tail with a dramatic spin of their robes. Steel flashed beneath, their swords naked with no sheaths. "Like I said, a joke. They're waiting to get me alone, make me an offer again. All so I can refuse *again*."

Sorasa declined to elaborate.

Dom cared more for the stone tiles beneath them, flat and worn, making up the raised the dais of the altar. He scuffed a boot over them.

"There's more beneath us," he said sharply.

"Nothing gets past you, Elder," Sorasa said, waving them all past the chipped altar. The dogs panted in their wake, watching with baleful eyes. Andry stooped to give one a scratch.

He caught Corayne watching and shrugged. "A criminal dog is still a dog."

A narrow stair hid behind the altar, cramped between the dais and the exterior wall. Another image of Tiber, his mouth spilling coins, loomed over the stairway. Sorasa gave him a familiar pat on the nose as she descended the steps. Corayne did the same, hoping for a blessing.

A square chamber, once a crypt, opened up below. Three of the walls had long rectangular openings, vaults for coffins. They were blissfully empty. Corayne swallowed, put off by the vaults, but at least no skeletons leered in the dim light.

On the only flat wall, a single torch burned, off center against the brick and mortar. When it flickered, Corayne could make out something like a doorway, nearly blending into the wall, visible only at the edges where it couldn't lie completely flush.

But Sorasa didn't go to the door. Instead she reached into one of the vaults, never hesitating, and rapped her knuckles on the back wall inside. It sounded like wood. After a hasty second, it slid back, and a pair of eyes appeared where a body once rotted.

"Five—" Sorasa said to the eyes, then stopped herself and

checked their number. Valtik was still upstairs. "Four. The witch is mingling."

"You know the rules: no more than two," came a raspy reply. The eyes darted. They were green and watery, surrounded by fat, pink flesh.

Sorasa bent closer. "Since when have rules meant anything around here?"

Before the eyes could answer, another voice sounded behind the sliding panel.

"Is that Sarn I hear?" a male voice said.

The eyes rolled. Before Sorasa could say another word, the panel snapped back into place, slamming shut.

Dom rumbled out a low laugh. "You have that effect on most people."

There was a grinding, a gear turning somewhere in the wall as a pair of latches pinged open. Corayne jumped when the door in the brick wall swung forward, heavy on great iron hinges. The chamber beyond was long, well lit by torches and streams of daylight.

Sorasa smiled in the Elder's face, or as close as she could reach. "I certainly do," she said, passing into the next room with a bounce in her step.

The original crypt extended the length of the church above, set with fat, cobwebbed columns and high, flat windows to bring in at least some natural light. It shifted, blue and white with the passing clouds. There were more vaults along the walls, all stuffed with crates, tools, and food stores, as well as miles of parchment and gallons of many-colored inks.

Corayne looked it over, noting wood blocks that looked

suspiciously like printing stamps, not to mention several cast-iron molds. Her eyes narrowed.

We're in a forger's workshop.

"Charlon Armont," Sorasa said, approaching the stubby young man bent over a workbench. She said his name with the characteristic Madrentine flourish, words swooping. "So nice to see you."

He looked up, one eye exaggerated by a magnifying glass. The other was mud brown, like the thick hair held back from his face by a tight braid. He straightened, revealing a strongman's gut and broad, rounded shoulders. He had the build of a laborer, sturdy as a wall. But his hands were thin and delicate, skillful. His skin was pale, unnaturally so, as if he spent most daylight hours down in the crypt. *It's probably true*, Corayne thought.

"Don't lie, Sarn. You're too good at it; it unnerves me," he said, lowering his eyeglass to let it dangle from the cord around his neck. Without looking down, he swept the papers on his desk into a box, hiding the contents from sight. Corayne tried to catch some of it, but he moved too quickly. "It isn't like you to come with company. Especially this kind of company," he added, eyeing the rest of them. His curiosity deepened as he glanced from Andry to Dom to Corayne, taking their measure.

Corayne did the same. Armont didn't look older than twenty, his face unlined by age, his skin smooth as marble and the color of honeyed milk.

His assistant, the owner of the green eyes, wavered nearby. She was small with a frizzy head of sandy hair. Charlon dismissed her with a nod, and she made herself scarce. The brick door shut behind her, the gears above it now clearly visible. It even had padlocks and a broad bar to be lowered into place.

He looks ready for a siege, Corayne thought.

"Strange days," Sorasa answered, her hands spread wide. Both her palms were as tattooed as her fingers. On her right hand, the sun; on the left, the crescent moon.

Charlon nodded. He removed the glass, shoving it into the tool belt around his wide-set hips. He looked like a bull. *A very nervous bull.* "Indeed, there's been odd talk."

"What sort of talk?" Corayne said sharply.

It felt like being home again in Lemarta, listening to sailors trade tales at the tavern, or merchants jaw in the market. She wanted to sink her teeth in, tear out something useful from the nonsense. Once, she'd have grabbed for a line on a treasury ship moving currency. Now, perhaps, some word of where Taristan was going next, or where he had been. *What Spindle will tear next, and which is already torn? What new dangers lurk on the horizon, waiting for us—and anyone else caught in the crossfire?*

Charlon eyed her and she eyed him back, unyielding. "Storms out of season," he answered. "Villages going quiet. Gallish troops on the move, and not to any war anyone knows about. Ships running aground out at sea," he added, moving a hand over his chin. The tips of his fingers were stained a dull, dark blue. *Years of ink.* "One of them limped in this morning, hull nearly cracked in two. And there's that whole fuss about the Queen of Galland marrying some no-name without gold or a castle."

Corayne flinched. *But he has an army.*

"News certainly travels fast around here," Andry said shakily. "By the way, I'm Andry Trelland," he added, extending his hand.

Charlon did not return the gesture, perturbed by his politeness.

"Good for you," he muttered. "What can I say, we're people of the realm. We like to stay in the know. Ain't that the truth of it, Sarn?"

A corner of Sorasa's mouth twitched, betraying a smile. "If you want information, come to Adira."

"And be prepared to pay for it," Charlon replied neatly. "So, what do you need?" He gestured to the vaults with a blue-tinged hand. "I've some fresh seals made for the Siscarian dukes, and with the mess in Rhashir, I've got a line on a genuine Singolhi mark-press. Not cheap, but easy. Run off your own Rhashiran notes. Wash the money for gold or land before their treasury knows what's what."

Corayne felt her jaw drop. *A mark-press from the Bank of Singhola, the treasury of Rhashir. Noble seals.* And, based on the vast collection of ink, paper, quills, and wax stuffing the shelves, a great deal more where that came from. *He could probably make letters of trade, privateer papers from every crown on the Long Sea, wax-sealed orders. As good as a shield to any ship, smuggler, or pirate on the water.* Her hands twitched as she eyed the shelves again. She saw the symbol of the Tyri navy, a mermaid holding a sword. *One stamp of that in blue wax and Mother could run any fleet blockade or enter any port without so much as a wink.*

"See something you like?" Charlon followed her gaze, taking a step closer. He narrowed his eyes. "If you have the coin, I've got the means."

Only then did Dom stir, moving to loom over them both. Stout Charlon craned his neck, looking up. "You must have money on you, with a bodyguard like this," he said nervously.

"We're not looking for seals or forgeries," Sorasa said sharply, bringing them back to the task at hand. "We're looking for *you*."

Charlon barked out a dry laugh. He wagged a finger at her. "The days really are strange. I don't think I've ever heard you tell a joke in all your life."

"She isn't joking, sir," Corayne said, wrenching herself away from the wall of iron seals.

"'Sir,'" he chuckled. Again he waved a hand at Sorasa, as if scolding her. "Well, are you going to explain what you're going on about? So I can tell you again why I can never leave the walls of this city?"

Sorasa didn't hesitate. She opened her mouth to explain, but Corayne felt a shiver down her spine. She swallowed and raised a hand, cutting the assassin off.

"Let me," she said, shrugging off her cloak.

It took a long moment, but she managed to unbuckle the sword belt from her shoulders. *I'm getting better at this.* Charlon went round-eyed as she drew the Spindleblade from its sheath. It was still heavy, and her hands trembled around the hilt, but it felt familiar now. *My father's sword.*

Even in the forger's crypt, the steel gleamed strangely, etched and marked by a realm lost. It fed on the underground light, brightening as the rest of the chamber darkened, until it was the only thing in Corayne's world, a mirror of cold flame. When she finally pulled her eyes away from the blade, she found Charlon staring just as deeply, his keen focus trained on the sword. He was a craftsman. He knew delicate, intricate, and ancient work when he saw it.

"That's no ordinary steel," he breathed. He didn't step forward or reach out, though he certainly looked like he wanted to. "Not Treckish. Not Elder." His eyes darted to Dom again, the wheels in his head turning with obvious motion.

Corayne shook her head. "This is a Spindleblade," she murmured, and his face went paler than she thought possible. "Forged in a forgotten realm, the land of my ancestors."

"You're from the lines of Old Cor." Charlon stopped staring at the sword to stare at her. "Spindleblood."

She returned his gaze. "I am."

"Not too many of you still walking the Ward," he said.

Corayne pursed her lips and slid the sword back into its sheath. The blade sang the length of the leather. "There won't be much of anything walking the Ward if we fail."

"What?" Charlon said, the smile still floating on his face.

She saw Taristan in her mind, looming over her, reaching for the sword, with no concern for anything but his own desire. In her head, the blue scars were already there, dragged along his cheek, the only mark on his fair skin. She wanted to claw him to pieces, expel him from the Ward and her fears.

"You're right. The Queen of Galland has married a man with no titles and seemingly no purpose," Corayne said plainly. "No purpose but the destruction of Allward, the entire realm, ripped apart at her Spindles. Burned, broken, and conquered, beneath the Queen, beneath him, and beneath What Waits."

She could smell them again, the corpses, even if they had only been sendings of Valtik's magic. Echoes of a real threat. Like the red presence in her dreams, shifting behind shadows. She felt its weight now, the grip tightening as she thought of What Waits and His growing influence through the realm. If Charlon could see terror written on her face, she did not know. But she saw it in the others: in the flash of Andry's eyes, the pull of Dom's mouth, the fall of a mask over Sorasa's face, to hide the rush of emotions beneath.

The forger drummed his fingers on the work desk, his smile curdling at the edges. She expected him to laugh. Instead he watched their faces, seeing their fear.

"Oh, is that all?"

After suffering what Corayne had to say about her uncle, her warning of a children's villain made real, not to mention Dom and Andry's recollection of the battle at the Spindle temple, Charlon demanded air. He set a manic pace through the Priest's Hand and out into the streets. He led them down to the waterfront, muttering to himself and casting scowls at Sorasa, who weathered them all with disinterest. Valtik caught up with them somewhere outside the church, the smell of cold following in her wake.

"And who's this one?" Charlon demanded, eyeing the witch.

"Don't ask," they said in unison.

It began to drizzle, bringing the mist up the hill and into the city. By the time they reached the port, a gray curtain dragged across the Bay, eating up the ships anchored in deeper waters. Despite the weather, the streets quickened with people as the day wore on and the docks spat out sailors.

The Adira port jutted over the water, fat planks hammered together to make a square. It bridged the main peninsula and a set of rocky islands, each one no bigger than a cathedral. The islands were land unto themselves, built up. One had an onion-domed roof painted pale orange, the telltale sign of a Treckish church. A palisade walled another, the planks painted woad blue with white-and-green knots marked over them. *Jydi symbols.* Charlon led them toward an island with a flat top, crowned in a verdant garden and a small bell tower, its white and yellow-gold pennant flags looping from roof to roof.

An Ishei district. Corayne's heartbeat doubled. Isheida was the edge of the map, the end of the Ward, farther even than the old Cor borders. Not even Hell Mel had been there, its jagged lands far from the tides of the Long Sea.

The island smelled of sweet flowers and cooking meat, undercut with a rich swell of tea. Isheida ruled the mountains and the Crown of Snow, a kingdom of peaks north of Rhashir. Her sailors were few, and they congregated here, trading news beneath the eaves of cookhouses and tea shops. There were priests too, with white robes and long, glossy hair combed straight down their backs. Each looked bathed in moonlight, even under the gray clouds. The Ishei had high, flat cheekbones and dark eyes. Their faces varied in color, ranging from porcelain to bronze and dusk, but all were black-haired, with long eyelashes and easy smiles. Corayne stared, unable to check her wonder. She didn't speak Ishei, but she could have listened to them talk all afternoon, jotting notes in her ledger. Sorasa nearly had to seize her by the collar to drag her along.

To her delight, Charlon led them into a tea shop with a cheery hello to the keepers. He must have been a regular. The three other patrons, two Ishei and one Ibalet in wrapped silks, offered him nods from the long bar set down the middle of the shop.

For the first time since setting foot in Adira, Andry seemed at ease, lulled by the smell of brewing tea. He relaxed when they sat, planting his back against the sturdy wall. With the rain outside and the cocooning warmth of the tea shop, Corayne felt as relieved as he looked. Before she could even think to ask, there was a cup in her hand and a pot on the table, steaming gently.

Charlon plucked a flower from the vase, blue petals in the shape of a star. He crushed them in his fist and added them to his cup before drinking. "So the realm stands on the brink of destruction. It might have tipped already. And for some reason, you need me to join this . . ." He glanced down their line. This time his scrutiny felt like an insult. "Merry band of heroes?"

Sorasa snorted into her tea.

"The witch said seven," Corayne answered. "Sorasa led us to you. I trust her judgment."

It was Dom's turn to snort. The Elder didn't quite know how, and it came out like a wet snarl.

"I'm still not clear on the whole witch thing." Charlon looked from the table to the eaves of the shop, open to the street. Valtik didn't sit, choosing instead to stand at the curb, collecting rainwater in her empty teacup.

"Neither are we," Dom replied.

Charlon sipped his tea again. "And you, Elder, where do you stand on this?"

"Our number is sufficient," Dom said stiffly. "In fact, I think we could do with one less."

"One big happy family, then." The young man laughed. "Well,

regardless of why you need me in whatever you're planning—"

"Close the next Spindle torn open," Corayne said sharply.

"Wherever it is," Andry said, almost under his breath. He glanced at Corayne, eyes soft but not apologetic. She felt torn between annoyance and agreement. There was still so much they did not know, so much higher to climb.

But we can't be daunted by the size of it, or we're done for.

"I'm in Adira for a reason." Charlon laid his hands on the table, one finger jabbing at the wood in his fervor. He seemed plain outside his crypt, unremarkable. It was almost too easy to forget his shop full of seals and ink, his fingers stained blue. "No laws means no crowns. No bounties. I might get my throat slit tonight, but no one's going to drag me out of these walls and back into crown territory to face judgment or execution. Adira is her own, and the streets will turn on anyone who turns on her. I'm safe here. I can shut my eyes without worrying that that Temur wolf is going to snap me up."

Andry tipped his head. "Temur wolf?"

"I can handle Sigil," Sorasa cut in before Charlon could explain.

Sigil?

Charlon blustered, flapping his lips. "As much as I'd like to see that, I'm not willing to risk my head for it. She'll have me in chains before sundown, on my way to the gallows for whichever kingdom set the highest price."

"That's a long list," Sorasa said, unamused. She sat oddly in her seat, turned to the room. An assassin always, waiting for an attack or planning her own. It set Corayne's teeth on edge.

"It's good to take pride in your work," Charlon said with a

shrug. "And I'd like to keep working, which I won't be able to do without a head. I will not set foot outside these walls."

"You really think Sigil of the Temurijon is camped out in the marsh waiting for the likes of you? You have a very high opinion of yourself, Charlie." The assassin laughed coldly, a sharp sound. "She's the finest bounty hunter in the realm. Last I heard she's rounding up bandits for the Crown Prince of Kasa, terrorizing the Forest of Rainbows. A world away."

Some tension was released from Charlon's shoulders.

He's right, Corayne thought with the shadow of triumph. *Sorasa is very good at lying.*

"I know someone who is waiting for you, though," she added, lowering her voice. Her eyes wavered, moving from Charlon's face to his hands. They clenched on the table, knuckles standing out white.

"Don't, Sarn," he growled. Again he reminded Corayne of a bull. This time, one who saw a red flag waving in front of his face. "Don't talk about him."

Sorasa was undeterred.

"If the Ward burns, so does he."

A cord wound behind Charlon's eyes. His bared his teeth. "Don't talk to me about Garion," he growled, suddenly as danger-ous as any other criminal in Adira.

Sorasa was undeterred, a predator on the hunt, smelling a kill. "I saw him, you know. In Byllskos."

Charlon went white, his already pale cheeks turning to alabas-ter. "Is he well?" he murmured, leaning into the assassin without regard. Corayne saw the desperation in him plain as the rain pouring down outside. Whoever Garion was, he was very important to the forger.

"As well as usual," Sorasa said with a dismissing wave. "Preening, overly proud. Pissed with me for stealing his contract."

The cord broke, unfurling, and he nodded. His lethal edge disappeared, receding like a curtain drawn away. "Good," he said in a small voice, running a finger over his lips. "I don't suppose you can . . . entice him to join your endeavor too?"

It was Sorasa's turn to harden. "That's not something I can do anymore."

"Fine," Charlon said, his eyes on the table. "Fine." Then he glared at Corayne, his voice forceful again. "What do you think, Cor girl?"

Corayne blinked, taken off guard.

"About all this," he clarified. "Your quest to save the realm, and my place in it?" He gestured to the sword on her back.

She felt it down her spine, cold steel and leather. Most of the time it was a deadweight, an anchor. Now it reassured her, and she leaned into it, hoping to bring some of its steel into her bones.

Corayne raised her head, tossing back her braid of black hair.

"I think we're being hunted by a kingdom and a devil. The devil, there's not much you can do about that." *So far to climb, but I cannot look up, or look back.* "But the kingdom, an army . . . it will be good to have someone like you to smooth the way."

That seemed to agree with Charlon. He leaned back, clapping his hands together. "I can get you passage papers by the end of the day. Diplomatic envoy seals. Marks of travel. No city gate will be barred, no palace closed; no patrol would dare stop you. Only the

Queen herself could demand your arrest. All at a price, of course," he added, cutting a glance at Dom.

The Elder scowled. "I'll have sold Iona before all is said and done."

"But what good is that to a Spindle burning in the wild? *Two* Spindles?" Charlon added, asking the question they all had. "What good will I be?"

Sorasa didn't seem to share his sentiment. "We'll certainly find out."

"But I'm not going," Charlon added sharply. "And you don't even know where you're headed!"

"Leave that to us," Corayne heard herself say.

Leave that to me.

Already the threads were pulling together, inch by inch. She needed only weave them into something that made sense, a simple direction.

She felt Sorasa's copper-flame eyes. The assassin did not smile, but there was victory in her all the same. She reached across the tea table, taking Charlon by the shoulder.

"Would I be here if this weren't real?" she murmured, leaning so she was all he could see. Her voice dropped an octave, stern. "Would I risk my life for anything less than the end of the world?"

The forger's jaw tightened. "No, you wouldn't," he said thickly, then fell silent. Sorasa let him think, giving him a long moment to make his decision. "What of Garion? He must be warned."

The assassin fought the smile on her lips. "Between the two of us, I'm sure we can figure out a way to get a message through," she offered. "He doesn't exactly bother to cover his tracks."

VICTORIA AVEYARD 399

A corner of Charlon's mouth lifted. "No, he does not."

"I'll help you pack up, Charlie," she said, pulling him to his feet with a pat on the back.

In the street, the rain hissed.

"I bet you will, Sarn."

Corayne and the others stayed in the tea shop, bent over a pot that never seemed to go empty. The Ishei keeper was a diligent man, quick with his hands. Andry happily engaged him in a whispered conversation about brewing. What sort of spices, which roots, what did the Ishei use to clear the chest or encourage sleep? Over the brim of her cup, Corayne watched him chattering animatedly.

He doesn't belong here with us, as much as he tries to. The end of the world is no place for Andry Trelland. He doesn't deserve it.

The squire felt her examination and glanced over his shoulder. Goose bumps rose along his forearms. They were toned and leaned, corded with muscle from years of squire work and sword training. He rubbed them smooth, fingers working.

"What is it?" he muttered, looking back to her.

Corayne tightened her grip on her cup, trying to draw the warmth into herself. It warred with the cold down her spine. She shook her head.

The tea shop was quiet and peaceful. Too much for her liking. She wanted noise, activity. She wanted to see and hear what was going on.

"The Long Sea is quiet in the summer," she finally said, chewing over Charlon's words back in the crypt. "Few storms at all, but shipwrecks? Running aground out at sea? Impossible. There are no reefs, no shoals. And what did Charlon say about Gallish soldiers on the move? Where are they going? Why would Erida send them beyond her own borders?"

"Well, she is hunting us," Andry offered.

"I doubt she's hunting in the wrong place. We aren't exactly hard to follow, and we were obviously going in a certain direction." *We rode west. But where are the armies going?* Her mind lit on fire, the blaze leaping up from always-burning embers. "She's sent soldiers after us, but there are more elsewhere. Looking for something. Or *guarding* something. Perhaps both."

Dom grasped his cup so tightly a crack broke down the clay side, like a black streak of lightning. "The second Spindle."

"It could be."

Corayne ran a hand through her hair, exasperated. It was like chasing the sunset. Impossible, just out of reach, even in the fastest ship or astride the swiftest horse. Something brushed the edge of her fingertips before dancing beyond her grasp again.

"Valtik?" she said, raising her voice to catch the witch, who was still examining the rainy sky. She swilled the rain in her cup. "What do the bones tell?"

The old woman responded in a loud tangle of Jydi, too fast for Corayne to decipher, or even to pick out a single word. It sounded like a melody, the rhythm soothing. *And useless.*

With a huff, Corayne began to stand. "Valtik—"

But another spill of Jydi cut her off. Spoken not in the old woman's voice, but in a booming one. Deep, masculine, joyful. *Familiar.*

Corayne fell back into her seat with a painful *thunk*, the backs of her thighs digging into the hard bench. She dropped her face, dropped her eyes, dropped her hood, trying to curl into herself as quickly as she could. Suddenly the quiet shop was too loud, the walls closing in. She wanted to disappear; she wanted to stand up and draw as much attention as she could. Her body felt torn in two.

Warm hands took her shoulder, Andry's fingers closing over the corner of her cloak. "Corayne, what's wrong?"

Dom spread his arms wide, bracing himself against the table. He looked to the doorway, hawk-eyed, ready for anything. An assassin, an army, even Taristan himself.

Instead there was Valtik, grinning her strange smile, jabbering away in the rain. She craned her neck, looking up into the face of a bald-headed Jydi raider, every inch of his exposed skin scarred or tattooed in complicated knots. He answered her rhymes eagerly.

"His name is Ehjer," Corayne murmured beneath her hood. *Recruited ten years ago, loyal to my mother. A pirate. A raider. An old friend.* "The one next to him is Kireem, a Gheran navigator from the Tiger Gulf."

Indeed, a smaller man stood at Ehjer's side, half his size, one eye covered by a patch swirling with chips of black stone. Scars bled out beneath the patch, the purple lines violently dark against his ocher skin. *Smart as a unicorn, he can read the stars even on blackest night.*

The two had been together as long as Corayne remembered. Relationships among the crew were tolerated so long as they didn't interfere with the ship, and the pair kept a fine balance. Now away from their duty, they should've relaxed.

Instead Corayne had never seen them more on edge.

The Jydi passed Valtik, entering the shop with the patch-eyed man. They beelined for the tea bar, settling in alongside the other patrons, putting their backs to the room.

"Are they a threat?" the Elder murmured, never taking his eyes off them.

Corayne shook her head once.

"You know their crew," Andry breathed, close enough to feel his heat. She glanced out from under her hood, meeting his wide, dark eyes like pools of still water.

"As well as I know myself. The *Tempestborn* is here," she whispered.

And so is my mother.

If I get up now, they won't notice. I can cross the square, hunt the docks. It will only take a moment. She imagined her boots, each step faster than the one before, until they pounded over the planks and up the gangway, into her mother's waiting arms. There would be yelling, arguments, perhaps the locked door of the captain's cabin. But Meliz an-Amarat was here. *Hell Mel* was here. *We could be gone with the tide. To whatever horizon we choose. Toward danger, or away from it.*

Corayne knew which her mother would choose for them.

And it would be the world's ending.

It took everything to stay in her seat, gripping the edge of the bench lest she bolt away.

"Should we get out of here?" Andry said, his hand on her shoulder again.

Corayne didn't answer, her focus on the Jydi's broad back. Swallowing hard, she brought a finger to her lips, gesturing for quiet.

"I've never known you to be a tea drinker, Ehj," Kireem said, his voice musical, the Paramount accented by his native Gheran. He shrugged out of her salt-worn coat.

Ehjer laughed heartily on his stool. "The storm rang my head like Volka's bell. I don't think I could touch Mother's mead, let alone stomach whatever *yss* they serve up in the Adira taverns," he said, hissing out the Jydi curse. *Piss*, it meant. One of the first words Corayne had ever learned in his language. "Many thanks, friend," he added, raising his fresh cup to the tea keeper. "So, will the ship live?"

"Lost a mast, barely salvaged the hull." Kireem crushed flowers into his own pot, stirring idly. "What do you think?"

Lost a mast and nearly the hull. Corayne's heartbeat quickened. She tried to picture the proud and fierce *Tempestborn* limping into the port like a wounded animal. *Nearly broken in two*, Charlon had said, describing some poor ship Corayne had barely pitied. Now she knew better. Now she knew fear for that galley and its crew. Under the table, her knuckles went white.

Until there was not the bench beneath her fingers, but skin, darker than her own, warm where her flesh went numb. She squeezed Andry's hand gratefully.

"You know better than I," Ehjer blustered, in his booming

version of a whisper. "The Captain tells you things."

"A few weeks, if the supplies can get in. But with the Sea the way it is . . ."

"Never seen the Sarim like that." Ehjer slurped his tea. "Whirlpools, waterspouts, thunder . . . it was furious. The gods themselves warring in the water."

Kireem didn't touch his cup, his single eye fixed on the steam rising from the liquid. He traced it, transfixed or dazed. "I've never seen anything like that *thing*," he hissed. The navigator had been with Hell Mel for as long as Corayne lived, and nothing had ever unsettled him so.

"Where did it come from?" The big Jydi was just as agitated.

Kireem shrugged. "You're the godly one between us, Ehj."

"That doesn't mean I understand why the goddess of the waters sent a monster to devour us."

Corayne ripped her eyes from her mother's crewmates, looking to Dom with lightning speed. He was already glaring back, his mouth set into a thin line. *A monster. The goddess of the waters.* Her stomach churned like the angry ocean.

Kireem dropped his voice again. "Did you see what the captain cut out of its belly?"

"I was busy chopping a tentacle off Bruto. The beast was still choking him even while it bled to death."

The other patrons of the shop were clearly listening, as was the tea keeper. Everyone froze, dropping all pretense of pretending not to eavesdrop. Corayne felt as if she might forget to breathe.

Tentacle.

"Three Ibalets, sailors of the Golden Fleet," Kireem hissed.

His fingers wound around Ehjer's wrist, nails like claws. "In full sail armor and dyed silk, half eaten. All there out on the deck with the creature's rotten guts."

Ehjer gingerly nudged his tea away. "Meira of the Waters is ravenous."

"I can't believe that," Kireem scoffed, but his eye said something different. Wide and worried, it darted wildly, searching Ehjer for an answer he could not accept.

"You don't have to believe it," Ehjer answered. Licking his lips, he brushed his fingers over the tattoos on his cheeks, tracing the swirls of ink. The action soothed him somewhat. "*Gud dhala kov; gud hyrla nov. The gods walk where they will, and do as they please.*" Then he raised his voice to his usual roar, gesturing to the tea-shop eaves, where Valtik still stood. "Ah, *Gaeda*, sit, have a cup," he said, beckoning to her. "Tell me tales of home! I sorely need them!"

Without a glance at her compatriots, Valtik all but bounced into the shop, the raindrops running from her braids. Corayne did not know it was possible for the old witch to act even stranger, but somehow Valtik accomplished just that. She preened in Jydi again, patting Ehjer on both cheeks, tracing the tattoos he had.

It was distraction enough.

Corayne moved quickly out into the street, one hand pulling her hood low, the other cold without Andry's skin. They followed her in silence, but she heard the questions rolling from their bodies. She scrambled for answers, trying to make sense of what she'd heard—and which ship was waiting nearby, wounded beyond measure.

Weave the threads, she told herself, drawing a breath through her teeth. *Fit the pieces.*

Again, she wanted to run. The *Tempestborn* would be easy to find. Battered, riding low among the proud ships and galleys of the port.

Hell Mel, Meliz an-Amarat, Mother. She wanted to scream each name and see which would draw an answer. *She's nearby; I can feel it. Maybe in the dock market, bartering for supplies. And doing poorly without me.*

The wetness on her cheeks could not be rain. Raindrops didn't sting your eyes.

Her next words came hard, like a knife drawn from her own body.

"I know where the second Spindle is."

24

THE WOLF
Domacridhan

Again Dom loomed at Corayne's shoulder while she shopped, trading his Ionian coin freely as evening fell over Adira. The night market was lively, blooming as the sky darkened. In her haste, Corayne didn't bother to haggle too much. She made sure Andry outfitted himself with a good sword and belt, and found a long, thrusting dagger for herself. The Spindleblade was still of little use, too unwieldy in unskilled hands. Dom had his Ionian sword, centuries old and Vederan-made, her steel as sharp as the day she was forged. His bow had been lost back in Ascal, so he chose another for himself and, after a long, begrudging moment, for Sorasa too. His was overpriced but well made, a double bend of black yew. It was not from his homeland, but the fine swoop of wood reminded him of the glens all the same.

After the weapons, Corayne drifted to provisions. Dried meat,

408 REALM BREAKER

hard biscuits, skins of fortifying wine, a pouch of salt, beans, a sack of apples. Things that would keep for the voyage.

And the desert.

Dom's throat went dry. He could already feel the sand, gritty on his skin, stinging in his eyes. He was a son of Iona, born to rain, mist, and glens green with life. He did not favor heat and he disdained the thought of Ibal. The dunes like mountains, the sun furious and without mercy. Nor did he want to accompany Sarn to her home, where she would gloat over his discomfort, if not make it worse.

They returned to the Priest's Hand in good time. Corayne had a head for direction, navigating the streets well. Dom felt a bit like a pack horse, laden with their supplies, bags slung over each shoulder. He expected chatter, but Corayne kept silent, shadowed in her hood. It worried him, to see her shuttered. Andry hovered at her shoulder, trying to coax something out of her, but she fended off all attempts at conversation with a few sharp words.

Her pace never broke, even in the crowds. She walked like something might catch her if she stopped. She looked back at the port a few times, her depthless eyes hunting.

No one followed us, Dom wanted to say, if it would quiet her mind. But even he knew better. *The* Tempestborn *is here. Her mother's ship, her mother's crew. Every piece of her life until the moment I found her.*

He might have suggested lingering a moment if there had been time, if the realm had not been relying on their next steps. *Too many ifs to count.* An overwhelming prospect for an immortal, whose entire life stretched into centuries of unchosen paths. Dom had enough ifs of his own to weather. He could not stomach Corayne's as well.

Charlon and Sorasa were in the yard outside the Priest's Hand when they arrived, surrounded by their horses and one very grumpy mule. The long-eared beast curled its lip as Charlon adjusted its saddlebags, shoving another sheaf of parchment into place.

"I expected more of a fight from you," Dom said to him, "if the danger is as you say."

The danger, of course, being just punishment for what seems like a great many crimes against a great many kingdoms.

Charlon grinned in return, patting the mule. "Got the feeling Sarn would slit my throat if I argued too much. And if Sigil does decide to come hunting, I wouldn't mind seeing the pair of them try to kill each other. Neither would you, I wager, eh, Elder? Or do you prefer Veder? That's what you call yourselves, don't you?"

"I have little preference," Dom replied in a brittle voice. He imagined leaving Sarn behind at almost every turn, but found he could not picture her battling a bounty hunter to death, and certainly not over someone as unimportant as Charlon Armont.

The forger was built like a young man squashed, with short legs and a round belly, his arms oddly long for his frame. Among the bags of parchment, quills, seals, and stamps, Dom didn't miss the flash of a hand ax and a shortsword. Not to mention a wicked-looking hook on a loop of rope. For someone who seemed like an afterthought in a quest to save the world, he was certainly equipped to do it.

"I like to be prepared," Charlon offered, following Dom's eye.

"Good," Dom replied. "But every turn of this path has been less than predictable."

Every step from Iona, since the Monarch sent me forth into the harbinger shadows of coming doom. Dom nearly threw himself into the saddle to keep the memories at bay, jolting the horse beneath him. The cloak fell around his shoulders. *It no longer smells like home, like clean rain and old stone.*

The yard of the Priest's Hand used to be a cemetery, but most of the gravestones had been torn up like rotten teeth. Now it served as a meeting square outside the market, teeming with traffic. Still Dom heard Corayne's voice, low as it was.

She stood by the crooked fence, staring up at Sorasa, who was already in the saddle.

"The second Spindle is in Ibal," she whispered.

The assassin leaned down to meet her. To Dom's confusion, Sarn did not smile or even seem pleased. Her copper eyes clouded. She set her teeth. "How can you be sure?"

"I'm sure" was all Corayne said in reply, her voice like iron.

With her back to him and hood raised, Dom could not see her face. He judged Sarn instead, as her brow furrowed, her eyes downcast and searching. She faltered, looking for any misgiving in Corayne. Dom did not trust Sorasa Sarn, with his life or anyone else's. But he trusted the assassin with her own survival. Sarn would not risk herself, not without cause.

"Fine," she muttered, tightening the reins in hand until her horse tossed. "We'll ride west, stop at the crossroads before finding passage over the Long Sea."

Dom winced at the thought of another voyage, let alone one

in such close proximity with this steadily growing band of shabby travelers. *At least I won't spend this one shoved below deck like a corpse in a steadily rocking tomb,* he thought.

"We should get passage here," Corayne hissed back. She glared over her shoulder for a second, once again looking toward the port. Her eyes flared. "There are ships enough."

"You said before, you trust my judgment. Trust it again. We'll head south within a few days, be on the sands as fast as the winds can carry us."

There was something in Sarn's voice that Dom had not heard before. In the many long days since he'd found her in Byllskos, she'd been frustrated, annoyed, weary, enraged, and mostly bored. Never desperate. *She is desperate now,* he realized, reading the carefully masked motions of her face. In spite of himself, the immortal knew her enough to note the pull of her lips, the hard clench of her jaw, the minuscule narrowing of her tiger's eyes.

"All right," Corayne said, spinning on her heel. By the time she mounted her own horse, the saddlebags full to bursting, her golden cheeks were moon pale.

Pale with fear or with frustration, Dom had no idea. *Mortals are impossible to fathom, especially Sorasa Sarn.*

He urged his mount alongside Sorasa's as they trekked from the old cemetery. She didn't acknowledge him at first, focused on checking her saddlebags too many times. He saw her whip, a great many flashes of steel and bronze, alongside small packets he vaguely recognized. A few were blue, some green, one of them a tiny square of black covered in Ishei writing. Clearly she had stocked up on supplies of her own.

By the time they reached the Adira gate, she huffed a sigh.

"Just say what you're going to say, Elder."

It felt like victory. A corner of Dom's mouth curled into a smirk. He leveled his eyes on Charlon, swaying on his mule a few yards ahead, planted firmly between Andry and Valtik. He didn't favor either for company.

Dom pointed his chin at the forger. "You're using that young man as bait."

It was meant to be an insult. Sarn took it as anything but.

"Catching on, are you?" she said, spurring her horse down to the marsh.

Larsia was a sea of tall yellow grass and gentle hills, the dirt too poor for much planting. As night fell, Dom's eyes perceived the empty, sloping lands, without forest or farm, all but barren. The emptiness rankled. A pang of longing shot through him. He had never been so far west, the travels of his long life having taken him only to the Gallish border. His days were not well spent under harsher suns in distant lands, away from home. He ached for woods, for glens, for rivers swollen by rain and snowmelt. A stag beneath the boughs of a yew tree, its antlers indistinguishable from branches. The old gray stone of Tíarma, the proud ridge thrust out of the fog, her windows like glowing eyes. The Monarch in her silver gown, waving from the gate. Ridha, smiling in the stable yard, her armor cast away, her sword forgotten and unneeded.

Will I ever see them again?

The stars above gave no answer, veiled by cloud and doubt.

The Cor road was still too dangerous. They rode a dirt track instead, a path older than the empire, rutted by centuries of cart traffic. Every step took them farther from Ascal and the lands of the Queen. Even so, Dom felt Taristan breathing down his neck again, his voice hateful and gloating.

Shall I kill her in front of you too?

The leather of the reins cracked between Dom's hands, threatening to tear. He wanted to do it, to feel something break that wasn't his own heart.

The sun rose and the sun set and still they moved on, shadow-eyed and tired. The others dozed off and on, heads lolling with the rhythm of the horses. All but Corayne. Even as the hours passed, the dawn sliding into day, she did not sleep, her pulse disquieted. The sword was a gargoyle on her back, misshapen under the cloak. It made her slump.

Dom wanted to take it from her, to ease her burden. And claim what little of her father remained on the Ward.

It's not for you to wield, he scolded himself sharply. He wished for Corayne's questions or Andry's gentle platitudes. Sarn's hissing retorts, sharp and quick as the whip coiled on her saddle. Even Valtik's rhymes, annoying as they were, would be better than his own thoughts.

There were no settlements but Adira this close to the border, all having been either razed or abandoned in the many skirmishing centuries. Dom couldn't even spot a village or castle on the horizon. It wasn't until afternoon, when the sun dipped toward the distant ridge of the Ward Mountains, that he saw a smudge far off, trailing smoke. *A tavern or an inn,* Dom knew as it came into sharper focus, the thatched roof and stonework chimney stark against the sky. It was shaped like a horseshoe, at the intersection of two tracks. *A crossroads.*

A mile off, the sour scent of beer wrinkled his nose. *I do not think I will enjoy this,* he thought as they approached, the sun sinking behind the mountains.

When Sarn ushered them through the tavern door, he knew he wasn't wrong.

The interior stood in stark contrast to the empty road and empty landscape outside. All manner of folk gathered within the boisterous common room: travelers and merchants, priests and wanderers, crossing paths as the tracks crossed outside. Judging by the full stable, it was a busy evening, and the barkeep didn't break stride when they entered, barely glancing over their strange party.

In this part of the world, where the east and west began to collide, it was difficult to seem out of place, even for them. An immortal Veder, a Jydi witch, a copper-eyed assassin, a royal squire, a criminal fugitive, and the pirate's daughter, the Ward's hope. *What a mess we are,* Dom thought as Sarn claimed a corner of the room.

Her glare and Dom's bulk were enough to send a few patrons scuttling for alternate seats, leaving them a nook of space to cram into. Far too tight for Dom's liking, so he leaned against the wall instead, feeling like a statue, wishing he could be one.

Corayne dropped her hood as she sat, planting herself in the narrow corner between the table and the wall. She braced her back, taking some of the blade's weight off her shoulders.

Dom expected Andry to slide in next to her, if his stolen

glances were any indication. Instead the squire sidled up to him instead, his expression gentle but shadowed with exhaustion.

"How are the ribs?" he said, glancing at Dom's side.

The flesh had healed over and caused him no more pain. But he could still feel the knife between his ribs, tearing as it went in and tearing as it went out.

"Better" was all Dom could say.

Andry didn't push and offered a tight-lipped smile. "You'll have a hell of a scar."

"The Vedera don't scar," Dom said quickly, without thought. Then he remembered his face, the long, jagged lines he would never be rid of. Weapons and monsters of the Spindles did not cut Vederan flesh in the way he knew. "Not usually."

At least I'm not alone in these, he thought, remembering Taristan's face again. The lines down his cheek, torn by Jydi magic and Corayne's own hand. *He has scars to match me now.*

It wasn't like Squire Trelland to fidget. But his fingers twitched and his eyes darted, not to their table or even to the bar, where any young man might wish to stray. Instead he eyed the stairway, bending up and around to the bedrooms upstairs.

"If you'd like to retire, no one will stop you," Dom said softly, looking down at the boy.

As in Ascal, Andry was torn between duty and desire. *The squire will march and fight and carry on until he drops. Until someone gives him permission to stand back, and be a little less strong.*

Dom felt a burning in his chest when he remembered Cortael at his age, and his same dogged, sometimes misguided resolve.

"You're no use to anyone half-asleep, Trelland," he said, putting a hand on the squire's shoulder. "I'll be sure to wake you if any trouble arises."

A wash of relief fell over Andry and he sagged, the last few days pulling on his shoulders. He gave Dom a grateful nod, and with only a single glance back to their table, fled the common room. Though the squire was mortal, he had a grace to him that most did not, even with lanky limbs and overlong strides. He dodged tables and took the stairs two at a time, disappearing to the next floor with his pack and cloak.

Dom turned back to their corner, satisfied with himself. "We should do the same," he said to the others, now sprawled around their pitted table. "Rest is what we all need right now."

Four cups were slapped down on the table, sloshing with ale and foam. Dom sighed, watching the mortals eagerly reach for their drinks. Charlon grabbed the first, downing it in one gulp. Corayne was quick to follow.

She glanced up at Dom over the rim of her cup. "It's not just sleep he's after," she said. "I don't think taverns agree with him."

"A squire who doesn't like taverns or barmaids or drinking on another man's coin," Charlon laughed, gesturing for another beer. "Rare as a unicorn, that boy. Not that I'm exactly clear on what that boy is bringing to the table, if I'm being honest."

"Andry Trelland is the reason we have the Spindleblade and even a chance of saving the realm," Corayne answered coldly, her Cor eyes inscrutable.

Charlon raised a hand in placation. "All right, all right. *Ca galle'ans allouve?*" he muttered, raising an eyebrow at Sarn.

Dom failed to hide a smirk. He did not speak Madrentine, but by now he knew that Corayne most likely did. With the same twist of her lips, Sarn met his eye, sharing his sentiments for once.

Corayne's face flushed, her grip closing on her drink. "I can think of nothing more ridiculous than being lovestruck in times such as these," she said tightly. "And if you'd like to talk about me, I suggest you do it in Jydi. I can follow in almost everything else."

Valtik cackled merrily into her cup.

And Charlon laughed too, his face flushing with surprise. He laid a hand on his chest, blue fingers bare. "Well, *m'apolouge*." He sounded truly sorry.

Unless he can lie to faces as well as he lies on parchment.

"So, why Ibal?" Sarn said, her voice sharp, turning them back to the great task at hand. As if it could really be far from anyone's mind. She took her first gulp of ale and pulled a face, setting the cup aside with an Ibalet curse.

In the yard of the Priest's Hand, she'd looked just as disgusted by the prospect of returning home. For what reason, Dom could not say. *But I would do well to find out, before we set foot in the sands, and she brings whatever she fears crashing down on us.*

"I heard enough in Adira." Corayne darkened like a storm cloud, her voice low as conversation turned to the Spindle. "A pirate galley nearly sank in the Long Sea, on the Sarim current along the Ibalet coast."

Charlon frowned. "Is that odd?"

"Something with tentacles tried to tear the ship apart. Yes, I'd say that's odd," Corayne said. Across the table, Charlon lost his jovial manner, his eyes narrowing in disbelief. "It had sailors from the Golden Fleet in its belly."

"Worn to bones, worn to blood," Valtik crooned, upending her empty cup. She motioned for another with wrinkled fingers. "A Spindle torn for flame, a Spindle torn for flood."

Sarn gritted her teeth, frustration written all over her tensing body. *I don't blame her.*

"Some months ago," Corayne pushed on, ignoring the witch, "I heard word the Ibalet court had moved from their palace in Qaliram. Heading to the mountains. I thought it was nothing—strange, but nothing."

"I heard the same." Sarn nodded. "You think they knew something was wrong, knew long before any of us?"

"Ibal did not become the wealthiest country upon the Ward by being foolish," Corayne said, nodding. "Taristan could've torn the desert Spindle before the Companions ever went to the temple. Or he did it soon after, racing south when Dom and Andry escaped. That Spindle has been open for gods know how long, spewing its bile into the Long Sea. Somewhere on the coast, or a river." Corayne clenched her jaw, her eyes sliding out of focus as her mind left the tavern. It was obvious where it went, flying over waves and water. "I didn't know there were sea monsters in the Ashlands."

"There aren't," Charlon said, ruddy in the candlelight. "That is a burned realm. If what you heard is true, if creatures of the deep are coming through a Spindle and into the Long Sea . . ." He trailed off, eyes flashing. "You're talking about Meer."

A chill went down Dom's spine, and he pushed off the wall, shifting closer to the table. "The realm of oceans," he said, saying what they all knew. His brow furrowed. "But why would Taristan choose a doorway to a realm he doesn't control? Beyond the influence of What Waits?"

"If he's only tearing what he can find, then there's not much choice to it," Charlon answered, shrugging. "According to scripture, the goddess Meira came to us from Meer, bringing with her the waters of the realm and every creature below the waves. The truth of that remains to be seen, but the realm itself—clearly it's real. And it's here."

Dom felt a muscle twitch in his jaw. He wished he'd paid more attention in his lessons half a lifetime ago, when Cieran had lectured the young immortals on the gods and Glorian, on the lost crossings to their realm and so many others. His mind had been in the glens, in the training yard, in the rivers. Not the classroom.

He shook his head. "Then Taristan does not care what he's tearing, so long as it is torn."

"Or he knows exactly what he's doing," Corayne broke in. "And he means to fill the Long Sea with monsters, cutting off half the realm from the rest." Her fist clenched. "Ibal, Kasa, Sardos, Niron, their armies, their fleets. Any help they might offer," she hissed, her exhaustion giving over to anger. "It's a good strategy."

"And weakens the Ward, no matter which realm he tears to," Charlon said, heaving a breath. It was like throwing a heavy shadow over their number, darker even than the shadows before. "Every Spindle forced open is a balance unmade. An abomination to the gods." His eyes tight, Charlon kissed his palms and raised them quickly, hands open to the sky. A holy gesture.

"You were a priest once," Corayne murmured, eyeing his hands.

Charlon winked. "For a little while. But that vow of celibacy," he said, grinning, "wasn't for me."

As the others laughed, Dom heard the creak of wood beneath heavy feet, felt the shift of air from a moving body. He turned to see a broad woman, nearly his height, striding across the common room.

She carried herself well, in boiled-leather armor and greaves, her boots knee-deep in mud, an ax slung across her back as easily as a cloak. The woman was of the Temurijon steppes, judging by the armor and her high-boned face, her skin a deep bronze like polished coin. Her hair was raven, cut short but still thick, falling over one brow. Her eyes narrowed, keen as a bird of prey, fixing on a single figure. She had the look of his fallen Companion, Surim of Tarima enclave, who rode half the realm just to die.

The room cleared a path for her, travelers pushing out of her way before she could remove them. Her face was known and respected here, if not feared. Dom stood to bar her way, but she stopped short, bearing a smile like a knife.

"A pity you went from illuminating manuscripts to forging them, Charlie," she sneered, bracing a hand on her hip. Her fingers were scarred and knobbled, broken and healed a dozen times.

Charlon seemed unsurprised by her presence. He only shook his head again and reached for Sarn's abandoned ale, pouring it down his throat. "Hunting bandits in the Forest of Rainbows, eh?" he sighed, tsking at the assassin.

"I suppose I was misinformed," Sarn said calmly. "Sigil, have a seat."

Dom stayed rooted, reluctant to let the strange woman

anywhere near Corayne. Or to take orders from the likes of Sorasa Sarn.

Sigil, the Temur wolf, did not seem bothered by his bulk. She held her ground too. "Another time, Sarn. I've business with the Ink King."

"The Ink King," Charlon sniggered under his breath. "What a stupid nickname."

Sarn took no notice. "I'm busy saving the realm, Sigil. Your business can wait."

"Charlon Armont," Sigil said, her voice drained of emotion, as if she were reciting a prayer at an altar, "dedicant priest of the Madrentine Order of the Sons of Tiber, there is a bounty upon your head, and it is my sworn duty to see it fulfilled."

A bounty hunter. Dom looked her over again, trying to read the Ward on her. She must have been watching the gates, waiting for her prey to emerge.

"Now, to which kingdom is she going to drag you, that's the question," Sarn muttered with a half smirk. "Tyriot?"

Charlon kissed his palms again. This time it felt like a rude gesture, and Sigil bristled. "Nah, that was just a spot of illegal export. It'll be the homeland for certain."

The bounty hunter forged on. "You are wanted by the crown of Madrence—"

Charlon grinned, elbowing Sarn. "See?"

"—for trespassing, thievery, arson, destruction to holy property, forgery, banditry, bribery of a priest, bribery of an officer, bribery of a noble, bribery of a royal, attempted murder, and murder," Sigil reeled off, in perfect intonation. "By royal and holy writ, I, Sigil of the Temurijon, have been appointed to return you to the court at Partepalas and see you face justice for your many crimes."

The charges were grave indeed. *Attempted murder. Murder.* Dom was sorely tempted to get out of Sigil's way and take Corayne with him. Not that she would go. Corayne looked like a child enthralled by a play, hardly afraid of anyone, let alone the fallen priest. She looked between them, owl-eyed, sipping at her ale.

The unremarkable Charlon seemed a bit more remarkable now, an odd gleam in his eye. His grin took on a shadowed edge.

Sarn crossed her arms, putting a foot up on the empty seat Sigil had refused. "I'm so glad I don't have to recite anything when I kill someone."

"Careful, or I'll drag you in too," Sigil drawled with little bite, her eyes never leaving Charlon. "Let's go, Priest. Make it easy on yourself."

"I think it's you who want to make things easy, Sigil." Again, the assassin tried to wave her down. Her booted foot tapped against the chair. *"Take a seat."*

The bounty hunter loosed the ax, dropping it smoothly into her hand. "I'll be taking the criminal and nothing else. Besides, I don't think you have room for us all," she added, running a hand through her short hair, sweeping it back from her face.

In the far corner, a man stood. He was, as the mortals would say, big as a house.

By the hearth, two men turned, though they could have passed for bears with their looming bodies and furry brown beards.

At the kitchen door, a cook with an apron smeared in pig's

blood stepped out, his carving knife clutched in a fist.

And so it went. The whole world fell silent, the travelers and merchants and weary nobodies going round-eyed at the brewing conflict. Six other men stood around the tavern, some on the stairs, some coming in from the yard. Armed and monstrous, big enough to put a lick of fear in anyone. Even an immortal.

Dom snapped his head back, looking to Sarn. Hoping she saw, hoping she knew.

The assassin wore her mask again, features still and unreadable, cold and unmoving as stone. She unfastened her cloak, letting it drop. Her whip coiled on one hip, the curved sword and daggers at the other. Her pouches of tricks ran along her belt. She met his gaze with that familiar, lethal flicker in her eyes.

Corayne tried to shrink back in her seat but found nowhere to go. She looked to Dom, and a plan already spun in his mind, a simple one: *Get her out of here.*

"I'm telling you the truth, Sigil." Methodic, Sarn began unspooling her whip, her eyes passing from the bounty hunter to the men gathering behind her. "The realm of Allward faces destruction. And I need you to help me save it."

"You should listen to her," Dom heard himself rumble, drawing up to his full six-and-a-half-foot height. Next to Sigil, it only gave him a few inches, but he used them well.

She sneered up at him, taking in his sword. "You're going soft, Amhara. Never knew you to need a bodyguard."

Dom braced his fingers on the sword hilt. His grip closed. "I am Prince Domacridhan of Iona, a son of Glorian Lost. I guard no

424   REALM BREAKER

one but the Realm's Hope."

"This is a waste of time, Sigil," Sarn sighed, drawing her dagger.

The bounty hunter faltered, only for a second, running her teeth over her lips.

"An immortal?" she said, looking to her hired thugs. "That sounds like even odds."

Finally, Sarn stood. Next to her, Charlon did the same, the glint of steel wedged between his knuckles. Their chairs fell to the ground with a clatter.

Corayne pressed herself into the corner, her throat bobbing over the collar of her cloak. She balanced between fear and fascination.

Dom sucked in a fortifying breath. *I just hope I am not stabbed again*, he thought, catching the first blow of a hammer-hard fist. The thug behind him yelped as the immortal's grip crushed his hand, snapping finger bones like dry twigs. He struck again, jabbing the man in the throat, leaving him writhing on the floor, gasping for air. *That's one of you sorted.*

He went for Sigil next, but the bearded bears caught him around the middle, heaving with all their strength. All three went toppling to the floor, crashing through a bit of wall little more than thin wood and paint. Dom caught a glance of a naked couple in the adjoining bedroom, both of them shouting. Instinctively, he muttered an apology, only to have one of the bears put an arm around his throat. The thug squeezed, intending to crush his windpipe. It was a bit uncomfortable, and Dom forced himself to stand, lifting the man clear off the floor. He elected not to draw his sword and threw an elbow instead, catching the man in the center of his chest. The bone cracked under his force. *Another.*

In the common room, the other occupants of the tavern fled or joined in, some with ale in hand. One very old, very toothless man attempted to bash Sigil with a pewter tankard, but she swatted him off. Meanwhile, Sarn wound her whip around the ankles of another thug, using it to pull him off his feet. Her dagger was a snake fang, striking swift and lethal. Blood sprayed across her face while more stained Charlon's hands. He didn't have his hand ax, only a finger blade, a tiny triangle of steel. He punched with his fist, sinking the sharp edge into the cook's eye. Charlon helped him slide to the floor, his lips moving quickly as he spoke a prayer in Madrentine.

The thugs were brutish, but poorly trained. Men who got what they wanted by standing tall and looking gruff. Only their number stood in the way, as did Sigil, who was easily worth the remaining five of them.

Sarn's whip lashed out again, this time wrapping around Sigil's armored forearm. The bounty hunter smiled her ruthless grin and pulled, dragging the assassin into her grasp. Sarn slid over the floor, her boots slick on the spilled ale, the momentum carrying her forward too quickly. She smiled too, using Sigil's pull to her advantage. With the whip still in hand, she snapped back, leaping, both booted feet coming off the floor. They caught Sigil in the jaw, her head cracking to the side as boot met skull. Dom winced. *She's either dead or out cold.*

Sigil of the Temurijon was neither.

She rolled her shoulders, spitting blood, her teeth painted a gruesome red. "Good to see you, Sarn," she snarled, tossing the whip away.

426   REALM BREAKER

Sarn rolled into a crouch, one hand braced against the floor-boards, the other raised like a scorpion's stinger, her dagger bronze and bloody. The black powder around her eyes smeared, running like dark tears.

Dom doubted Sorasa Sarn had ever shed a tear in her life.

"And you, Sigil."

Before he could wade between them, a thug lunged at Corayne, still pressed against the wall. Dom threw the table clear out of the corner, sending cups spilling and rolling.

Valtik let the brawl break around her, unbothered as she sipped her ale.

The thug reached and Corayne lashed out, her long knife in hand, cutting in wild arcs as she tried to scramble away. A star-burst of fear flared in Dom's chest, only for a moment, before he caught the thug by the neck and tossed him to the floor.

The wild noise of the tavern was a storm, thundering with the rumble of breaking bones and furniture, cracking with the lightning of a shriek or a yelp or a cackle. Sigil and Sarn danced, each landing blows, but never enough to incapacitate the other. They had a familiarity. They knew weaknesses and strengths, and played to both. Sarn was quicker, more agile, but no match for Sigil's brute force. They circled, Sigil pressing toward Charlon, and Sarn keeping her at bay. The priest spent most of the brawl praying, going from body to body, with little regard for the chaos around him.

"I think they're enjoying this," Corayne gasped, safely tucked under Dom's arm. She watched as Sarn dodged a plate. In the corner, Valtik clapped her hands, delighted.

"We don't have time for Sarn's amusement," Dom rumbled. He glared over the common room, brawl-battered, the hearth spitting smoke, the tables smashed, the barkeep cowering among his barrels, his patrons jeering along or using the opportunity to settle old scores.

Three of Sigil's hired men remained, advancing on Charlon. They were white-faced, with thick necks and stupid eyes, each holding a hand ax.

Dom gritted his teeth. *Sarn is still occupied, Valtik is useless, Corayne can barely swing a blade, and Andry is somehow sleeping through everything.* With a sigh, he pushed Corayne to Valtik and set to ending this mess of an evening.

He did not enjoy violence. It was the skill, the challenge, the graceful arc of steel, the strategic dance in mind and body that drew Dom to fighting. In Iona, in the training yards, that was more than reason enough. There was artistry to it. Out in the Ward, there was purpose: blood spilled for a reason, and not spilled often. But then he'd seen more blood in the last year than he had in centuries, and it sickened him. He made their defeats quick, and he made them gentle.

The first received a single good blow to the head, which snuffed him out like a blown candle. The second lost the ability to stand, his knee dislocated. The third Dom caught around the throat, holding his arms at an angle, until his eyes slid shut and his heartbeat slowed.

"Enough," Dom growled as the thug slid to the floor with a limp thud. "Enough."

The rest of the tavern shrank away from the blond-haired,

green-eyed behemoth in their midst. Some froze mid-grapple, fists raised and collars grabbed. The thugs still living groaned on the floor, inching away like worms.

Sigil and Sarn took no notice, the latter wrapped around the former, trying to squeeze the life out of the bounty hunter with her thighs. Sigil laughed, seizing Sarn around the waist, and threw her into the wreckage. Sarn landed hard, a hiss of pain smoking through her teeth.

Then Sigil was up against the outer wall, all stone, no give, Dom's forearm braced against her throat, under her chin. He stared into her face, all his thoughts narrowing to one.

"Enough," he said again, unyielding, even when she kicked him over and over.

Her face began to purple as he cut off her air, pressing harder. Still on the floor, moving slowly, Sarn raised her head.

"I'm willing to trade, Sigil," she said. Though they had won, the bounty hunter and her thugs incapacitated beyond measure, there was defeat in Sarn's voice.

It sent a shudder through Dom and surprised the Temur wolf. But it worked.

The bounty hunter gave a nod, as much as she could. Her legs dropped, her arms went slack. Dom stepped away, letting her find her feet. Her hand flew to her throat and she gasped, sucking down air. Her sharp eyes darted to Charlon, his stained fingers drawing holy symbols in the air over the cook, then to Sarn.

Sigil swallowed hard. "Let's talk."

In her chair, Valtik cackled, first in Jydi, and then in the common tongue they all knew. "Hammer and nail, the Companions are now seven, wind and gail, bound for hell or bound for heaven."

By now Dom was well accustomed to the witch's rantings, but he felt a shudder up his spine all the same.

The footsteps on the stairs were light, well balanced, barely a brush of feet. Dom turned to see Andry leaning down, his jaw slack and eyes puffy. He looked over the hurricane that was once the tavern.

"What did I miss?"

25

TEARS OF A GODDESS
Erida

Erida expected nightmares. Some judgment, from the gods or her inner self. Remorse or regret for her choice. This was not just a marriage, but an alliance with a man she could not trust. But she had seen Taristan's skin, cut by blade, healed in seconds. She had read the harried reports of her best scouts, their descriptions of his army like none other upon the Ward. And the hunters of the fleet had sent word as well. Monsters spotted in the Long Sea, creatures not seen for centuries, better suited to myth or the pages of a children's book. Everything Taristan had promised, the gifts of the Spindles, had come to fruition. What she desired was in her grasp, closer by the second, with every Spindle torn.

And the guilt never came.

The Queen slept soundly, without nightmare or dream. Even on the road, when rest was usually difficult. She found herself reinvigorated every morning she awoke in her tent or carriage. It was oddly easy to keep moving, and her convoy's pace reflected her ambitious manner.

Autumn crept closer, the heat of summer breaking when they left the lowlands. Green hills rose as the procession climbed out of the fertile valley of the Great Lion, heading east. A fresh north wind rode the landscape, carrying the smell of pine from the Castlewood. It would be colder still at the Madrentine border, the winds angled by the mountains.

The final morning was crisp. Erida took advantage of it, electing to ride her horse rather than shutter herself up in the massive but stifling carriage. The cold air made her alert as a falcon, the hood of her emerald velvet cloak thrown back, her gloved hands tight on the oiled leather reins.

While some of her ladies were just as happy to escape their rolling box, a few grumbled, their voices low behind their hands. Erida heard them anyway, well accustomed to eavesdropping. She listened from her saddle, keeping her eyes on the Cor road ahead.

"The Queen sets a quicker pace than most armies," Margit Harrsing, one of Lady Bella's many nieces, chittered to her companions. Fiora Velfi, the daughter of a Siscarian duke, hmm-hmmed in her high voice, in neither agreement nor contradiction. The dark-haired young woman was better suited to intrigue than the rest, raised in the royal villa at Lecorra, a pit of vipers. She very rarely, if ever, gave her true opinion on anything.

The fourteen-year-old Countess Herzer, with ringlet curls as stupid as her instincts, didn't bother to check her tone. "Her Majesty is eager to see her husband again," she said, sending a smattering of laughter through the ladies. "I think it's romantic."

432   REALM BREAKER

A tongue of fire went down Erida's spine. She kept straight and still, but her lips pressed to nothing, her teeth clenched behind them, as she weighed her options. *A woman in love is a woman in weakness, not to mention far from the truth,* she thought. *It won't do for my ladies, and by extension my court, to think their queen reduced to a simpering, starry-eyed girl trailing after the first man to touch her.*

But it is not useless either. Taristan stands in a precarious position. My favor keeps him steady, keeps him important. And that helps me maintain control over him, at the end of it all.

She elected not to answer, in either direction. Countess Herzer meant to be heard and wanted to draw a response. Erida of Galland would not give her the satisfaction. There was too much else at stake to be drawn into small-minded games.

Besides, she had not missed the way the ladies seemed to whisper about Taristan. Their conversations varied, assessing everything from his appearance to his stoic manner, but always returned to the way he had seemingly bewitched the Queen, winning her hand at first sight. *For reasons you cannot fathom.* It was frustrating, but ultimately, she was glad for their ignorance. And their expectations. It made her endeavors easier, if no one expected them of her.

The border with Madrence loomed, somewhere over the forested hills and down into another river valley. Erida imagined it like the lines on her map, starkly drawn, with a row of Gallish castles built up along the river, her soldiers strung between them like ropes of pearl. Their lines had held for years, the border country precarious, a stack of dry kindling that needed only a few sparks to burst into flame. Erida carried that candle with her now, ready to set all alight.

Madrence was a soft country made strong by flanking mountains and gentle neighbors. Siscaria cared only about its storied history, looking inward for glory, while Calidon kept to itself, hemmed within its own mountains and deep glens. Galland needed only reach out, now that the timing was right. Push south to the sea, storm the castles and the capital with such speed and force that their aging king could not help but surrender. Such a victory had not been won in decades, not since her grandfather's time. Erida pictured raising the Lion over the Madrentine shores, at every palace and castle. *How the people will love me then.*

Taristan's letter rode inside the lacings of her riding habit, the parchment brushing against her bare skin so Erida might not forget it. As if she could ever do such a thing. The jagged writing was like a scar, the ink burning her fingers as his hands had burned her skin.

We ride for your shifting borderlands. Ronin leads us to a hill with a broken castle, its slopes overgrown with thorns. Find me there.

The message had come only two weeks after he left, dispatched with speed.

No wonder my ladies talk, Erida admitted to herself. *It took me only hours to follow.*

The Queen blamed her haste on the hunger that lived in her, and in every ruler of Galland. The want for conquest, for more.

It rose in her with every mile forward, ravenous and all-consuming.

Castle Vergon was a ruin, her walls and towers having collapsed two decades prior. Her stones were grown over with moss, and a young forest sprung up in her halls, roots climbing through cellars and dungeons. After weeks on the road, Erida was glad to see the hollow wreck of the castle, her remaining walls black against the blue sky, the hill crowned in thorns. Like the rest of the hulking line of Gallish fortresses, she guarded the valley of the Rose River, called the Riverosse across the border. Erida smiled at the silhouette, knowing that Castle Herlin and Castle Lotha were twin shadows, one at either end of the horizon. Their front was unbroken now, her strength gathered.

With more to be unleashed.

She had seen this border only once, accompanying her father on a campaign when she was a child. He had won a great victory near the Rose's north branch, claiming a valuable pass into Calidon. Erida remembered that it had been winter, the air freezing on her cheeks as the wind blew sharp off the Watchful, where raiders prowled. This was different, in every respect. The air was crisp but warm enough for light clothing. The army waiting was her own to command. Her father was dead and gone. The battle was not yet won, a victory unseen.

But close enough to taste.

The Third Legion held the border always, ten thousand soldiers honed and perfected by years on tempestuous ground. The First had recently joined them, doubling their number. It was as if a city had sprung up overnight, the tents clustered in the shadows of the castles, hiding most from any spies across the river. While Madrence knew that Erida's army was amassing its force, they could not know to what extent, not without sneaking across the river and risking Galland's wrath. A caught scout was cause enough for war, if utilized properly. The smaller country would not give Erida another reason to fight. She had enough already.

Erida thought of Lord Thornwall and his words in the council chamber, when he'd given her his measure of the Madrentine campaign. It felt like looking back across a canyon. As if her life were split in two: before Taristan's proposal, his promise, her choice—and after.

They turned from Cor road at the last moment they could, maneuvering the Queen's great procession off the wide, ancient byway and onto rockier ground. The shadow of Vergon fell over them, but Erida did not feel its cold. She smiled up at the ruined castle and slid gracefully from horseback.

Taristan was nowhere in sight at the base of the hill, nor on the narrow path cut through the thorns to Vergon above. His own guard, a detachment of grizzled soldiers from the Ascal garrison, busied themselves with widening the thorn path. They hacked at the bloomless vines with swords and axes, making more of a mess.

When she approached, they jumped to attention, each man freezing in place. Their captain was easy to pick out, a green-edged cloak over his shoulder.

"Your Majesty," he said, dropping to a knee as best he could in full plate.

Erida nodded. "Captain," she said. "I assume my husband is in the ruins?"

"He is, Your Majesty," the captain answered hurriedly. "His

Highness requested we wait here," he added, almost apologetic. His teeth worried at his lip.

She fixed on her brilliant smile, tugging the corners of her mouth toward her ears. "You were good to obey the prince consort," she said with courtly grace.

The captain heaved a sigh, relieved, as Erida turned to her companions. They hung back on their horses or at the door of the coach, peering out at the landscape with fascination.

"Ladies, there's no need for all of us to ruin our skirts," the Queen called to them. "You may wait here with the captain. I'm sure his men will take good care of you all."

Judging by the captain's flush and the sly glances passed around her ladies-in-waiting, no one would object.

That left only the Lionguard to accompany her, the six knights in their golden armor, their green cloaks like spring among the dark thorns. More than a few snagged on the climb up the hill.

Again, Erida felt Prevail in her hand, the marriage sword planted between herself and her husband, their defense against the world. And each other.

A vaulted arch remained where the doors to Vergon's great hall used to be, half choked by an ash tree. Its leaves were tinged yellow, another herald of autumn. She paused, laying a hand against rough bark.

"I'll call for you if needed," she said, glancing at her escort.

The knights stared back, stern beneath their helms. They wanted to refuse, she knew. Before the changing of her world, she would have heeded their judgment. But the Lionguard could do little if Taristan and the wizard turned on her. Her husband could not be harmed by weapons of the Ward. His accomplice was Spindletouched, crawling with magic. It made no difference if her knights followed at close range or waited for her screams, to come charging to glory and death.

Sir Emrid made a noise low in his throat when she turned her back, stepping through the archway. He was only a year older than the Queen, the newest recruit to the Lionguard, and the least disciplined. She kindly ignored his attempt to check the Queen of Galland, leaving her knights behind.

The roof of the great hall was gone, broken all over the ruins in ragged piles of stone and mortar. Moss lay across everything in a velvet blanket, the stone blocks like lumps beneath. It was springy under her feet, soft to walk on. Her boots left light indentations. So had his.

She followed the footprints.

Erida felt the all too familiar sensation of being watched. She wondered if the ghosts of the people who used to live here still clung to the stones. Were they following her now, whispering about the Queen of Galland as the rest of the world did?

She imagined what they might say. *Married to a nobody. Four years a queen with nothing to show for it. No conquest, no victory.*

Just wait, Erida told them. *There is steel in me yet.*

She found Taristan and the wizard in the old chapel, in front of the single intact window, its glass blue and red and golden. The goddess Adalen wept sapphire tears over the body of her mortal lover, his chest torn open by hounds of Infyrna, a realm of fire and judgment. Their forms retreated in the back of the glass, burning and unholy. Erida knew the scriptures. Adalen's mortal gave his life to save the goddess from the fiery hounds. Strange, the scriptures never gave him a name.

Red Ronin knelt near the window but did not pray to it. Instead he put his back to the goddess while he whispered, eyes shut, his voice too low to hear. In the shadows of the chapel wall, Taristan prowled, a tiger with naked claws. His courtly attire was abandoned, traded for rough leathers and the same weatherworn cloak he'd first arrived in. He looked as far from queen's consort as a man could be. The Spindleblade flashed in his hand, drawn from its sheath. The steel was clean, a mirror to the blue-and-white sky.

His eyes met Erida's like lightning finding the earth.

She stopped walking, holding her ground. The air crackled between them, the work of a Spindle. Torn or close enough to feel. Burning or willing to burn. She sucked in a breath of air, wanting to taste it.

"Is it done?" she said, her eyes darting.

But the chapel looked unremarkable. Old stone, broken rocks, moss and roots. The trees weren't old enough to form a new roof. She saw nothing out of place, nothing to hint at a Spindle torn, a realm opened, another gift given, be it an army or a monster.

"Not yet," Taristan answered, his voice as deep as she remembered. She could still feel his fingers in her hair, still see his blood on her bed.

Erida glanced to Ronin, then back to the broken castle around them.

She took another breath. She couldn't taste a Spindle, but she tasted truth. "An earthquake destroyed this place two decades ago. People said it was the will of the gods, or a simple act of nature. But that isn't true, is it?" Sunshine filled the window, making Adalen glow. "There is a Spindle here, closed but waiting. It broke the castle, not anything else."

The wizard's eyes snapped open, his prayers cut off. "Your histories said as much, for anyone with the mind to see it," he hissed. "Even the echoes have power."

His red-rimmed glare ran over Erida's skin from her wrists to her neck. It was like a glowing poker, close enough to throw off cloying heat, but not enough to burn. She raised her chin. The wizard would not best her with tricks.

It was Taristan who stepped between them, breaking Ronin's raw-eyed stare.

"I thought you'd like to watch," he said, silhouetted against Adalen's tears.

Overhead, a cloud passed over the sun, plunging them all into shadow. The wind found them in the corpse of the castle, pulling at her traveling clothes with invisible fingers. It stirred the hair falling from the braided crown around her head, blowing a curtain of ash brown across her vision.

She held Taristan's gaze.

"Indeed I would."

He turned on his heel, stalking to the stained-glass window, his empty hand raised in a gloved fist. Without so much as a grunt, he punched clean through the goddess's face, shattering blue and white onto the mossy ground. A few shards punctured his knuckles and he picked them out with a wince.

He still feels pain.

Erida looked on, filled with fascination.

"When you first came to me, I wondered if this was all a trick," she murmured. A few drops of blood welled up in Taristan's cuts, falling to the grass before the skin knit together again.

He tested his fist. Not even the glimmer of a scar remained. "Does this look like a trick to you?" he rumbled, glowering.

The ground muffled her footsteps as she moved, skirts wheeling around her legs. "A con man and his pet wizard," Erida said, turning his fist over in her grasp. The blood was still there, but nothing else. "Using petty magic to ensnare a queen."

"Petty magic," Ronin spat, his scarlet robes like a gown around him. He rose smoothly to his feet, his face flushed like his clothing. "You know not of what you speak."

Erida glared, her gaze like a volley of arrows. Very few upon the Ward would dare speak to her with such a tone. "Then enlighten me, Wizard."

It was Taristan who answered, raising the sword in his other hand, the hilt clutched in his fist. It reflected his face, the scratches below his eye turned to pearly white scars. "I took this sword from the vaults of Iona, winding deep beneath an Elder fortress. They called me a thief for retrieving what was mine, wielded by my ancestors, even when my own brother carried its twin."

He ran a finger down the strange steel, etched with runes in a language Erida could not read. She tried to picture the Elder enclave, hidden from the world, surrounded by mist. *And ruin crawling within, a Corblood mortal with a deathless grudge and iron will.*

"That day was long in coming. It was Ronin who found me, told me what I was. The red wizard pulled a mercenary from the mud of a Treckish war camp and made him a conqueror," Taristan continued, his voice low but strong, reverberating in Erida's chest. He passed the sword through the air errantly, without thought. "I knew in my bones I was not the same, not a man like the ones beside me, content to fight and fuck and farm, drinking their money and pissing their lives into nothing. I wanted the horizon more than I wanted any cup or coin or concubine."

Ronin raised his chin, looking on Taristan as he would a beloved son. He passed by him, brushing a white hand over his shoulder. "Such is the way of Old Cor. Of all your like," the wizard said, moving on. "It's the Spindle in your blood."

"You are children of crossing," Erida offered, remembering her lessons as best she could. As the heir to Galland, she had been taught the tales of Old Cor as much as any other part of her birthright. Her father used to tell them at night, like any other bedtime story. *Children of crossing, children of conquest. Destined to rule every corner of the Ward, but they fell. They failed. We are their successors.*

And I will prove it, the Queen believed.

Taristan turned, silhouetted against the broken window. He stared into the ruins of Castle Vergon, but Erida knew he looked farther. Backward. Into his own past.

"The Elders took my brother, older by minutes, chose him for nothing but a few seconds of life. He would be their champion, their emperor, their dog, their sword to cut a path back home." The words ripped from him, and color rose in his pale cheeks. The son of Old Cor cut a vicious line in the moss, splitting the green like flesh. Though he stood tall and whole, a prince of Galland, a prince of Old Cor, immune to harm, unbothered by pain, Erida could not help but feel pity for him. *No, not for Taristan today. But for the boy who grew up alone, abandoned, with nothing but the road beneath his feet.* "They left me screaming in the wilderness. And I became someone else's sword, someone else's beast."

Her heartbeat sputtered. *Mine*, she thought too quickly.

Taristan met her eyes again but said no more, a muscle working in his jaw. Some part of him hesitated, holding back. Her gaze trailed down his neck. White veins stood out at his collar, visible beneath the ties. They had grown since last she'd seen him, like the roots of a tree.

Ronin moved, passing between the royal pair. He leered at Erida, showing small teeth.

She swallowed back a burst of revulsion. *Get away from me, you rat*, she thought.

"You serve your gods, your silent judges in their stained-glass prisons, dead but for their priests speaking for bones long turned to dust," the wizard said. "If they were ever bones at all."

Her body ran hot, a sweat breaking along her neck like fever, like sickness. The Queen chewed his words, turning them over and over.

"And who do you serve, Taristan?" she asked, her voice shaking.

Her husband lowered his black eyes.

"You know Him as What Waits."

Her first instinct was to laugh, but to laugh at Taristan of Old Cor felt like signing her own death warrant. Her second instinct was to call her knights. Sacrifice as many Lionguard as she could to get away from the madman she had foolishly chained herself to.

The third instinct settled deeper than the others, stronger, darker.

I know What Waits as a ghost story, a villain in the fables, the shadow under the bed or the creak behind the door. He varies from tale to tale. The Red Darkness, the Torn King of Asunder. He is each and nothing. He is not real.

He is not real.

But staring into Taristan's eyes, she could not say that aloud. Again she saw the odd sheen, the scarlet moving in the black, barely a flash or a reflection. She glanced down, then behind. There was nothing red before him, only green and gray and blue. *How can this be?*

What have I done?

What more will I do?

Again, she expected regret, remorse. It did not come. *My ambition is stronger than any shame.*

"What Waits," she heard herself say, shaping the words. Her ladies would giggle to hear her voice tremble. Lord Konegin would gloat. *And their opinions mean nothing.* "So you *are* a priest, wizard. After a fashion."

Ronin smiled a hateful grin. "To the only god this realm will ever know."

"What of you, Erida?" Taristan asked, drawing close again, until there were only inches between them. Air and steel, hot breath and Spindleblade. "Will you serve Him as we do?"

Do I have a choice? Somehow, looking up into the eyes of Old Cor, she knew she did. Taristan stared down at her, unmoving. His black eyes, usually so unreadable, filled with a dark and wretched hope.

Her fingers brushed the scars on his face, her touch fleeting and featherlight. His white skin felt hot as flame. "There are breakers of castles, breakers of chains, breakers of kings and kingdoms," she said, her voice iron.

"Which am I?"

Power surged through her veins, delicious and seductive. She wanted more; she needed more. "You are a realm breaker, Taristan. You would crack this world apart and build an empire from its ruins."

Flames burned at her wrist as his rough hand grazed hers.

Erida stood without her throne, without a crown, without any of the trappings of the ruler she was born to be. And, somehow, she'd never felt more like a king.

"So would I."

His smile reminded her of a wolf, a lion, a dragon. Every predator upon the Ward, made in one face, with all their ferocious beauty and danger. She felt the wind on her teeth, her grin matching his own.

Leather and iron were nudged into her grasp before Erida knew it, and her fingers tightened around the hilt of the Spindleblade. The sword pointed outward, its tip inches from Taristan's own heart. He leaned for a second, pressing his leather-clad chest into the sharp edge. One inch further and he would bleed.

Erida smiled wider, enjoying the feel of a sword.

With deliberate motions, never breaking her gaze, Taristan laid a palm to the keen blade.

"Let me bleed for you," he murmured.

The Queen needed no more coaxing, and she drew against his skin, cutting a gash down his palm. The blade ran darkly red, his blood like syrup, coating the sword.

"Here," Ronin said, staring into Adalen's shattered face. The sun glowed through, its rays swirling with dust so thick they seemed solid enough to touch. The wizard did just that, reaching out a white hand to run it through the sunbeams, his fingers trembling as he did.

Taristan reclaimed the sword without a word, both hands wrapped around the hilt. He stalked to Adalen's window and raised it high, like a woodsman before a tree.

The Spindleblade cut through open air, the sun flashing against it for a second as it crossed through the rays.

And then the light itself splintered, shattering like the stained glass, into shards of yellow and white. A crackling filled the air, the sound of a red-hot iron plunging into water, or the soft tear of silk, or the ripping of parchment—Erida could not say. It was nothing she knew, nothing she'd heard before. The sound echoed in the air, in her bones, rattling up her spine until she felt she might choke on it. The air on her face seemed to prickle, tingling her cheeks like the first breath of frost. Her mouth dropped open, gasping, and she tasted iron and blood both.

She had imagined a Spindle all her life, like most children. The stories varied; the histories were vague. It had been a thousand years: only Elders remembered, and they had not been forthcoming these last centuries. Even now, she pictured a great column like a lightning bolt, veined purple, frozen in its brilliance, with an archway to the next realm. An open doorway. A pillar. Something gigantic and beautiful enough to hold such rare power.

She was wrong.

The thread hung in the air, seven feet high, slim as a needle, and easy to miss at the wrong angle. It glimmered, gold then silver, wavering as sunlight on the surface of gentle water.

Taristan stared, transfixed, the thread reflected in his coal-black eyes, splitting their darkness. He didn't bother to clean his sword, sheathing it back at his hip before running a hand as close to the Spindle as he dared. It bowed, arcing toward his skin, coming within an inch.

The Queen clenched her jaw and took a small step backward. Anything might come through, and it would not be loyal to her. She swallowed hard, trying not to show fear.

Her husband felt her discomfort anyway. He looked away from the Spindle, finding her face. She felt herself pale.

"Have I frightened you?" he said, his voice too soft. "You are not foolish, and only a fool would be unafraid."

Erida wanted the lie. Admitting weakness was not a luxury queens enjoyed.

"I'm terrified," she forced out.

The Spindle gleamed at her, beckoning. Her insides twisted in reply, every nerve singing a warning. The gold and silver flashed. Within them, there was another color. At first she thought it to be black, but on closer inspection it proved to be darkest, most lethal red. She felt it like breath on skin, gentle and foreboding. A promise. It was watching.

What Waits.

She raised her chin. "And I intend to use that terror to my advantage."

"Good." Pride laced through Taristan's face, and he dropped his hand. "Fear should never be ignored, only controlled. I learned that lesson long ago. It's good I don't have to teach it to you."

"Where does this doorway lead?" she asked, taking another step. This time forward again, her feet moving of their own accord even as her mind flew through all the reasons to stay far away. The Spindle set the hairs on her neck on end. "What comes? Another army?"

She stared at it, closer now, expecting to see a sliver of what lay beyond. But she saw nothing, not even the red presence. The Spindle hissed, a snake warning away enemies.

"The blessings of What Waits," Ronin murmured.

He shifted so he stood alongside Taristan. The man of Old Cor dwarfed him, but Ronin did not seem small despite his slight frame. The Spindle filled him with something, a power Erida could not name. He nudged Taristan.

"Take what is offered," the wizard said, urging him on.

The Spindle glowed in Taristan's eyes. He stared, unblinking, and plunged a hand into the thin, shining thread.

Erida expected the Spindle to burn or cut, to harm him in some way. Instead his fingers passed through it as easily as the divide in a wall of curtains, pushing aside the planes of this realm to reach the next. Then his hand disappeared, and his wrist, until he was well past the elbow of his arm. On the other side, there was nothing but empty air.

448 REALM BREAKER

His mouth tightened, his teeth clenching together as his body jerked once. If he was in pain, he did not show it.

"Taristan," she heard herself murmur. To the Queen's surprise, she grabbed his opposite shoulder, fingers working into his leathers, trying to pull him out.

The Spindle gave him back without difficulty.

Diamonds, big as eggs, flawless and without peer, spilled from his hand, rolling over his fingers and onto the grass. At first Erida thought they were blocks of ice, some rough, some clear, too massive and too many to be jewels. She grabbed one, expecting it to be frozen. Instead she felt hard stone, heavy on her palm.

"Irridas," Ronin breathed, stooping to inspect the stones. "The dazzling realm."

"Home to Tiber, the god of riches," she said reflexively, remembering scripture.

The gems were marvelous, but Erida was queen of a wealthy kingdom. It was difficult to impress a woman like her with jewels. She straightened, a diamond in her fist, watching Taristan's face.

When his thin lips spread into a smile's shadow, she swallowed. "What else?"

"Nothing gets past you," he replied, taking the jewel from her. His bare skin was already pale, but Erida did not miss the steady spread of white veins in his flesh. They matched those already on his chest, growing and branching, as something grew and branched in him.

His fingers closed, the diamond in his grip. His knuckles went hard and sharp, bones standing out beneath his skin, and the gemstones crumbled to dust, sifting like starlight between his fingers.

This time, he smiled with white teeth, like a predator closing in on a kill.

Her flesh burned when he raised his palm to her face, cupping her cheek. His blood smeared, sticky on her skin, but somehow she didn't mind.

In the Spindle, something growled.

26

PAIN AND FEAR
Corayne

Sigil rode a horse as a bird flew. Second nature, with incredible, impossible ease. The people of the Temurijon were legendary equestrians, nearly born in the saddle, and Sigil was no exception. Her mount was no steppe pony, but a chestnut hunter, with long legs and a white star down its face.

She kept a rope from the pommel of her saddle attached to Charlie's, forcing him to keep pace, dragging him along with a grimace. He bounced on his mule like a sack of potatoes, and every time they stopped, he walked gingerly, wincing. Like Corayne, he wasn't exactly comfortable in the saddle, and Sigil needled him for it. Their relationship was strange, gruff but tolerating, despite Sigil's endeavors to bring Charlie to execution. Even so, they shared old jokes and even older insults. Clearly she'd been chasing him for a very, very long time.

"I must say, I'm glad to get out of that marsh," Sigil said, raising her face to the sun as they trotted along a country lane. Freckles dotted her cheeks. She led them southwest, leaving the Adiran mists behind. Though Corayne knew the map as well as anyone, she had no idea where they were going.

Sorasa swayed with the rhythm of her horse, her cowl raised again. "I can't believe you wasted so many days squatting in the mud, waiting for such a sorry excuse for a bounty," she said, cutting a glance at Charlie.

Sigil drew herself up proudly. "I've never failed to bring a charge to justice."

Charlie sneered next to her, huffing. "And never failed to collect a blood price."

"Blood price? Don't act so moral, Priest," she shot back, grinning. "I believe one of your charges is murder."

On his own horse, Andry coughed, doing his best to hide a disapproving grimace. *His best isn't very good,* Corayne noted, watching the squire squirm next to her. Dom was stone-faced, trying to hide his own disapproval. *You're surrounded by criminals now, Prince,* Corayne thought.

"It was him or me," Charlie said airily, waving a hand in the air. The movement almost made him slip from the saddle. "Garion of the Amhara taught me well."

Another Amhara? Before Corayne could open her mouth to ask, Sorasa peered out from her hood, a mischievous glint in her eye.

"I'd say you taught him a few things too," she wheedled, loosing her sharp, reserved laugh.

Charlie blushed a furious red but laughed with her, the pair exchanging meaningful glances. *Another odd history, longer than we know.* Corayne couldn't help but be amused watching them both. They reminded her of the *Tempestborn* crew, a collection of killers and rogues, at home with each other and no less lethal for it.

Craning her neck, the bounty hunter looked back, twisting her body in her leather-bound armor. Her own smile was brittle. "I'm surprised Garion wasn't waiting in the marshes, same as me. You didn't exactly make yourself difficult to find."

His smile disappeared in an instant, replaced with a pained frown. With unsteady motion, he slipped from the saddle, landing hard in the dirt of the road. "I think I'll walk for a bit," he grumbled, stumbling on uneasy legs to put some distance between them.

Sigil let him fall back.

"That was unkind," Sorasa said in a flat voice, without judgment. A simple statement of fact.

Sigil shrugged. "No one pays me to be kind."

At Corayne's shoulder, Andry leaned, closing the distance between them. "She might be harsher than Sorasa," he said out of the corner of his mouth.

At the rear of their line, Dom scoffed. "I did not realize there was a competition for worst personality," he crowed.

Sorasa didn't hesitate. "It's not a competition with you around, Elder."

On the road, Charlie jabbed a thumb over his shoulder, his discomfort forgotten. "Do all immortals have sticks up their asses or just him?"

Their joined laughter carried through the Larsian fields,

rustling the tall grass. To Corayne's delight, even Dom's lips twitched, betraying a smile.

"Get up."

Corayne opened her eyes with a jolt of terror, expecting her uncle, or the red wizard, maybe even What Waits himself, a looming shadow set to rip her apart. Instead she found Sorasa bending over her sprawled form, the weak fire dancing in her copper eyes.

Shaky, Corayne rose up on her elbows, looking around their camp. Embers glowed in a ring of stones. Charlie sat over it, his cloak wrapped around his body as he poked the flames, barely awake. Sigil watched over him, alert as a hawk. The moon was gone, but the stars still hung in the sky. The eastern horizon was barely tinged in blue.

"Sorasa, it's still dark," she protested, scrubbing at her face. "I'm not on watch—"

But the assassin took her by the shoulder, hauling her to her feet. The night air bit cold when her cloak fell away.

"Hurry up. We don't have much time until they come back," Sorasa said, half marching her toward the fire, where Sigil loomed. Corayne stumbled along, trying to get her bearings as sleep faded away. "I should've done this a long time ago."

Done what? Corayne wondered, her mind snapping awake. She opened her eyes fully to Sigil, whose attention shifted from the fugitive priest to Corayne's own face. Doubt bled through her, its edges tinged with fear. With a jolt, she realized Dom and Andry were gone, their sleeping spaces empty.

"Where's Dom?" she asked, uneasy and wary. As much as her

protectors chafed, she felt bare without them, too vulnerable. "And Andry?"

Sorasa let go of her arm, planting them both in the center of the camp. She crossed her arms over her chest and settled back, tapping one boot. "The walking scowl and the noble squire are hunting for breakfast."

Corayne nearly jumped when Sigil began circling her like she was a horse at auction. With a gulp, Corayne shifted to keep her in sight, turning steadily. "Can I help you with something, Sigil?"

"The Spindleblade is too big for her to ever use properly," Sigil finally said, taking Corayne by the shoulders. She balked, surprised, as the bounty hunter gave her a shake. "She doesn't have enough heft for an ax either. What about finger blades?"

It took Corayne a second to realize Sigil wasn't speaking to her at all.

"She's too slow," Sorasa answered, also sizing her up. "Archery is out of the question too."

Corayne squinted between them, at a loss for once. Then the pieces slotted together, all at once. "Are—are you going to teach me to fight?"

Firelight gleamed on Sorasa's teeth. "If I had a year, yes. I could make you passable," she answered, smirking. Then she shook her head, looking Corayne up and down. "If I ever meet your mother, I'll certainly have words for her. What a lesson to neglect."

My fighting skills are not the only thing she neglected, Corayne thought bitterly.

"Even when it isn't the end of the world, the realm is a dangerous place for women," Sorasa added, gesturing between herself and the bounty hunter.

Sigil grinned broadly. "And so we became dangerous."

"Care to dance with us?" Sorasa extended a hand, gesturing like a partner at a ball. "We who belong nowhere?"

Any anxiety or annoyance over her disrupted sleep quickly faded. Corayne nodded eagerly, thinking of the Spindleblade in its sheath, and the long dagger from Adira. *We who belong nowhere.*

"Teach me," she said, breathless.

She tasted dirt before she knew what was happening, knocked over without so much as a warning. "What the f—" she wheezed, fighting to her feet.

Only to get knocked down again, the assassin moving in a blur of limbs.

Corayne fell, flat on her back, sputtering as the air rushed from her lungs. Huddled in his cloak, she heard Charlie laugh beneath his breath. Sigil did not join them, content to watch in silence.

Sorasa bent over her, as she had some minutes before, a shit-eating grin on her face. With a wriggle of tattooed fingers, she put out her hand, offering it.

"This is the easy way?" Corayne forced out, gasping for her lost breath.

Pulling hard, Sorasa hauled her to her feet. "Absolutely," she said. "Now shift your weight. Balls of your feet. You'll balance better and have an easier time changing direction."

The assassin demonstrated, transitioning from a flat-footed stance to her toes, both knees bending slightly. She swayed back and forth, her shoulders square to her knees. Corayne did the same, mimicking Sorasa's body as best she could. This time, when Sorasa lunged, she managed to keep standing for three whole seconds, until the assassin dropped her again.

Corayne winced, her back beginning to ache. "Sorry," she gritted out, feeling the embarrassed sting of failure.

"Better" was all Sorasa said, tugging her up again.

"Maybe I should just go back to sleep," Corayne said, massaging her shoulder. Still, she kept on her toes, ready should Sorasa try her again. "Leave the fighting to the people who know how?"

Sorasa pretended not to hear her.

"I don't think we have a sword light enough for her." Sigil began to circle again. She wasn't wearing her armor yet but seemed no less gigantic. "Unless you want to give her yours?"

"I'd rather give her a limb," Sorasa scoffed before turning back to Corayne. "The long knife you bought in Adira will have to do." She drew the blade from Corayne's saddlebags. It winked in the ember light, a plain thing, with a sharp edge and a leather-wrapped hilt. Sorasa gave it a testing swing and thrust. "Good weight—you can use one hand or both. I'd say both if you want to really make it hurt."

The blade continued to dance, sliding around her fingers in a blur of motion.

"Show-off," Charlie rumbled, taking a pull from a waterskin. *No, that's wine,* Corayne realized, watching something black drip from his lips.

"Here." Sorasa snapped her back to attention, pressing the dagger into Corayne's unsteady hands.

She set her jaw, locking her teeth as she locked her fingers around the hilt. While the Spindleblade was too heavy for her, it felt familiar, at least. This was odd, a stranger in her grasp.

Sorasa hardly gave her a moment to adjust, already fixing her grip. She rearranged Corayne's hold on the dagger, wrapping her fingers one by one. "Tight but not too tight, see? Don't lock your joints, in your hands or anywhere else."

Again Corayne flushed. She hated getting things wrong, and had little experience with it. *At least I used to, until the realm decided to crash down on my head.*

"Good." Sorasa nodded, eyeing her hand. Her own dagger, one of many, flashed before Corayne even knew it was drawn. She blanched, falling back a step. "Don't worry," Sorasa said, "You're generations away from crossing blades with me. Just watch, mimic, memorize. You're good at that, aren't you?"

I am, Corayne thought, her flush giving over to a tentative smile.

The drills were not difficult, built on repetition and memorization. *Draw, parry, stab, slice, twist, double-grip, backhand, switch.* Corayne didn't have the same strength behind her blows, and her form was nothing compared to an Amhara, fallen or otherwise. *But it's something where there was nothing before,* she thought, wiping away a bead of sweat.

"Excellent—at least I know how to hold a dagger now," she said when Sorasa slowed, dropping her weapon back into her belt.

The assassin smirked. "If only you knew how to hold your tongue."

Until now, Sigil had been content to watch, but no longer. She rolled her shoulders, waving Sorasa out of the way. "Let's see if you know how to throw a punch, Corblood," she said, dropping her guard and bending so that her face was within reach. "Go ahead."

Behind her, Charlie gestured a blow. "She's not kidding."

"Don't tuck your thumb, unless you want to break your hand," Sorasa added, taking a seat next to him, leaning back on the grassy ground.

Corayne blinked at them both, then at Sigil. The bounty hunter only stared back, expectant, the edge of her jaw like an anvil.

"Is this how the Temur show affection?" Corayne said weakly, squaring her shoulders. *Shift your weight*, she thought, adjusting her stance.

"We Temur are free with our love and free with our anger," Sigil answered, matter of fact. She tipped her head, presenting her face for a blow.

When her knuckles connected, Corayne realized what a very, very bad idea this was. She howled in pain, feeling fire in her hand, and nearly fell to the ground, clutching her wrist. "By the Spindles," she cursed, shaking out her fingers. Her knuckles were already red, close to swelling. "Adalen's tears," she yelped, and continued to swear in every language she knew.

Sigil chuckled, standing up straight.

"Well?" Sorasa asked, an eyebrow raised.

"Honestly, not as bad as I thought," Sigil answered, sounding shocked.

It didn't lessen Corayne's pain, but it did make it easier to bear. "You're not the first person I've ever punched," she hissed through her teeth, shaking her hand again. "Just the most painful."

Proud, Sigil slapped a hand against her jaw, then beat a fist on her broad chest. "The iron bones of the Countless will never be broken," she boasted, a rally cry of the Temur.

Charlie didn't let her gloat long. He tipped his head, pretending to think. "Didn't I break your arm in Pennaline?"

"*You* did not break my arm; your paramour did," Sigil snapped, flexing the arm in question. Corayne saw no evidence of injury. "And he had to use a hammer to do it."

"Ah yes. Such happy memories," Charlie said, looking wistful.

It felt wrong to laugh when so much hung in the balance, but Corayne laughed all the same. "Has anyone told you how strange you all are?"

Sigil winked. "How strange *we* are, Cor girl. And you're far from finished," she said, gesturing for Corayne to start again. Reluctant, the girl did as told, squaring off with a bounty hunter twice her size.

"Punch here. One," Sigil said, raising her right hand, palm out. "Punch here. Two." The left hand. "And keep those feet moving. Duck when I strike."

"I'd rather you didn't strike," Corayne mumbled, her hand still smarting.

Sigil didn't give her any more time to grumble, both hands dancing in succession. "One, two, two, one, two, one, one." She raised each in succession, catching Corayne's blows in her massive hands.

When she yelled, "Duck!" Corayne was ready, dropping under a swipe from her long arm, with a grin.

"Good!" Sigil cried out, her smile wide, showing big teeth.

"Good concentration. You've got focus; you know where to keep your eyes. That's something." She tapped Corayne on the forehead. "Now *duck*," she cackled.

I suppose I should be used to the ground by now, Corayne thought, hitting the grass with a painful thud. She heaved a shaking breath. Sigil struck like a charging horse and her head spun. The corner of her mouth smarted, wet with a trickle of blood.

"Are you afraid?" Sorasa's face wheeled above her, crowned in dizzying stars.

Corayne didn't have the strength to lie. "Yes."

Judging by Sorasa's smile, it was the right answer.

"Fear is a well-honed instinct, useful as any steel edge," she said. "It's kept me alive more times than I care to count. So let that fear in, let it fill you up, let it whisper and guide. But do not let it rule."

Corayne shakily nodded her head. "I won't let it rule."

The assassin looked satisfied. "There are no greater teachers than fear and pain."

"By the wings of Baleir, what are you doing?"

A blur of golden hair and emerald-green eyes shouldered Sorasa out of the way, pulling Corayne to her feet. She wavered, unsteady, clutching an arm for support. There was pain, but she leaned into it. *The pain means I learned something.*

Sorasa snarled, a tiger before the hurricane. She jabbed a finger into his chest, color rising in her cheeks. "What we should've done since the second we found her."

Dom eagerly rose to the challenge, snarling right back. "Corayne is the hope of the realm, the only thing standing between Allward and complete destruction."

The assassin threw up her hands, exasperated, losing her infinite control piece by piece. "*Exactly!* She should know how to defend herself when we can't."

Someone dabbed at her lip and Corayne turned to find Andry standing close, a kerchief in hand, the edge of it stained red. She took it gratefully, holding the cloth to her bleeding mouth.

"It's fine. They're good teachers," she said, stepping between Dom and Sorasa. *Almost as good as pain and fear.* "Even if I'm bad at almost everything."

The Elder and the assassin glared at each other, breaking at precisely the same time, turning on their heels to stalk away. *Thank the gods,* Corayne thought.

While the rest set to cooking breakfast, Andry hesitated, remaining close.

Corayne checked her lip with her fingers, then realized she was probably covered in dirt. She felt oddly self-conscious in front of him, though Andry Trelland had seen her in all states by now.

"Your horsemanship could use some work as well," he mumbled, scuffing a boot.

When she struck his shoulder, she was careful to keep her thumb untucked.

27

SERPENT
Andry

They boarded the trader at a fishing village, this time under Sigil's advice. She seemed to know everyone Sorasa did not, and passage on a ship bound for Almasad came cheap.

"Another godsdamned boat," Dom sputtered, staring into the sea below.

After two days on the water, Andry was thanking his lucky stars that he was not plagued with seasickness, doomed to empty his guts over the side of the ship rail as Dom did. The Elder was better today, but still green as his cloak, his infinite focus fixed on the waves lapping against the side of the Larsian galley. The others gave him a wide berth, though Charlon kept offering him wine, which Dom kept refusing. Valtik said a charm over him, which possibly made things worse. Sorasa ignored him entirely, deep in conversation with Sigil at the prow of the ship, the women as starkly different as night and day.

Sigil was broad and tall, her face turned skyward, reveling in the daylight. Not like Sorasa, who was a shadow next to the Temur wolf. Her lips barely moved as she spoke, her face a mask, while Sigil was quick to grin or scowl.

Andry wanted to eavesdrop, if only to pass the time.

Corayne was certainly trying. She stood as close as she dared, halfway down the long, flat deck of the galley, hidden behind a pile of crates netted to the ship.

She smiled when Andry sidled up to her, leaning against the rail.

"Honorable squire, are you joining me to eavesdrop?" she said, nudging him with her elbow.

His arm buzzed at her touch. "I think they'd skin me alive if I tried," he answered, and he meant it. "What about you? Have you figured it out yet?"

"I'm smart, but I'm not a mind reader, Trelland." Corayne narrowed her eyes at the prow, her brows furrowed in concentration. "Whatever she promised the bounty hunter must be big. Someone with a higher price than Charlie."

Charlie. Corayne's familiarity with the Madrentine fugitive was no surprise. After all, she was more accustomed to criminals than anyone else. And besides, she spent half the night going through the forger's seals and markers, trying to memorize them for her own use. They'd become quick friends, the fallen priest and the pirate's daughter.

"Maybe she offered herself?" Andry suggested. "Certainly an assassin has a price on her head."

Corayne barked a laugh. "I think Sorasa would sell every person on this ship before risking herself."

Andry grinned. "She'd sell Dom twice," he said, pleased when Corayne chuckled again. "But not you," he added, without much thought. It was the truth, after all.

Her smile disappeared as if he'd thrown a bucket of cold water over her. She turned her face into the wind, searching the vast blue horizon. The sun bounced off the waves, dappling her face in shades of gold. Her eyes remained inscrutable, black as pitch, a hole to swallow the world.

"They all hover over me like I'm some kind of child," she murmured, her fist closing on the rail.

Andry chewed his words. If he could have conjured a cup of tea for Corayne, he would have. *But mint and honey won't change her circumstance.*

"Are they wrong to?" he said carefully, watching her face. Her brow tightened. She didn't move, but he could tell by the angle of her body that she wanted to touch the sword hidden beneath her cloak. "If you don't make it to the Spindle, then all this is for nothing."

Corayne looked to him sharply, her teeth bared. "There are others. I'm not the only Corblood idiot walking the Ward."

"And where are they?" he prodded, still gentle. Andry Trelland had seen enough spooked horses and hot-blooded squires in the training yard to know how to maintain some semblance of calm. *Even if Corayne an-Amarat is more terrifying than either.* "You're the best hope we've got. That comes with consequences."

She huffed, crossing her arms over her chest. "Does one of them have to be a brooding immortal listening to my every heartbeat?" she growled, nodding at Dom only a few yards away.

"If it keeps you alive, yes." Heat spread across his cheeks, a flush blooming over his brown skin. *That was forward, Trelland.* "I mean, we need you alive—"

Corayne threw up her hands. "*We* don't even know how *this* works. My blood, the blade. Then what? Wave it around?" She pulled back her cloak for effect, revealing the sheath across her back for a second. Her face spotted with color and, frustrated, she ran a hand through her unbound hair. The black locks curled in the sea air, clinging to her neck.

"We'll cross that bridge when we come to it," he muttered, wrenching his eyes away. "We've got Valtik, and Charlon—Charlie—seems to know what he's talking about too, even if he is a bit young to be a priest *and* a fugitive—"

She only pushed closer, setting her stance so he was backed against the crates. Andry's mouth clapped shut.

"You've actually seen one, though. You were there. With the Companions."

Wood pressed into his shoulder blades as warmth spread over his body. No amount of squiring had prepared him for a girl like Corayne. Noble ladies, perhaps, shy behind their hands or scheming in their silks. But not the girl in front of him, with a sword on her back and maps in her pockets, the starless night in her eyes.

"I'm with the Companions now," he said, trying to change the subject.

She glared up at him, mouth half open. "You were there," she said again, softer this time.

I don't want to remember. I see it enough in my nightmares. But her eyes were impossible to deny. He felt his teeth grind together,

466 REALM BREAKER

bone on bone. The creak of wood and rope and lapping waves faded, until the wind on his face turned too hot, and all he could hear were screams. He tried not to hear them, tried to see the time before it all, when the world was different. When he was still a boy.

It was beginning to rain. The clouds pushed down above us. The temple doors were shut, everything quiet. They were all alive.

"I didn't see it, but I could feel it," he said, a blackness dropping over his vision as his eyes squeezed shut. There was a cool touch on his hand as Corayne brushed against his palm, her fingers small and deliberate. "Like lightning before it strikes."

He remembered feeling the hairs on his arms stand up, the vibrations of that place unsettling his deepest core. *Like the world was off balance.* Her fingers tightened, and he felt it all again.

Andry forced his eyes open, half expecting to see Taristan before him, not the girl who would undo all his evils. There was only Corayne. This close, he could see a dusting of freckles on her nose, the shade of a long-worn tan over her cheeks. She looked like her father and uncle, and also nothing like them at all.

A gull called, breaking his concentration.

His hand twisted out of her grasp. "You think you can find the Spindle?" he said, putting his elbows to the rail. Shutting her out.

She pursed her lips and mirrored his movements, putting space between them. "Ehjer said they were in the Sarim, a coastal current." Her tone shifted, hardening. It was easy to picture her on the deck of another ship, papers in hand, commanding crew and merchants. "Near Sarian's Bay, if they were able to make it to Adira. And the monster had devoured sailors of the Golden Fleet."

Andry sighed, rapping his knuckles against the wood. "How can you narrow that down? Ibal has the largest navy in the world."

"Divided into fleets. The Crown Fleet patrols the Strait of the Ward and off Almasad, the Jewel Fleet the southern coast, where the gem mines operate. The Storm Fleet hunts raiders as far as the Glorysea. The Golden Fleet defends the Aljer, the Jaws of Ibal." Her nails drummed the rail. "I'd bet every coin in the realm the Spindle is near there, in the water or close to it."

The squire didn't know the Ward as well as a pirate's daughter, but his teachers had not neglected geography. Ibal was vast, a mighty kingdom of mountains, deserts, rivers, and coastlines, its cities like jewels in a shield of hammered gold. The grand port of Almasad was said to rival Ascal, and its capital, Qaliram, was even more magnificent, a wonder of monuments and palaces along the Ziron. Sacred horse herds moved through the landscape like storm clouds, moving from grassland to desert under the protection of Ibalet laws. There was the Great Sands, a sea of dunes like cresting waves, cut by canyons and salt flats. The countless oases, some large enough to support cities of their own, some little more than a few palm trees. And then the famed Ibalet coast, cliffs and gentle slopes above pale green waters, patrolled by the greatest navy in the realm. The Cors conquered ancient Ibal once, but at great cost, and their kings lived on, second only to the emperors of the north. His heartbeat quickened at the thought of seeing such things, such marvelous places, so far from the land he knew as home.

He shook his head. "That's still a lot of ground to cover."

To his surprise, Corayne shrugged. She looked delighted by the challenge, not daunted. "Like you said, we've got Valtik and now

Charlie. Maybe they have something to say about that. If Taristan was able to track down an old Spindle, why can't they?"

Andry looked over the experts in question. Both were currently occupied. Charlon crouched in the shadow of the sail, his tongue between his teeth, his eyeglass screwed in, as he painstakingly went over a piece of parchment with quill and ink. Documents of passage for when they arrived in Ibal. He looked like an overlarge toad, sweating in the shade. Surprising no one, Valtik had caught a daggerfish, striped and spiny. She deboned it bloodily on the deck, ignoring the glares of the crew. Most of the fish she ate raw, her smile red as she sang to herself, counting ribs.

Hardly a convincing sight.

The trade ship cut through the water on a sharp wind, prow breaking through undulating waves. Andry had never been out of sight of land before, and he sucked in a gasp of salt air. He expected to feel unnerved by the journey, but only hunger stirred in his belly.

He could feel Corayne's eyes hard on his face, watching him instead of the sea. "Your mother will be in Aegironos by now," she said, the wind in her hair again. "The ships bound for Kasa replenish supplies in the Gulf of Farers. Safe waves. A beautiful city."

He tried to picture it. Tried to see his mother smiling beneath a warmer sun, her skin glowing again, even as she curled in her chair. He knew she wanted this, wanted to see home again, and had for years. *She's getting her wish,* he told himself, trying to ease the shame beneath every inch of his body. *And she'll be safe.*

"Have you been to the southern continent?" he asked.

Corayne shook her head, her lips in her teeth. "My mother has southern blood and so do I, but I've only heard stories of the world, from the people allowed to see it."

"You're seeing it now."

She gave him a withering look. "I don't think this counts, Trelland."

"Maybe after." He shrugged. *After* seemed so foolish and impossible, far beyond reach. They would probably die trying to save the realm, or in the doom that followed their failure. But the hope of after, distant as it was, felt like a balm on fevered skin. Andry leaned into it, chasing the sensation.

"I can't exactly be a squire anymore." *Not for a queen trying to kill me.* "Before he died, one of the Companions—a knight of Kasa, his name was Okran—he invited me to Benai." *Perhaps my last happy memory, before everything went to ashes.* Andry wished he could step back, take Okran's horse by the reins, drag him away from the temple and his doom. "He promised to show me the land of my mother, and her people."

A stillness crossed Corayne's face, only her eyes moving. Andry felt searched. She read him like her maps, connecting one point to another, reaching a conclusion he could not see.

All the same, he saw understanding. Corayne thirsted for the world more than he did. She knew what it was to look to the horizon and want.

"Maybe after," she murmured. "Your mother can show you herself."

The hope guttered in his chest, slipping through his fingers. It left behind an ache. Something told him that dream would never come to pass.

470   REALM BREAKER

* * *

Andry did not sleep down below, where the air was tight and the sailors stank, belching and breaking wind all night. Only Charlon and Sigil could bear it, though perhaps the bounty hunter kept close should her fugitive take any opportunity to attempt escape. Even if they were in the *middle of the sea*. Valtik was gods-knew-where, somehow able to disappear even on a trade galley. *Probably hanging from a rope over the side, luring turtles for their shells.*

Instead, Andry slept on deck. The ship rocked in an easy lull. He felt himself suspended between sleep and waking, reluctant to dream of the temple, the feel of the sword, and the red, ruined hands on his skin. In his nightmares, the horse faltered. The sword fell. He slipped from the saddle and was eaten, the hope of the realm dying with him. Starlight bled through his eyelids, brighter than he had ever seen. So far from land, from smoke and candlelight, the stars were like needles through the heavens, pinpricks from their realm to the heaven of the gods. He tried to ignore Corayne dozing only a few yards away, half obscured by Domacridhan sitting next to her. She was little more than a lump in her cloak, the sword half hidden beside her, a spit of black hair curling out of her hood.

The first jolt felt like nothing. An errant wave. A gust of wind filling the sail.

Andry opened his eyes to find the sail flat, the sea calm. *A trick of sleep*, he thought. *Like when you think you're falling.* Even Dom didn't stir, the constant sentinel staring at his boots.

Andry settled back again, warm in his cloak, the salt air cool on his face. *I don't know why people complain about sailing so much. It's quite pleasant.*

The second jolt made the hull creak, the ship tipping beneath Andry's body. Still gentle, an easy, steady movement. One of the crewmen on watch whispered to another, their Larsian harsh and hissing with confusion. Another looked over the side of the galley, staring into the black waters.

Andry narrowed his eyes as Dom straightened. His white face paled in the dim light; his lips twitched beneath his golden beard. The Elder stared toward the prow, where Sorasa slept upright, her arms folded over her body in a tight embrace.

Something unfurled in the dark, outside the weak spheres of light swaying from the mast, prow, and stern. Andry stared, squinting.

The Elder was on his feet in a second, his voice raised in warning, already lunging.

For once, the immortal was not quick enough.

A muscular arm of green and gray snapped out of the darkness, curling around a sailor's chest. It was slick and gleaming, reflecting the light like the belly of a slug. The man choked out a wet gasp, the air crushed from his lungs before he went overboard.

Andry blinked.

What an odd dream.

Then the ship heaved, Dom shouted, and another sailor went over the rail, alive enough to scream, his ankles tangled in a meaty, curling vine of wet flesh. The sound of his voice was abruptly cut off the by the slap of the waves as he was pulled under.

Andry tried to stand but was caught in his cloak, his limbs still heavy from sleep. "What is it?" he heard himself rasp.

The lanterns swung with the motion of the ship, out of rhythm

472 REALM BREAKER

with the waves. Something was pushing them, bobbing the galley like a toy.

Corayne blinked, bleary-eyed, as Dom hoisted her to her feet and pressed the Spindleblade into her arms. Her eyes found Andry, the same question on her lips as the ship swayed beneath them.

Her words died with the next member of the crew, a curling tail like a whip wrapping around his throat and yanking him overboard. Andry watched, slack-jawed, as the two-hundred-pound Larsian disappeared into the sea.

"The Spindle," the squire breathed, feeling terror claw up his throat. *Was it here? In the waves beneath them?* But there was no telltale brush of lightning, of wrongness. Only the night filling with screams. The Spindle was still far away, but its monsters had spread wide.

Sailors shouted back and forth, springing into action. Pulling ropes, tying off sails. Most grabbed weapons: swords and long, hooked spears better suited to fishing. One shouted into the hold, calling for the captain and the rest of the crew.

Sigil emerged before anyone else could, pushing the fugitive priest along, her face grim. Her ax spun in her free hand.

Andry fought to his feet and rushed to the mast. The Elder backed Corayne against it, his body set broadside to the rail. "I should tie you down," he said, grimacing at the mainsail.

"Don't you dare," she snapped. "I have a vested interest in not drowning."

The Elder ignored her, running out a length of rope and looping it around her middle. "You'll only drown if the ship sinks. And if we sink with a sea serpent, you're as good as dead anyway."

Her golden face went pale in the lantern light. She didn't fight when the rope tightened, backing her to the mast. Instead she glanced at Andry. He expected to see the same terror he felt in his heart. But there was only cold resolve in Corayne an-Amarat.

"My blood is as much saltwater as it is Spindle," she said, grim.

The squire wished he could say the same. Night pressed in from all sides of the ship, the lanterns a weak defense against the beast curling in the water.

"Sea serpent," Andry managed to breath.

The ship rails bristled with armed sailors, their hooks and short ship swords brandished like needles. They peered at the water, ready for the next strike.

"Better than a kraken," Valtik singsonged, dancing over the deck with her dirty bare feet. The full, cleaned skeleton of a fish dangled from her belt. "We are not forsaken."

Sigil scowled. Her ax flashed. "Does she always do that?"

"Unfortunately," Sorasa answered, stepping into the light of the mast lantern. Her bronze dagger leered. "Well, Witch. Immortal." She glanced from Valtik to Dom. "Any suggestions?"

The old woman grinned toothily and tied herself in next to Corayne, looping rope over her wrists.

"Survive," Dom answered, grave.

The assassin's eyes rolled. "I don't know which one of you is more useless."

"Get some more lanterns lit; keep your eyes open," Sigil called, her voice commanding. Though Andry knew little of the bounty hunter, her presence was familiar and calming, like one of the knights or instructors training him to the sword. She stalked to the rail as she barked orders, her boots hammering the deck. At the prow, the Larsian captain echoed them, his face gray with fear. "Captain Drageda—" she called in sudden warning.

Only to see the serpent's great head rise up behind him, yellow eyes slitted, the sheen of sharp, white teeth in its jaws. It struck, devouring the captain headfirst before darting back into the safety of the water. Spears glanced off its scaled hide; hooks failed to find purchase. Only Dom's sword broke the creature's skin, drawing black blood that splattered the decks.

It rained, dark as oil, down the length of his steel.

"Run out the oars—we need to make for land!" one of the sailors shouted, his panic rising. A few others agreed, dropping their hooks in haste.

Andry gritted his teeth, the newly bought sword heavy at his hip. His hands shook as he drew it. He breathed heavily, trying not to think of the last time he'd raised a sword for battle. "Hold your ground!" he shouted, sounding bolder than he felt.

"Stow the oars—that thing will snap them like matchsticks!" Corayne roared, her voice so strong it caught even the sailors off guard. She strained against the ropes keeping her safe. "Use the sails but protect the masts at all costs!"

The sailors had no idea who Corayne was and were not inclined to obey a teenager on their ship. A few still ran for the hold and the oardeck, their boots sliding over the spray of seawater. It was Charlon who turned them back, blocking the way.

"You heard her," he said, wagging an ink-stained finger.

Sigil's eyes flashed, filling with light as lanterns flared all down the galley. "Defend the masts, men," she snapped, all business.

The bounty hunter in armor, an ax tight in her fist, was more difficult to ignore than Corayne. She formed up first, putting her back to Corayne, letting Dom hold the opposite side. They moved in unison, circling slowly, their eyes on the darkness beyond the ship. Andry fell in without question. This he understood. The squire had trained all his life to fight side by side.

A dark shape crawled overhead and he jumped, startled, raising his sword only to find Sorasa clambering nimbly up the mast. She had a bow over her shoulder, a quiver of arrows dangling precariously from her hip. Her dagger flashed in her teeth, the sail snapping around her as the winds kicked up. She wasn't bothered, nestling herself into the cross of the mast and yard.

The serpent returned in earnest, still bleeding as it looped over the ship in a graceful, terrible arc. Its eyes blazed, jaws wide as it crashed through the sailors on the opposite rail. Wood splintered and bones broke; hooks tore in vain at thick scales. Dom surged, sword raised with a battle cry of Iona. An arrow flew past him, close enough to ruffle his long hair. It needled into the serpent as it dove back into the water, taking two sailors with it, their weapons abandoned on the deck.

Andry wished for sunrise. Daylight. The blackness pushed in, no matter how many lanterns they lit along the ship. The serpent struck again and again, darting with its tail or diving up and over. The galley listed with each blow, threatening to topple over under the sheer force of the beast. Only the wind saved them, filling the sails with a gale that moved them forward, howling beneath the stars. It blew shudderingly cold.

The sailors dwindled, one by one, abandoning the rail to ring the main mast. The monster hissed at them, coiling once around the prow, threatening to snap it apart. It nearly got an arrow to the eye for the trouble and slipped away as Dom and Sigil charged, their weapons flashing in tandem. Andry followed, his muscles remembering how to fight even if his mind still could not believe *what* he fought.

The serpent was longer than the ship, thick around as an oak tree, spitting and bleeding and flooding the deck with seawater at every turn. Andry nearly lost his footing, and salt stung his eyes as he swung his sword, the scales passing just out of reach. His vision blurred but he kept his eyes open, narrowed to slits, as the beast wriggled up and over the ship. This time it came within snapping distance of Corayne, its fangs the length of her arm.

Charlie threw crate netting at the beast's head, grunting as he did so. The serpent seemed to sneer, dodging the ropes, its tail lashing across the deck. Another part of the rail splintered under its force, and waves lapped over the deck, foaming white.

Without thought, Andry made for the gap in the rail, his clothes soaked through. But he never lost his grip on his sword.

A voice screamed his name but he didn't stop, sliding into place to block the serpent's retreat. Behind him, there was nothing but open air and the devouring waves.

The serpent fixed him with a glowing, yellow stare, its breath hissing between fangs. Its massive body coiled and turned on the deck, gathering to strike. Andry set his feet, though the deck was slick, his boots useless.

"With me," he growled under his breath, meeting the horrific yellow gaze.

The ax and arrow struck in unison, the first at the neck, the second through one giant, lamp-like eye. The serpent's scream was like nothing Andry had ever heard before. It shrieked as it writhed, both a wailing hurricane and an old woman.

Sigil hooted a cry of joy, wrenching her ax from the scales with an arc of black blood. She wasted no time striking again, cutting like a lumberjack hacking at a dead old tree.

Enraged, the serpent lashed with all its strength, its coiling body and tail undulating over the deck, knocking aside sailors and cargo, spilling both into the Long Sea. Andry froze as it whipped toward the mast with enough force to cut it in two.

Dom's sword fell to the deck, splashing against the flooded planks, as the Elder moved with immortal swiftness, his arms stretched wide. He caught the snapping tail with a grunting roar, his teeth gnashing together as his boots scuffed over the deck. It was enough to save the mast, even as the serpent tightened, wrapping itself around the Ionian prince.

Corayne screamed, fighting against her ropes, reaching weakly for the immortal.

Arrows fell like shooting stars. They needled the serpent as Sorasa leapt to the deck, tossing aside her empty quiver. She danced toward the creature, bypassing every lash of its head. Her dagger cut with abandon, slicing lengthwise, opening a long gash in the monster's throat.

Still it coiled and pulsed, until only Dom's face could be seen, his teeth working in what could only be agony. A mortal would already have broken, and Dom was close to breaking.

Andry ran, his sword flashing, the point level with the thickest part of the serpent. He aimed true, missing Dom's body by inches as he plunged the sword to the hilt, through hard muscle and scale. On the other side, Sigil did the same, her ax working with blinding speed.

The coils loosened a little, the serpent bellowing, its blood pouring over the galley, the deck blacker than the night sky. Andry felt it, hot and gushing, as it spurted around his hands. He didn't relinquish his grip, grunting as he worked the sword, trying to twist it, inflicting as much damage as possible.

The serpent lost its other eye to Sorasa's dagger, its wail pitiful and keen. Dom snarled as the tight spirals of the monster fell away. Andry shoved at the scales, pushing them off the immortal, his arms caked in fresh blood.

"Thank you," he heard the prince murmur, one hand pawing at his shoulder. Sorasa leapt to his side, coaxing the Elder to sit back on the deck.

Blind and torn apart, the serpent curled and shuddered, wailing a death song on the deck of the trader. The surviving sailors jeered, prodding it toward the broken rail. It flinched and slid, slower by the second.

"Get it off the ship," Corayne called over the noise of the dying monster and the roaring wind. "Before it drags us down with it."

Charlie braced his back against the meat of the beast, brave enough to push the still-breathing serpent. "A little help, please?" he snapped at the crew.

Together with Sigil, they eased the doomed creature into the sea. As soon as the serpent hit the waves, the wind guttered and died, the sail falling loose.

Andry collapsed to his knees, exhausted and stunned. The blood was still there, staining his clothes up to his waist. He took little notice, his breath coming in short gasps.

"Thank you," Dom said again, breathless, lying back against the deck.

As soon as he was down, Sorasa stalked to the mast. The assassin loosed Corayne with a few cuts from her dagger. Corayne lunged forward, sliding to Andry's shoulder, her hands shaking as she looked him over.

"I'm fine," he murmured, sounding anything but.

Still willfully tied, Valtik cocked her head, leering around at the survivors. "Did anyone manage to grab a tooth?" she said, as if asking for a second mug of ale. "The fang of a serpent is poisoned in truth."

No one had the strength or will to respond.

28

THE HIGHEST BIDDER
Corayne

Smashed rails on either side of the galley. Lost cargo. A dead captain, along with a dozen members of the crew. All in all, not so bad for a battle with a sea serpent.

Corayne assessed the damage with a keen eye before settling in with the ship's navigator, who was now the de facto captain. The stout little man reminded her of Kastio. Together they charted a course to take advantage of the Strait's winds and currents. Her fingers danced over the parchment maps spread out like a carpet. The sun glowed warm; the air was clean and full of salt. This was where she belonged.

Once again, Dom found himself among the injured, stripped to the waist, his torso a mess of black-and-blue bruises, patterned like scales. He made no sound as Sigil examined his chest, her fingers prodding for signs of internal bleeding. Sorasa loomed over the pair, a long welt down one side of her face from the serpent's snapping tail. The Elder kept his mouth shut, but his annoyance was infinitely clear. Only a cup of tea from Andry's kettle settled him somewhat, as the squire made his rounds, offering up the sweet-smelling brew to the sailors.

By the time night fell, they were ready with a watch crew, the ship swinging with lanterns. The darkness passed without incident, as did the following evening. Nothing else rose out of the deep, but everyone remained on edge, stealing glances at the waves.

No ship had ever been so relieved to spot the Crown Fleet of Ibal, the gallant warships spaced across the narrowest point of the Long Sea like teeth in a lion's mouth. Their flags danced in the wind, royal blue and gold. The trader ran out its Larsian flag, a white bull on pale blue, and every sailor gave up a cheer or a wave.

Corayne did not share the sentiment. Instead she watched Charlie set the last touches to their papers of passage. The seals looked perfect: Tyriot aquamarine set with the warrior mermaid, her scales patterned in real gold ink. How Charlie had managed to draw up something so beautiful on the deck of a ship, Corayne could not say. She marveled at the diplomatic papers, letters to mark them as agents of a Tyri merchant company.

"Not my best work," Charlie said, his teeth gritted as she peered over his shoulder. "It would be better to have some variety. You can pass for Ibalet or Ahmsarian, same as Sarn. But I didn't have time to make a fresh seal."

"These will do fine," she answered. "What matters is the cut of our shoulders, not the cut of the seal."

Never far away, Dom sidled up next to them, his focus on the horizon. His lips moved as he counted ships. "I am a prince of Iona," he said, folding his arms. "Certainly that counts for something?"

Charlie had tact enough not to respond, in word or expression.

"The Crown Fleet is an impossible blockade to run without intricate planning or sheer luck," Corayne answered. *And while the crowns of the Ward might still marvel at Elders, the captain of a fleet ship would hardly care, let alone believe you exist at all.* Her mother contended with the guardians of the Strait of the Ward every time she sailed west, and Corayne was careful to avoid complications. "Everyone who passes pays a toll of travel. Either your papers are good enough to warrant the usual price, or you have to scramble. Some captains can be bribed in a pinch, but there's no telling which ship will meet you on the waves."

They sailed on toward the fleet. One of the ships hung low in the water, heavier. Corayne felt her mother's hunger flare in her chest. The fat, triple-masted galley squatted like a toad on a pond. It would be filled with coin and letters of promise, signed marks from well-known nobles, diplomats, or even royalty bound to pay the treasury at Qaliram. Meliz an-Amarat often fantasized about capturing a toll ship, but their voyages were heavily guarded. Too great a risk, even for such a prize.

Corayne's heart pounded as an Ibalet ship sailed up alongside them, her deck crowded with fine sailors in light, airy silk the color of blue mist. They had no use for real armor, both on the waves and in the southern heat. Ibalet's sailors were talented swimmers and swordsmen. Heavy plate would only slow them down. Like

VICTORIA AVEYARD 483

Sorasa's, their swords and daggers shone bronze, gleaming in the daylight, an open show of strength.

The navigator met with the Ibalet captain, his purse and papers clutched in his fist. Judging by the way the navigator spoke, his hands curling and undulating in rolling paths, Corayne guessed he spoke of the serpent. It was enough to give the captain pause, and he barely rifled through their forged papers. He glanced over the crew still ragged from battle but did not linger. Not even for Sigil, clearly not of Tyri descent, nor Valtik, better suited to the grave than a trade vessel.

It only took a few moments to be on their way again, sailing for the Ibalet coast.

The grand city of Almasad followed.

Ibal was a land veiled in soft light, made hazy by the sun dipping in the west. The coast was green, lined with massive palm trees and succulent gardens, verdant as any forest of the north. Corayne marveled. The banks were thick with reeds and pale blue lotus along sandy beaches. A line of yellow glimmered on the horizon, where the dunes began. Villages and cities clung to the coastline, on cliffs or at the waterside, growing larger with every passing mile. Fishermen teemed in the shallows. Boats moved along the coast like carts upon a Cor road, ranging from war galleys to little skiffs poling through the shallows.

Then Almasad appeared out of the shimmering air, the port city fanning out on either side of the mighty Ziron. This wasn't Ibal's capital, but it was marvelous anyway, filled with sandstone monuments and gleaming pillars of limestone. The river was too wide for bridges, and barges crossed it like ants crawling back and forth. As Sorasa said, its cothon put Ascal's to shame. The circular docks for the navy was a city itself, walled and patrolled by sailors in water silks. Corayne tried to count the dozens of ships in port, but could hardly keep up with the many sails and glimmering flags of Ibal and her fleets.

Raised causeways ridged the city like the arms of a sunbeam, carrying both freshwater and travelers through the many sectors of Almasad. They were not like the ruins of Old Cor, broken and chipped away. The limestone gleamed white under the sun, bright as a shooting star. Palatial compounds, citadels, and paved plazas ran along either side of the riverbank, patterned in soft yellow, green, and bright blue. A royal palace sat on the only hill, surrounded by sandstone walls and towers tipped in winking silver. It looked down on the Ziron, its many windows and balconies empty. As Corayne knew, the royal court of Ibal was not here or even in the grander capital. They were farther south, in the mountains, hiding or biding their time. *They know something is wrong*, she thought, clenching her teeth.

Statues of ancient kings flanked the river, taller than a cathedral spire, their faces worn by the ages. The galley passed through their shadows, cast for thousands of years.

"Are those emperors?" Corayne said at the rail, looking on them with wonder. As in Siscaria, as in Galland, the ancient empire ruled here once. She searched their facades, looking for some hint of her father, of herself. But found none. "Old Cor?"

Sorasa leaned into the warm wind, looking at the water, not

the bank. "Do those look like northern conquerors to you?" she said with a proud smile.

Indeed, the statues did not, their features and clothing different from any emperor across the Long Sea. Each sat astride a fine stallion, with a cloak of patterned silk and peacock feathers. *They looked more like my mother,* Corayne thought, seeing the same lips and cheekbones.

Leaning into the warm breeze, Sorasa straightened her spine. Whatever fear she felt at returning to her home seemed to disappear. "Ibal was born before Cor and still lives long after it died."

For certain, Ibal was truly *alive*. Different parts of the riverbank crowded with boats or splashing children or the knobbled form of a crocodile. Long-necked white birds flapped overhead, hunting shining copper fish. People traveled the causeways on foot or carriage or horseback, fading into the distance in every direction. The Ibalets of the coast were golden, their faces a prism of color in every shade of sunlight. Those from the south and east were darker, their faces the rich, reddish color of carnelian or black jet. They hailed from farther lands—Sapphire Bay, Kasa, or even distant Niron, a kingdom nestled in the Forest of Rainbows. Their voices rose in every language of the south, some familiar to Corayne, some foreign as Ishei.

Where Ascal stank and overwhelmed, a riot upon the senses, Almasad was a balm. The air was sweet, perfumed by the lotus gardens adorning the Ziron. Music drifted through the streets, from performers in their plazas or private homes along the river. And the water itself ran clean, not like the fetid canals of Queen

486   REALM BREAKER

Erida's capital. Corayne almost wanted to dive into the water as
they eased toward shore, the clear green current inviting as any
fine bath.

Another inspector met their ship at the docks. Corayne
thought of Galeri back in Lemarta, bribes jingling in his pockets,
his ledger full of falsehoods. The Ibalet officer seemed far more
alert, her light, cream-colored clothing set with several badges of
office looped together with gold chain.

Again, the navigator took up the captain's mantle and met the
officer as the crew unloaded in the usual chaos. The pair went
over their surviving cargo, inspecting crates.

Corayne and the others gathered at the rail, watching the traffic below. Another galley was in port beside them, looking worse
for wear, with torn sails and snapped oars sticking out like the
quills of a porcupine. It listed to one side, leaning drunkenly, while
its crew disembarked as swiftly as they could.

Corayne read the ship. *Sardosi, black-and-white sails—a grain
galley*. The crew hastily rolled great barrels onto the dock, lest the
ship sink right then and there with all its cargo.

"This is going to be a mess," she said in a low voice, looking to
Dom and Andry at her side. "Dock officers care more about cargo
than passengers. We can give them the slip, move in pairs."

Another barrel bounced down the gangplank, landing hard.
After a second, its wood hoops burst, the barrel splitting open
with a hiss of shifting grain. Both crews, well as the Ibalet officer
and her inspection team, shouted in dismay.

On the rail, Sorasa slipped a slingshot back into her belt, her
expression open and blank. "You first," she said, grabbing Corayne

by the arm. "Meet at the Red Pillar, the *takhan*," she added to the rest, nodding at the impossibly tall obelisk rising from the city skyline. It was only half a mile away, Corayne judged, but through the densest part of the city.

Dom fell in at her shoulder, his bulk like a solid, comforting wall. Together, they marched her down the gangplank as the opposite galley groaned, her port side sinking fast.

The Ibalet officer did not stop them, her hands more than full as another barrel cracked open like a broken egg. They made it up the dock splits and onto the main plaza, retreating into the crowded port district. Flowers bloomed from seemingly every window and empty corner, with low stone pots of sweet-smelling oil and fat candles set at intervals. An ingenious way to combat the horrid smells of a city.

Sorasa knew the way and led them in a beeline, the Red Pillar dead ahead through the maze of clay and stone buildings. Weary travelers passed by, seeking stone-walled inns or cool courtyards shaded with trees. Despite the many taverns and wine bars, Corayne noted very few drunks or beggars. The Almasad streets were kept remarkably clean, both by sweepers and roving patrols of soldiers in silk and mail.

They passed a fish market with a rainbow of stalls, each one selling a different catch from the Ibalet coast and the winding Ziron. Corayne recognized most—oily catfish, massive river carp, crocodile tale, spiny puffers. Her heart thumped at the shadow of a curling tentacle, displayed proudly by a muscular fisherman. But it was only the arms of an octopus, inky black. The sea monsters of the Spindle had not made it here.

Sandwiched between Dom and Sorasa, Corayne heaved a breath. For a split second, she was back in front of her cottage, beneath the blue night of a Siscarian summer. The road lay before her, begging to be walked.

Her choice was already made.

Valtik and Andry trailed at a distance, the squire easy to pick out. He was nearly a head taller than most and darker-skinned than the Ibalets, not to mention dressed like a northerner. While most Ibalets wore flowing robes and head coverings to combat the heat and sun, Andry still had his tunic and leather leggings, with a cloak over his shoulder. Nodding, he met Corayne's eye before she turned a corner, losing sight of him.

She blinked, confused, as another face stared out at her.

Her own.

The old brick wall surrounding the docklands was centuries old, set with a dozen open gates. Unlike the causeways, it crumbled where exposed. The rest was glued over with old paper. Notices, advertisements, fading letters in all languages, but mostly in swooping, artful Ibalet. The faces of criminals and fugitives glared from the brick wall, their misdeeds written beneath their names.

Corayne didn't bother to read the many crimes listed beneath the drawings of herself, or Dom, or Andry, but their names were clear enough. CORAYNE AN-AMARAT. DOMACRIDHAN OF IONA. ANDRY TRELLAND. There was even a rough sketch of Sorasa, her eyes lined with black, menacing as a nightmare.

"'Wanted by the Gallish Crown,'" Sorasa said softly, reading the words scrawled over all their heads. They moved closer, drawn to themselves like a ship pulled into a whirlpool. "'For crimes against Galland. Reward for information, capture, or corpse.'"

Corayne's fingers met her sketched face, her lips too thin, her jaw too sharp. Andry's and Dom's faces were more accurate. She suspected that Taristan had guided an artist through their portraits, if he hadn't done them himself.

The paper was slick under her hand, still wet.

"These are fresh," she said, her voice trembling.

Sorasa growled to herself, cursing. "Plastered in every port of the Ward, in every kingdom that fears or loves Galland. We're being hunted, in every corner of the realm."

"By men and beasts, both," Corayne murmured. It didn't matter who held the sword to her neck, a skeletal demon or a watch officer following the orders of a queen. It would still end in the world's ruin.

Dom's voice was low, guttural. "We need to get out of this city."

"For once, I agree with the troll," Sorasa replied, tearing the posters from the wall.

Almasad was one of the largest ports of the Long Sea, its docks bunched together, needling out from the banks. But only a few streets inland, the city relaxed, stretching out in wider arcs and less crowded lanes. Many homes and buildings were walled, islanded by palm and cypress gardens. The great avenues were wide as canals passing beneath the causeways. Some had canopies, canvas as big as ship sails, ready to be pulled out on great lines and wood frames. The shadows were cool and inviting, the streets clearly designed to minimize the southern heat. Unfortunately, easy, quiet neighborhoods were more difficult to pass through without notice. Especially for anyone with a bounty on their head.

The Red Pillar stood in the center of a plaza, carved from a single block of rust-colored granite. It was more than a hundred feet high, a square column that tapered to a point like a pyramid. A carved face of Lasreen, goddess of sun and moon, night and day, life and death, stared out from each side.

They hurried past it, hoods raised and heads down. When a troop of Ibalet soldiers passed, clad in silk and armor, Sorasa ushered Corayne into a basement dwelling cramped beneath a structure of apartments that looked more like a child's blocks. It was dim and smoky; Corayne's eyes stung as they adjusted to the light.

Once she could see, she realized they stood in a dirt-walled root cellar, the ceiling so low Dom had to stoop. Doors and archways branched off from all sides, leading into cramped darkness.

"I take it you know what you're doing," Corayne said. Dried herbs and bushels of plants hung from the ceiling, perfuming the air. Footsteps thumped from the dwelling above them.

The assassin kept one eye on a crack in the door. A single beam of sunlight split her face.

"Somewhat," she replied. "This is a bit of a way station for the underbelly of Almasad. Thieves, pickpockets, the occasional assassin. And, now, fugitives of Queen Erida."

"My aunt will not abide this." Dom braced the side of his head against the roof. "I am a prince of Iona. To hunt me so openly is to court war with my enclave."

Corayne tried not to roll her eyes. She investigated the cellar, turning over the plants with disinterest.

The assassin didn't move from the door, her voice flat. "Your enclave refused to fight for the sake of the entire Ward, but they would fight for *your* life? Somehow I doubt that."

"Just because you have no concept of honor or duty does not mean others do not," Dom answered hotly. Sorasa replied with a withering glare, sunlight illuminating one copper eye.

A twist of lavender crumbled between Corayne's fingers, filling the cellar with its heady, floral scent. She breathed it deeply, hoping for some calming effect. It didn't work.

"I don't know where we go from here," Corayne said, shouldering between them. "The Spindle will be close to the Jaws, but that's days into the desert. And no ship will take us by sea, not with our faces plastered all over the port."

"Let's figure out where we're going before we figure out how to get there," Sorasa replied. Without a sound, she slipped out the door, leaving motes of dust swirling in her wake.

"Good riddance," Dom muttered. He drew up a crate and sat, straightening out his neck.

"You'd still be wandering up and down the Ward looking for me, if not for Sorasa," Corayne said, brushing lavender off her hands. "You can at least pretend not to hate her."

The immortal heaved a dramatic sigh and leaned back against the wall. "I do my best not to lie."

Before Corayne could laugh or snap, Sorasa returned with Valtik and Andry in tow. The squire was flushed, his hood drawn up, his body coiled with tension. Somewhere, the witch had picked up a colorful scarf, patterned with scales, and wrapped it around her hair.

"Did you see?" Andry demanded, pointing back to the street with a shaking finger. "That's us out there. Already."

"We saw the posters, Squire," Sorasa said, holding the door ajar for Charlie and Sigil, who trooped in with a little less concern. "That's why we're hiding instead of enjoying the sunshine."

Corayne went to the old witch and took her by the hand. Her flesh felt so light, her skin thin as paper. "Valtik, what do the bones tell?" she said, pushing all her worry into her eyes. Valtik stared back, her gaze that same vivid blue. "I know they tell you something. Anything."

"Don't bother," Dom said. "The witch has a way of being useless precisely when we need her most."

Sorasa shut the door tight, plunging them all into shadow. "Something you two have in common?"

To Corayne's relief, Dom ignored the jab and Valtik quirked a grin. Her free hand strayed to her belt, loosing the pouch of bones with a single pull of a string. They spilled around her feet, yellow and white, scrubbed clean of blood and muscle.

"Let's see, shall we?" Valtik said, watching as they fell into place, seemingly at random. The others looked on, hunting for a pattern only Valtik could see. She didn't stare long. Whatever she saw in the bones was clear as day. "We're in the right land." She turned her cornflower eyes back on Corayne. They bored into her. "But we must find a mirror—mirrors on the sand."

"Why do we tolerate this Jydi nonsense?" Sigil hissed. Her bronze face had gone red in the heat, but it was nothing compared to Charlie, who was already sunburned. "And how long are we going to cower here?" The bounty hunter also needed to crouch, lest she crack her head on the roof. "It's only a matter of time before one of your own comes along and sells us out."

"Take heart, Sigil. The Amhara would rather kill me themselves then let a northern queen do it," she said lightly. "But yes, we should be moving. Almasad is not Ascal. Criminals are not so easily overlooked." She bit her lip. "Mirrors on the sand, eh, Valtik? Any ideas on what that could mean?"

The witch had no more to give. She ran her fingers over the dirt floor, scooping the bones back into her purse.

Charlie watched, bright-eyed even in the dim light. He kissed both palms as he had in the crossroads tavern. "Strangeness follows Spindles. It clings to their locations, before they open and even after they close. Scripture calls it the shadow of the gods. It's how the Spindletouched are born, brushed with magic," he said, gesturing to the old woman scrabbling on the floor. She seemed anything but magical. "If there were a Spindle open in this land, there would be a sign."

"But some of us can't exactly walk all over Almasad eavesdropping and looking for such signs." Corayne said.

"It's not my face on those posters," Sigil offered. "I can make the rounds, see what I hear. Hopefully bring back something the rest of you can piece together."

Sorasa offered her a rare, true smile. "Thank you, Sigil."

"I'm a simple woman, Sarn," the bounty hunter said with a shrug. "I serve the highest bidder. That's currently you."

The assassin took it in stride. "The ruins of Haroun, on the outskirts. Dusk," she declared. "Charlie, you can walk free too.

Can you get us horses? Ready by the Moon Gate?"

Before the fallen priest could acquiesce, Dom shook his head, still braced against the wall. "And what if they abandon us?" he said, eyeing both Sigil and Charlie.

It isn't a foolish thing to wonder. Corayne bit her lip, trying to fight down her own trepidation. Across the floor, Andry frowned. *We've made enough mistakes so far. Will trusting two criminal strangers be another?*

Sorasa's eyes flashed, a warning. "Then they abandon the Ward to ruin, and themselves to doom."

"Cheerful to the last, Sarn," Charlie said, wrenching open the door. It spilled light so bright Corayne winced. Sigil's silhouette flared across the floor, a giant behind her.

"Either way," Corayne muttered, "we don't have much choice in the matter."

Sorasa slammed the door behind them, scowling. "That's the spirit."

They wouldn't last much longer in the cellar. Sigil was right: it was only a matter of time before the Ibal patrols or some criminal element discovered their ragtag band. Even a common thief wouldn't balk at turning them in, should he manage to escape Sorasa's blade. So Sorasa led them east, through a damp, muddy passage that surfaced in an overlooked alleyway strewn with hung laundry. To Corayne's dismay, Sorasa was jumpier than a rabbit, double-checking every corner, avoiding alcoves and sewers like they might snap shut on her body.

"Is it just me, or is Sorasa Sarn scared?" Andry murmured.

"Terrified," she answered.

"There's an entire sea between us and Taristan, his army, the other Spindle." He adjusted his steps, matching her stride. "What could she fear?"

"Her own," Corayne said, coming to realization even as she spoke.

A fallen Amhara, forsaken, broken. *Osara*. It must also mean *doomed*.

Corayne's blood chilled, her skin prickling even in the dry, desert heat of Ibal. She licked her lips, tasting sweat and salt. *Not long now*. Dusk approached, the sky overhead going hazy pink. *We'll meet Charlie and Sigil. We'll have horses. We can leave this place and those posters behind. There aren't any patrols in the dunes. There isn't anyone at all.*

Sorasa's caution got them through the alleys without trouble, her internal compass winding them away from the hustle and bustle. It took hours of careful navigation, avoiding patrols and crowded markets, but eventually the buildings grew sparse. The causeway overhead sloped downward, its arches lower and lower until it ran into an avenue of paved stone. Almasad bordered the Great Sands and had no use for walls beyond the port. No army could assault the city from the desert. The roads and streets simply disappeared, swallowed by ever-shifting dunes. Even the scent of flowers grew weak, replaced by the smell of hot, dusty sand and the underlying drift of some herb Corayne couldn't name.

The ruins of Haroun were not a temple, as Corayne had suspected, but a massive tower at the edge of the city, fallen like a tree broken in half. All that was left was a hollow column, a single spiral stair reaching up the middle like a spine, leading to nothing. The crown of the fallen tower was missing, torn from the rough sandstone.

"Stolen," Sorasa said, following Corayne's gaze. Her fingers fumbled at her arm, loosing her sleeve. "Haroun's Eye was taken before the tower fell, when the Cors defeated ancient Ibal. The rest, the bronze cap, was cut up piece by piece after the tower collapsed. Melted into weapons, coin, jewelry. Northerners do not honor the past as we do in the south."

Corayne furrowed her brow, looking over the ruins again. She tried to imagine it long ago. "Why would they build a lighthouse this far from the sea?"

"Well seen," Sorasa said, baring her forearm. The black lines on her fingers continued over her wrist, forming the lashes of an open eye halfway to her elbow. The pupil held the moon and sun, a crescent fitted around flame. "It wasn't for sailors. Haroun's Eye blazed night and day, guiding caravans home across the Sands."

"I wish I could have seen it," Corayne replied, a lament all too common in her life.

Sorasa covered up her tattoo again. Another flashed on her inner arm, some kind of bird. "Let that wish go, Corayne. It won't do you any good."

If only it were that easy.

"It's past dusk," Dom grumbled. He glared at the sky, the light waning into purple. "Your priest better get those horses. I can walk the desert to hunt Spindles, but can any of you?"

"Of course, go ahead," Sorasa snapped, waving her hand at the dunes. "We'll catch up."

Again, Valtik plopped onto the ground. She traced her nails in the sand, drawing Jydi spirals and knots. "Sand and rain, salt and grain, much to lose, much to gain," she chanted.

"Valtik, please," Corayne sighed, her nerves fraying.

The first star gleamed directly above, straight out over the desert. Corayne tried to name it and found she could not. *I don't know the stars here. I don't know the way forward. I don't even know the way back.*

If she squinted, the dunes could be the Long Sea, their rolling backs like waves. She tried to picture the cliffs of Siscaria, Lemarta in the distance, the cottage behind. Her mother's ship on the horizon, returning. *How fare the winds?* Corayne thought, her lips moving without sound. The breeze that played in her hair was nothing like what she remembered, too hot and dry. Still, she could pretend. *Fine, for they bring me home.*

Andry kept his distance, pacing, wearing tracks closer and closer to the collapsed ruin of the tower. She was glad for the space, oddly comforted by the gap between them. Through long weeks on the road, Corayne had never been truly alone. She wasn't now either, but felt better than being loomed over night and day.

Oddly, the Spindleblade seemed lighter. Or at least she took less notice of the giant sword on her back. It wasn't any more comfortable, and she sweated where the leather pressed against her clothes. But somehow it felt less. More like a limb than a piece of metal. She reached back over her shoulder, fingers grazing the hilt. It was still worn to her father's hand, the grooves fitted to a dead man. *They will never fit me*, she thought, pulling back.

The sun disappeared completely, the disc of gold slipping

498 REALM BREAKER

beneath the western horizon to leave smudges of red and purple. Though the day had been hotter than any Corayne could recall, the night was almost immediately cold, the sand quickly losing its warmth. Blue and then black came, like a blanket drawn from one end of the sky to the other, pinpricked with more stars. As they winked into existence, Corayne breathed a sigh of relief. *There is the Dragon. There is the Unicorn.*

The Ward was still her own. Any navigator could find the way now. *And so will I.*

Mirrors on the sand.

"Sorasa!" she shouted, tearing back over the sandy ground. Her companions whirled to the sound of her voice.

Dom caught her first. "What is it?" he said, eyes wide with worry.

She looked to Sorasa. "The Eye was a mirror, wasn't it?" Corayne demanded, heaving a breath. "An enchanted mirror? Special? *Spindletouched?*"

"It was." Sorasa clasped her arm through her sleeve, instinctively touching the tattoo. "Glowing without flame, bright as a second sun."

"Where did it come from? Here?" Corayne demanded, grabbing at the assassin.

Sorasa furrowed her brow. "No, not Almasad," she muttered, racking her memory. "Priests of Lasreen found it, in the desert. At an oasis."

"An oasis. Does it have a name?" She felt Valtik staring, silent, her eyes blue and cold. "*Where*, Sorasa?"

The arrow thwipped between them before Sorasa could

answer, and Corayne was thrown bodily to the ground, half buried in the sand, half crushed by Dom's weight. He didn't let her up, using one hand to keep her down, the other to draw his sword. Corayne glanced up through her wild hair to see his eyes trained on the city. Another arrow whizzed past his head, missing by inches, fluttering the long hair tucked behind his ear. This time it came from the tower, the opposite direction of the first.

Ice bled through Corayne's gut.

Ambush.

She squirmed under Dom's grasp, trying to get up, but his hand was a deadweight on her spine. Sand choked her mouth, tasting of heat. She craned her head, looking for Andry, only to spot Sigil emerging from the ruins of the tower, a contingent of soldiers with her. Corayne gnashed her teeth, so angry she couldn't even scream.

In a second, she counted forty troops approaching from the tower. Twenty of Ibal, with their bronze swords and pale rose silk over steel. Twenty of Galland, their green cloaks unmistakable, their pale, pig-eyed, sweating faces grim beneath their helms. Sigil stood between them, her weapons abandoned on her hips. She raised two fingers to her lips and whistled, a keen, sharp sound that made Corayne's ears hurt.

Another forty soldiers appeared from the outskirts of Almasad, all of them Ibalet, arrows nocked to every bow.

A stream of Ibalet curses spilled from Sorasa's lips like blood from an open wound. Soldiers surrounded her, their blades drawn, as Sigil approached.

Sorasa spat heartily, her aim true.

"Don't take it personally, Sarn," Sigil drawled, wiping a hand over her face. "You know what I am, and I know what you are. Tell me you wouldn't have done the same?"

Sorasa's voice was a serpent's hiss. "To the highest bidder."

29

THE BEAR OF KOVALINN
Ridha

The princess of Iona missed the sand mare, but the frigid north would have been a cruel punishment for so loyal a horse. She'd been bred for speed in the Ibalet sands, not trekking through frozen fjords. Ridha set her loose before crossing the Watchful Sea, sailing on the rare Jydi ship bound for trade and not raiding. In frostbitten Ghald, she purchased a stockier, long-haired pony, as well as a musty fur cloak that would serve her better in the wilds of the Jyd.

Though she was Vedera, immune to most discomforts of the mortal world, Ridha did not enjoy being so cold. The Jyd was positively freezing, even though it was only early autumn.

As she sailed the Glorysea, she saw Jydi longboats under the white sail of peace. Ships of trade and travel. Raiders sailed beneath gray sails, iron cold as the winter sky. But Ridha spotted none. It was as the thieves in the tavern had said: no Jydi were raiding. *Not rare*, she thought as the she rode the rocky coast. *Impossible.*

Kovalinn sat in the Vyrand, the great, wolf-shaped mountain range that formed the spine of Jyd. Ridha remembered the enclave of her northern cousins from a diplomatic journey in her youth, some centuries before, when she'd accompanied her mother. Domacridhan had been left at home, too young to go with them. He'd been little more than a child then, still growing, and he'd wept on her shoulder before she left.

She sorely wished he could have been with her now, a shield as much as a crutch.

The Jydi mortals were not ignorant of the Vedera like their southern neighbors, and they were far less intrigued by woman carrying weapons. When Ridha passed through villages on her way north, few children of the Jyd balked at her presence. Most were fair, blond or ginger-haired, but the Jyd welcomed all who took up the ax, the shovel, or the sail. Black skin, bronze skin, porcelain, every shade from white to ebony was present in the frigid north, from Ghald to Yrla to Hjorn, in every village and on every farm.

It was the same in Kovalinn.

When she reached the river mouth in the Kova fjord, a Veder was already waiting, stoic as an old oak. She was reedy and tall, wrapped in furs, with skin like glowing topaz, her black-and-silver hair braided into locks tied with fine chain. Ridha did not know her, but raised a hand in greeting, her palm white as the early snow clinging to her eyelashes.

How they knew of her coming, Ridha could easily guess. *Mother must have made another sending, this time to the monarch of the snows.* She tried not to think of Isibel of Iona, a wisp of magic with silver hair stirring in a phantom wind. *Come home. Come home.*

Is it an echo or a memory? Ridha could not say.

"I am Ridha of Iona."

She searched the woman's face. *If Mother has already contacted Kovalinn, this might be for nothing.*

The other Veder dipped her brow. "I am Kesar of Salahae, right hand to the Monarch of Kovalinn. He bids you welcome in his lands and is eager to speak with you."

"As I am eager to speak with him," Ridha answered.

In the distance, a cold wind blew, stirring up the steady fall of snowflakes. The way up the fjord cleared for an instant, showing a jaw of granite and snowy ground, a waterfall plunging its way to the river and the sea. At its peak, at the crest of a zagging pathway cut into the rock, was Kovalinn. Even from a distance she saw the bears carved into its gate, their fur chipped from black pine.

Beneath her cloak and steel, Ridha shivered. The wind blew again, and the enclave disappeared into the snows.

The great bear was the sigil of Kovalinn, set into her gates, woven into tapestries, carved from towering pines to loom down the length of the great hall. It was also a living guardian. One slept soundly by the seat of the Monarch, its massive paws curled over its face, the ridge of its back like a mountain. It snored softly, nuzzling its snout against the feet of the boy who ruled this enclave of the Vedera. The redheaded child bent down from his chair, scratching the animal behind the ears. Its head was nearly the size of his body.

Dyrian of Kovalinn, his eyes pearl gray, smiled at his pet fondly. He was only a century old, the youngest Veder to rule upon the Ward. His white face was spattered with freckles; his clothing was plain: a brown cloak trimmed in black sable, the bear on his tunic picked out in amber, jet, and swirling jasper. There was a twisted circle of gold around his throat to match one on his wrist, but he wore no crown. In his lap there was a living pine bough, its needles a lush hunter green.

Ridha knelt, her fur cloak over one shoulder, the steel of her armor still cold from the ride up the fjord. She watched him keenly, weighing his youth.

The boy was not alone: advisors fanned around him, either seated or standing. Kesar stood at his right hand, unbothered by the sleeping bear. On his left was clearly his mother, her hair as red as his own, gathered into two long braids beneath a circlet of hammered iron. She was broad, similar in build to Ridha, a cloud of white fox fur around her shoulders, a chain-mail gown pouring over her crossed legs. Her eyes were flint, unblinking.

The princess of Iona weighed the Monarch against his diplomats. *Who commands the enclave? Who speaks for Kovalinn? Who do I have to convince?*

"He's larger than usual," Dyrian said, straightening in his chair. It was too big for him; his fur boots dangled over the flagstones of the raised dais. He looked younger than his decades, his face still clinging to fat. There was a sword at his side and a dagger in his boot, suited to his small size.

"Putting on fat for the winter sleep," he added, smiling a toothy grin, showing a gap between his teeth.

The smile did not reach his eyes.

Ridha raised her chin. Her focus narrowed to the Monarch, and not the others, who lived thousands of years between them.

"And what of you, my lord?" she said. "Do you intend to sleep as well?"

Behind him, his mother's mouth twitched but did not open. As Ridha had guessed, no one spoke for Dyrian but Dyrian.

The boy rested his hands on the arms of his chair, the wood carved in the likeness of his pet.

"I was told Ionians dance around the point," he said, amused. His gray-white eyes belonged to a wolf, not a child. "Not you, Princess."

"Not me," she answered.

Her skin crawled with a shiver. The great hall of Kovalinn was a long room beneath a thatched roof, the walls made of cut lumber. Today it served as the Monarch's throne room, emptied of onlookers but for his council. Two open pits ran the length of the chamber behind her, shimmering with hot coals and lit flames, but the great doors were swung wide, letting in the echoes of winter. Snow danced along the flagstones, swirling around her boots.

Ridha tried to ignore the cold. "What did my mother tell you in her sending?"

He tapped a finger against his lips, thinking. "Enough," he finally answered. "A Spindle torn, the rest in danger. Blood and blade in the wrong hands, serving What Waits and his devouring hunger."

Her insides twisted. It was a song she knew well, but she winced every time it was sung.

Dyrian leaned forward, bracing his hands on his knees. His wolf eyes flashed. "A calamity already beyond our control."

Ridha stood gracefully, her jaw set. "I disagree."

The boy grinned again, looking sidelong at his mother. Her eyes sparked to his, conveying a message Ridha could not read.

"Oh, I thought you were here for a social visit," he said, shrugging. "So, then, Ridha of Iona, what do you want of us?"

No, those with endless years tend not to worry about time lost. Even when they should, Ridha thought, biting her tongue. Again she looked over the advisors, weighing their influence as she weighed Dyrian's. *I'm not a diplomat*, she thought. *I'm no good at this.*

Dom would be far worse.

"I want you to fight," she bit out, laying a hand on her sword. Her eyes dropped to the pine bough in his lap. "Lay down the branch, take up the ax." She felt desperate. She sounded desperate. Ridha hated it but would not stop. *If I have to beg, so be it.* "The Ward is not yet lost. And I don't think it's worth losing."

"Not like your mother does," Dyrian muttered. "The Monarch of Iona is Glorianborn. I cannot fault her for seizing any opportunity to return to the land of our ancestors, the realm that sings in her blood. She aches for home, as so many do." He turned in his chair, assessing the other immortals. A few were silver-haired, thousands of years old, their hearts in another realm too. They stared, silent, their faces like a stone wall no one could ever climb.

Ridha felt sick, her stomach twisting.

Then the Monarch looked back to her, his wolf eyes alight.

"I do not," he said sternly.

She felt the breath leave her body. "My lord—"

His mother stood, her dress of mail shimmering like scales on a fish. She was near seven feet tall, milk-skinned, a warrior queen with scars on her knuckles.

"What brought you here?" she demanded. There was a strange rasp to her voice, unnatural. Ridha gulped, spotting another scar, a pearly line of white cut across her throat. "Of all the enclaves? We are not the strongest nor the largest. The journey is not easy, even before the winter, even for an immortal such as you. Why us, Ridha of Iona?"

"The raiders of the Watchful Sea have not raided; no gray sails fly," she said simply. It was no use to tell them she heard this at a no-name tavern, from mortals already fading to dust.

"Their longboats haven't been spotted this season. The towns and villages of the southern kingdoms have not burned." It had been decades, but Ridha still remembered the sight of longboats on the water, emerging from a cloud of smoke with flame at their backs. Like dragons rising out of the sea.

The Vedera of Kovalinn did not answer.

Ridha crept forward. If this was victory, she could feel it in her fingers, nearly slipping. "What are they running from?"

"Running?" Dyrian scoffed. He eyed his mother, still standing, nearly a bear herself. "No, the raiders of the Jyd do not run."

Fear lanced down Ridha's spine. Fear . . . and hope. Her voice shook. "Then what are they preparing to fight?"

On the floor, the bear stirred, yawning his fearsome jaws. His teeth were three inches long, yellow and dripping. He looked up at his master and blinked sleepy, warm eyes. Again, Dyrian scratched his fur, earning a satisfied hum from the bear's throat.

This time, the Monarch did not smile. He did not look like a child anymore.

"The enemy we all must face," he said. "Whether we choose to or not."

30

AGAINST THE GODS
Sorasa

There were three prisons in Almasad. One on the water, the cells half flooded at high tide, with crocodiles tearing at the bars. One on the outskirts, between the city and the dunes, the cells open to the sun, so that prisoners burned and blistered within hours of captivity. The third was buried beneath the citadel fortress of the city's central garrison, its cells dark and cool and sepulchral, secure as a tomb. The first two were unpleasant, but manageable. Sorasa Sarn had swum and climbed her way out of both.

She gritted her teeth as they were led, bound and gagged, to the third. *Taltora*, she knew, cursing its name.

Sorasa kept her face lowered. It wasn't difficult to look defeated. After all, Sigil had betrayed them.

I should have known, she thought as their footsteps echoed. *She never saw the corpses on the hill. She never saw Taristan of Old Cor, the red wizard at his side. Sigil is of the Ward, still existing within the rules she understands.*

And she's right, Sorasa thought. *In another time, I would have done the same.*

The Ibalet officers brought them to a guardroom below the prison fortress, flaring with torches, its walls lined with shelves and trunks. The Ibalets wasted no time stripping away their weaponry, relieving Dom and Andry of their swords. Corayne grimaced in the flickering light, her eyes too wide as they removed her cloak and tossed it away. She fought weakly, choking against her gag, when they unbuckled the Spindleblade and took it gingerly from her back.

Dom bucked against his captors, but six men and a heavy iron chain around his wrists and ankles were enough to keep the Elder from escape. *Sigil warned them*, Sorasa cursed, watching him writhe in vain.

The bounty hunter was nowhere in sight, and neither were the Gallish soldiers in their cloaks. While the soldiers patted down Valtik, puzzling at her trinkets, Sorasa imagined Sigil in the soldiers' mess, surrounded by the northern troops. Or perhaps in the warden's office, collecting a seal of merit to be presented for payment in Ascal. *The latter, most likely. Sigil enjoys nothing until her business is completed.*

When it was her turn, Sorasa leaned into the shadow, trying to obscure her face. She winced when a guard with a badge of office examined her, his eyes narrowing beneath full, dark brows. He had the hawk face of a noble Ibalet, his eyes a warm, syrupy brown. She recognized his black beard, shaved and oiled into perfect curls beneath his cheekbones. Without removing the gag, he grabbed her by the chin, turning her head from side to side. Then his gaze dropped, taking in the tattoos at her neck and the lines on her fingers.

He sighed aloud, sounding fatigued. "Back so soon, Amhara?"

Sorasa smiled, working the gag out of her mouth, using a combination of her tongue and lips in a well-practiced trick. "Bar-Barase, I see you made lieutenant," she sneered, nodding to his badge. "Congratulations."

The soldier clenched his teeth. "Put the rest in the cells; space them evenly. Keep the immortal chained," he said wearily, without joy or zeal. "Strip this one bare. Search every inch."

Across the room, Corayne made a small noise behind her gag, trying to take a step. A single guard stopped her. Dom himself fought harder, nearly overpowering his six guards, until a seventh caught him around his neck. They struggled even as they were marched away, nudged along at spear and sword point.

Sorasa shrugged as they went, her hands still bound. "The sooner we get this started, the sooner we can finish."

The lieutenant's lip curled and he waved forward two of the female guards, both of them hardened enough to have been carved from the granite of the Red Pillar. Sorasa let them work, her muscles tight with tension. She stared at the lieutenant's back, hating him.

There is nothing so frustrating as an honest officer.

It didn't take long. Sorasa Sarn had been strip-searched since childhood. It was a regular occurrence in the Guild, where acolytes were encouraged to steal food, money, or whatever else they could get away with. She barely noticed as they checked over her body, looking for hidden weapons from her scalp to her toes.

She counted the cells as she passed, and every hairpin turn. Taltora was a labyrinth beneath a fortress, the air dry and cool. They took everything—her belt, her sword, her bow, her daggers, every pouch of precious powder, and, worst of all, the coin purse strapped along her thigh. All that Ionian gold, gone to the vaults of Taltora, where it would only gather dust under the watchful eye of dutiful Lieutenant Bar-Barase. *The stiff-necked fool won't even use it for himself*, Sorasa lamented, marching along the passage.

Four guards marched her along, their swords drawn and raised. Subduing them wouldn't fix anything. Another six would come running, and she'd end up unconscious and chained in a deeper cell, without even the hope of a candle. No, Sorasa was a model prisoner, her wrists tied behind her back, her leggings, boots, and shirt hastily donned again. Her black hair hung loose over one shoulder, ragged from their journey.

She heard Valtik around the fourth turn, the old witch rambling in Jydi again. Her voice echoed off the dirt floor and stone roof, a ghost haunting its mausoleum. For once, Sorasa was glad to hear her squawking. She wagged a finger as Sorasa passed, grinning with too many teeth.

Around the next turn she found Corayne and Andry, an empty cell separating each from the other. Sorasa looked them over, expecting a blubbering mess, especially from the squire. Both stood at the bars, flint-eyed and bold, their gags torn away.

"Did they hurt you?" Corayne demanded, her fists clenching on the iron.

Sorasa tossed her head. "Does it look like it?"

The Elder's cell faced the others, alone across the aisle. He was half obscured in the dim light, chained against the wall like a rabid animal. Even his neck was bound, forcing him to stand awkwardly straight, his back braced to the stonework. He shifted, clinking his chains.

"A bit much, don't you think?" Sorasa said to her guards. "He's a puppy dog."

Dom scoffed, struggling with the chain around his throat.

The guards did not respond, opening her own cell with the grate of metal on metal, jamming a key in the snarling lock. They shoved her in, wrists still bound, and slammed the cell door before marching back into the passage.

Their footsteps died away, leaving the five of them in the quiet dark, the only light coming from a single torch. Between the empty cells and the long aisle, no one could brush fingertips, let alone help each other. And with Dom bound as he was, there was little hope of smashing their way out. Their brooding battering ram was no more.

"This is less than ideal," Dom growled to the ceiling.

Corayne kicked up a spray of dirt, exasperated. "That's one way to put it," she snapped. "You trusted the bounty hunter."

Sorasa took the accusation in stride. She paced her cell, examining the bars for any flaw. "Charlie's still on the outside."

Andry's scoff echoed. "Oh yes, he'll certainly come back for us."

"He could draw something up," Corayne offered, looking between them. "A writ or a diplomatic letter to buy us some time?"

"He won't get anything past Sigil." Sorasa kept up her inspection. The bars were dug in, hammered into the ceiling and the dirt floor. She scuffed at the bottom, trying to make a hole. The iron reached too deep. "She's going to drag us all the way back to Ascal." *Another voyage across hostile seas, to die on the executioner's block or in the maw of a sea serpent. Exhausting.* "Unless we do something about it."

"We're forty feet underground, Sarn," Dom said in a flat voice. He strained again, his pale face going red with exertion. The bonds didn't budge.

"Locked in cages. Chained," Corayne added, waving a hand at the Elder. "I doubt even you can do something about that."

"You're right," Sorasa said. Then, with a huff of breath, she jumped straight up, tucking her knees, drawing her bound wrists around her feet. When she landed on her toes, her hands were in front. It was an old trick, taught to every acolyte at the citadel. "Ibalets are just jailors but Taltora is a bitch of a dungeon. The air shafts are too small even for a child. Trust me, I've seen it tried."

She began to move her wrists over themselves, pulling with each pass of skin on skin. The restraints were good rope, braided and tight, but the knots needed work. Inch by inch, she made room against her flesh. The rhythm was slow, steady, even hypnotic. She sank into it as easily as a warm pool.

"The only way out is the way we came in. Down the cells, four turns through four rows. Then the guardrooms, the antechamber, and up the gut of the citadel itself. Where you have to charge through the courtyard of the barracks and garrison offices before reaching the street. Then it's a race to the desert, which few can survive on foot, if they manage to not get run down by mounted cavalry before they hit the dunes." The others winced as she listed each obstacle, but Sorasa only shrugged, her wrists turning. "Be grateful we're not in a Treckish prison pit, half-buried in our own refuse. Or Ascal, for that matter, at the mercy of pig-idiot guards who forget to feed their prisoners. No, Taltora is kind compared to those."

Her right hand loosed first, squeezing between the bindings. The left followed with a slip, and she tossed the rope around her neck. It would come in handy later, should she need to strangle someone.

The others watched, wide-eyed.

"You've been in prison before," Andry said in a flat voice.

"I've been in *this* prison before," Sorasa replied. With her hands free, she rolled up the sleeve of her left arm, exposing an intricate tattoo of a bird's wing.

"Well?" Corayne leaned her forehead against the bars. Hope flared in her eyes. It was so easy to coax the girl into flame, Sorasa was almost jealous. *The ability to hope was driven from me long ago.* "We don't exactly have time to waste. It's been hours already."

Sorasa drummed along the feathers, feeling the flesh of her arm. She stopped at the wing tip and put her teeth to her own skin. "The guards are wise to my ways by now," she said out of the corner of her mouth.

After a moment, she felt the metal nub of the pin and latched on. It slid from her skin easily, the steel of the thick needle shining crimson. It wasn't long, the length of a single finger joint. She ignored the sting and the single drop of blood marring her tattoo.

"But they still can't figure out how to check a body properly," she added, triumphant, the needle in her teeth.

Dom stared in disgust. "Are you going to fix a hole in a shirt?"

Sorasa didn't answer, pulling a second pin from another spot in the bird's wing.

"Oh, well done," Andry said, gasping in fascination.

"Thank you, Trelland. It's nice to be appreciated," she answered as she set to picking the cell lock with her bloody pins.

Her heart pounded as the door swung open, the hinges mercifully silent. *Now what, now what, now what* drummed to a crescendo in her head. The guards hadn't taken her lockpicks, but they had taken everything else. Her gear, Dom's Elder sword, the *Spindleblade*. Not to mention there were probably a hundred soldiers between themselves and the street, one of them Sigil of the Temurijon. Sorasa gritted her teeth, trying to remember a more precarious position she had been in and escaped.

Well, I've never tried to save the realm before, so nothing comes to mind.

Dom's voice grated in her ears. "What's next, Sarn?"

She wanted to slip through his bars and tighten the chain around his neck until he couldn't breathe, let alone speak. Instead she crossed the aisle, setting to work on Andry's cell.

"If your life didn't depend on getting out of here, I'd say you were gloating, Elder," she snapped over her shoulder.

His chains clinked. He drew up his chin as best he could. "The Vedera do not gloat."

Andry pushed open his cell door with a grateful nod.

"Valtik?" he said, looking to the witch. "Any tricks?"

Still on the dirt floor, Valtik shrugged her narrow shoulders. "Listen for the bells," she said. For the first time since they met, Sorasa thought the old woman sounded tired, her voice matching her advanced age. "So the bone tells."

Andry winced, reaching through the bars to help her to her feet. His expression darkened like a storm cloud. "I've had enough of bells to last a lifetime."

The picks turned in another lock and Corayne's cell opened. She spilled out, a whirlwind, a mad horse kicking up dirt. "We can't go anywhere without the blade," she said. Her body leaned, compensating for a weight she no longer carried. Without her cloak, without the sword on her back, she looked small and young, a child plucked from her bed.

Then she gnashed her teeth, stepping into Sorasa's way. The assassin stared, the child melting away before her eyes.

"The Spindleblade, Sorasa," Corayne said, her eyes black as jet.

"I know," she hissed, making quick work of Valtik's lock.

"Do you think Charlie is still waiting?" Corayne followed close on her heels. Desperation rolled off her in waves.

"I really can't say," Sorasa forced out, prying open the final cell. Dom glowered at her from the wall, awkwardly splayed within his chains. The assassin approached him with her picks bared, raised like daggers. "Try not to bite, Elder."

"Why would I?" he snarled back. "Your blood is probably poison."

His first wrist came free, then the second. The neck was more difficult: she had to push his hair away to find the padlock holding the chains in place.

She chuckled to herself, unlocking his feet. "Only a little," she said as he fell to the floor, a heap of sore muscles.

Corayne was right: there was no time to waste. But Sorasa found herself wishing they were deeper in the cells of Taltora, if only to buy a few more seconds to think. They were running into oblivion, with no plan and no hope of finding the light on the other side. It was well into the night by now, but that would mean little until they made it outside. Past the guardrooms, the garrison, the citadel itself . . .

Her mind spun, hunting for opportunity.

For the first time in her life, Sorasa Sarn found none.

The door loomed, cedar planks banded with iron, its hinges fat and heavy. She imagined it splintering under Dom's weight, opening onto a room full of soldiers armed to the teeth.

Our only hope is surprise. Get a sword, get a dagger, get any weapon we can. Fight until numbers are back on our side. Let Dom do the heavy lifting. I could manage the rest.

And above all else, she knew, *keep Corayne an-Amarat alive.*

Dom stared at the door, his face pulled in concentration. Sorasa knew he was listening, trying to figure out exactly who and how many were on the other side.

"I'll take down whoever I can," he murmured, staring around at them. Even Valtik stood in front of Corayne, with Andry shifting to protect them both, his long arms stretched out.

The squire met the Elder's eye, exchanging stern nods.

"With me," the boy said, resolute.

"With me," Domacridhan of Iona echoed, taking as many steps back from the door as he dared. Two, three, ten. Until long yards stretched between himself and the wood.

He lunged, a blur, sprinting so quickly Sorasa felt the air stir around her. She braced, willing him through the door, telling herself to follow, as close as lightning to thunder.

The door gave beneath his shoulder, cracking on its hinges, falling flat like a drawbridge. He kept his balance, staying on his feet to pound through, nearly colliding with an oak table. Instead he leapt over it, spinning, lithe as a deer in the forest.

Sorasa burst into the room, clamping down on the fear rattling between her teeth. She waited for the sting of swords, the cut of daggers, the bashing blow of a shield or fist.

Nothing came.

Sigil sat in a chair, her overlarge boots resting on the table, legs crossed at the ankles. She had a chicken leg in one hand, a smear of grease over her lips. A forelock of dark hair fell over one eye. She looked from the Elder to Sorasa, a smile in her eyes as she sucked meat off the bone.

"Two hours to get out of a cell," she chuckled. "Sarn, I think you're losing your touch."

Their weapons fanned over the tabletop, the Spindleblade safe in its sheath. Sorasa's blood soared, singing with adrenaline. Her mask of indifference slipped, showing a true smile.

"Sleeping draft?" she said, angling her head at the ceiling.

"You're not the only one who knows her way around poison and powder," she answered. "These soldiers certainly can drink. The entire garrison went down like a baby."

"Good you came to your senses, Bounty Hunter. To betray us is to betray the realm, and your own survival." Dom glowered, snatching his weapons from the table.

Sigil basked in his judgment. "I didn't betray you, Elder. Or, at least, I didn't betray you for long," she added.

"And what did you learn from two hours with the citadel garrison?" Corayne asked, returning the Spindleblade to her back. She breathed a sigh of relief as it slid home, her shoulders dropping. "That was your aim, right?"

"Smart girl," she answered. "The Gallish soldiers had a chatty captain, not to mention stupid. He was happy to trade news—I think he wanted to share in my earnings, or my bed. I had no interest in either, of course." Sigil fiddled with the edge of her ax. "But he did say they aren't the only Gallish troops in Ibal. Two hundred soldiers arrived a week ago, sailing right into Almasad."

Andry balked. "The Queen can't send that many soldiers into a foreign kingdom, not without a declaration of war."

"I doubt she minds," Corayne muttered. "Did he tell you where they were going?"

Sigil raised her chin, catching Sorasa's eye. After so many years, they shared an understanding, a familiarity. The assassin saw reluctance in the bounty hunter, perhaps even fear.

"An oasis on the Aljer coast," she said. "Called Nezri."

Sorasa felt that fear too, and let it be her guide.

Mirrors on the sand.

It had been years since the daughter of Ibal had ridden its deserts, a sand mare beneath her, flying over the dunes she was born to.

There was nothing quite like it. Not standing at the prow of a ship, nor the bed of a chariot. Not even leaning into the wind at the edge of a cliff, the entire realm splayed out like a blanket of green and blue, all the world in your teeth. In the heart of Sorasa Sarn, there was no thrill to match a desert at night, moving swiftly below clearest stars, the cold, clean wind in her hair, the only sound her heartbeat and the shifting of ancient sand.

She lay back in the saddle, thighs clenched tight to keep her seat as her spine hit leather, her eyes on the heavens. The oil-black sand mare shuddered beneath her, galloping in perfect, steady rhythm. With the breeze on her face and the stars above, Sorasa cleared her mind, emptying her head of Spindles and Elders, Corblood girls and enchanted blades. It was a Guild tactic, to seek clarity through peace.

Sorasa had never been much good at it.

She sat up again, the reins back in hand and her boots in the stirrups. The mare surged beneath her, eager to run. The other mounts responded in kind, the horses' hooves like meteors across the sand.

How Charlie had procured seven sand mares, black and red and golden, Sorasa did not know. But she was certainly glad he had. There was no creature so fast, no beast so hardy. The miles passed in a blur, the sky wheeling toward dawn.

With the right provisions and good planning, the Great Sands of Ibal were easy to navigate. *It's the sun that'll kill you, not the stars.* They set their course by the constellations, thundering a line over the dunes. Sigil took the lead, with Dom at her side. They rode neck and neck, testing each other, her hair flattened to her skull, his trailing like a flag of hammered gold.

They raced toward a Spindle torn open, spilling forth the monsters of Meer.

The realm of oceans, surrounded by a sea of sand dunes. Sorasa could not comprehend it, but so much was beyond her understanding these days. She narrowed her focus to what she could control and could accomplish. Another Guild tactic. *All I can do now is ride and outrun a doom like the rising sun.* She felt it now, a sword at her neck. Taristan and What Waits, their hands outstretched to seize the realm. And another blade hung over her, closer and closer with every second.

Return and I'll pick your bones clean.

She heard Lord Mercury's voice in her head, clear as the stars in the inky black. Their citadel was to the north, too far to see, miles off on the coast, where sands met cliffside. But she dared not look. The horse might shift beneath her, the path might change. Sorasa Sarn might lose all control and bring her bones home.

Dawn was a curtain of heat like the opening of an oven. Sorasa kept them moving as long as she could, pushing the outlanders to their limits. Until the sun was too high, too strong, the shadows pocketed in the dunes nearly gone. The horses gleamed with sweat, flagging in their perfect steps. Even Dom breathed a sigh of relief when Sorasa called for camp.

She dismounted into sand hot enough it seared through her boots. A scrabble of rocks at the base of a dune provided good shade. It was still boiling hot but bearable, and the others used their cloaks to prop up little tents for more shadow. Andry was asleep in an instant, snoring as soon as he lay down. Charlie was quick to join him, while Dom took watch, his face buried in the dark of his hood. Valtik dug at the sand, building herself a nest in the cooler layers below, before waving at Corayne to join her. Sorasa quirked a brow at her, but did not bother asking how a northern witch learned desert ways.

"They'll have a watch on the canyon," Sigil murmured, shucking off her armor. She was just as big without it, all muscle and thick limbs. "Archers, crossbows. It won't be pretty."

Sorasa shaded her eyes and squinted at the horizon, the bright, blue sky meeting shimmering gold. Though she wore muted clothing, black and brown and dirty gray, blue and gold were her favorite colors. The royal blue of the flag. The gold of sand. The clear cerulean of the endless sky. The yellow wink of coin. They were Ibal. They were home.

It was early autumn now. The others could not feel the change in the winds, the miniscule drop in temperature. But a daughter of Ibal certainly did.

"I can handle the canyon," she said, patting Sigil on the shoulder.

The bounty hunter replied with a gruff laugh. "Good. I'd rather not have to save your skin again."

As they made their way forward, they slept through the worst heat of the days, rousing before dusk. It was exhausting, even for Sorasa, who had been long from home. Corayne's lips cracked and bled. Dom swathed himself from head to toe, sweating in his cloak and hood. Poor Charlie nearly fainted every morning, ruddy from fingertips to toes. Sigil sweated through her armor, her face shining, and Andry didn't drop his hood for days, shading his eyes. Only Valtik was somehow unaffected by the heat or sun, her ivory skin never changing, her head bare and eyes wide open. *Some Spindlerotten trick,* Sorasa assumed.

The sun sapped their strength, leaving their nights quiet and swift. A week passed in near silence, their waterskins growing lighter, their stores of food running low. The apples bought in Adira were long gone, the sweetness of them only a memory.

Sorasa did not worry. It was no longer summer and the red line appeared on the horizon as it should, growing with every passing hour. The cliffs cast long shadows, bathing the desert in cool air, the earth cracked by a seasonal lake. It would be months before winter rains brought it back. A few hardy plants still wormed up through the cracks in the dirt, fed by an underground water supply, seeping through the dirt and sand. The sand mares tried to nose at them as they walked, lips reaching for any hint of green.

"Either you intend to go around," Dom said one morning, his immortal eyes on the cliffs still miles off. They stretched the length of the horizon, jagged from north to south, a wall of rusty stone. "Or go through."

"Around would take weeks. The Marjeja rings the Aljer like a crescent moon. We'll take the canyon." The horse's flank was smooth beneath her hand, steadying as an anchor. The sand mare shuddered at Sorasa's touch, leaning into it. "And we won't be the only ones."

Sorasa finished braiding her hair into a tight bun at the nape of her neck. With a will, she raised her eyes to stare at the horses spread across the dry riverbed, the canyon a gash in the wall of cliffs half a mile on. Though she was still, her heart rammed in her chest and her stomach twisted. There were two hundred Shiran at least, in all colors, from cream to sand to blood red and even a few obsidian black. They grazed across the cracked earth, hunting in the growing shadows of the cliffs. There were only a few stallions, the rest intelligent mares and colts still growing into their gangly limbs. They looked akin to sand mares, but any Ibalet knew them as a beast apart, stronger and faster and infinitely more wild than their domestic cousins. *This is wrong,* Sorasa thought, feeling shame already. *This is unholy, a strike against the gods and the realm.*

The others stared with her, sweating against the dawn.

"Are we going to look at them all day or . . . ?" Charlie said, trailing off with a half grin.

"That is a Shiran."

Sorasa's skin crawled at the thought of what they had to do.

"After the gods, there is nothing so sacred to Ibal as these herds. They are the wind made flesh, faster than a storm, fiercer than sand wolves. In the days of Old Cor, the empire raided them, dragging wild Shiran screaming across the sea. Most died so far from home. Not so anymore." Her mouth went dry. "To disturb or capture a wild Shiran is punishable by death."

Corayne shifted in the saddle. "Something else for the posters," she grumbled.

"They are a testament to the gods, to the Ibalet kings, to the great and terrible glory of Ibal, who was conquered but never killed." Sorasa felt sick but forged on. *At least I must make them understand.* "These lands are their own to wander, from coast to riverbed, cliff to grassland, mountain to oasis shade.

"They are truly free," she murmured, feeling the wind in her air, the judgment of the gods in her bones. And Dom's emerald eyes on her, soft for once, without his usual glare.

"We will not harm them," he rumbled, bowing his head low. "You have my word."

Sorasa could only nod, her mouth too dry as he urged his mare forward, descending the dunes with Sigil close beside him.

Saydin nore-sar.

Gods forgive me.

Saydin nore-mahjin.

Gods protect us.

She worried more for the sacred horses than for most of her human companions. *Somehow, the witch manages to survive everything. Andry will be fine too. He is a good horseman, easy in the saddle. Charlie not so much, but if he is trampled, so be it. His blood isn't saving the Ward anytime soon.* It was Corayne she looked to, reading the tension in the girl's shoulders, the tightness of her fingers on the reins of her horse, a sand mare the color of garnet gemstone.

"Keep your grip," Sorasa said to her. "Whatever you do, don't let go. One arm over the saddle, both feet in one stirrup. I'll be right next to you; so will Dom. No one will let you fall."

Corayne dipped her chin in a firm nod, her face a picture of strength. The trembling in her hands told a different story. For once, the Spindleblade was not across her back. It would have sent her off balance. For the run, they'd strapped it to her horse's saddle, angled out of the way, lashed as tightly as they dared.

If we lose that horse . . . , Sorasa thought. Her mind tried to chase down every possible outcome and mistake they might face. There were too many to follow, too many variables to anticipate. And not enough time to plan for any, let alone all.

Sigil knew how to move horses. She'd cut her teeth on the steppes among the stocky, stout ponies of the Temurijon. She urged her horse between the Shiran mares, aiming for a stallion standing apart, his neck arched and ears twitching.

In the dunes above, Sorasa wound the reins into her hands, her heels and thighs tightening around her mount.

The battle cry of the Countless, the great army of the Temur emperor, went up from the herd, a shriek like the crashing of metal and lightning. Combined with Sigil's galloping mare and the flash of her ax, it was enough to send the stallion bolting. Muscle shuddered beneath his flank, a ripple over water, beautiful for a moment, as if he were forged from metal instead of flesh. He went for the plain but found Dom in his way, his sword bright with sunlight, startling the wild horse.

Together they drove the stallion toward the canyon, his voice braying over the riverbed. The herd screamed with him, kicking up dust, exploding to follow his thunderous path.

"Don't let go," Sorasa said again, leaning over to strike Corayne's mare on the flank.

They raced down the sand, pelting into the thick of the Shiran, the smell of dust and wild horse in the air. Sorasa's heart leapt with the horses, their hooves beating a rhythm to match her pulse. It was like joining a storm, falling into a tempest. Sorasa shuddered and jarred as her sand mare found pace with the herd, their bodies pressing closer together to follow the stallion as he charged. She galloped with Corayne, their knees nearly touching. As for the others, Sorasa could not say. There was only Corayne and the Spindleblade, the scarlet flank of her horse like a beacon at the corner of Sorasa's eye.

The cliffs loomed, the canyon a narrow split of rock. All the world shrank to the red walls and the drumbeat of a thousand hooves, the rhythm of her blood, adrenaline rattling through her body. Corayne bent low over her mare's neck, clawed to the horse, her teeth bared and gnashing. A familiar shade of gold flashed somewhere, joined by the snap of dark green. Dom pulled up alongside Corayne's other flank as the shadows of the cliffs fell over them, the cool air a dropping curtain, the sound of the herd echoing off stone in a deafening roar.

"Now!" Sorasa tried to yell, her voice lost in the din. She could only hope the others saw her and followed.

Hands tight on the reins and the hard pommel of her saddle, she swung her left leg out of her stirrup, passing it up and over the horse's back in a smooth arc. Her muscles pulled, tensing as she balanced one boot in the stirrup, wedging the other alongside as best she could. The horse didn't break stride, urged on by the pace of the herd. Centuries of breeding could not outweigh pure instinct, and sand mares were Shiran somewhere down their lines. It wasn't easy, keeping herself tight against the horse's side, her head tucked to the saddle. The dusty ground flowed beneath her like water, cragged with rocks, uneven and worn. She tried not to look down or imagine being trampled. Instead she glanced left and right, back and forward, searching through the waves of roiling horseflesh.

Her stomach turned when she saw soldiers in the high rocks, their silhouettes sharp on the cliffs. Archers, all of them, watching the canyon. She flinched, expecting a fiery bolt of pain at any moment. An arrow through the neck. It never came.

It's working, she thought, almost losing her grip in shock. Instead she strengthened her resolve, pulling herself closer to the horse.

First she spotted Andry, his head pressed to the side of his bay mare. He was taller than Sorasa, and had to curl his body to keep his legs from dragging along the ground. He met her gaze, his mare weaving among the Shiran. The squire did not falter, his brow set in a dark line. Sigil was behind, also too tall. She wrapped herself around the horse, one arm and leg thrown over its back, the others passing under. Valtik and Charlie were nowhere to be found, lost in the sea. At least if she couldn't see them, any Gallish scouts certainly wouldn't either.

Corayne was still on her right, the girl's breath coming in hard, fast gasps. Her knuckles went white on the reins and saddle, fingers scrabbling to keep hold. She dangled close to Dom, the Elder gripping his horse with only one giant hand. The other held Corayne's horse by the saddle, keeping them in pace together. He braced the Cor girl against his chest, his immortal grace holding them both up and out of crushing death.

The horses ran at breakneck speed, their manes like flags in the wind, their hooves kicking up stones and dust. A cloud followed the herd, hazy and pink, obscuring the heights of the cliffs. The figures faded, the archers lost in the dust. Sorasa allowed herself a small burst of triumph. If they held on long enough, the herd would carry them through.

The canyon seemed to stretch, endless. It widened and narrowed with each turn, forcing the herd to adjust, and their mares with them. Sorasa winced as another horse clipped her, nearly crushing her against her mare's ribs. A cry of alarm went up somewhere. It sounded like Charlie. Sorasa tried to pray, willing him to hold on, willing the scouts not to listen. All she could do was clench her teeth and keep steady, her own grasp on the saddle slipping.

While the entrance to the canyon was a dark gash, the way out blazed bright as any star, a white column of daylight. It appeared around the next bend, and Sorasa nearly crowed in relief, her body bruised and weakening. She willed the herd to move faster, begging any god who might be listening.

Dom and Corayne pulled ahead, their horses running in tight formation. The Elder had a foot in Corayne's stirrup and his one hand on either saddle, with Corayne braced against his chest, her face pressed into his cloak. His back faced forward, allowing his cloak to flow around them and keep her hidden.

It also kept him blind.

The assassin drew a sharp, almost shrieking breath when she saw the path split around a boulder thrusting out of the earth like a dagger. The herd broke around it, maneuvering easily. But not Dom and Corayne, their mares held together, the whites of their eyes furious, both horses blowing hard. They charged, screaming, trying to pull apart, but Dom was stronger, his fingers wormed beneath the girths of both saddles.

Sorasa was on the back of her horse again without thinking, her heels digging into the sides of her mare. The horse whinnied and bolted, outstripping the Shiran around them, a darting black arrow. If the scouts could see her, she didn't care.

"Reach for me!" she shouted, coming up on the Elder and the Cor girl.

They looked up at her in shock, Dom's face red from exertion. And now anger.

"You'll kill us—" he began, but Sorasa ignored him, stretching out her hand.

The boulder loomed, closer with every second, a hammer to split them in two.

She looked to Corayne, who raised her head, all terror. But her eyes were the same. Blacker than the night sky. The eyes of another realm.

"REACH FOR ME!" Sorasa screamed again, already feeling the crush of rock on bone. Her fingers stretched, touching open air. Something thwipped by. *An arrow*, she thought idly, knowing the sound all too well.

Then Corayne's hand was in her own, Dom shouted, and Sorasa pulled as hard as she could, her shoulders screaming under the sudden weight. For a second, time suspended, slowed to nothing. Corayne drifted toward her, arms wide, her eyes filled with terror as the rock passed within inches. Behind her, Dom moved in a blur, kicking off one horse to land on the other, one arm thrown over the Spindleblade to keep it from falling loose.

The rock passed between them, Dom never breaking their gaze. Sorasa felt his focus like a spear through her gut, his eyes that stormy, unyielding green. But not as angry as she knew, not as disgusted. They rode apart, weaving around the break before colliding back together, Corayne sprawling between them, the girl shuddering against Sorasa's back.

A shout sounded above, the barking voice of a soldier. Another volley of arrows peppered the herd, needling the horses around them. Sorasa felt the arrows as keenly as if they were embedded in her own flesh. Her heart bled for the Shiran, now bleeding for her. She loosed a curse under her breath and snapped the reins, kicking the sand mare to her limits.

"Faster," she hissed, to herself and the horse. "Faster."

The canyon opened out onto desert, the sand here whiter than the gold of the dunes. They rode with the Shiran, the great stallion pulling his herd along. The soldiers would follow. They were probably already clambering down the cliffs or signaling to the rest of their company. Whatever element of surprise Sorasa hoped to use had disappeared.

But we are alive. And that is enough.

The water was a few miles ahead, the gulf of the Aljer so close she thought she could smell it. After days in the desert, the salt tang of seawater was impossibly heavy on her tongue. But the oasis stood between, a dark smudge a mile ahead. The shadow whispered of palm trees, cool water, and a small outpost town for caravans and pilgrims. A blessed place, Spindletouched.

And now Spindletorn.

"Keep going," she shouted, to anyone who could hear her, to anyone who made it through the canyon.

Corayne's grip shifted on her waist, the pressure fleeting but unmistakable. To their right, Dom had the sword. Sorasa nearly wept in relief, choking out a triumphant cry.

We are enough.

She dared not look back, lest she see the others broken or trampled.

On the horizon, the oasis glimmered. An odd sight, like the edge of a blade laid against the earth. Steel. Silver. Mercury.

Her breath caught.

Mirrors on the sand. The Eye of Haroun.

And this.

The sand turned to liquid, her horse's hooves kicking up water instead of dust. But the mares kept on, the Shiran never stopping, every horse plunging into the shallow layer of water laid across the harshest desert upon the Ward.

It was shockingly cold.

Sorasa shivered as she never had before. The merciless sun of Ibal beat down on her face while the water of Meer splashed around her, lapping up the legs of her mare.

"I think this is the right place," Corayne said weakly in her ear.

31

BLOOD AND BLADE
Corayne

Corayne flinched as a spray of water broke across her face, stinging her eyes and spurting up her nose. It tasted too cold, and a gray edge to the water left streaks on her skin. She tried to wipe them away, staining her hands. She'd never seen anything like this. The oasis was flooded, a new lake forming across hot sand, turning everything to sucking mud. She could barely make out the slight hills of the oasis, palm trees bending brown and green. The town nestled within, small and unassuming, its buildings blue paint and decorated white stone. She heard crashing waves somewhere, or a waterfall, or both. *This doesn't make sense,* Corayne thought, blinking at the shining water, nearly blinding as it reflected the sun overhead.

But there was no time to wonder. The Gallish soldiers guarding the canyon would pursue, and there were more in Nezri, to protect the Spindle. She leaned forward, pressing her cheek against Sorasa's warm back. The assassin's firm, steady heartbeat grounded her.

"Did we make it?" Corayne panted, fighting to be heard over the splashing hooves.

The Shiran fanned out, snorting and tossing their heads. Their formation lost its tightness without the canyon, and Corayne felt like she could breathe again, no longer surrounded. She searched the horses, looking for riders, in the saddle or dangling from it.

There was no one behind them but the dust cloud and, in it, the telltale flash of sun on steel. *The Lion is already coming.* Corayne hissed through her teeth.

"We're here!"

Andry panted as he rode up alongside their mare, back in the saddle, his face streaked with red dust. Blood bloomed along his sleeve, seeping from some wound. Corayne's eyes flickered to it.

"One of the horses bit me," he said, catching his breath. "Could've been worse."

Another mare joined their number, breathing hard beneath the weight of Charlie Armont. "No shit. I nearly *died*," he crowed, his face purple. There were angry burns on his arms, lines from the reins. *He must've been dragged all the way through the canyon.* "I nearly lost my *supplies*! My ink, my seals . . ."

Sigil rode out of the mirrored sand, her figure rippling into solid form. The horse danced beneath her. "A child could outride you, Priest," she said dryly. "What of the witch?"

Corayne could not say what swelled in her, an instinct or a feeling or something deeper. But she didn't bother looking for Valtik, in the herd or on the horizon. "She'll come when we need her."

Sorasa tightened under her hands, glancing over her shoulder. "I think we need her now."

Soldiers ahead, soldiers behind. A Spindle between them.

Corayne looked to Dom, one hand on his reins, the other on her Spindleblade. He followed her gaze and dipped his brow. Again she saw him on the cliffs of Lemarta, kneeling on the road and begging her forgiveness. *Asking me to save the world.*

The water deepened the closer they rode to Nezri, until it was up to their horses' knees, forcing them to slow to a trot. The Shiran pranced and bucked, snorting at the strangeness in their lands. Whatever protection they'd offered disappeared as the sand mares left the herd behind.

"Mirrors on the sand," Sorasa murmured, the sun reflecting in her eyes. The strange water flecked her cheeks. She raised a hand to shade her gaze, inspecting the outpost ahead.

Corayne did the same, peering around the assassin's shoulder. The palms sparkled, jeweled with dark droplets. A column of water like a gigantic fountain spouted into the air, a hundred feet high, wide as a tower, an impossible spring exploding out of the oasis basin. It roared with the crashing of a hundred waves, raining down on the city beneath. Like the water on the ground, it had an odd gray color, like oil or corruption. Corayne could feel it on her skin, tracking dirty lines down her face and neck.

Nezri was otherwise vibrant, but there was no one on the outskirts that Corayne could see. No citizens, no merchant caravans or pilgrims to the oasis temple. *Perhaps the Spindle drove them away—or Erida's men killed them all.*

"There are at least two hundred men of Galland in that

town," Sorasa growled, pulling her bronze sword from the sheath strapped to her saddle. "Stay fast; don't stop. Find the Spindle and get Corayne to it."

Blades sang loose. An ax bit the air. A hook on a string swung in a lazy circle. Corayne felt for her stabbing dagger, somehow still at her hip. The hilt was unfamiliar, wrong in her hand, despite the little training she'd had from Sorasa and Sigil.

Seven against two hundred soldiers of Galland, a Spindle at their backs. Impossible, but then so was everything else up to this moment. *We've overcome impossible before*, Corayne told herself, trying to believe it, trying to be brave. For her mother somewhere, for her father dead. For her friends around her, and the realm threatening to collapse on them all.

"Dom, the sword?" she said, trying not to tremble. Her voice wavered but her hand did not, stretching across open air, her palm raised.

The Spindleblade shone, its etchings filled with the desert sun. Again, Corayne could feel the cold radiating off the ancient blade, as if its heart were frozen and not forged. Dom held it out to her, passing it between their mares.

Her fingers brushed the hilt, the leather soft.

A screaming mouth full of fangs rose up between their horses, spooking them down to the bone. The sea serpent was young, its scales a cloudy white, its eyes red and weeping black. Its jaws snapped inches from Corayne's fingers, and Sorasa yanked her back out of its reach.

Dom changed his grip, flipping the blade through the air to take it by the hilt, swinging in the same motion. His horse reared and he missed, the Spindleblade chopping through open air instead of serpent flesh.

The mares tossed as the water foamed and rippled, splashing not from their hooves but from the quivering mass of serpents rolling over themselves, coiling and unfurling, white and black and red, gray and green and blue, scales like iridescent crystal or slick oil. The serpents circled, more and more drawn to the commotion, their movements like hunting waves.

There is no sound like screaming horses.

Corayne screamed too, as fangs snapped in her face.

The Companions broke apart, without aim, without a plan, at the mercy of their mares and the monsters beneath the surface. It was all Corayne could do to keep her seat, her arms locked around Sorasa's waist while the assassin fought to keep the horse alive, let alone standing.

Only Sigil had any luck, roaring the cry of the Countless again. It thrummed in the air, spurring her horse into a charge. She rode with the fury of a hurricane, ax in one hand, sword in the other, leaning back and forth to use both with abandon. Serpent heads flew behind her, their sliced necks spurting black blood to stain the waters.

"Follow me!" she cried, cutting a path into the oasis, serpent corpses floating in her wake.

For someone terrified of the bounty hunter, Charlie was the quickest to follow, his legs drawn completely out of the stirrups, lest a serpent catch him by the ankle. With his red face, he made quite a sight.

"Why did I agree to this?" he howled to no one.

Sorasa's mare spurred to action, getting her head and her bearings. The horse sprinted in the water, kicking at anything close in her haste to reach the palm trees and the outpost city.

The assassin chanted to her, the Ibalet language soothing the beast, calming her into focus. Water foamed around them, and Corayne swung, the dagger odd in her grip, its edge clumsy. She stabbed for a coil of serpent scale and nearly lost her balance, her stomach dropping.

"Just stay with me, Corayne; I'll handle the rest," Sorasa said, urging the mare into the palm trees.

Even flooded, Nezri looked charming, albeit deserted. The oasis was built around what had once been a placid, shining pool, the palm trees shading inviting streets. A domed and spired temple, small but intricately patterned in green paint and white mosaic, glimmered between the trees. Its prayer bell hung silent. There was a market plaza too, its stones flooded, the arches of adjoining bazaar choked with debris. Beautifully woven carpets lay forgotten, ruined in the water. As in Almasad, a causeway rose up and around the original banks of the oasis, standing on elaborate limestone columns, their crowns carved in the likeness of regal animals. It was smaller than the stone paths in the city, and abandoned.

The sun shone too brightly for so strange a day, jarring against the gray water and the tidal wave of sea serpents twisting over the sandy waterbed.

Corayne turned, searching for the others, but searching above all else for the Spindle. *I don't even know what I'm looking for,* she cursed. *Where it could be, what it looks like. Nothing.*

Sorasa maneuvered between the buildings, splashing down a narrow street to leave the serpents behind. Doors hung off their hinges, and windows dangled open, the apartments and shops long abandoned by their owners.

A man leaned out of one, his armor good steel, his sword flashing, his tunic a hideous, hateful green. Only Sorasa's lightning reflexes kept their heads attached to their bodies, and she yanked the mare's reins so forcefully the horse toppled, screaming as she went.

They fell, Corayne plunging into the water. She sputtered and fought to stand, her cloak too heavy. Sorasa growled somewhere, and Corayne whirled to find the Gallish soldier on top of the assassin, his longsword pointing at her throat.

Corayne did not know she could move so quickly or with such force until her dagger pulled back, red in her hand, coated to the hilt in fresh blood.

She froze, rattled, forgetting how to breathe, forgetting how to think, as the soldier fell to his knees, clutching his side. He looked at her, gasping for one last breath, spraying blood into the air.

His face was young, unlined. *He isn't much older than me.*

I'm sorry, Corayne tried to say, but the words never came.

"Run!"

The assassin hauled them both, crashing through the water, toward the center of the oasis. Corayne couldn't stop herself from looking back. A serpent, its scales an oily scarlet, swallowed the soldier whole, his eyes still open, staring without seeing.

"Domacridhan!" Sorasa's voice echoed, a roar, a scream, a desperate plea.

They fought through the flood, up to their waists in gray, their cloaks floating behind them. Sorasa hunted, sword raised, watching the water for any ripple of movement not their own.

"Domacridhan of Iona, I know you can hear me!" she yelled again, begging.

Corayne slammed back against the wall of a stone house, panting hard. The dagger was still in her hand, her grip on it painful. The blood on the blade throbbed, brighter and brighter. Her breath came too quickly, and then not at all, her throat threatening to close as her vision spotted. The world spun.

"Defend the Spindle. Defend the Queen!" someone shouted, his voice met with the confident roar of a dozen voices.

The roof above them bristled with Gallish troops, their spears long and wicked. The sun burned behind their heads, turning the soldiers into silhouettes, figures with no faces and no names. Inhuman. Soldiers of What Waits, not warriors for a mortal queen. Corayne lunged and darted, trying not to lose her balance as their spears rained down. Her dagger dropped from her hand, lost to the waters.

Something splashed behind her, crashing along the flooded street—a serpent or a soldier, she did not know. All she could do was run, Sorasa at her shoulder, fleeing in whatever direction they could.

Until strong arms scooped her around the waist, lifting her up and out of the water as if she were only a doll. Corayne balled her fists, aiming to swing, only to find herself slung belly down over Sigil's saddle, the Temur woman towering over her.

"Easy, I have you," the bounty hunter said, using her hips to guide the horse.

The mare ran as best she could, galloping for the causeway steps, climbing up and out of the water. Her hooves clattered on stone, and Corayne's teeth rattled so hard she though they might fall out. The causeway was meant for foot traffic and not a charging horse, but Sigil kept the mare in hand, taking sharp turns in swift stride.

The geyser of Meer roared up alongside them, spitting gray water like rain. Corayne gaped as they galloped, Sigil holding her steady. In the heart of the geyser, something thrashed.

More serpents, she thought at first. Until one of the things coiled into view, the mist parting to show a fat, long tentacle, its underbelly patterned with suckers, the end flat and probing. Another unfurled out of the water, gigantic, the length of a cathedral spire. They waved in unison, a sick, pale purple, snapping through the air, obliterating palm trees with every swipe. It pushed forward, outward, easing from its realm into their own.

Still she could not see the Spindle, but even so, she knew.

"I need the sword," Corayne murmured, unable to blink, unable to do anything but stare. All thoughts but the Spindleblade melted away.

This was what Mother's ship met on the Long Sea. This nearly sank the Tempestborn *and killed her crew. Killed my mother.* A monster was being born before her eyes. *How many ships will it sink? How many mothers will it steal?*

These things are going to cut the Ward in two.

"I need the sword, Sigil!" she shouted, wriggling, her voice stronger.

"What does it look like I'm doing?" Sigil growled, spurring the horse over the walkway, her hooves a rain of hailstones.

What drew the kraken, Corayne did not know. But the arms twitched, changing direction, as more of its lumbering bulk shifted from the geyser, tentacles wriggling free. The first arm crashed down, then the second, the weight of them cracking straight through the stone walkway.

"Sigil!" Corayne shouted as the woman kicked the horse, snapped the reins, and gave a sharp "hyah!" in perfect unison.

As the walkway crumbled under the mare's hooves, she gave a mighty leap, sailing through the air while the structure collapsed, sending up a spray of water. They landed hard, sliding over the flat roof of the nearest house, cluttered with empty pots and a thatched canopy.

The poor mare collapsed to her knees, shuddering and breathing too hard, her eyes rolling in her head. Corayne tumbled onto shaky legs, every nerve in her body aflame. Sigil had more grace, stopping to give the mare a swift pat down the neck. She murmured a Temur word Corayne did not know, but she could guess.

Thank you.

They flew down the steps of the house, Sigil leading the way as they reluctantly plunged back into the water. Corayne finally ripped her cloak away, leaving it to the oasis as they ran.

"Dom!" Corayne screamed, cupping her hands over her mouth. A swell of fear threatened to consume her. If the Elder could not hear her, if he could not come . . . *Only death would stop him. Only death would keep him from me.* "DOMACRIDHAN!"

She tried not to think of the others, or their fates. Sorasa, on the other side of the town. Charlie, probably hiding on a rooftop. *Andry.* The noble squire who betrayed his country, his duty, all he ever worked for. Who left his mother to save the realm, and broke his own heart to do it.

Andry.

He appeared at the far end of the lane, still on horseback. His sword dripped red, his face a ruin of rage and sorrow. Corayne knew that look. She felt it in herself, in her hands, in her blade as it cut through a man's life.

"Corayne!" Andry shouted, his mare fighting through the water, her neck high and nostrils flaring. He stood in the stirrups, extending a hand as he rode.

"It's the geyser!" she heard Sigil shout, the bounty hunter's big hands going to Corayne's hips. With a groan she all but tossed her into the air and Andry's waiting arms.

He took her weight in stride, shoving her into the saddle in front of him, his arms around her. "We need the sword," Corayne gasped, knotting her hands in the mare's mane.

"I know," he answered, kicking the horse to higher ground. She picked up speed, circling the oasis town while the echo of hissing snakes and clattering steel rose to rival the geyser's roar.

Nezri was a simple ring, her streets fanning out, wide enough for camel caravans—and now wide enough for the roiling monsters of Meer. Corayne searched as they rode, her heart in her teeth. Her stomach flipped when she saw the river, a deluge of water flooding down the hill from the oasis, carrying with it a school of sea serpents and whatever else might burst through the Spindle.

It wound over the sand in a speedy current, rushing towards the Aljer. An easy path through the gulf and into the Long Sea.

Andry spotted the flash of gold before Corayne could, pulling the horse down an abandoned lane and back into deeper water. The mare tried to fight but he kicked her on, cursing colorfully under his breath.

"If we survive this, remind me to scold you for that unseemly language," Corayne said wearily.

His chest moved against her back, rising and falling with stilted laughter. The warmth of him took her by surprise. "I certainly will."

They found Dom in a circle of soldiers, the Spindleblade in one hand, his own sword in the other, both blurs of flashing steel. Corpses fell like scythed wheat, the green of Galland stained scarlet as the soldiers died. Serpents feasted, kept at bay by the steady supply of flesh.

"Take this," Andry forced out, gesturing to the sword sheathed to his saddle. "Swing. Smooth arc. Let the horse help your movement."

Corayne wanted to vomit at the thought of killing another man, but clenched her jaw, pulling Andry's sword loose. She held it in a double-fisted grip, leaning as they rode, the steel edge already crimson.

It curved in an arc like the crescent moon, and a head followed, still crammed into an iron helmet. She refused to look as Andry wheeled them around for another strike. The Elder hardly noticed, making mincemeat of the troops standing against him. This time, Corayne missed, but the mare didn't, barreling down on a pair of soldiers, their bodies disappearing into the gray water foaming with blood. Behind them, Dom roared the battle cry of Iona, his language foreign to every ear. It was enough to send the surviving men scuttling away, bleeding and white-faced, terrified by the immortal mountain of rage.

His chest rose and fell, his dark green cloak torn to tatters, the embroidered stags a ruin of thread. There was blood in his golden hair, blood in his beard, blood to his elbows. Corayne almost expected his eyes to be bloody too, but they were still that steady, hard emerald. Unchanged. His breath came ragged, his chest rising and falling heavily.

Numb, Corayne sheathed Andry's sword and slid down from the saddle, her boots splashing.

Dom stared at her, dazed, nearly overcome by the bodies piled around him. Then he shuddered, came back to himself, and held out the Spindleblade. "Your sword," he said in a shaky voice.

This time, no serpent came between them.

There was only the bellow of the kraken, wet and endless, so deep Corayne felt it in her ribs, in the hollows of her chest. She wanted to fall to her knees.

Instead her hand closed on the sword, the jewels of her father's blade winking red and purple, the language of her lost realm blazing down its length. She could not read the runes, but she did not need to. They meant little in this moment. There was only the Spindle, her blood, and the blade in her hand.

They waded forward, a trio, Andry and Dom chopping at serpents as she walked her road. Sigil howled in laughter somewhere, her triumph echoing as a pair of soldiers fled her ax. Another fell from a roof, a bronze dagger in his neck, a tiger-eyed shadow watching him die.

The water slowed everything, each step harder than the one before. Corayne's body ached; her mind bellowed. She wanted to lie down and let the water take her. She wanted to charge, screaming like Dom, like Sigil, to rattle the air with the storm in her chest. She settled for another step. *Another. Another.*

Until they stood at Nezri's ruined core, the great column of water churning into the air. The water around her knees was black and red, the geyser spewing, the kraken still forcing its way out of the Spindle as in some unholy birth. Corayne squinted and saw a thread of gold shining between the sprays of water, the kraken's tentacles curling out from the razor-thin doorway to another realm. Its bulbous and slimy body heaved, pressing through, a single eye the size of a shield rolling in its socket. The edges were red and yellow, corrupted, poisoned. The beast smelled worse than old catch under the hot sun, stinking of rot and spoiled fish. It was gigantic, bigger than a galley and still growing, still pushing. It screamed again, blowing a foul wind over the oasis.

The Spindleblade was heavy in her hands, the point dragging through the water. She could barely lift it, let alone cut her way through a forest of tentacles to the glimmer of gold rippling through the kraken. Her heart faltered. Corayne felt her body flag, her limbs threatening to give out. Exhaustion fell in a heavy curtain. She gritted her teeth, fighting to stay upright, to stay moving.

On the other side of the oasis, among the palms, a figure crossed the water, letting it ripple around her waist. No soldier or snake followed. She was alone.

Gray water, gray hair, gray clothing. Hands like the gnarled roots of a white tree. Eyes like the clearest sky.

Valtik.

The old witch faced the kraken without hesitation, her face upturned to meet its glare. Her braids were undone, woven with bones and palm. Her ratty old dress floated behind her, somehow too long. The sun reflected on the water, dappling her with an odd glow of light. Her hands spread wide, fingers splayed like the points of a star.

She chanted, the Jydi language filling the oasis, the hum of it sharp and visceral. It shuddered through the beast, curling its tentacles inward.

"The gods of Meer have spoken," Valtik said, raising her voice and her chin as she switched to words they all understood. "The beasts of their waters awoken." Though she didn't move, the water around her rippled, pushed by something. "These lands are not your own; I bind you and banish you by rite of blood and rite of bone."

The kraken howled, the sound shredded and deafening. Corayne held her grasp on the sword, fighting the instinct to cover her ears.

She couldn't believe her eyes as the beast obeyed, even against its own will. It trembled, shifting, pulling backward inch by inch, the flesh of its body disappearing back into the Spindle.

Corayne took a step forward.

Valtik curled her fingers until her hands became claws, her wrinkled brow tightening as she grimaced, her voice never stopping.

"Be gone, be gone, be gone," she growled, in seemingly every language. The words of the witch were as a hurricane blowing, breaking over the infernal monster. It twisted and fought, the worms of its body slapping against the flooded ground, sending up sprays of foul water.

Corayne kept moving, the others beside her. She saw the flash of their steel, felt the air stir as they moved, the water flowing around her knees. Sand slid under her boots, turned to mud. It sucked at her steps, grasping her ankles, trying to hold her back.

"These lands are not your own!" Valtik wailed.

A shadow passed over the sun and a tentacle fell like a collapsing tower, the kraken shrieking its killing blow. Until Dom's sword wheeled, cutting through stinking flesh, sending the appendage plunging into the water, the end still thrashing.

The kraken's eye rolled and disappeared into the thread, the last of its wriggling tentacles weak and coiling.

"I bind you and banish you by rite of blood and rite of bone."

Even the geyser sputtered, its whitewater force pulsing.

Corayne felt her skin and muscle part as she ran her hand down the edge of the Spindleblade. Her blood joined the rest, a glittering crimson, carrying with it the hope of the realm. The hope of her father. The hope of herself.

The gash in her palm smarted as she returned her grip to the hilt, blood welling between her fingers. Another tentacle squirmed toward her, reaching like a vine, but Andry knocked it away, his sword dancing. She kept walking, the water cold, the wind cold, the sword cold.

The Spindle, needle thin, winked like a star. It caught its own light, too bright to stare at for long. Corayne expected a glimpse of another realm, the mighty oceans of Meer crashing beyond. There was nothing but the kraken, trying to battle its way into Allward. It weakened, its screams distant and echoing, the jolting motion of its tentacles going slow. One brushed her cheek, barely the touch of a hand. She ignored it. There was nothing else but the Spindle, the call of it a hook in her heart, tugging her in.

"For the Ward," she murmured. *For us all.*

The Spindleblade rose and arced, cutting across kraken flesh and Spindle thread, trailing black blood and unraveling gold, the geyser raining down on her in a waterfall. It collapsed and fell to nothing, slapping against the flooded land, drenching them all to the bone. The kraken screamed again from somewhere far away and was suddenly silent, the tear of the Spindle wiped clean out of the air, like the gap in a curtain pulled closed. The remaining tentacles sank in the water, neatly cut from a body now realms away.

Without the steady flow of the geyser and Meer's gateway, the flood melted, sucked into desert sand parched for centuries.

All over the oasis, hissing echoed, the serpents wailing a lament for their lost realm. Corayne slumped, leaning hard on the sword. She expected the sting of a fang at any moment.

It never came.

Her head lolled against a warm shoulder, and arms tightened around her body, holding her steady. She glimpsed dark amber eyes, a kind mouth, a gentle face.

She tried not to lose focus, keeping her eyes wide. But the sky darkened anyway, the sun losing its brilliance. Figures surrounded them, indistinguishable. Enemies or allies, she couldn't say.

"It's over," she heard Dom mutter, his voice distant and fading. "It's over."

Andry felt closer, a hand brushing her arm. His body was warm against hers. She tried to cling to him, her grip too weak. "With me, Corayne. Stay with me."

Her eyelids drooped, the Spindleblade falling from her wounded hand. "That's one down," she murmured, slipping into darkness.

32

THE ORPHANS
Erida

For a man who could crush diamonds in his fist, his touch was featherlight, his fingers gentle on hers.

Queen Erida let Taristan escort her from her horse to the staging ground at the top of the hill, the Madrentine border and the Rose River spread out before them. On the banks, the First and Third Legions formed up like silver beetles in ranks, crawling inexorably forward to the hastily constructed barge bridges anchored in the current. Despite her husband's glowering presence beside her, not to mention her assembled council of generals and war advisors, Erida could not tear her eyes away from the river. Twenty thousand men marched below, cavalry and infantry and archers, pikemen, knights, squires, and peasants pressed into service with their feudal lords. Men and boys, enamored of war or terrified of it. Rich, poor, or somewhere between. *Their hearts beat for me this morning.* She breathed deeply, as if she could taste their steel. The moment shimmered in her mind, already a treasured memory.

When I am old, an empress without equal, I will remember this day. When it all began.

She felt Konegin's glare, familiar as her own face. He had no cause to be angry. He wanted this war as much as any other good son of Galland. Madrence was weak, unworthy of its lands and wealth. It needed a stronger master. *He only wishes he were me, his feet in my shoes, my crown on his head.* And what a crown it was this morning: her father's own, made for battle, a circle of gold hammered into a steel cap. Her hair hung loose beneath it, falling over her shoulders in waves. Erida was not accustomed to steel, but her armor was light, made from precious metal, meant for ceremony rather than war. She had not bothered with a sword, even for show.

"A beautiful morning, Cousin," she said, drinking down another gasp of crisp autumn air. In the foothills, the leaves were turning, edges going red and gold.

Konegin huffed a noise in his throat, low and wet. "I'll weigh the morning when evening comes," he answered, folding his arms over his golden breastplate. It matched his luxurious beard, every hair combed into place. He looked the part of a king.

But so does Taristan, she thought, his hand still supporting her own.

Again he wore blood red beneath his armor, which was crimson and scarlet with a cloak edged in gold. The colors reflected oddly in his eyes, giving them a sheen like rubies. He brushed his hair back, slicking the dark red locks against his scalp. By now she noticed that one of his eyebrows had a split in it, cut by the tiniest white scar.

The cuts were still on his cheek, thin but unmissable, the same blue as the veins in her wrist. She wanted to trace them, one finger to each.

"You'll lose a thousand men by nightfall," Taristan muttered, his eyes never leaving the river. His wizard was not with them, cooped up with his own doings back at Castle Lotha. "The Madrentines are dug in between their forts. Their trench lines are as deep as our own. Even if we outnumber them five to one, it will be a killing field."

His voice was flat, without accusation.

"A thousand men for the border," Erida answered. "A thousand men for a clear road to Rouleine, and then Partepalas, and then the coast."

A clear road.

They both knew what that meant.

Though the Spindle was back in the ruins, guarded by an encampment of five hundred men, she could still hear the growl within it, the shuddering cascade of gems and teeth.

"For the glory of Galland," Konegin rumbled, putting a fist over his heart.

Though she despised him, the Queen didn't mind echoing his words, the battle cry that had lived in her since birth. "For the glory of Galland."

The others followed suit, the great generals and lords cheering for their country. Their voices swelled as one, thunderous to meet the first echoing clash of steel at the river.

Only Taristan remained silent and staring, his eyes rimmed in red, his fingers soft in Erida's own.

The Madrentine campaign headquartered at Lotha, the grander of the two castles close to the first assault. Once the field was won, they would move further downriver, keeping the Rose between themselves and danger. More legions would follow, already marching from the corners of Galland to bolster their conquest through the soft valleys of Madrence.

Erida had never been on campaign before, not truly. The morning began with battle and the night ended with feasting, the great lords toasting each other and their splendid performance on the field. Beer flowed and wine spilled along the tables of the Lotha hall, every head spinning with drink or battle or both. Indeed, a thousand men had been lost through the day, but miles had been gained, the Madrentines driven out of the forests and into their crumbling fortress to await siege. The day had been a rousing success.

And tomorrow will be another, Erida thought, bringing a third glass of wine to her lips. She surveyed the feasting chamber laid out before her, her version of a battlefield.

Lotha was no palace—built to defend the border, not entertain royalty—but it was comfortable enough to pass the days. The hall was tiny compared to Erida's own back in Ascal, and crammed with Gallish nobility, most of them falling over themselves this late in the evening. Many toasted the Queen, shouting her blessings, praising her boldness and courage. Her kingdom had not conquered in years. She was hungry. She was ready, an eager horse pawing at the gate. Erida felt it in herself, as she felt it in her crown.

Her husband did not enjoy feasts, or most of the posturing required of a royal consort. He sat in silence, eating little, drinking little, speaking to a select few and only when forced. It was the same tonight, his eyes lowered to the plate of wild boar set in front of him.

"Will Ronin be joining us this evening?" she muttered, careful to angle her voice. Konegin was never far from her side, separated by only a few seats, and he often weaseled his way into their conversations, scrabbling for crumbs.

The corners of her husband's mouth pulled downward into a frown. "He will come in his own time," he answered. The shadow in his eyes burned red. "Whenever that might be."

Erida leaned closer, hiding her mouth with the goblet. "Is something wrong?"

"I don't know," he said, voice flat as his stare. It was the truth, without adornment. Then he raised an eyebrow, his lips curling. "Are you going to scold me again? Tell me to make friends among your simpering nobles?"

The Queen scoffed into her wine, taking another sip. It tasted of cherries. "Allies, not friends. There are no friends to be had here," she said quickly, almost in singsong. The same creed had been hammered into her since childhood. "Besides, I'm growing accustomed to your taciturn manner."

"Taciturn."

"It means—"

"I know what it means," he said, leaning back in his seat. It put some distance between them, and Erida found herself disliking it. He carried a heat with him, a comfort in the cold stone of an old, dreary castle. She watched, waiting for the telltale flash of red anger in his stare. It never surfaced, his gaze on his plate, his eyes like obsidian. "Orphans can grow to intelligence, even those raised in the mud."

Her hand lay on the wooden table, inches from his fingers. She did not dare move it, either closer or farther away.

"You forget I'm an orphan too," Erida said hotly, feeling the now-familiar lick of anger Taristan always drew up her spine. Her cheeks warmed and she turned away, hiding her flush. If he noticed, he gave no indication.

She chewed her lip and shifted from one frustrating topic to another. "I received a letter from Bella Harrsing today," she said, looking at him sidelong.

Though Taristan did his best to remain unbothered by the workings of a royal court, she saw a muscle feather in his cheek. He forced another bite of boar. "And why does that concern me?"

"She asked about our progress. Toward an heir."

His eyes flashed. This time, the red was there. "That seems rude."

"She's an advisor," Erida offered, shrugging her shoulders. "It's her job to ask. Just like it's our job to provide one." *Provide a child, as if they are simply plucked off trees.* Yes, it was a queen's duty to birth children, and a monarch's duty to solidify the chain of succession. These were facts of life, as real and undeniable as the glass in her hand.

Taristan said nothing, his own goblet undisturbed and filled to the brim. He contemplated it but did not drink. Erida wished she could crack his head open and peer inside. An impossible want, largely because any blow would probably glance right off his skull, thanks to the blessings of his demon lord. She would have to be direct instead. It made her skin crawl.

"Will you visit tonight?" she asked quietly, hating herself for being so blatant. *It's not like me to maneuver so poorly.*

And it was not like Taristan to flinch. His eyes snapped to hers, his teeth parted to draw a surprised breath.

"I prefer to go where I am wanted," he finally said, searching her face.

Erida nearly laughed. She had never heard anything so strange. And yet . . . it made her wonder. She could still feel his hands in her hair, his nails along her scalp. The drag of his fingers over her collarbone as he disheveled her shift, pushing her to sit on a rumpled bed. The heat in her cheeks burned again and words escaped her, any response dying in her throat. This time, she found she could not turn away, hooked to his gaze as though a Spindle burned within it, gold and glimmering, undeniable.

The Queen of Galland drew a fortifying breath, settling her mind.

"The sea fills with monsters, the hills with skeletons, the river with blood. Our strength is growing, Taristan," she said, imagining each. Taristan did the same, his brow furrowing as he licked his lips. "An empire is within our grasp."

"For Him," her husband answered. Suddenly their fingers were closer on the tabletop, though her hand had not moved. "And for us."

When the wizard slunk into the hall, Erida wanted to hurl her goblet at his little white head. He festered in his red robes, hands wringing as he hastened past the crowded tables.

Taristan broke their stare, sensing Ronin, and moved to stand.

Only to look up at Konegin instead, looming over them. Her royal cousin motioned for two more goblets of wine, the smile beneath his mustache weak and forced. He dipped his head. For once there was no circlet, not even a jeweled chain hanging from shoulder to shoulder. He seemed smaller than his usual self.

Perhaps, for all his blustering, war does not agree with him, Erida thought, relishing the idea. *It agrees with me fine.*

"Your Majesty," he said, easing into a shallow but steady bow. "So many of our noble friends have made toasts here tonight, in honor of the Queen and her army, as well as our victory today."

A cheer went up among the tables as men jumped to their feet, banging their cups. They swallowed up Ronin, obscuring his red robes and white face.

"I thought it fitting I make another, to His Royal Highness, the prince consort," Konegin continued, his hand extended. A servant in reversed livery, green lion on gold, pressed an ornate chalice into his hand, the brim spilling with deep, red wine.

The servant then offered the same to Taristan, who took it with an obliging scowl, his lips curled over his teeth in a frightful attempt at a smile. A woman with less restraint would have howled with laughter, but Erida contained herself.

"To Prince Taristan of Old Cor, husband to our beloved queen, father to the future of Galland. The son and sire of empires!" Konegin shouted, raising his cup to the room. Then, with a leering grin, he looked back at Erida's consort, blue eyes sparkling. Like a man dying of thirst, he gulped at his wine.

"To Taristan!" rippled out among the crowd, Ronin still livid among them.

Erida reached for her own glass, tipping it to her husband in amusement. "To Taristan," she echoed, drinking deeply.

The Corborn man kept his grasp tight on the chalice, his fingers working up the stem of the intricate metalwork.

Erida's smile weakened, her delight dulled by exasperation. *Is he really going to embarrass us both? Now? Over nothing?* She almost kicked him under the table. *Drink, you fool.*

To her relief, Taristan relented, as if this were some battle to be sacrificed.

Lord Konegin beamed, showing wine-stained teeth, the liquid still dripping in his mustache.

Taristan forced down a healthy swallow and pushed back his chair, rising to his full height. They were nearly the same size, though Konegin was older, gone to fat around his middle. They glared at each other, like a pair of archers trading arrows.

Her instincts flared. Something was not right.

In the crowd, Ronin shoved his way forward, knocking noblemen aside. A few balked while the rest watched the scene at the high table, their voices falling into silence.

"Taristan?" the Queen said, putting down her glass. It echoed too loudly for a feasting hall.

Her husband didn't react. Instead he put out his hand, the chalice gripped in his fingers. "Share in this with me, my lord," he said. Torchlight gleamed on the cup and in the wine, shining a dim and syrupy red.

Konegin snorted, shoving his own cup back to his servant. The one in the reversed livery. *His own man*, Erida knew, feeling a wave of cold settle over her limbs.

"I've had my fill, Taristan," he answered, still smiling with red teeth. "So have you."

"Very well," Taristan answered, knocking back the rest of the chalice, the wine running over his chin and chest, never blinking, never breaking his gaze on Konegin's face.

Beneath his mustache, her cousin's smile fell.

"What are you?" hissed from his mouth.

Erida leapt to her feet, the pieces snapping together in her head. *Treason. Betrayal. Poison.* She knocked the cup from her husband's hands and pointed to her royal cousin, her fingers shaking. "Arrest him," she blurted out, nearly a scream. "Take Lord Konegin into custody—put him in chains."

The lord quivered, still watching Taristan, his face torn between confusion and dread. "What are you?" he said again, stepping off the dais.

"Arrest him!" Erida shouted, and the hall exploded into noise. "He has tried to poison the prince!"

Her knights surged, eager to obey, even if the orders bewildered them. Konegin was beloved by many, a potential king to a young, untested queen. He had supporters among the nobles, many in the hall. Many in the army. Erida felt her knees tremble as he plunged into the crowd, his own entourage following him quickly. Even his idiot son managed to flee, scurrying after his father as quickly as his legs would carry him.

Poison, she thought again, coming back to herself.

There was a warmth beneath her hand, another around her back. She tore herself from the disarray of the feasting hall to look down, to her own fingers flush against Taristan's coat, pressing firmly into his chest. She blinked, dumbfounded. It was his arm around her waist, keeping her close.

He looked down at her, his lips and chin red. She imagined him like a beast, a predator feasting on prey.

"Poison," she said aloud, raising a shaking finger.

He caught it before she could touch his lips, pushing her away.

"I am immune," he ground out. "You are not."

The Lionguard moved in pursuit, most of them charging after Konegin and his men. They disappeared through the doors at the far end of the hall, streaking for the courtyard and the gates of Castle Lotha. Erida wanted to gather her skirts and follow. To pin Konegin down herself and cut his throat for his treachery.

Instead she remained at the high table, a statue to all who saw her, though her bones were shaking.

I'll need to explain, she thought idly, eyeing the room. Her loyal subjects were in a frenzy, too drunk to understand or too confused to do anything more than shout. Her remaining knights bristled at the base of the dais, pushing back any who attempted to pass.

All but Ronin.

They knew better than to cross the wizard.

He glowered, his body twitching in an odd manner, his face whiter than Erida could ever remember it being. Like fresh snow, like a corpse drained of blood. The whites of his eyes were lined with blood vessels, some broken.

Taristan wiped at his face with his sleeve, scrubbing the poison away. "What is it?" he snarled, looking down on his wizard.

Ronin dropped his head, his hands raised like a priest begging forgiveness. "We've lost Meer," he murmured. "We've lost a Spindle."

The chalice, made of pure silver, cracked apart in Taristan's hands.

Erida felt his rage. It mirrored her own.

"Lost," she breathed. *As if someone has simply misplaced it.* Blood roared in her ears and she met Taristan's eye, catching his wrists before he could tear the table into pieces. "Lost," she said again, snarling.

He glared, the fire burning in his eyes, a dull red edged in gold. Somewhere, Erida smelled smoke. "I'll kill her," he hissed.

"I'll help you," she answered.

ACKNOWLEDGMENTS

Writing this novel has been a cathartic experience. It was a welcome escape from increasingly frustrating times, and I hope to pass that on to readers. But what became an escape began as a step backward, to the girl I was at thirteen, searching for myself in stories but never finding her. Everything I loved didn't seem to love me back. I hope, as the years roll on, that sentiment becomes more and more rare, for all children.

As always, I must thank my parents first, who continue to love and support me through life. I would never be here without them, and they are the foundation everything I make is built on. My brother will recognize many things in this book and probably pick out their exact inspirations better than anyone else. I look forward to your thoughts, Andy. I hope to hear them in person. To Granddad George, I love you and I'll see you soon. To my extended family of cousins, aunts, and uncles, too many to name, thank you for your continued support and constant love.

I'm lucky to have another family out here in California, comprised of many, many friends who have stuck together through the strange decade after college. I am so grateful for this circle. And while many things change, we haven't, for better or worse.

I never imagined having friends like Morgan, Tori, and Jen, my dearest girls, who build me up and break me down in every way I need. I feel truly lucky to have all three of you and don't know what I did to deserve your love. As Morgan read the first draft of *Red Queen*, Tori was the first to finish *Realm Breaker*. Her immediate response was my first breath of relief. *Someone* liked this book. I did my job. I can't wait to be under the same moon with you all again.

My love and thanks to Jordan, for seeing me through this. I'm glad I share the moon with you.

Once again, I have to write a quick thank-you to my sunbeam of a puppy, Indy. I carry no shame for writing my dog into my acknowledgments and never will. We almost lost her during the course of this book, and every second more is a gift.

Few people get to have colleagues like mine, who not only became valued friends, but are incredibly talented role models to look up to and poorly emulate. I will not list them all, because it feels like bragging. But I must thank my Patties—Susan, Alex, and Leigh—for their friendship, advice, humor, and commiseration. Soman, whose shadow I am overjoyed to live in. Jenny and Morgan, I'll meet you in Paris. Emma, we're in the trenches together and I hope we always will be. And Sabaa, my constant through this strange journey.

I'm glad to have many swords and shields in this industry, because you need many. Sharpest of all is Suzie Townsend, who continues to cut through the world so I can forge my path. All my love and thanks to her and the rest of the New Leaf team, who somehow manage to be both the best and kindest people in the business. To Pouya, Jo, Meredith, Hilary, Veronica—I hope I never get to stop thanking you all. An extra thank-you to Dani, without whom we would all be headless chickens. I could never forget my shield, also known as my lawyer, Steve Younger.

Once again, my name is on a book published by HarperCollins, and I could not be prouder of what we've made together. I'm so privileged to be able to work with Alice Jerman and Erica Sussman and hope for many more collaborations. Thank you for giving me the room to bring this story to life. And thank you to the countless, tireless, incredible copy edit team who somehow managed to keep track of everything when I couldn't. Alexandra and Karen, thank you. I always look forward to your style sheets, but this one most of all. Thank you to the Harper marketing magicians, the Epic Reads mavens, the publicity artists—Ebony, Sabrina, Michael, Tyler, Shannon, Jennifer, Anna, and so many more who somehow manage to make something a cave person scratched up into a shiny thing people want in their homes. A special thank-you goes out to my cover designers, who have done so well by me all these years and continue to knock it out of the park. Thank you to Alison, Catherine, and Jenna for making *Realm Breaker* so stunning.

Another thank-you to my sensitivity readers, who were so thoughtful and encouraging, and deepened this new world in ways I could not fathom.

My deepest thanks goes to you readers and bloggers and teachers and librarians and booksellers, to anyone who holds a book and passes it on, or eats it up. Stories cannot live without you. Thank you for giving life to anything I might briefly carry.

This is the part where I should list my inspirations, but there are far too many watersheds for this river. I will only thank J. R. R. Tolkien here, for throwing me into Middle-earth, for giving me so much—and yet so little. For making me want. For making me hungry.

I'm grateful my grandmothers were able to see me published, and while they aren't with me anymore, I hope this story is with them, somehow.

My love to you all,

Victoria